A
Christmas Night

CHRISTINE MERRILL

MILLS & BOON

mark owner
registered
ce for
tries.

rs, Ltd

Books S.A.

The Mi... ... ...Merrill
A Regency Christmas Carol © 2011 Christine Merrill

ISBN: 978-0-263-30257-8

MIX
Paper from
responsible sources
FSC® C007454

This book is produced from independently certified FSC™ paper to ensure responsible forest management.

For more information visit: www.harpercollins.co.uk/green

Printed and bound in Spain
by CPI, Barcelona

THE MISTLETOE
WAGER

To Jim and the boys. Christmas comes
but once a year.

But it lasts twelve months.

Chapter One

Harry Pennyngton, Earl of Anneslea, passed his hat and gloves to the servant at White's, squared his shoulders, and strode into the main room to face his enemy. Nicholas Tremaine was lounging in a chair by the fire, exuding confidence and unconcerned by his lesser birth. To see him was to believe he was master of his surroundings, whatever they might be. He reminded Harry of a panther dozing on a tree branch, ready to drop without warning into the lives of other creatures and wreak havoc on their nerves.

And he was a handsome panther at that. In comparison, Harry always felt that he was inferior in some way. Shorter, perhaps, although they were much of the same height and build. And rumpled. For, no matter how much time or money Harry spent on his attire, Tremaine would always be more fashionable. And he did it seemingly without effort.

On the long list of things that annoyed him about the

man, his appearance was at the bottom. But it was on the list all the same.

The room was nearly empty, but Harry could feel the shift in attention among the few others present as though there had been a change in the wind. Men looked up from their cards and reading, watching his progress towards Tremaine. They were curious to see what would happen when the two notorious rivals met.

Very well, then. He would give them the show they hoped for. 'Tremaine!' He said it too loudly and with much good cheer.

His quarry gave a start and almost spilled his brandy. He had recognised the voice at once, and his eyes darted around the room, seeking escape. But none was to be had, for Harry stood between him and the door. Harry could see the faint light of irritation in the other man's eyes when he realised that he would have no choice but to acknowledge the greeting. 'Hello, Anneslea.' Then he returned his gaze to the paper he had been reading, showing no desire for further conversation.

How unfortunate for him. 'How goes it for you, old man, in this most blessed of holiday seasons?'

The only response was a nod, followed by a vague grunt that could have indicated satisfaction or annoyance.

Harry smiled and took a chair opposite the fire, facing Tremaine. He took a sip from the brandy that a servant had rushed to bring him. He examined the liquid in the glass, holding it out to catch the firelight. 'A good drink warms the blood on a day like this. There is a chill in the air. I've been tramping up and down Bond Street all morning. Shopping for Christmas gifts. Tailors, jewellers, whatnot. And the fixings for the celebration, of course. What's not to be had in the country must be brought back with me from town.' He waved his hand at the foolishness of it. 'I do not normally take it upon myself. But now that I am alone…' He could almost feel the ears of the others in the room, pricking to catch what he would say next.

Tremaine noticed as well, and gave a small flinch. It was most gratifying.

Harry looked up from his drink into Tremaine's startled face. 'And, by the by, how is Elise?' It was a bold conversational gambit, and he was rewarded with a slight choke from his opponent.

The other man turned to him and sat up straight, his indolence disappearing. His eyes glittered with suppressed rage. 'She is well, I think. If you care, you should go and ask her yourself. She would be glad of the call.'

She would be no such thing. As he remembered their last conversation, Elise had made it plain that if she never saw Harry again it would be too soon. 'Perhaps I will,' he answered, and smiled as though they were having a pleasant discussion about an old friend and nothing more.

It must have disappointed their audience to see the two men behaving as adults on this most delicate of subjects. But their moderate behaviour had not quelled the undercurrent of anticipation. He could see from the corner of his eye that the room had begun to fill with observers. They were reading newspapers, engaging in subdued chat, and gazing out of the bay window while sipping drinks. But every man present was taking care to be uninterested in a most focused fashion, waiting for the cross word that would set the two of them to brawling like schoolboys.

If only it were so easily settled. If Harry could have been sure of a win, he would have met his opponent on the field of honour long before now. The temptation existed to hand his jacket to the nearest servant, roll up his sleeves, raise his fists and lay the bastard out on the hearth rug. But physically, they were evenly matched. A fight would impress no one, should he lose it. And Elise would think even less of him than she did now if he was bested in public by Nicholas Tremaine.

He would have to strike where his rival could least defend himself. In the intellect.

Tremaine eased back in his chair, relaxing in the quiet, perhaps thinking that he had silenced Harry with his indifference. Poor fool. Harry set down his empty glass, made a great show of placing his hands on his knees, gave a contented sigh and continued the conversation as though there were nothing strange about it. 'Any plans for the holiday?'

'Has Elise made plans?' There was a faint reproof in the man's voice, as though he had a right to take Harry to task on that subject. Harry ignored it.

'You, I mean. Do you have plans? For Christmas?' He smiled to show all the world Elise's plans were no concern of his.

Tremaine glared. 'I am most pleased to have no plans. I intend to treat the day much as any other.'

'Really. May I offer you a bit of advice, Tremaine?'

He looked positively pained at the idea. 'If you must.'

'Try to drum up some enthusiasm towards Christmas—for her sake, at least.'

In response, Tremaine snorted in disgust. 'I do not see why I should. People make far too big a fuss over the whole season. What is it good for, other than a chance to experience diminished sunlight and foul weather while in close proximity to one's fellow man? I find the experience most unpleasant. If others choose to celebrate, I wish them well. But I do not wish to bother others with my bad mood, and I would prefer that they not bother me.' He stared directly at Harry, so there could be no doubt as to his meaning.

Perfect. Harry's smile turned sympathetic. 'Then I wonder if you will be any better suited to Elise than I was. She adores this season. She cannot help it, I suppose. It's in her blood. She waits all year in anticipation of the special foods, the mulled wine, the singing and games. When we were together she was constantly dragging trees where they were never intended to be, and then lighting candles in them until I was quite sure she meant to burn the house down for Twelfth Night. I doubt she will wish to give that up just to please you. There is no changing her when she has an idea in her head. I know from experience. It is you who must alter—to suit her.'

A variety of emotions were playing across

Tremaine's face, fighting for supremacy. Harry watched in secret enjoyment as thoughts formed and were discarded. Should he tell Anneslea what to do with his advice? It had been offered innocently enough. Accuse him of ill treatment in some way? Not possible. Should they argue, Tremaine would gain nothing, for society would find him totally in the wrong. Harry's only offence was his irrational good humour. And Tremaine was at a loss as to how to combat it.

At last he chose to reject the advice, and to ignore the mention of Elise. 'I am adamant on the subject. I have nothing against the holiday itself, but I have no patience for the folderol that accompanies it. Nor am I likely to change my mind on the subject to please another.'

'That is what I thought once.' Harry grinned. 'And now look at me.' He held out his arms, as if to prove his honest intentions. 'I'm positively overflowing with good will towards my fellow men. Of course, once you have experienced Christmas as we celebrate it at Anneslea Manor…' He paused and then snapped his fingers. 'That's it, man. Just the thing. You must come out to the house and see how the feast is properly done. That will put you to rights.'

Tremaine stared at him as though he'd gone mad. 'I will do no such thing.'

The other men in the room were listening with obvious interest now. Harry could hear chuckles and whispers of approval.

'No, I insist. You will see how the season should be shared, and it will melt your heart on the subject. I doubt there is a better gift that I could offer to Elise than to teach you the meaning of Christmas. Come to Lincolnshire, Tremaine. We are practically family, after all.'

There was definitely a laugh from somewhere in the room, although it was quickly stifled. And then the room fell silent, waiting for the response.

If it had been a matter of fashion, or some caustic witticism he was directing at another, Tremaine would have loved being the centre of attention. But today he hated the idea that he was the butt of a joke, rather than Harry. There was a redness creeping from under Tremaine's collar as his anger sought an outlet. At last he burst out, 'Not in a million years.'

'Oh, come now.' Harry pulled a face. 'We can make a bet of it. What shall it be?' He pretended to consider. 'Gentlemen, bring the book. I am willing to bet twenty pounds to Tremaine, and any takers, that he shall wish me a Merry Christmas by Twelfth Night.'

Someone ran for the betting book, and there was a rustling of hands in pockets for banknotes, pens scratching IOUs, and offers to hold the stakes. It was all accompanied by a murmur of agreement that hell would freeze before Tremaine wished anyone a Merry Christmas, so well known was his contempt for the season. And the chance that anything might induce him to say those particular words to Harry Pennyngton were equal to the devil going to Bond Street to buy ice skates.

But while the room was raised in chaos, the object of the wager stared steadfastly into the fire, refusing to acknowledge what was occurring.

Harry said, loud enough for all to hear over the din, 'It does not matter if you do not wish to bet, Tremaine, for the others still wish to see me try. But it will be easier to settle the thing if you will co-operate.' Then he addressed the room, 'Come out to my house in the country, all of you.' He gestured to include everyone. 'Bring your families, if you wish. There is more than enough space. Then, when Tremaine's resolve weakens, you will all be there to witness it.' He stared at the other man. 'And if it does not, if you are so sure of your position, then a wager on it will be the easiest money you could make.'

The mention of finances brought Tremaine to speech—just as Harry had known it would. 'I no longer need to make a quick twenty pounds by entering into foolish wagers. Especially not with you, Anneslea. A visit to your house at Christmas would be two weeks of tedious company to prove something I already know. It would be an attempt to change my character in a way I do not wish. It is utter nonsense.'

Harry grinned. 'You would not find it so if the wager were over something you truly desired. Now that you have received your full inheritance, I suppose twenty quid is nothing to you. I have no real desire to spend a fortnight in your company either, Tremaine. For I swear you are one of the most disagreeable fops in Christendom. But I do care for Elise's happiness. And if she means to have you, then you must become a better man than you are.' He touched a finger to his chin, pretending to think. 'I have but to find the thing you want, and you will take the wager, right enough.' Then he reached into his pocket and pulled the carefully worded letter from his breast pocket. 'Perhaps this will change your mind.'

He offered it to Tremaine and watched the colour drain from the man's face as he read the words. Others in the room leaned forward to catch a glimpse of the paper, but Harry stepped in to block their view.

'For Tremaine's eyes only, please. This is a matter between gentlemen.' For a moment he gave vent to his true feelings and let the words drip with the irony he felt at having to pretend good fellowship for the bastard in the seat in front of him. Then he turned back to the crowd. 'The side bet will in no way affect our fun. And it will be just the thing to convince our victim of the need to take a holiday trip to Anneslea.'

Or so he hoped. Tremaine was still staring at his offer, face frozen in surprise. When he looked up at Harry their eyes locked in challenge. And it was Tremaine who looked away first. But he said nothing, merely folded the paper and tucked it into his own pocket before exiting the room.

Harry smiled to himself, oblivious of the chaos around him.

And now he had but to wait.

Chapter Two

Elise Pennyngton straightened her skirt, smoothed her hair, and arranged herself on the divan in her London sitting room so that she could appear startled when the door to the room opened. Her guest was in the hall, just outside, and it would be careless of her to let him find her in true disarray. With a little effort she could give the impression that she awaited him eagerly, without appearing to be desperate for his company.

As he paused in the open doorway, awaiting her permission to enter, she looked at Nicholas Tremaine and steeled her nerves. Taking a lover was the first item on her list, if she truly wished to be emancipated from her husband. And if she must have male companionship, Nick was the logical choice. In her mind, he had been filed under 'unfinished business' for far too long. He was as elegantly handsome as he had been when he'd first proposed to her.

And she'd turned him away and chosen Harry.

But, since Harry did not want her any more, she was right back to where she had started.

'Nicholas.' She pushed the annoying thoughts of Harry from her mind, and held out her hands to the dashing gentleman before her.

He stepped forward and took them, raising her fingers to his mouth and giving them a brief touch of his lips. 'Elise.' His eyes were still the same soul-searching blue, and his hair just as dark as the day they'd met, although it had been more than five years.

There was no grey in her hair, either. And she took special care that when they met she looked as fresh and willing as she had at eighteen. Her coiffure was impeccable and her manner welcoming. And her dress was dotted with sprigs of flowers that perfectly matched the blue of her eyes.

Or so Harry had always claimed.

She gave a little shake of her head to clear away that troublesome memory, and gazed soulfully at the man still holding her hands. She was not the naïve young girl he had courted. But surely the passage of time on her face had not been harsh?

If he noticed the change the years had made in her, he gave no reason to think it bothered him. He returned her gaze in the same absently devoted way he always had, and she could see by his smile of approval that he found her attractive.

'Come, sit with me.' In turn, she took his hands in hers, and pulled him down to sit on the divan beside her. He took a place exactly the right distance away from her body—close enough to feel intimate, but far enough away not to incite comment should someone walk in on them together.

She hoped that she had not misunderstood his interest. For it would be very embarrassing if he were resistant to the idea, when she had raised sufficient courage to suggest that they take their relationship to a deeper level. But she had begun to suspect that the event would not happen until she had announced herself ready. It would be so much easier if he were to make the first move. But he had made it clear that he would not rush her into intimacy until she was sure, in her heart, that she would not regret her actions.

For a well-known rake, he was annoyingly protective of her honour.

'Are you not glad to see me?' She gave a hopeful pout.

'Of course, darling.' And after a moment he leaned forward to kiss her on the lips.

There was nothing wrong with the few kisses they had exchanged thus far. Nicholas clearly knew how to give a kiss. There was no awkwardness when their mouths met, no bumping of noses or shuffling of feet. His hands held her body with just the right level of strength, hinting at the ability to command passion without taking unwelcome liberties. His lips were firm on hers, neither too wet nor too dry, his breath was fresh, his cheek was smooth.

When he held her she was soft in his arms, languid but not overly forward, giving no sign that he need proceed faster, but neither did she signal him to desist immediately.

The whole presentation smacked of a game of chess. Each move was well planned. They could both see the action several turns ahead. Checkmate was inevitable.

Of course if it all seemed to lack a certain passion, and felt ever so slightly calculated, who was she to complain of it? She had thought about Nicholas in the darkest hours of her unhappy marriage and wondered how different it might be had she chosen otherwise. Soon she would know.

And if it would ever be possible to gain a true divorce from Harry she must accept the fact that at some point she would need to take a lover, whether she wanted one or not. Her confirmed infidelity was the only thing she was sure the courts might recognise as grounds. But even then, whether she could persuade her husband to make the effort to cast her off was quite another matter.

The matter was simple enough, after all. Harry must have an heir. Since she had been unable to provide one for him, he would be better off free of her while he was still young enough to try with another. But she had grown to see a possible divorce as one more thing in her marriage for which she would need to do the lion's share of the work, if she wished the task accomplished. The last five years had proved that Harry Pennyngton could not be bothered with serious matters, no matter how she might try to gain his attention.

And now Nicholas had pulled away from her, as though he could not manage to continue the charade.

She frowned, and he shook his head in embarrassment. 'I'm sorry if I seem distracted. But the most extraordinary thing happened at White's just now, and we must speak of it. I received an invitation to Christmas.'

She stared at him with a barely raised eyebrow. 'Hardly extraordinary, darling. Christmas is less than two weeks away. It is a bit late, I suppose. You should have made plans by now.'

'Certainly not.' Nicholas, had he had feathers, would have ruffled them. 'I do not make it a habit of celebrating the holiday. It is much better to use the time productively, in reading or some other quiet pursuit, and to avoid gatherings all together. With so many others running about country drawing rooms like idiots, hiding slippers and bluffing blind men, it makes for an excellent time of peaceful reflection.'

Nicholas Tremaine's aversion to Christmas was well known and marked upon. She had commented on it herself. And then she had placed it on the list of things that she would change about him, should their relationship grow to permanence. 'You are most unreasonable on the subject, Nicholas. If someone has chosen to call you on it, it can hardly be a surprise.'

'But the invitation came from a most unlikely source.' He paused. 'Harry. He's asked me up to the house 'til Twelfth Night, and has bet twenty quid to all takers that he can imbue me with the spirit of the season. He says the celebration at Anneslea Manor is always top drawer, and that I cannot fail to bend. And he invited all within earshot to come as well.' He paused. 'I just thought it rather odd. He's obviously not keeping bachelor's hall if he thinks to hold a house party.' He paused again, as though afraid of her reaction. 'And to induce me to yield he gave me this.' He removed a folded sheet of paper from his pocket and handed it to her.

She read it.

I, Harry Pennyngton, swear upon my honour that if I cannot succeed in making Nicholas Tremaine wish me a Merry Christmas in my home, by January the fifth of next year, I shall make every attempt to give my estranged wife, Elise Pennyngton, the divorce that she craves, and will do nothing to stand in the way of her marriage to Nicholas Tremaine or any other man.

It was signed 'Anneslea', in her husband's finest hand, and dated yesterday.

She threw it to the floor at her feet. Damn Harry and his twisted sense of humour. The whole thing had been prepared before he'd even entered into the bet. He had gone to the club with the intent of trapping Nicholas into one of his stupid little jokes, and he had used her to bait the hook. How dared he make light of something that was so important? Turn the end of their marriage into some drawing room wager and, worse yet, make no mention of it to her? Without thinking, she reverted to her mother tongue and gave vent to her frustrations over marriage, divorce, men in general, and her husband in particular.

Nicholas cleared his throat. 'Really, Elise, if you must go on so, please limit yourself to English. You know I have no understanding of German.'

She narrowed her eyes. 'It is a good thing that you do not. For you would take me to task for my language, and give me another tiresome lecture in what is or is not proper for a British lady. And, Nicholas, I am in no mood for it.'

'Well, foul language is not proper for an English gentleman, either. Nor is that letter. If you understood the process, Elise… He is offering something that he cannot give. Only the courts can decide if you are granted a divorce, and the answer will often be no.'

'We will not know until we have tried,' she insisted.

'But he has done nothing to harm you, has he?' Nick's face darkened for a moment. 'For if he has treated you cruelly then it is an entirely different matter. I will call the man out and we will finish this quickly, once and for all, in a way that need not involve the courts.'

'No. No. There is no reason to resort to violence,' she said hurriedly. 'He has not hurt me.' She sighed. 'Not physically.'

Nicholas expelled an irritated sigh in response. 'Then not at all, in the eyes of the court. Hurt feelings are no reason to end a marriage.'

'The marriage should not have taken place at all,' she argued. 'There were no feelings at all between us when we married. And as far as I can tell it has not changed in all these years.' *On his part, at least.*

'It is a natural thing for ardour to cool with time. But he must have felt something back then,' Nicholas argued. 'Or he would not have made the offer.'

Elise shook her head and tried not to show the pain that

the statement brought her. For she had flattered herself into believing much the same thing when she had accepted Harry's offer. 'When he decided to take a wife it was no different for him than buying an estate, or a horse, or any other thing. He did not so much marry me as collect me. And now he has forgotten why he wanted me in the first place. I doubt he even notices that I am gone.'

Nicholas added, in an offhand manner, 'He enquired after you, by the way. I told him you were well.'

'Did you, now?' Elise could feel the temper rising in her. If Harry cared at all for her welfare, he should enquire in person, not make her the subject of talk at his club. 'Thank you so much for relaying the information.'

Nick looked alarmed as he realised that he had mis-gauged her response to his innocent comment. 'I had to say something, Elise. It does not do to ignore the man if he wishes to be civil about this. If you truly want your freedom, is it not better that he is being co-operative?'

'Co-operative? I am sure that is the last thing on his mind, no matter how this appears. He is up to some-thing.' She narrowed her eyes. 'And how did you respond to his invitation?'

Tremaine laughed. 'I did not dignify it with a response. It is one thing, Elise, for us to pretend that there is nothing unusual between us when we meet by accident in the club. But I hardly think it's proper for me to go to the man's home for the holiday.'

She shook her head. 'You do not seriously think that there was anything accidental in your meeting with my husband, Nicholas? He wished to let me know that he is celebrating in my absence. And to make me wonder who he has for hostess.' She furrowed her brow. 'Not his sister, certainly.' She ran down a list in her head of women who might be eager to step into her place.

'Harry has a sister?' Nicholas asked, surprised.

'A half-sister, in Shropshire. A vicar's daughter. Far too proper to give herself over to merriment and run off to Anneslea Manor for a house party.'

Nicholas frowned. 'You would be surprised what vicar's daughters can get up to when allowed to roam free. Especially at Christmas.'

Elise shook her head. 'I doubt it is her. More likely my husband is trying to make me jealous by sending the hint that he has replaced me.' And it annoyed her to find that he was succeeding.

'It matters not to me, in any case,' Nicholas replied. 'A tiresome sister is but one more reason for me to avoid Anneslea—the Manor and the man.'

If Nick refused the invitation then she would never know the truth. A lack of response, an unwillingness to play his silly game, would be proper punishment for Harry, and might dissuade him from tormenting her, but it would do nothing to settle her mind about her husband's reason for the jest.

And then a thought occurred to her. 'If we are doing nothing wrong, Nicholas, then there can be no harm in a visit, surely?' Perhaps if she could persuade him to go she would discover what Harry really intended by extending the offer.

Nick was looking at her as though she were no more

trustworthy than her husband. 'I see no good in it, either. Harry is all "Hail fellow, well met," when we meet in the club, darling. He is being excessively reasonable about the whole thing. Which is proof that he is not the least bit reasonable on the subject. He wants you to come home, and is trying to throw me out of countenance with his good humour. And he is succeeding. I would rather walk into a lion's den than take myself off to his home for the holiday. God knows what will happen to me once he has me alone.'

'Do not be ridiculous, darling. It is all decided between Harry and me. There was nothing for us to do but face the facts: we do not suit.' She put on her bravest smile. 'We are living separately now, and he is quite content with it. I suspect we will end as better friends apart than we were together. And, while I do not doubt that he has an ulterior motive, I am sure he means you no real harm by this offer.'

'Ha!' Tremaine's laugh was of triumph, and he pointed to her. 'You do it as well. No truly content couple would work so hard to show happiness over their separation. It is a façade, Elise. Nothing more. If I go to Harry's little party in Lincolnshire, I suspect we will be at each other's throats before the week is out. The situation is fraught with danger. One too many cups of wassail, and he will be marching me up a snowy hillside for pistols at dawn.'

'Harry challenge you over me?' She laughed at the idea. 'That is utter nonsense, Nicholas, and you know it.'

'I know no such thing.'

'If Harry were the sort to issue challenges, then it is far more likely that I would be there still, celebrating at his side. But he has given no evidence of caring at all, Nicholas, over what I say or do.' She tried to keep the pain from her voice, for she had promised herself to stop hurting over that subject long ago. 'It is possible that his invitation was nothing more than it sounded. I know the man better than anyone alive, and I can find many defects in him, but I do not fault his generous spirit.'

He had certainly been generous enough to her. After a two-month separation he was still paying all her bills, no matter the size. If he truly cared he would be storming into her apartments, throwing her extravagances back in her face, and demanding that she remove from London and return home immediately. She gritted her teeth.

'But his sense of humour leaves much to be desired. Inviting you for the holiday could be nothing more serious than one of his little pranks. It is a foolish attempt to be diverting at Christmas.'

Tremaine nodded. 'As you will. I will thank him for the generosity of his offer, which has no ulterior motive. And if what you say is true he will be equally polite when I decline it.'

'You will do no such thing. Accept him at once.'

He stared at her without speaking, until she began to fear that she had overstepped the bounds of even such a warm friendship as theirs.

'I only meant,' she added sweetly, 'that you will never know what his true intentions are until you test them. And if we are to continue together, the issue will come up, again and again. If he is mistaking where I mean to make my future, the sooner Harry learns to see you as a part of my life, the better for all concerned. And you need to see that he can do you no harm once he has accepted the truth.'

'But Christmas is not the best time to establish this,' Tremaine warned. 'In my experience, it is the season most likely to make fools of rational men and maniacs of fools. There is a reason I have avoided celebrations such as this before now. Too many situations begin with one party announcing that "we are all civilised adults" and end with two adults rolling on the rug, trading either blows or kisses.'

'I had no idea you were so frightened of my husband.' She hoped her sarcasm would coax him to her side.

'I am not afraid, darling. But neither do I wish to tempt fate.'

She smiled. 'If it helps to calm your nerves, I will accompany you.'

He started at the idea. 'I doubt he meant to invite you, Elise.'

'Nonsense again, Nicholas. It does not matter what he meant to do. I do not need an invitation to visit my own home.' And it would serve Harry right if she chose to put in an appearance without warning him. 'It is not as if we need to go for the duration of the party, after all. A day or two…'

'All three of us? Under the same roof?' Tremaine shuddered. 'Thank you, no. Your idea is even worse than his. But if you wish to visit Harry, you are free to go without me.'

'If I visit Harry alone, then people will have the wrong impression,' she insisted.

'That you have seen the error of your ways and are returning to your husband?'

'Exactly. But if we visit as a couple then it will be understood. And we will not go for the holiday. We need stay only a few hours at most.'

He covered his brow with his hand. 'You would have me traipsing halfway across England for a visit of a few hours? We would spend days on the road, Elise. It simply is not practical.'

'All right, then. We will stay long enough to win Harry's silly bet and gain his promise that he will seek a divorce.' She tapped the letter with her hand. 'Although he probably meant the offer in jest, he has put it in writing. And he would never be so base as to go back on his word if you win.'

If Harry was willing to lose without a fight, then she had been right all along: their marriage was of no value to him, and he wanted release as much as she wished to set him free. But she would never know the truth if she could not persuade Nicholas to play along.

Then a thought struck her, and she gathered her courage along with her momentum. 'And afterwards we will return to London, and I will give you your Christmas present.'

'I have given you my opinion of the holidays, Elise. It will not be necessary to exchange gifts, for I do not mean to get you anything in any case.'

'I was thinking,' she said, 'of a more physical token of gratitude.' She hoped that the breathiness in her tone would be taken for seduction, and not absolute terror at making the final move that would separate her permanently from the man she loved. But if her love was not returned, and there were no children to care for, then there was no reason to turn back. She ignored her rioting feelings and gave Nicholas a slow smile.

Nicholas stared at her, beginning to comprehend. 'If we visit your husband for Christmas? You cannot mean…'

'Oh, yes, darling. I do.' She swallowed and gave an emphatic nod. 'I think it is time to prove that my marriage is every bit as dead as I claim. If you are convinced that Harry carries a torch for me, or that I still long for his attention, then see us together. I will prove to you that your ideas are false. And if it is true that he wants me back, your presence will prove to him that it is hopeless. We will come away from Lincolnshire with everything sorted. And afterwards we will go somewhere we can celebrate in private. I will be most enthusiastically grateful to have the matter settled.' And she leaned forward and kissed him.

There was none of the careful planning in this kiss that had been in the others, for she had taken him unawares. She took advantage of his lack of preparation to see to it that, when their lips parted from each other, his defences were destroyed and he was quite willing to see her side of the argument.

When he reached for her again, she pulled out of his grasp. 'After,' she said firmly. 'We cannot continue as we are with this hanging over our heads. After we have settled with Harry, we will come back to town and make a fresh start. You may not enjoy Christmas, but I shall make sure that the New Year will hold pleasant memories.'

Chapter Three

Harry crossed the threshold of Anneslea Manor with his usual bonhomie. It had always been his way to treat everyone, from prince to stablehand, as though he were happy to be in their presence and wished them to be happy as well. If Rosalind Morley had not been in such a temper with him, she could not have helped but greet him warmly. She could feel her anger slipping away, for it was hard not to be cheerful in his presence.

Although his wife had managed it well enough.

'Dear sister!' He held out open arms to her, smiling.

She crossed hers in front of her chest and stood blocking his entrance, in no mood to be charmed. 'Half-sister, Harry.'

'But no less dear for it.' He was not the least bit dissuaded, and hugged her despite her closed arms, leaning down to plant a kiss on the top of her head. 'Did you receive my letter?'

'I most certainly did. And a very brief missive it was.

It arrived three days ago, missing all of the important details, and strangely late in the season. I wish to know what you are about, sending such a thing at such a time.'

He tipped his head to the side. 'Sending plans for Christmas? I should think this would be the most logical time to send them. It is nearing the day, after all.'

'Aha!' She poked him in the chest with a finger. 'You know it, then? You have not forgotten the date?'

'December twentieth,' he answered, unperturbed.

'Then you do not deny that in the next forty-eight hours a horde will descend upon us?'

'Hardly a horde, Rosalind. I invited a few people for Christmas, that is all.'

'It will seem like a horde,' she snapped, 'once they are treated to what is in the larder. You said to expect guests. But you cannot tell me who, or when, or even exactly how many.'

'It was a spur-of-the-moment invitation, to the gentlemen at the club,' he said, and his gaze seemed to dart from hers. 'I am not sure how many will respond to it.'

'And what am I to give them when they arrive? Napoleon had more food in Russia than we have here.'

'No food?' He seemed genuinely surprised by the idea that planning might be necessary before throwing a two-week party. If this was his normal behaviour, then Rosalind began to understand why his wife had been cross enough to leave him.

'With Elise gone, Harry, the house has been all but shut up. The servants are airing the guest rooms, and I have set the cook to scrambling for what is left in the village, but you cannot expect me to demand some poor villager to give us his goose from the ovens at the baker. We must manage with whatever is left. It will be thin fare.'

'I am sure the guests will be content with what they have. We have a fine cellar.'

'Good drink and no food is a recipe for disaster,' she warned, trying not to think of how she had learned that particular lesson.

'Do not worry so, little one. I'm sure it will be fine. Once they see the tree they will forget all about dinner.'

'What tree?' She glanced out of the window.

'The Christmas tree, of course.'

'This is some custom of Elise's, is it?'

'Well, of course.' He smiled as though lost in memory. 'She decorates a pine with paper stars, candles and gingerbread. That sort of thing. I have grown quite used to it.'

'Very well for you, Harry. But this is not anything that I am accustomed to. Father allows only the most minimal celebration. I attend church, of course. And he writes a new sermon every Advent. But he does not hold with such wild abandon when celebrating the Lord's birth.'

Harry rolled his eyes at her, obviously amused by her lack of spirit. 'It is rather pagan, I suppose. Not in your father's line at all. But perfectly harmless. And very much fun—as is the Yule Log. You will see.'

'Will I?' She put her hands on her hips. 'I doubt I shall have time to enjoy it if I am responsible for bringing it about. Because, Harry, someone must find this tree and have it brought to the house. And there is still the question of finding a second goose, or perhaps a turkey. If I am to feed a large group, one bird will not be enough.'

'And you must organise games. Do not forget the games.' He held up his fingers, ticking things off an imaginary list. 'And see to the decorations in the rest of the house.'

She raised her hands in supplication. 'What decorations?'

'Pine boughs, mistletoe, holly, ivy. Elise has a little something in each room.' He sighed happily. 'No matter where you went, you could not forget the season.'

'Oh, it is doubtful that I shall be able to forget the season, no matter how much I might try.'

He reached out to her and enveloped her in another brotherly hug. 'It will be all right, darling. You needn't worry so. Whatever you can manage at such short notice will be fine. Before I left London I filled the carriage with more than enough vagaries and sweetmeats. And on the way, I stopped so that the servants might gather greenery. When they unload it all you will find you are not so poorly supplied as you might think.'

Rosalind took a deep breath to calm herself, and tried to explain the situation again, hoping that he would understand. 'A gathering of this size will still be a challenge. The servants obey me sullenly, if at all. They do not wish a new mistress, Harry. They want Elise back.'

His face clouded for a moment, before he smiled again. 'We will see what can be done on that front soon enough. But for now, you must do the best you can. And look on this as an opportunity, not an obstacle. It will give my friends a chance to meet you. They do wonder, you know, that you are never seen in London. I think some of them doubt that I have any family at all. They think that I have imagined the wonderful sister I describe.'

'Really, Harry. You make me sound terribly antisocial. It is not by choice that I avoid your friends. Father needs me at home.'

He was looking down at her with a frown of concern. 'I worry about you, sequestered in Shropshire alone with your father. He is a fine man, but an elderly vicar cannot be much company for a spirited girl.'

It was perfectly true, but she smiled back in denial. 'It is not as if I have no friends in the country.'

He waved a hand. 'I am sure they are fine people. But the young gentlemen of your acquaintance must be a bit thick in the head if they have not seen you for the beauty you are. I would have thought by now that there would be men lined up to ask your father for your hand.'

'I am no longer, as you put it, "a spirited girl", Harry. I do not need you to act as matchmaker—nor Father's permission should any young men come calling.' And she had seen that they hadn't, for she had turned them all away. The last thing she needed was Harry pointing out the illogicality of her refusals. 'I am of age, and content to remain unmarried.'

He sighed. 'So you keep telling me. But I mean to see you settled. And if I can find someone to throw in your path…'

'Then I shall walk politely around him and continue on my way.'

'With you so far from home, you could at least pretend to need a chaperon,' he said. 'Your father made me promise to take the role, and to prevent you from any mis-alliances. I was quite looking forward to failing at it.'

Her father would have done so, since he did not trust her in the slightest. But she could hardly fault Harry for his concern, so she curtseyed to him. 'Very well. I will send you any serious contenders for my hand. Although I assure you there will be no such men, nor does it bother me. I am quite content to stay as I am.'

He looked at her critically, and for a change he was serious. 'I do not believe you. I do not know what happened before your father sent you to rusticate, or why it set you so totally off the masculine gender, but I wish it could be otherwise.'

'I have nothing against the masculine gender,' she argued. In fact, she had found one in particular to be most to her liking. 'I could think of little else for the brief time I was in London, before Father showed me the error of my behaviour and sent me home.'

'You are too hard on yourself, darling. To have been obsessed with love and marriage made you no different from other girls of your age.'

'I was still an ill-mannered child, and my rash be-haviour gave many a distaste of me.' She had heard the words from his lips so many times that she sounded almost like her father as she said them. 'I am sure that the men of London breathed a hearty sigh of relief when

I was removed from their numbers before the season even began.' At least that was true. At least one of them had been more than glad to see the last of her.

'But it has been years, Rosalind. Whatever it was that proved the last straw to your father, it has been forgotten by everyone else. I think you would find, if you gave them a chance, that there are many men worthy of your affection and eager to meet you. There are a dozen in my set alone who would do fine for you. But if you insist on avoiding London, then I must bring London to you.'

'Harry,' she said, with sudden alarm, 'tell me you have not done what I suspect you have.'

'And whatever is that, sister dear?'

'You have not used the Christmas holiday as an opportunity to fill this house with unattached men in an attempt to make a match where none is desired.'

He glanced away and smiled. 'Not fill the house, precisely.'

And suddenly she knew why he had been so cagey with the guest list, giving her rough numbers but no names. 'It is all ruined,' she moaned.

'I fail to see how,' he answered, being wilfully oblivious again.

'There should be a harmonious balance in the genders if a party is to be successful. And it sounds as though you have not invited a single family with a marriageable daughter, nor any young ladies at all. Tell me I will not be the lone partner to a pack of gentleman from your club.'

He laughed. 'You make them sound like a Barbarian invasion, Rosalind. You are being far too dramatic.'

She shook her finger at him. 'You will see the way of things when we stand up for a dance and there is only me on the ladies' side.'

He ignored her distress. 'I do not care—not if you are presented to best advantage, dear one. This party will give you a chance to shine like the jewel you are.'

'I will appear, if anyone notices me at all, to be a desperate spinster.'

'Wrong again. You assure me you are not desperate, and you are hardly old enough to be a spinster.' He held her by the hands and admired her. 'At least you certainly do not look old enough.'

'That has been the problem all along,' she said. 'When I came of age I looked too young to consider.'

'Many women long for your problem, dear. When you are too old, I expect they will hate you for your youth. It is something to look forward to.'

'Small comfort.'

'And you needn't worry. You will not be the only female, and I have not filled the house to the roof with prospective suitors. I believe you will find the company quite well balanced.' He smiled as though he knew a secret. 'But should you find someone present who is to your liking, and if he should like you as well, then I will be the happiest man in England. And to that end, I wish you to play hostess to my friends and to try to take some joy in it for yourself, even though it means a great deal of work.' He was looking at her with such obvious pride and hope for her own welfare that she felt churlish for denying him his party.

'Very well, Harry. Consider my good behaviour to be a Christmas gift to you. Let us hope, by the end of the festivities, that the only cooked geese are in the kitchen.'

For the next two days, Rosalind found herself buffeted along with the increasing speed of events. Harry's carriage was unpacked, and servants were set to preparations. But they seemed to have no idea how to proceed without continual supervision, or would insist that they knew exactly what was to be done and then do the tasks in a manner that was obviously wrong. It was just as it had been since the moment she had stepped over the threshold and into Elise's shoes. At least she'd managed to gain partial co-operation, by begging them to do things as Elise would have wanted them done, as proof of their loyalty to her and in honour of her memory.

It sounded to all the world as if the woman had died, and she'd been left to write her eulogy instead of run her house. But the servants had responded better to her moving speech then they had to anything she could offer in the way of instruction. At some point, she would have to make her brother stir himself sufficiently to retrieve his wife from London. For Rosalind was not welcome in the role of mistress here, nor did she desire it. But it must wait until after the holidays, for she had made Harry a promise to help him for Christmas and she meant to stick to it, until the bitter end.

At last the house was in some semblance of readiness, and the guests began to come—first in a trickle and then a flood. Arrivals were so frequent that the front door was propped open, despite the brisk wind that had arisen. A steady fall of snow had begun in the late afternoon and followed people across the stone floor in eddies and swirls. She busied herself with providing direction to servants, and praying that everyone would manage to find their way to the same room as their baggage.

Couples and families were talking loudly, shaking the snow from their coats and wraps and remarking in laughing tones about the deteriorating condition of the roads and the need for mulled wine, hot tea, and a warm fire. It seemed that Rosalind was continually shouting words of welcome into an ever-changing crowd, promising comfort and seasonal joy once they were properly inside, making themselves at home. Just to the left, the library had been prepared to receive the guests, for the sitting room would be packed solid with bodies should she try to fit all the people together in that room. The great oak reading tables had been pushed to the edges of the room and heaped with plates of sandwiches and sweets, along with steaming pots of tea, carafes of wine and a big bowl of punch.

There were sounds of gratitude and happiness in response, and for a moment she quite forgot the trouble of the last week's preparation. And although at times she silently cursed her brother for causing the mess, she noticed that he was behaving strangely as he moved through the hubbub, making many restless journeys up and down the stairs. It was as if he was anticipating something or someone in particular, and his pleasure at each new face seemed to diminish, rather than increase, when he did not see the person he expected.

And then the last couple stepped through the open doorway.

'Rosalind!' Elise threw her arms wide and encompassed her in an embrace that was tight to the point of discomfort. 'So you are the one Harry's found to take the reins.'

'Elise?' The name came out of her as a phlegm-choked moan. 'I had no idea that Harry had invited you.'

'Neither does Harry,' Elise whispered with a conspiratorial grin. 'But how can he mind? This was my house for so long that I think I should still be welcome in it, for a few days at least. And since he made such a kind point of inviting my special friend, he must have meant to include me. Otherwise he would have left me quite alone in London for the holidays. That cannot have been his intention.'

'Special friend?' Elise could not mean what she was implying. And even if she did, Rosalind prayed she would not have been so bold as to bring him here. If Elise had taken a lover, Rosalind suspected that it was very much Harry's intention to split the two up.

'Have you met? I doubt it. Here, Nicholas—meet little Rosalind, my husband's half-sister. She is to be our hostess.'

When she saw him, Rosalind felt her smile freeze as solid as the ice on the windowpanes. Nicholas Tremaine was as fine as she remembered him, his hair dark, his face a patrician mask, with a detached smile. It held none of the innocent mirth of their first meeting but all of the world-weariness she had seen in him even then. And, as it had five years before, her heart stopped and then gave an unaccustomed leap as she waited for him to notice her. 'How do you do, Mr…?'

But it was too much to hope that he had forgotten her. 'I believe we've met,' he said, and then his jaw clenched so hard that his lips went white. He had paused on the doorstep, one boot on the threshold, snow falling on his broad shoulders, the flakes bouncing off them to melt at his feet. His clothing was still immaculate and in the first stare of fashion. But now it was of a better cut, and from more expensive cloth than it had been. It hardly mattered. For when she had first seen him, Nicholas Tremaine had been the sort of man to make poverty appear elegant.

If his change in tailor was an indication, his fortunes had improved, and wealth suited him even better. In any other man, she would have thought that pause in the doorway a vain attempt to add drama to his entrance, while allowing the audience to admire his coat. But she suspected that now Tremaine had seen her he was trying to decide whether it would be better to enter the house or run back towards London—on foot, if necessary.

The pause continued as he struggled to find the correct mood. Apparently he'd decided on benign courtesy, for he smiled, although a trifle coldly, and said, 'We met in London. It was several years ago, although I cannot remember the exact circumstances.'

Liar. She was sure that he remembered the whole

incident in excruciating detail. As did she. She hoped her face did not grow crimson at the recollection.

'But I had no idea,' he continued, 'that you were Harry's mysterious sister.'

Was she the only one who heard the silent words, *Or I would never have agreed to come?* But he was willing to pretend ignorance, possibly because the truth reflected no better on him than it had on her, so she must play the game as well.

'I am his half-sister. Mother married my father when Harry was just a boy. He is a vicar.' She paused. 'My father, that is. Because of course Harry is not…' She was so nervous that she was rambling, and she stopped herself suddenly, which made for an embarrassing gap in the conversation.

'So I've been told.'

'I had no idea that you would be a guest here.' *Please*, she willed, *believe I had no part in this.*

If the others in the room noticed the awkwardness between them, they gave no indication. Elise's welcome was as warm as if there had been nothing wrong. 'How strange that I've never introduced you. Rosalind was in London for a time the year we…the year I married Harry.' She stumbled over her own words for a moment, as though discovering a problem, and Rosalind held her breath, fearing that Elise had noticed the coincidence. But then the moment passed, and Elise took Tremaine's arm possessively. 'I am sure we will all be close friends now. I have not had much chance to know you, Rosalind, since you never leave home. I hope that we can change that. Perhaps now that you are old enough, your father will allow you to come to London and visit?'

'Of course,' she replied, fighting the temptation to remind Elise that Rosalind was her senior by almost two months. Her age did not signify, for her father would never let her travel, and certainly not to visit her brother's wife. If Elise meant to carry on a public affair, no decent lady could associate with her. And the identity of the gentleman involved made an embarrassing situation into a mortifying one.

Elise continued to act as if nothing was wrong. 'I am glad that you have come to stay with Harry. He needs a keeper if he has taken to engaging in daft wagers for Christmas. And this party will be an excellent opportunity for you to widen your social circle.'

'Wagers?' She looked at her sister-in-law with helpless confusion. And then she asked, 'What has Harry done now?'

Elise laughed. 'Has he forgotten to tell you, little one, of the reason for this party? How typical of him. He's bet the men at the club that he can make Mr Tremaine wish him a Merry Christmas. But Nick is most adamant in his plan to avoid merriment. I have had no impact on him, and you know my feelings on the subject of Christmas fun. It will be interesting to see if you can move him, now that you are in charge of the entertainments here.'

'Oh.' This was news, thought Rosalind. For at one time Nicholas Tremaine had been of quite a different opinion about the holiday, much to their mutual regret.

But there was no reason to mention it, for Tremaine seemed overly focused on his Garrick and his hat, as though wishing to look anywhere than at his hostess.

Now Elise was unbuttoning her cloak, and calling for a servant, treating this very much as if it was still her home. It was even more annoying to see the servants responding with such speed, when they would drag their feet for her. It was clear that Elise was mistress here, not her. Rosalind's stomach gave a sick lurch. Let her find her own way to her room, and take her lover as well. She signalled to the servants to help Tremaine, and turned to make an escape.

And then she saw Harry, at the head of the stairs. The couple in the doorway had not noticed him as yet, but Rosalind could see his expression as he observed them. He saw Tremaine first, and there was a narrowing of the eyes, a slight smile, and a set to the chin that hinted of a battle to come. But then he looked past his adversary to the woman behind him.

Resolution dissolved into misery. The look of pain on his face was plain to see, should any observe him. Then he closed his eyes and took a gathering breath. When he opened them again he was his usual carefree self. He started down the stairs, showing to all the world that there was not a thing out of the ordinary in entertaining one's wife and her lover as Christmas guests.

'Tremaine, you have decided to take up my offer after all.' He reached out to clasp the gentleman's hand, and gave him a hearty pat on the back that belied his look of a moment earlier. 'We shall get you out of the blue funk you inhabit in this jolly time.'

Tremaine looked, by turns, alarmed and suspicious. 'I seriously doubt it.'

'But I consider it my duty,' Harry argued. 'For how could I entrust my wife to the keeping of a man who cannot keep this holiday in his heart? She adores it, sir. Simply adores it.' There was the faintest emphasis on the word 'wife', as though he meant to remind Tremaine of the facts in their relationship.

'Really, Harry. You have not "entrusted" me to anyone. You speak as though I were part of the entail.' Pique only served to make Elise more beautiful, and Rosalind wondered if it was a trick that could be learned, or if it must be bred in.

'And Elise.' Harry turned to her, putting a hand on each shoulder and leaning forward to kiss her.

She turned a cold cheek to him, and he stopped his lips just short of it, kissing the air by her face before releasing her to take her wrap. 'This is most unexpected. I assumed, when you said that you never wished to set foot over my threshold again…' he leaned back to stare into her eyes '…that you would leave me alone.'

Elise's smile was as brilliant as the frost glittering from the trees, and as brittle. 'When I heard that you wished to extend your hospitality to Nicholas, I assumed that you were inviting me as well. We are together now, you know.' There was a barb in the last sentence, but Harry gave no indication that he had been wounded by it.

'Of course. And if it will truly make you happy, then I wish you well in it. Come in, come in. You will take your death, standing in the cold hall like this.' He looked out into the yard. 'The weather is beastly, I must say. All the better to be inside, before a warm fire.'

Tremaine cast a longing glance over his shoulder, at the road away from the house, before Harry shut the door behind him. 'Come, the servants will show you to your rooms.'

'Where have you put us?' Elise asked. 'I was thinking the blue rooms in the east wing would be perfect.'

Rosalind swallowed, unsure of how she was expected to answer such a bold request. Although Harry might say aloud that he wished for his wife to have whatever made her happy, she doubted that it would extend to offering her the best guest rooms in the house, so that she could go to her lover through the connecting door between them.

Before she could answer, Harry cut in. 'I am so sorry, darling. Had I but known you were coming I'd have set them aside for you. But since I thought Tremaine was arriving alone, if at all, I had Rosalind put him in the room at the end of that hall.'

'The smallest one?' Elise said bluntly.

'Of course. He does not need much space—do you, old man?' Harry stared at him, daring him to respond in the negative.

'Of—of course not,' Tremaine stuttered.

Harry turned back to Elise. 'And I am afraid you will have to take the room you have always occupied. The place beside me. Although we are full to the rafters, I told Rosalind to leave it empty. I will never fill the space that is rightly yours.'

The last words had a flicker of meaning that Elise chose to ignore. 'That is utterly impossible, Harry. I have no wish to return to it.'

His voice was soft, but firm. 'I am afraid, darling, that you must make do with what is available. And if that is the best room in the house then so be it.' He turned and walked away from her, up the stairs.

Elise hurried after him, and Rosalind could hear the faint hiss of whispered conversation. Nicholas Tremaine followed after, his retreating back stiff.

Chapter Four

By the time they reached the door to her bedroom, Nicholas had made a discreet exit. And for the first time in two months, Elise was alone with her infuriatingly reasonable husband.

'But, my dear, I cannot give you another room, even if I might wish to. On my honour, they are all full.'

Harry was smiling at her again, and she searched his face for any sign that he had missed her, and had orchestrated the situation just to have her near. But in his eyes she saw not love, nor frustrated passion, nor even smug satisfaction at having duped her to return. He was showing her the same warmth he might show to a stranger. He held a hand out to her again, but made no attempt to touch her.

'I am offering you the best I have, just as I have always done. And you will be more comfortable, you know, sleeping in your own bed and not in a guest room.'

He was being sensible again, damn him. And it was

likely to drive her mad. 'It is not my own bed any longer, Harry. For, in case you have forgotten, I have left you.' She said it with emphasis, and smiled in a self-satisfied way that would push any man to anger if he cared at all for his wife or his pride.

Harry responded with another understanding smile. 'I realise that. Although it is good to see you home again, even if it is only for a visit.'

'If you were so eager to see me you could have come to London,' she said in exasperation. 'You were there only last week.'

Harry looked confused. 'I was supposed to visit you? If you desired my company, then you would not have left.' He said it as though it were the most logical thing in the world, instead of an attempt to provoke her to anger.

'You tricked Nicholas into coming here for Christmas with that silly letter.'

'And he brought you as well.' Harry beamed at her. 'I would hardly call my invitation to Tremaine a trick. I promise, I meant no harm by it. Nor by the arrangement of the rooms. Can you not take it in the way it is offered? I wish Tremaine to have a merry Christmas. And I wish you to feel at home. I would want no less for any of my guests.' If he had a motive beyond that she could find no trace of it—in his expression or his tone.

'But you do not expect the other female guests to share a connecting door with your bedroom, do you?' She had hoped to sound annoyed by the inconvenience. But her response sounded more like jealous curiosity than irritation.

He laughed as though he had just remembered the threshold he had been crossing regularly for five years. 'Oh, that.'

'Yes. That, Harry.'

'But it will not matter in the least, for I have no intention of using it. I know where I am not welcome.' As he spoke, his cordial expression never wavered. It was as though being shut from his wife's bedroom made not the slightest difference in his mood or his future.

And with that knowledge frustration got the better of her, and she turned from him and slammed the door in his face.

Nick made it as far as the top of the stairs before his anger got the better of *him*. In front of him Harry and Elise were still carrying on a *sotto voce* argument about the sleeping arrangements. In truth, Elise was arguing while her husband remained even-tempered but implacable. In any case, Nick wanted no part of it. And he suspected it would be the first of many such discussions he would be a party to if he did not find a way back to London in short order.

But not until he gave the girl at the foot of the stairs a piece of his mind. Rosalind Morley was standing alone in the entryway, fussing with the swag of pine bows that decorated the banister of the main stairs. She was much as he remembered her—diminutive in stature, barely five feet tall. Her short dark curls bobbed against her face as she rearranged the branches. Her small, sweet mouth puckered in a look of profound irritation.

It irritated him as well that even after five years he fancied he could remember the taste of those lips when they had met his. It was most unfair. A mistake of that magnitude should have the decency to fade out of memory, not come running back to the fore when one had troubles enough on one's hands. But he doubted she was there by accident any more than he was. And she deserved to know the extent of his displeasure at being tricked by her again, before he departed and left Elise to her husband. He started down the stairs.

She was picking at the boughs now, frowning in disapproval and rearranging the nuts and berries into a semblance of harmony. But her efforts seemed to make things worse and not better. As he started down towards her, the wire that held the thing in place came free and he could see a cascade of needles falling onto the slate floor at her feet, along with a shower of fruit.

'Damn,' she whispered to herself, sneaking a curse where she thought no one could hear her.

'You!' His voice startled her, and she glanced up at him, dropped the apple she had been holding, and stared fixedly at it as it rolled across the floor to land against the bottom step.

'Yes?' She was trying to sound distant and slightly curious, as though she were talking to a stranger. But it was too late to pretend that she had no idea what he meant by the exclamation, for he had seen the panic in her eyes before she looked away.

'Do not try to fool me. I know who you are.'

'I did not intend to hide the fact from you. And I had no idea that you would be among Harry's guests.'

'And I did not know, until this moment, that you were Harry's sister, or I'd never have agreed to this farce.'

'Half-sister,' she corrected.

He waved a hand. 'It hardly matters. You were more than half-loyal to him the day you ruined me.'

'I ruined you?' She laughed, but he could hear the guilt in it.

'As I recollect it, yes. You stood there under the mistletoe, in the refreshment room at the Granvilles' ball. And when you saw me you held your arms out in welcome, even though we'd met just moments before. What was I to think of the offer?'

'That I was a foolish girl who had drunk too much punch?'

He held up a finger. 'Perhaps that is exactly what I thought, and I meant to caution you about your behaviour. But when I stepped close to you, you threw your arms around my neck and kissed me, most ardently.'

Rosalind flinched. 'You did not have to come near to reprimand me, or to reciprocate so enthusiastically when I kissed you.' She stared down at the floor and scuffed at the fallen pine needles with her slipper, looking for all the world like a guilty child.

He shook his head, trying to dislodge the memory. 'Believe me, I regret my reaction, no matter how natural it was. That little incident has taught me well the dangers of too much wine and too much celebration.'

'So you blame me, personally, for ruining Christmas for you?'

'And my chances with my intended, Elise. For when she got wind of what had occurred she left me and married another.'

Nicholas was surprised to see the girl start, as though she was just now realising the extent of her guilt and the chaos her foolish actions had caused. 'You were engaged to Elise? The woman who was in the entry with us just now? My sister-in-law?' Rosalind shook her head, as though she were misunderstanding him in some way.

'The woman who married your brother after you so conveniently dishonoured yourself and me.'

She gave a helpless little shrug. 'But I had no idea, at the time, what I was doing.'

'Because you were inebriated.' He held up a second finger, ticking off another point in his argument. 'And on spirits that I did not give you. So do not try to tell me I lured you to disaster. Although you appeared fine to the casual observer, you must have been drunk as a lord.' He puzzled over it for a moment. 'If that is even a possible state for a girl. I do not think there is a corresponding female term for the condition you were in.'

She winced again. 'I was sorry. I still am. And I paid dearly for it, as you remember.'

'You were sick in the entry hall before your father could get you home.'

If possible, the girl looked even more mortified, as though she had forgotten this portion of the evening in question. 'I meant when I was sent off to rusticate. I never had the come-out that my father had promised, because he said he could not trust me. I am unmarried to this day.'

'You are unmarried,' he said through gritted teeth, 'because your father could not persuade me that it was in my best interests to attach myself for life to a spoiled child.'

'I never expected that you would marry me,' she assured him. 'And I had no wish to marry you. We had known each other for moments when the incident occurred. It would have done no good to pile folly upon folly trying to save my reputation.'

He smiled in triumph. 'Miss Morley, I think I know very well what you expected. For now that I have come to this house the picture is suddenly clear to me. You expected Elise would get word of it and that she would choose your brother over me. And that is just what occurred.'

'Half-brother,' she corrected. 'And I did no such thing. To the best of my knowledge, Harry knows nothing of the happenings of that night. Father kept the whole a secret, and does not speak of it to this day. Harry does not enjoy the company of my father, and seldom visited his mother. We had only just arrived in London, and I did not get a chance to call on him before my behaviour forced the family to leave again. Even now, all my brother knows of that visit is that I did something so despicable that I was sent from London in shame, and that the family is forbidden to speak of it. We could not have the thing fall from memory if it was a continual topic of conversation.'

'You expect me to believe that you were not in collusion with Harry to ruin my engagement to Elise?' He arched an eyebrow at her and glared, waiting for her resolve to break under his displeasure.

She raised her chin in defiance. 'Do you honestly think that my brother would destroy my reputation so casually in an effort to defeat you?'

'Half-brother,' he corrected.

'Even so,' she allowed. 'You may not like him, but do you think Harry is the sort of person who would behave in such an underhanded fashion as to get me foxed and throw me at you? It is not as if he does not care for me at all. He would have no wish to hurt me.'

He paused and considered the situation, trying to imagine Harry Pennyngton as the mastermind of his destruction. While he could imagine Harry viewing an affair of the heart with the same shrewdness he brought to his business dealings, he would never have orchestrated the disaster with Rosalind Morley. More likely, when he had discovered that Elise was free, he had simply capitalised on an opportunity, just as she assumed.

At last, he admitted, 'Harry has always been the most even-handed and honourable of fellows. Elise comments on it frequently.'

'See?' Rosalind poked him smartly in the chest with a holly branch she had pulled from the decorations during her agitated repairs, and a leaf stuck in the fabric of his jacket. 'If he'd had wind of it at the time it is far more likely that he'd have called you out for it, or helped to cover the whole thing up, just as my father wished to do. And he'd have never invited you here while I was hostess, even after all this time. If Elise had learned anything about it she would not have greeted me as warmly as she did just now. I doubt that either of them has a clue as to what happened.' She blinked at him, suddenly worried, and whispered, 'And I would prefer that it stay that way. Which will be difficult, if you insist on arguing about it in a public room.'

Nick took this information in and held it for a while, examining it from all sides before speaking. If it was in any way possible that the girl told the truth, then he must give her the benefit of the doubt. Revelation of the story at this point would turn a delicate situation into a volatile one. He said, 'I have no desire to unbury any secrets during this visit, if it is true that we have managed to keep them hidden. What's done is done. We cannot change the past.'

'This meeting was none of my doing, I swear to you,' she said earnestly, before he could speak, again. 'I would never have agreed to any of it had I known…' He could see the obvious distress in her eyes, and she twisted the holly in her hands until the leaves scratched her fingers and the berries had been crushed. 'I never meant to hurt you or anyone else by my actions. Or to help anyone, for that matter. I simply did not think.' She looked down at the destruction, dropped the twig, and hurriedly wiped her hands on her skirt. She held them out in appeal. 'I am afraid I am prone to not thinking things through. But I have worked hard to improve my character, and the messes I make are not so severe as they once were.'

He nodded, though her unexpected presence still filled him with unease. 'I understand. I am beginning to suspect we are both here for reasons that have little to do with our preference in the matter and everything to do with the wishes of others.'

She said, 'I think Harry hoped that I would have the opportunity to impress eligible male guests with my ability as a hostess. I doubt that will be the case, since my skills are nothing to write home about. In any case, the single gentlemen he promised have failed to materialise. There is you, of course, but if you are with Elise...' She trailed off in embarrassment, as she realised that her babbling had sounded like an invitation to court her.

He watched her for a time, allowing her to suffer a bit, for it would not do for the girl to think he was interested. Whatever Harry had planned for him this weekend, he doubted it would include courting his sister. Rosalind could not tell by looking at him what his real feelings might be for Elise, and he had no wish to inform her of them. But if Elise learned the truth before he could escape, there would be hell to pay.

He said, 'It is very awkward for everyone concerned. Elise wished to come and speak with Harry, and she did not want to come alone. Now that my job as escort has been done, I mean to stay no more than tonight— whatever Harry's plans might be. I suspect I will be gone shortly after breakfast, and I will trouble you no more.'

Rosalind glanced out of the window at the fast-falling snow. 'You do not know how treacherous the local roads can be after a storm such as this. You may find travel to be impossible for quite some time. And you are welcome until Twelfth Night in any case.'

But she looked as though she hoped he would not stay, and he did not blame her. 'Thank you for your hospitality. I trust you will not find it strange if I avoid your company at breakfast?'

She nodded again. 'I will not think it the least bit odd. As a matter of fact, it is probably for the best.' She hesitated. 'Although I do wish to apologise, one last time, for what happened when we first met.'

'It is not necessary.'

'But I cannot seem to stop. For I truly regret it.'

He gave a curt bow. 'I understand that. Do not concern yourself with it. We will chalk it up to the folly of youth.' And how could he fault her for that? For he had been guilty of folly as well, and was paying for it to this day.

'Thank you for understanding.'

'Then let us hear no more apologies on the matter. Consider yourself absolved.'

But, while he might be able to forgive, he doubted he would ever forget her.

Chapter Five

ELISE glared through the wood of her bedroom door at the man in the hall. She had not thought when she made this trip that she would end up back in her own room. She would be alone with her memories, and scant feet from her husband, while Nicholas was stowed in the remotest corner of the guest wing like so much discarded baggage. Though he showed no sign of it, she was sure that Harry had anticipated her appearance and sought an opportunity to separate them.

But if he did not want her, then why would he bother? So Harry did not mean to come and take her in the night? Fine. It was just as she'd feared. She meant nothing to him any more. And telling her the truth, with that annoying little smile of his, had removed all hope that he had been harbouring a growing and unfulfilled passion since her precipitate retreat from his house. If he cared for her, an absence of two months would have been sufficient to make him drag her back to his bed the first chance he got, so that he might slake his lust. But to announce that he meant to leave her in peace for a fortnight while she slept only a room away…

She balled her fists in fury. The man had not left her alone for a fortnight in the whole time they had lived together. But apparently his visits had been just as she'd feared: out of convenience rather than an uncontrollable desire for her and her alone. Now that she was not here he must be finding someone else to meet his needs.

The thought raised a lump in her throat. Perhaps he had finally taken a mistress, just as she'd always feared he would. It had been some consolation during the time that they had been together to know that he was either faithful or incredibly discreet in his infidelities. For, while she frequently heard rumours about the husbands of her friends, she had never heard a word about Harry.

And to have taken a lover would have required equally miraculous stamina, for even after five years he had been most enthusiastic and regular in his bedroom visits, right up to the moment she had walked out the door. Then, his interest in her body had evaporated.

If they had not married in haste, things might have been different between them. She should never have accepted Harry Pennyngton's offer when she had still been so angry with Nicholas. She had been almost beyond reason, and had hardly had time to think before she had dispensed with one man and taken another.

But Harry's assurances had been so reasonable, so comforting, that they had been hard to resist. He had said he was of a mind to take a wife. And he had heard that she was in desperate straits. That her parents were returning to Bavaria, and she must marry someone quickly if she wished to remain in England. If so, why could it not be him? He had described the house to her, the grounds and the attached properties, and told her of his income and the title. If she refused him he would understand, of course. For they were little better than strangers. But if she chose to accept everything he had would be hers, and he would do all in his power to assure that she did not regret the decision.

He had laid it all out before her like some sort of business deal. And although he had not stated the fact outright, she had suspected that she would not get a better offer, and would end up settling for less should she refuse.

That should have been her first warning that the marriage would not be what she'd hoped. For where Nicholas had been full of fine words of love and big dreams of the future, Harry had been reason itself about what she could expect should she choose to marry him.

It had been quite soothing, in retrospect, to be free of grand passion for a moment, and to give her broken heart a chance to mend. Harry had been willing to give without question, and had asked for nothing in return but her acceptance.

They had been wed as soon as he'd been able to get a licence. And if she'd had any delusions that he wished a meeting of hearts before a meeting of bodies, he had dispelled them on the first night.

Elise had thought that Harry might give her time to

adjust to her new surroundings, and wished that she'd had the nerve to request it. For intimacy had hardly seemed appropriate so soon. They had barely spoken. She hadn't even learned how he liked his tea, or his eggs. And to learn how he liked other things before they had even had breakfast? It had all happened too fast. Surely he would give her a few days to get to know her new husband?

But as she had prepared for bed on her wedding night, she had reached for her nightrail only to have the maid pull it aside. 'Lord Anneslea says you will not be needing it this evening, ma'am.'

'Really?' She felt the first thrill of foreboding.

'Just the dressing gown.' And the maid wrapped her bare body in silk and exited the room.

What was she to do now? For clearly the staff had more instruction than she had over what was to occur. And it was not likely to be a suggestion that they live as brother and sister until familiarity had been gained.

There was a knock at the connecting door between his bedroom and hers. 'Elise? May I come in?'

She gave him a hesitant yes.

He opened the door but did not enter. Instead he stood framed in the doorway, staring at her. 'I thought tonight, perhaps, you would join me in my room.' He stepped to the side and held a hand out to her.

When she reached to take it, his fingers closed over hers, and he led her over the threshold to his room.

It was surprisingly warm for a winter's night, and she could see that the fire was built to blazing in the fireplace. 'I did not want you to take a chill,' he offered, by way of explanation.

'Oh.'

Then he helped her up the short step that led to his bed, and jumped up himself to sit on the edge beside her. He brushed a lock of hair off her face, and asked, 'What have you been told about what will happen tonight?'

'That it will go much faster if I lie still and do not speak.'

His face paled. 'I imagine it will. But expediency is not always the object with these things. If you wish to move at any time, for any reason, then you must certainly do it. And by all means speak, if you have anything to say. If I am causing you discomfort I will only know if you tell me. And if something gives you pleasure?' He smiled hopefully. 'Then I wish to know that as well.'

'Oh.'

'Are you ready to begin?'

'I think so, yes.' She was still unsure what it was that they were beginning. But how else was she to find out?

He kissed her, and it was a pleasant surprise, for other than one brief kiss when he had proposed, and another in the chapel after the wedding, he had offered no displays of affection. But this was different. He rested his lips against hers for a moment, moving back and forth, and then parting them with his tongue.

It was an interesting sensation. Especially since the longer he kissed her the more she was convinced that she could feel the kiss in other parts of her body, where his lips had not touched. When she remarked on it, he offered to kiss her there as well, and his lips slid to her chin, her throat, and then to her breast.

It was wonderful, and strange, for it made the feelings even more intense, and he seemed to understand for his lips followed the sensation lower.

She scrambled away from him, up onto the pillows on the other side of the bed. Because she understood what it was he meant to do, and it was very shocking. It was then that she realised her robe had come totally undone and he was staring at her naked body. The feeling of his eyes on her felt very much like the intimate kiss she was avoiding, so she wrapped the gown tightly about her and shook her head.

'I have frightened you.' He dragged his gaze back to her face and looked truly contrite. 'Here, let us start again.'

He climbed past her on the bed, and reached for a pot of oil that rested on the night stand. It was scented with a rich perfume, and he took a dab of the stuff, stroking it onto the palm of his hand.

'Let me touch you.'

She tensed in anticipation of his caress. But he sat behind her this time. He slipped his hands beneath the neck of the robe to stroke her shoulders, kissing her neck before rubbing the ointment into the muscles there.

'See? There is nothing to be afraid of. I only mean to give you pleasure.'

And there certainly did not seem to be anything to fear. It was very relaxing to feel his hands sliding over her body, and she found it almost impossible to resist as he pushed the fabric of her robe lower, until he could reach the small of her back.

She was bare to the waist now. And even though he was behind her, and could not see them, she kept her hands folded across her breasts. But soon she relaxed her arms and dropped them to her sides. When he reached around her to touch her ribs, the underside of her breasts and her nipples, she did not fight him. It felt good. And then she leaned back against him and allowed him to play.

When he heard her breathing quicken he put his lips to her ear and kissed her once, before beginning to whisper, in great detail, just what it was he meant to do next.

For a moment her eyes opened wide in alarm, but his hands slipped down, massaging her belly, as his voice assured her that it would be all right. He nuzzled her neck. One hand still toyed with a breast, while the other slid between her legs and teased until her knees parted. The sensation was new, and intense, but he seemed to know just how to touch her until she moaned and twisted against him.

He explained again how wonderful it would feel to be inside her, and demonstrated with his hand, his fingers sliding over her body, inside and out again, over and over, until her head lolled back against him and her back arched in a rush of sensation.

He released her and turned her in his arms, so that he could kiss her again. And then he laid her down on the pillows. And she could see what it was that had been pressing against her so insistently as he had stroked her. She enquired after it.

He explained the differences in their bodies, but assured her that he would enjoy her touch just as she had enjoyed his. Then he kissed her again, and lay down beside her, guiding her hand to touch him.

It gave her a chance to observe him as she had not done before marriage. His own dressing gown had fallen away, and he was naked beside her on the bed. His body was lean and well muscled, although he had never given her the impression of being a sportsman or athlete. His eyes were half closed, and a knowing smile curled at the corners of his lips. He was a handsome man, although she had not thought to notice when he had made his offer to her. His hair was so light a brown as to be almost blond, and he had a smooth brow. His strong chin hinted at power of will, although his ready smile made him appear an amiable companion. There was no cruelty in his green-grey eyes, but a sly twinkle as he reached for her and, with a few simple touches, rendered her helpless with pleasure all over again.

Then he draped his hand over her hip and pulled her close, so her breasts pressed against his chest. His other hand slipped back between her legs, readying her. Her hand was still upon him, stroking gently, and she helped him to find his way to her, then closed her eyes.

He kissed her, and it was almost apologetic as he came into her and she felt the pain of it. But then she felt him moving in her, and against her, and his strength dissolved into need. Finally there was something that she could give to him, an explanation for his generosity. And it all made sense. So she ignored the pain and found the pleasure again, kissed him back as he shuddered in release.

He held her afterwards, and she slept in his arms. The next morning he was cautious and polite, just as he had been before they had married. She remembered the intimacy of the previous night and found it strange that he was still so shy. But she assumed that over time the distance between them would fade.

Instead it was as though the divide between them grew with each rising of the sun. He was friendly and courteous. He made her laugh, and was never cross with her over small things, as her own family had been. He did not raise his voice even when she was sure he must be angry with her.

But he never revealed any more of his innermost thoughts than were absolutely necessary. If he ever had need of a confidante he must have sought elsewhere, for he certainly did not trouble his wife with his doubts or fears.

In truth there was nothing about their relationship that would lead her to believe she was especially close to him in any way but the physical. At first, she thought that he had chosen her because he could find no other willing to have him. He had been too quick to offer, and with such minimal affection. Perhaps his heart was broken, just as hers had been, and he had sought oblivion in the nearest source?

But as time passed he spoke of no previous alliances, and showed no interest in the other women of the ton, either married or single. She had frequent opportunity to see that he could have married elsewhere, had he so chosen. And the compliments of the other girls, when they'd heard that she was to marry him, had held a certain wistful envy. Although he had offered for her, he had treated them all with the utmost courtesy and generosity, and they would have welcomed further interest had any been expressed.

They had done well enough together, Elise supposed. But he had never given her an indication, in the five years they had been together, that he would not have done equally well with any other young woman of the ton, or that his marriage to her had been motivated by anything other than the fortuitous timing of his need for a wife when she had desperately been in need of a husband.

When night came, there had been no question of why he had married her—for his passion had only increased, as had hers. It had been easy to see what he wanted, and to know that she pleased him, and he had taken great pains to see that she was satisfied as well. To lie in his arms each night had been like a taste of paradise, after days that were amiable but strangely empty. Even now she could not help but remember how it had felt to lie with him: cherished. Adored.

Loved.

It was all she could do to keep from throwing open the door between them right now and begging him to hold her again, to ease the ache of loneliness that she had felt since the moment she had left him.

But what good would that do in the long run? She would be happy at night, when he thought only of her.

But at all other times she would not be sure what he thought of her, or if he thought of her at all.

He would be pleasant to her, of course. He would be the picture of good manners and casual affection—as he was with everyone, from shopkeepers to strangers. But he did not seem to share many interests with his wife. While he had always accompanied her to social gatherings, she did not think he'd taken much pleasure in them, and he'd seemed faintly relieved to stay at home, even if it had meant that she was accompanied by other gentlemen. He had showed no indication of jealousy, although she was certain that her continued friendship with Nicholas must have given him cause. Her husband had treated Tremaine with a suspicious level of good humour, although they should be bitter rivals after what had gone before.

In time, Nicholas had forgiven her for her hasty parting with him, and his level of flirtation had increased over the years, overlaying a deep and abiding friendship. She'd enjoyed his attention, but it had worried her terribly that she might be a better friend to another man than she was to her husband.

But if Harry had been bothered by it she hadn't been able to tell. He'd either seen no harm in it, or simply had not cared enough about her to stop it.

Most important, if their lack of children had weighed on his mind, as it had hers, she had found no indication of it. In fact, he'd flatly refused to speak of it. The extent to which he'd appeared not to blame her for the problem had left her sure that he secretly thought she was at fault. Her own father had always said that girl children were a burden compared to sons. She dreaded to think what he would have said had his wife provided no children at all.

It had been hard to avoid the truth. She had failed at the one thing she was born to do. She had proved herself to be as useless as her family thought her. Harry must regret marrying her at all.

And on the day that she had been angry enough to leave she had shouted that she would return to her old love, for he at least was able to give her an honest answer if she asked him a direct question about his feelings on things that truly mattered.

Harry had blinked at her. There had been no trace of his usual absent smile, but no anger, either. And he had said, 'As you wish, my dear. If, after all this time, you do not mean to stay, I cannot hold you here against your will.'

Elise had wanted to argue that of course he could. That a real man would have barred the door and forbidden her from talking nonsense. Or called out Nicholas long ago for his excessively close friendship to another man's wife. Then he would have thrown her over his shoulder and marched to the bedroom, to show her in no uncertain terms the advantages of remaining just where she was.

But when one was in a paroxysm of rage it made no sense to pause and give the object of that rage a second chance to answer the question more appropriately. Nor should she have had to explain the correct response he must give to her anger. For if she must tell him how to behave, it hardly mattered that he was willing to act just as she wished.

So she had stormed out of the house and taken the carriage to London, and had informed a slightly alarmed Nicholas that there was nothing to stand between them and a much closer relationship than they had previously enjoyed.

And if she had secretly hoped that her husband would be along at any time to bring her back, even if it meant an argument that would raise the roof on their London townhouse? Then it was positive proof of her foolishness.

Chapter Six

After a fitful night's rest, Nick Tremaine sought out his host to say a hasty farewell. He found Anneslea at the bottom of the stairs, staring out of the window at the yard. Nick turned the cheery tone the blighter had used on him at the club back upon him with full force. 'Harry!'

'Nicholas.' Harry turned towards him with an even broader smile than usual, and a voice oozing suspicion. 'Did you sleep well?'

The bed had been narrow, hard where it needed to be soft, and soft where it ought to be firm. And no amount of wood in the fireplace had been able to take the chill from the room. But he'd be damned before he complained of it. 'It was nothing less than what I expected when I accepted your kind invitation.'

Harry's grin turned malicious. 'And you brought a surprise with you, I see?'

Nick responded with a similar smile, hoping that the last-minute addition to the guest list had got well up the nose of his conniving host. 'Well, you know Elise. There is no denying her when she gets an idea into her head.'

'Yes. I know Elise.'

Anneslea was still smiling, but his tone indicated that there would be hell to pay if Tremaine knew her too well. Just one more reason to bolt for London and leave the two lovebirds to work out their problems in private.

He gave Harry a sympathetic pat on the back. 'And, since you do, you will understand how displeased she shall be with me when she hears that I've had to return to London.'

'Return? But, my dear sir, you've only just arrived.' The other man laid a hand on his shoulder. 'I would not think of seeing you depart so soon.'

Nick tried to shake off his host's friendly gesture, which had attached to him like a barnacle. When it would not budge, he did his best to ignore it. 'All the same, I must away. I've just had word of an urgent matter that needs my attention. But before I go, I wanted to thank you and wish you a M—'

Anneslea cut him off in mid-word. 'Received word from London? I fail to see how. It is too early for the morning post, and, given the condition of the road, I doubt we will see it at all today.'

Damn the country and its lack of civilisation. 'Not received word, precisely. Remembered. I have remembered something I must attend to. Immediately. And so I will start for London and leave Elise in your capable hands. And I wish you both a Mer—'

'But surely there is nothing that cannot wait until

after the holiday? Even if you left today you would not arrive in London before Christmas Day. Although you might wish to be a miserable old sinner for this season, you should not make your servants work through Boxing Day to get you home.'

Nick sighed, trying to manage a show of regret. 'It cannot be helped. I have come to tell you I cannot stay. Pressing business calls me back to London. But although I must toil, there is no reason that you cannot have a Merr—'

Before he could complete the phrase sliding from his lips, Harry interrupted again. 'Ridiculous. I will not hear of it. In this weather it is not safe to travel.'

Damn the man. It was almost as if he did not want to win his bet. Which was obviously a lie, for he had seen the look on Anneslea's face at the sight of his wife. The man was as miserable without her as she was without him. Nick stared out of the nearest window at the snow lying thick upon the drive. 'It was safe enough for me to arrive here. And the weather is much improved over yesterday, I am certain. If I depart now I will have no problems. But not before wishing you a M—'

'Not possible.' Harry gestured at the sky. 'Look at the clouds, man. Slate-grey. There is more snow on the way, and God knows what else.' As if on cue a few hesitant flakes began falling, increasing in number as he watched. Anneslea nodded in satisfaction. 'The roads will be ice or mud all the way to London. Better to remain inside, with a cup of punch and good company.'

Nick looked at the mad glint in his host's eye and said, 'I am willing to take my chances with the weather.'

There was a polite clearing of the throat behind them as a footman tried to gain the attention of the Earl. 'My Lord?' The servant bowed, embarrassed at creating an interruption. 'There has been another problem. A wagon from the village has got stuck at the bend of the drive.'

Anneslea smiled at him in triumph. 'See? It is every bit as bad as I predicted. There is nothing to be done about it until the snow stops.' He turned back to the footman. 'Have servants unload the contents of the wagon and carry them to the house. Get the horses into our stable, and give the driver a warm drink.' He turned back to Nick. 'There is no chance of departure until we can clear the drive. And that could take days.'

'I could go around.'

'Trees block the way on both sides.' Harry was making no effort to hide his glee at Nick's predicament. 'You must face the fact, Tremaine. You are quite trapped here until such time as the weather lifts. You might as well relax and enjoy the festivities, just as I mean you to do.'

'Is that what you mean for me?'

'Of course, dear man. Why else would I bring you here?'

The man was all innocence again, damn him, smiling the smile of the concerned host.

'Now, was there anything else you wished to say to me?'

Just the two words that would free him of any further involvement in the lives of Lord and Lady Anneslea.

Nick thought of a week or more, trapped in the same house with Elise, trying to explain that he had thrown over the bet and her chance at divorce because he had her own best interests at heart. 'Anything to say to you? No. Definitely not.'

Rosalind stared at the bare pine in the drawing room, wondering just what she was expected to do with it. Harry had requested a tree, and here it was. But he had requested decorations as well, and then walked away as though she should know what he meant by so vague a statement. The servants had brought her a box of small candles and metal holders for the same, sheets of coloured paper, some ribbon, a handful of straw, and a large tray of gingerbread biscuits. When she had asked for further instruction, the footman had shrugged and said that it had always been left to the lady of the house. Then, he had given her the look that she had seen so often on the face of the servants. If she meant to replace their beloved Elise, then she should know how best to proceed—with no help from them.

Rosalind picked up a star-shaped biscuit and examined it. It was a bit early for sweets—hardly past breakfast. And they could have at least brought her a cup of tea. She bit off a point and chewed. Not the best gingerbread she had eaten, but certainly not the worst. This tasted strongly of honey.

She heard a melodious laugh from behind her, and turned to see her brother's wife standing in the doorway. 'Have you come to visit me in my misery, Elise?'

'Why would you be miserable, dear one?' Elise stepped into the room and took the biscuit from her hand. 'Christmas is no time to look so sad. But it will be considerably less merry for the others if you persist in eating the *lebkuchen*. They are ornaments for the tree. You may eat them on Twelfth Night, if you wish.'

Rosalind looked down at the lopsided star. 'So that is what I am to do with them. Everyone assumes that I must know.'

'Here. Let me show you.' Elise cut a length of ribbon from the spool in the basket, threaded it through a hole in the top of a heart-shaped biscuit, then tied it to a branch of the tree. She stood back to admire her work, and rearranged the bow in the ribbon until it was as pretty as the ornament. Then she smiled and reached for another biscuit, as though she was the hostess, demonstrating for a guest.

Rosalind turned upon her, hands on her hips. 'Elise, you have much to explain.'

'If it is about the logs for the fireplace, or the stuffing for the goose, I am sure that whatever you plan is satisfactory. The house is yours now.' She glanced around her old home, giving a critical eye to Rosalind's attempts to recreate the holiday. 'Not how I would have done things, perhaps. But you have done the best you can with little help from Harry.'

'You know that is not what I mean.' Rosalind frowned at her. 'Why are you here?'

She seemed to avoid the question, taking a sheet of coloured paper and shears. With a few folds and snips, and a final twist, she created a paper flower. 'The weather has changed and I was not prepared for it. There are some things left in my rooms that I have need of.'

'Then you could have sent for them and saved yourself the bother of a trip. Why are you really here, Elise? For if it was meant as a cruelty to Harry, you have succeeded.'

Guilt coloured Elise's face. 'If I had known there would be so many guests perhaps I would not have come. I thought the invitation was only to Nicholas and a few others. But I arrived to find the house full of people.' She stared down at the paper in her hands and placed the flower on the tree. 'The snow is still falling. By the time it stops it will be too late in the day to start for London. We will see tomorrow if there is a way to exit with grace.' She looked at Rosalind, and her guilty expression reformed into a mask of cold righteousness. 'And as for Harry feeling my cruelty to him? It must be a miracle of the season. I have lived with the man for years, and I have yet to find a thing I can do that will penetrate his defences.' The hole in the next ginger-bread heart had closed in baking, so she stabbed at the thing with the point of the scissors before reaching for the ribbon again.

Rosalind struggled to contain her anger. 'So it is just as I thought. You admit that you are attempting to hurt him, just to see if you can. You have struck him to the core with your frivolous behaviour, Elise. And if you cannot see it then you must not know the man at all.'

'Perhaps I do not.' Elise lost her composure again,

and her voice grew unsteady. 'It is my greatest fear, you see. After five years I do not understand him any better than the day we met. Do you think that it gives me no pain to say that? But it is—' she waved her hands, struggling for the words '—like being married to a Bluebeard. I feel I do not know the man at all.'

Rosalind laughed. 'Harry a Bluebeard? Do you think him guilty of some crime? Do you expect that he has evil designs against you in some way? Because I am sorry to say it, Elise, but that is the maddest idea, amongst all your other madness. My brother is utterly harmless.'

'That is not what I mean at all.' Elise sighed in apparent frustration at having to make herself understood in a language that was not her own. Then she calmed herself and began again. 'He means me no harm. But his heart…' Her face fell. 'It is shut tight against me. Are all Englishmen like this? Open to others, but reserved and distant with their wives? If I wished to know what is in his pocket or on his calendar he would show me these things freely. But I cannot tell what is on his mind. I do not know when he is sad or angry.'

Rosalind frowned in puzzlement. 'You cannot tell if your husband is angry?'

'He has not said a cross word to me—that I can remember. Not in the whole time we have been married. But no man can last for years with such an even temper. He must be hiding something. And if I cannot tell when he is angry, then how am I supposed to know that he is really happy? He is always smiling, Rosalind.' And now she sounded truly mad as she whispered, 'It is not natural.'

It was all becoming more confusing, not less. 'So you abandoned your husband because he was not angry with you?'

Elise picked up some bits of straw and began to work them together into a flat braid. 'You would think, would you not, that when a woman says to the man she has sworn herself to, that she would rather be with another, there would be a response?' She looked down at the thing in her hands, gave a quick twist to turn it into a heart, and placed it on the tree.

Rosalind winced. 'Oh, Elise, you did not. Say you did not tell him so.'

Elise blinked up at her in confusion. 'You did not think that I left him without warning?'

'I assumed,' said Rosalind through clenched teeth, 'that you left him in the heat of argument. And that by now you would have come to your senses and returned home.'

'That is the problem. The problem exactly.' Elise seemed to be searching for words again, and then she said, 'After all this time there is no heat.'

'No heat?' Rosalind knew very little about what went on between man and wife when they were alone, and had to admit some curiosity on the subject. But she certainly hoped she was not about to hear the intimate details of her brother's marriage, for she was quite sure she did not want to think of him in that way.

'Not in all ways, of course.' Elise blushed, and her hands busied themselves with another bunch of straws, working them into a star. 'There are some ways in which we are still very well suited. Physically, for example.'

She sighed, and gave a small smile. 'He is magnificent. He is everything I could wish for in a man.'

'Magnificent?' Rosalind echoed. Love must truly be blind. For although he was a most generous and amiable man, she would have thought 'ordinary' to be a better description of her brother.

When Elise saw her blank expression, she tried again. 'His charms might not be immediately obvious, but he is truly impressive. Unfortunately he is devoid of emotion. There can be no heat of any other kind if a person refuses to be angry. There is no real passion when one works so hard to avoid feeling.'

Rosalind shook her head. 'Harry is not without feelings, Elise. He is the most easily contented, happy individual I have had the pleasure to meet.'

Elise made a sound that was something between a growl and a moan. 'You have no idea, until you have tried it, how maddening it is to live with the most agreeable man in England. I tried, Rosalind, honestly I did. For years I resisted the temptation to goad him to anger, but I find I am no longer able to fight the urge. I want him to rail at me. To shout. To forbid me my wilfulness and demand his rights as my husband. I want to know when he is displeased with me. I would be only too happy for the chance to correct my behaviour to suit his needs.'

'You wish to be married to a tyrant?'

'Not a tyrant. Simply an honest man.' Elise stared at the straw in her hand. 'I know that I do not make him happy. I only wish him to admit it. If I can, I will improve my character to suit his wishes. And if I cannot?' Elise gave a deep sigh. 'Then at least I will have the truth. But if he will not tell me his true feelings it is impossible. If I ask him he will say that I am talking nonsense, and that there is nothing wrong. But it cannot be. No one is as agreeable as all that. So without even thinking, I took to doing things that I suspected would annoy him.' She looked at Rosalind and shrugged. 'He adjusted to each change in my behaviour without question. If I am cross with him? He buys me a gift.'

'He is most generous,' Rosalind agreed.

'But after years of receiving them I do not want any more presents. Since the day we married, whenever I have had a problem, he has smiled, agreed with me, and bought me a piece of jewellery to prevent an argument. When we were first married, and I missed London, it was emerald earbobs. When he would not go to visit my parents for our anniversary, there were matched pearls. I once scolded him for looking a moment too long at an opera dancer in Vauxhall. I got a complete set of sapphires, including clips for my shoes.' She shook her head in frustration. 'You can tell just by looking into my jewel box how angry I have been with him. It is full to overflowing.'

'Then tell him you do not wish more presents,' Rosalind suggested.

'I have tried, and he ignores me. Any attempt to express displeasure results in more jewellery, and I am sick to death of it.' She began to crush the ornament she had made, then thought better of it, placing it on the tree and starting another. 'Do you wish to know of the final argument that made our marriage unbearable?'

'Very much so. For I am still not sure that I understand what bothers you.' Rosalind glanced at the tree. Without thinking, Elise had decorated a good portion of the front, and was moving around to the back. Since the Christmas tree situation was well in hand, Rosalind sat down on the couch and took another bite from of the biscuit in her hand.

'Harry had been in London for several days on business, and I was reading the morning papers. And there, plain as day on the front page, was the news that the investments he had gone to look after were in a bad way. He stood to lose a large sum of money. Apparently the situation had been brewing for some time. But he had told me nothing of the problems, which were quite severe.'

'Perhaps you were mistaken, Elise. For if he did not speak of them, they could not have been too bad.'

The tall blonde became so agitated that she crumpled the straw in her hand and threw it to the floor. 'I was in no way confused about the facts of the matter. They referred to him by name, Rosalind, on the front page of *The Times.*'

That did look bad. 'Surely you do not hold Harry responsible for a bad decision?'

'I would never do such. I am his wife, or wish that I could be. Mine is the breast on which he should lay his head when in need of comfort. But when he returned home, do you know what he said to me when I asked him about his trip?'

'I have not a clue.'

'He said it was fine, Rosalind. *Fine!*' Elise repeated

the last word as though it were some unspeakable curse. 'And then he smiled at me as though nothing unusual had happened.'

She paced the room, as though reliving the moment.

'So I went to get the paper, and showed him his name. And he said, "Oh, that." He looked guilty, but still he said, "It is nothing that you need to worry about. It will not affect your comfort in any way." As if he thought that was the only thing I cared about. And then he patted me on the hand, as though I were a child, and said that to prove all was well he would buy me another necklace.'

She sagged onto the settee beside Rosalind and stared at the straws littering the floor. 'How difficult would it have been for him to at least admit that there was a problem in his life, so that I did not have to read of it in the papers?'

'He probably thought that you were not interested,' Rosalind offered reasonably. 'Or perhaps there was nothing you could do to help him.'

'If I thought it would help I would give him the contents of my jewel case. He could sell them to make back his investment. They mean nothing to me if all is not well. And if that did no good, then I would help him by providing my love and support,' Elise said sadly. 'But apparently he does not need it. And if he thinks to keep secret from me something so large that half of London knows it, then what else is he hiding from me?'

'It is quite possible that there is nothing at all,' Rosalind assured her, knowing that she might be wrong. For she had often found Harry closed-mouthed about things that pained him greatly. It was quite possible that Elise's suspicions were well grounded. She wished she could slap her foolish brother for causing his wife to worry, when he could have solved so many problems by telling her the whole truth.

'And when I told him, in pique, that I quite preferred Nicholas to him, for he at least had the sense to know that I was capable of reading a newspaper, Harry smiled and told me that I was probably right. For Nick had finally come into his inheritance. And at that moment, he had the deeper pockets. But Harry said he could still afford to buy me earrings to go with the new necklace if I wished them. So I left him and went to London. And he bought me a whole new wardrobe.' The last words came out in a sob, and she stared at Rosalind, her eyes red and watery. 'Is that the behaviour of a sane man?'

Rosalind had to admit it was not. It made no sense to open his purse when a few simple words of apology would have brought his wife running home. 'He was trying to get on your good side, Elise. He has always been slow to speak of his troubles, and even slower to admit fault. It is just his way.'

'Then *his way* has succeeded in driving me away from him. Perhaps that was what he was trying to do all along. He certainly made no effort to keep me. I said to him that perhaps I was more suited to Nicholas, and that our marriage had been a mistake from the start.'

'And what did he say to that?'

'That he had found our marriage most satisfactory,

but that there was little he could do to control how I felt in the matter.'

'There. See? He was happy enough,' said Rosalind. She picked up the ornament from the floor and offered it back to Elise, thinking that the metaphor of grasping straws was an apt one if this was all the ammunition she could find to defend her idiot brother.

Elise sniffed and tossed the straw into the fire, then took a sheet of paper and absently snipped and folded until it became a star. 'He said it was *satisfactory*. That is hardly praise, Rosalind. And the way he smiled as he said it. It was almost as if he was daring me to disagree.'

'Or he could have been smiling because he was happy.'

'Or not. He always smiles, Rosalind. It means nothing to me any more.'

'He does not smile nearly so much as he used to, Elise. Not when you are not here to see. Harry feels your absence, and he is putting on a brave front for you. I am sure of it.' There was truth in that, at least.

'Then he has but to ask me to return to him and I shall,' she said. 'Or I shall consider it,' she amended, trying to appear stubborn as she busied herself with the basket of ornaments, putting the little candles into their holders.

But it was obvious that, despite initial appearances, Elise would come running back to Harry in an instant, if given any hope at all. And Harry was longing for a way to get her back.

Rosalind considered. While neither wished to be the

first to make an overture, it might take only the slightest push from a third party to make the reconciliation happen.

And so she began to plan.

Chapter Seven

Harry watched Tremaine retreating to the library. Merry Christmas, indeed. Apparently the miserable pest had seen through the trap and was trying to wriggle out of it, like the worm he was. But his hasty departure would solve nothing, and his forestalling of the bet would anger Elise to the point that there was no telling what she might do. If she got it into her head that she was being rejected by both the men in her life, she might never recover from the hurt of it.

Thank the Lord for fortuitous weather and stuck wagons. It would buy him enough time to sort things again, before they got too far out of hand. And if it gave him an opportunity to deal out some of the misery that Tremaine deserved? All the better.

'Harry.' Rosalind came bustling out of the drawing room and stopped her brother before he could escape. 'What is really going on here?'

'Going on?' He made sure his face showed nothing

but innocence, along with a sense of injury that she should accuse him of anything. 'Nothing at all, Rosalind. I only wished to entertain some members of my set for the holiday, and I thought…'

His little sister set her hands upon her hips and stared at him in disgust. 'Your wife is here with another man. And you do not seem the least bit surprised. As a matter of fact you welcomed her new lover as though he were an honoured guest.'

'In a sense he is. He is the object of a bet I have made with the other gentlemen. I guaranteed them that I could make Tremaine wish me a Merry Christmas.'

'Why on earth would you do that?'

He grinned. 'Perhaps my common sense was temporarily overcome with seasonal spirit.'

Rosalind frowned at him. 'Or perhaps not. Perhaps you have some plan afoot that involves ending the separation with your wife. Or did you bet on her as well? And what prevailed upon the odious Mr Tremaine to accept your challenge? I do not understand it at all.'

'Then let me explain it to you. I told Tremaine that I would facilitate the divorce Elise is so eager for, if he would come down to the country and play my little game. I knew he would take the information straight to Elise, and that she would insist they attend—if only for the opportunity to come back here and tell me to my face what she thought of the idea. I expect she is furious.'

'And you think by angering her that you will bring her closer to you? Harry, you do not understand women at all, if that is your grand plan.'

'But I know Elise.' He smiled. 'And so far it is going just as I expected it to.'

'If you know her so well, then you should have been able to prevent her from leaving in the first place. Do you understand what you have done to her to make her so angry with you?'

He was honestly puzzled as he answered, 'Absolutely nothing. As you can see from the house, her wardrobe, her jewels, she can live in luxury. And if this was not enough I would go to any lengths necessary to give her more. I treat her with the utmost respect. I do not strike her. I do not berate her in public or in private. I am faithful. Although I have never denied her her admirers, I have no mistress, nor have ever considered a lover. I want no one but her, and I am willing to give her her own way in all things.' He gestured in the direction of the library. 'I even tolerate Tremaine. What more can she ask of me? There is little more that I can think to give her.'

Rosalind paused in thought for a moment. 'You spoil her, then. But you must cut her off if she means to belittle you so. If she has a taste for luxury, deny her. Tell her that you are very angry with her over this foolishness and that there will be no more gifts. Tell her that you wish for her to come home immediately. That will bring her to heel.'

'Do not speak that way of her.' He said it simply for he did not mean to reprove his sister, since she got enough of that at home. 'Elise is not some animal that can be punished into obedience and will still lick the hand of its master. She is a proud woman. And she is my wife.'

'It seems she does not wish to be.'

'Perhaps not. But it is something that must be settled between the two of us, and not by others. And perhaps if you had lived her life…'

Rosalind laughed. 'I would gladly trade her life for mine. You will not convince me that it is such a tragedy to be married to an earl. Even in separation, she lives better than most ladies of the ton.'

He shook his head. 'You should understand well enough what her life was like before, Rosalind, and show some sympathy. For her parents were every bit as strict to her as your father has been to you. I met her father, of course, when I offered for her. Her mother as well. It would not have been easy for her if she had been forced to return home after the disaster with Tremaine. The man betrayed her, and so she broke it off with him. It was the only reason she was willing to consider my offer.'

Rosalind bit her lip, as though the situation was unusually distressing to her. 'A broken engagement is not the end of the world. And you saved her from any repercussions. It could not have been so horrible to have you instead of Mr Tremaine.'

He shrugged. 'Perhaps not. I have endeavoured to make her happy, of course. But in losing Tremaine she lost any dreams she might have harboured that her marriage would be based in true love. Her parents did not care what happened to her as long as her brother was provided for. It was for him that they came to England. They wished to see him properly outfitted and to give him a taste for travel. Her presence on the trip was little more than an afterthought.' He remembered her brother Carl, who was as sullen and disagreeable as Elise was charming, and gave a small shudder.

'Before I came into the room to speak to her father I heard him remonstrating with her before the whole family for her refusal of Tremaine. He called her all kinds of a fool for not wishing an unfaithful husband. Told her if her mother had seen fit to provide a second son, instead of a useless daughter, then the trip would not have been spoiled with tears and nonsense. Her father swore it mattered not to him who she might choose, and that if she wouldn't have me then he would drag her back home by her hair and give her to the first man willing to take her off his hands.

'When I entered, and she introduced me, I assumed he would show some restraint in his words. But he announced to me that if the silly girl did not take her first offer she must take mine, whether she wanted it or no. He complained that they had spent a small fortune in launching her at what parties were available to them in the winter. They had no wish to do it again in spring, when she might be shown to her best advantage and have a variety of suitors. She stood mutely at his side, accepting the abuse as though it were a normal part of her life.'

Harry clenched his fists at the memory, even after several years. 'If I was not convinced beforehand that she needed me I knew it then. How did they expect her to find a husband with the season still months away? My offer was most fortuitous.' He remembered the resignation with which she had accepted him, and the way she had struggled to look happy as he took her hand. 'And she has been most grateful.'

'Then why is she not living here with you, instead of at Tremaine's side in London?'

'While it was easy enough for her to break the engagement, it has been much harder to tell her heart that the decision was a wise one. And at such times as there is trouble between us, she cannot help but turn to him and wonder if she made a mistake.' He sighed. But he made sure that when he spoke again it was with optimism. 'But, since I can count on Tremaine to be Tremaine, if she thinks to stray, she always returns to me, sadder but wiser.'

'Is he really so bad, then?'

He made note of the curious look in Rosalind's eyes as she asked the question, as though she was both longing for the answer and dreading it.

'He is a man. No better or worse than any other. I imagine he is capable of love if the right woman demands it of him.'

A trick of the morning light seemed to change his sister's expression from despair to hope and back again. So he said, 'But Elise is not that woman and never has been. He was unfaithful to her, you know.'

'Perhaps the thing that parted them was an aberration. Things might be different should they try again.' Rosalind's voice was small, and the prospect seemed to give her no happiness.

He gave her a stern look. 'I'm sure they would be happy to know that their rekindled love has your support. But I find it less than encouraging.'

'Oh.' She seemed to remember that her behaviour was of no comfort to him, and said, 'But I am sure she could be equally happy with you, Harry.'

'Equally?' That was the assessment he had been afraid of.

Rosalind hurried to correct herself. 'I meant to say much happier.'

'I am sure you did. But I wonder what Elise would say, given the chance to compare? Until recently I could not enquire. For at the first sign of trouble, she rushed off to London to be with Nicholas Tremaine.'

Rosalind eyed him critically. 'And you sat at home, waiting for her to come to her senses?'

For a moment he felt older than his years. Then he pulled himself together and said, 'Yes. And it was foolish of me. For I knew how stubborn she could be. It is now far too late to say the things I should have said on that first day that might have brought her home. She has ceased arguing with me and begun to talk of a permanent legal parting. But despite what I should have done, or what she may think she wants, I cannot find it in my heart to let her go. There will be no offer of divorce from me, even if Tremaine can remain stalwart in his hatred of Christmas.' He frowned. 'Which he shows no sign of doing.'

He cast her a sidelong glance. 'This morning he seemed to think he could lose easily and escape back to London. But it does not suit my plans to let him go so soon. If there is any way that you can be of help in the matter…'

Rosalind straightened her back and looked for all

the word like a small bird ruffling its feathers in offended dignity. 'Is that why you invited him here while I am hostess? Because if you are implying that I should romance the man in some way, flirt, preen…'

He found it interesting that she should leap to that conclusion, and filed it away for further reference. 'On the contrary. I mean to make Christmas as miserable an experience for him as possible, and keep him in poor humour until Elise is quite out of patience with him. I was thinking something much more along the lines of an extra measure of brandy slipped into his glass of mulled wine. Enough so that by the end of the evening his mind is clouded. While good humour may come easy at first, foul temper will follow close on its heels in the morning. But the thought of you forced into the man's company as some sort of decoy?' He shook his head and smiled. 'No, that would never do. To see my only sister attached to such a wastrel would not do at all.' He watched for her reaction.

'Half-sister,' she answered absently.

He pretended to ignore her response. 'No, I think he should have more brandy than the average. I doubt laudanum would achieve the desired effect.'

'Laudanum?' She stared at him in surprise. 'Are you seriously suggesting that I drug one of your guests?'

'Only Tremaine, dear. It hardly counts. And it needn't be drugs. If you can think of a better way to keep him off balance…'

'But, Harry, that is—' she struggled for words '—surprisingly dishonourable of you.'

'Then, little one, you are easily surprised. You did not think I had invited the man down here to help him in stealing my wife? I am afraid you will find that I have very little honour on that particular subject. So I did not follow Elise to town to compete for her affections? What point would there have been? Look at the man. More town bronze than the statues at Westminster. He has so much polish I swear I could shave in the reflection. I did not wish to go to London and challenge the man, for I doubt I could compare with him there.'

Harry rubbed his hands together. 'But now we are on my home turf. He knows nothing about country living, or the true likes and dislikes of my wife. And he has no taste at all for the sort of simple Christmas diversions that bring her the most joy. It will take no time at all for him to wrongfoot himself in her eyes, and his disgrace will require very little help from me. When that happens I will be here to pick up the pieces and offer myself as an alternative, just as I did before. If you wish to help me in the matter of persuading Elise to return home, then I wish to hear no more talk of bringing her to heel. Help me by helping Tremaine to make an ass of himself. I will see to Elise, and things will be quite back to normal by Twelfth Night.'

Chapter Eight

Rosalind left her brother and his mad plans alone in the entry hall. If what he was saying was true, then their marriage must have been as frustrating as Elise had claimed. The man had no clue what was wrong or how to fix things. And, worse yet, he refused to stand up to his wife, no matter how much she might wish for it.

This would be more difficult than she'd thought.

As she walked past the door to the library she paused, noticing the mistletoe ball from the doorway had fallen to the floor. She stared down at it in dismay. That was the problem with bringing live things into the house in such cold weather. There was always something wilting, dying or shedding leaves. And even with the help of the servants, she was hard pressed to keep pace with the decay. She shook the tiny clump of leaves and berries, patting it back into shape and re-tying the ribbon that held it together. Then she looked up at the hook at the top of the doorframe. It was hardly worth calling a servant, for to fix the thing back in place would be the work of a moment.

She reached up, her fingers just brushing the lintel, and glanced across the room at a chair. She considered dragging it into place as a step, and then rejected the idea as too much work. The hook was nearly in reach, and if she held the thing by its bottom leaves and stretched a bit she could manage to get it back into place, where it belonged.

She extended her arm and gave a little hop. Almost. She jumped again. Closer still. She crouched low and leaped for the hook, arm extended—and heard the stitching in the sleeve of her dress give way.

The mistletoe hung in place for a moment, before dropping back on her upturned face.

'Do you require assistance?' She caught the falling decoration before it hit the floor and turned to see the head of Nicholas Tremaine peering over the back of the sofa. His hair was tousled, as though he'd just woken from a nap. And he was grinning at her, obviously amused. Even in disarray, he was as impossibly handsome as he had been the day she'd met him, and still smiling the smile that made her insides turn to jelly and her common sense evaporate.

She turned away from him and focused her attention on the offending plant, and the hook that should hold it. 'Have you been watching me the whole time?'

Tremaine's voice held no trace of apology. 'Once you had begun, I saw no reason to alert you to my presence. If you had succeeded, you need never have known I was here.'

'Or you could have offered your help and saved me some bother.'

He paused, and then said, 'If you wished assistance, you would have called for a servant. I thought perhaps you drew some pleasure from it.' He paused again. 'I certainly did.'

She reached experimentally for the hook again. 'You could at least have done me the courtesy to mention that you were in the room. Or in the house, for that matter. You said that you wished to be gone.'

He sighed. 'I assumed you had looked out of the window this morning and guessed the truth on your own. You were right and I was wrong. I am told by your brother that the roads are quite impossible, the drive is blocked, and I am trapped. So I have gone to ground here by the library fire, and I was doing my best to keep true to my word and stay out of your path.' She heard the rattle of china and glanced over her shoulder to see his breakfast things, sitting on the table beside the couch.

'When you realised that your plan was not working, you could have given me warning that I was being observed. It would have spared me some embarrassment.'

He gave a slight chuckle. 'It is not as if I am likely to tell the rest of the company how you behave when we are alone together.'

She cringed. 'I did not say that you would. I have reason to trust your discretion, after all.'

'Then are you implying that my presence here embarrasses you?' He let the words hang with significance.

It did. Not that it mattered. She turned back to look at him. 'Perhaps it is my own behaviour that embarrasses me. And the fact that you have been witness to more than one example of the worst of it.'

He laughed. 'If I have seen the worst of your behaviour, then you are not so very bad as you think.'

She gave him her most intimidating glare, which had absolutely no effect. 'Tell me, now: are you accustomed to finding Elise leaping at doorframes, like a cat chasing a moth?'

'No, I am not. But then, she would not have need to.' His eyes scanned over her in appraisal. 'She is much taller than you are.'

'She is tall, and poised as well, and very beautiful.' Rosalind recited the list by rote. 'She will never know how vexing it is to find everything you want just slightly out of reach. It all comes easily to her.' And Elise, who had two men fighting over her, would never have to cope with the knowledge that the most perfect man in London still thought of her as a silly girl. Rosalind glared at the hook above her. 'I must always try harder, and by doing so I overreach and end up looking foolish.'

'Perhaps you do.' His voice was soft, which surprised her. And then it returned to its normal tone. 'Still, it is not such a bad thing to appear thus. And I am sure most people would take a less harsh view of you than you do of yourself.'

She picked at the mistletoe in her hands, removing

another wilted leaf. Behind her, there was a sigh, and the creak of boot leather. And then he was standing beside her and plucking the thing from between her fingers.

She looked up to find Tremaine far too near, and grinning down at her. 'I understand your irritation with *me*, for we agreed to keep our distance,' he said. 'I have been unsuccessful. But what has that poor plant ever done to you, that you treat it so?'

She avoided his eyes, focusing on the leaves in his hand, and frowned. 'That "poor plant" will not stay where I put it.'

He reached up without effort and stuck it back in its place above their heads. Then he tipped her chin up, so she could see the mistletoe—and him as well— and said innocently, 'There appears to be no problem with it now.'

As a matter of fact it looked fine as it was, with him beneath it and standing so very close to her. For a moment she thought of how nice it might be to close her eyes and take advantage of the opportunity. And how disastrous. Some lessons should not have to be learned twice, and if he meant to see her succumb again he would be disappointed. 'Do not try to tempt me into repeating mistakes of the past. I am not so moved.'

He smiled, to tell her that it was exactly what he was doing. 'Are you sure? My response is likely to be most different from when last we kissed.'

Her pulse gave an unfortunate gallop, but she said, in a frigid tone, 'Whatever for? What has changed?'

'You are no longer an inexperienced girl.'

'Nor am I as foolish as I was, to jump into the arms of a rake.'

He smiled again. 'But I was not a rake when you assaulted me.'

'I assaulted you?' She feigned shock. 'That is doing it much too brown, sir.'

'No, really. I cannot claim that I was an innocent babe, but no one would have called me a rake.' He held a hand over his heart. 'Not until word got round that I had seduced some sweet young thing and then refused to do right by her, in any case.'

'Seduced?' The sinking feeling in her stomach that had begun as she talked to Harry was back in force.

'The rumours grew quite out of proportion to the truth when Elise cast me off. Everyone was convinced that something truly terrible must have happened for her to abandon me so quickly.'

Her stomach sank a little further.

He went on as though noticing nothing unusual. 'And it must have been my fault in some way, mustn't it? Although I was not exactly a pillar of moderation, I had no reputation for such actions before that time. But it is always the fault of the man, is it not? Especially one so crass and cruel as to refuse to offer for the poor, wounded girl because I was already promised to another. And then to deny her father satisfaction, for fear that I might do the man injury.' He leaned over her. 'For I am a crack shot, and a fair hand with a blade. And your father, God protect him, is long past the day when he could have hurt me.' He put on a face of mock horror.

'And when I refused to make a full explanation to my betrothed, or give any of the details of the incident? Well, it must have been because it was so very shameful, and not because it would have made the situation even more difficult for the young lady concerned.'

'You needn't have used my name. But I would not have blamed you for giving the truth to Elise. It was not your fault, after all.' She wished she could sink through the floor, along with the contents of her heart.

'When she came to me with the accusation, I told her that the majority of what she had heard was true. I *had* been caught in an intimate position with a young lady, by the girl's father. But I had not meant to be unfaithful to her, it would not happen again, and she must trust me for the rest.' He frowned. 'That was the sticking point, I am afraid. Her inability to trust. The woman has always been quick to temper. She broke the engagement and went to Harry. I happily gave myself over to sin. And thereby hangs a tale.'

'So you are telling me not only did I ruin your engagement, and spoil Christmas for ever, I negatively affected your character?'

'It is not so bad, having a ruined character. I have found much more pleasure in vice than I ever did in virtue.' He frowned. 'And after all this time the woman I once sought has come back to me.'

Her anger at him warred with guilt. Elise and Harry were in a terrible mess, and she might have been the cause of it all. But how could Tremaine stand there, flirting so casually, as though it did not matter? 'She might have come back, but she is foolish to trust you. What would she think of you, I wonder, if she found you and I here, alone together?'

'I think she would go running right back into Harry's arms, as she did once before.' He seemed to be considering something for a moment, before reaching out to brush his knuckles against her cheek. 'But enough of Elise. I know what she has done these past years, for we have been close, although not as close as I once wished. At no time did she ever mention that Harry had a sister.'

Rosalind cleared her throat, to clear her head, and stepped a little away from him, until he was no longer touching her. 'Half-sister.'

'Mmm.' His acknowledgement of her words was a low hum, and she thought she could feel it vibrating inside her, like the purr of a cat. 'If it was not a trick, as I first suspected, is there some reason that they kept you so well hidden?'

She swallowed hard, and when she answered her voice was clear of emotion. 'Harry and my father do not get on well. He was sent away to school when we were still young, and took the opportunity to spend all subsequent holidays with his own father's family, until he was of age. Then he came to London.' She hung her head. 'I remained at home, where I could not be an embarrassment to the family.'

He was still close enough that if she looked up she could admire his fine lips, see the cleft in his chin. And she remembered the feel of his cheek against hers, the taste of his tongue. She had lost her freedom over a few kisses from that perfect mouth. And somehow she did not mind.

She could feel him watching her so intently that she feared he could read her thoughts, and he said, 'What did you do in the country, my little black sheep? Did you continue in the way you set out with me? Were there other incidents of that kind, I wonder, or was I an aberration?'

Rosalind pulled herself together, pushed against his chest and stepped out of the doorway further into the room. 'How rude of you to assume that there were. And to think that I would tell you if I had transgressed is beyond familiar.'

He turned to follow her and closed the distance between them again. 'But that does not answer my question. Tell me, my dear Rosalind, have there been other men in your life?'

'You were hardly in my life. And I most certainly am not your dear…'

'Ah, ah, ah.' He laid a finger on her lips to stop her words. 'Whether I was willing or no, I was your first kiss. But who was the second?'

'There has not been a second,' she answered, trying to sound prim. But his finger did not move from her lips, and when she spoke it felt rather as though she were trying to nibble on his fingertip. His mouth curled, and she shook her head to escape from the contact. 'I learned my lesson, I swear to you. There is nothing about my conduct of the last years that is in any way objectionable.'

'What a pity.' He leaned away from her and blinked his eyes. 'For a moment I thought Christmas had arrived, in the form of a beautiful hostess every bit as wicked as I could have wished. But if you should have a change of heart and decide to throw yourself upon my person, as you did back then, I would make sure that you would have nothing to regret and much more pleasant memories.'

She turned away and looked out of the window, so that he could not see the indecision in her face. The offer had an obvious appeal. 'How dare you, sir? I have no intention of, as you so rudely put it, *throwing* myself upon your person.'

'Did you have that intention the last time, I wonder?'

'I have no idea what I thought to accomplish. It was the first time I had drunk anything stronger than watered wine, and I did not know my limitations. One cup of particularly strong Christmas punch and I lost all sense.'

He raised his eyebrows. 'And how is the punch at this house?'

'Nothing I cannot handle.'

'If you have returned to the straight and narrow, then you are no use to me at all.' He turned and walked away from her, throwing himself down on the couch as though he had forgotten her presence. 'Whatever shall I do now, to give Elise a distaste of me? For if that fool brother of yours does not come up to snuff soon and reclaim his wife, I am likely to end up married to her after all.'

She looked at him in surprise, and then she blurted, 'Do you not mean to marry Elise?' It was none of her business, but it turned the discussion to something other than herself, which suited her well.

'Elise is already married.' He said it flatly, as though stating the obvious, and stared up at the ceiling.

It was her turn to follow him. She stood before him, hands on hips, close enough so that he could not pretend to ignore her. 'Elise is separated from Harry. If she can persuade him, she will be divorced and free. What are your intentions then?'

'Divorce is by no means a sure thing,' he hedged. 'I would have to declare myself in court as her lover. And even then it might amount to nothing. But it would drag the whole affair into the public eye.'

'Do you have issues with the scandal of it?'

He shrugged. 'If I did, then I would be a fool to escort her now. It is no less scandalous to partner with her while she is still married.'

'Would you think less of her should she be free? Would she be beneath you? Because that would put things back to the way they were before I spoiled them.' She sighed, and dropped her hands to her sides, remembering the look in her brother's eyes when he had seen his wife in the doorway. 'Although it would hurt Harry most awfully.'

Nicholas gave her a tired look, and stretched out on the couch with his feet up and a hand over his eyes. 'There is nothing wrong with Elise, and no reason that I would find her unfit to marry if she were free. Save one.' He looked as though the words were being wrenched out of him. 'I do not love her.'

'You do not…' Rosalind looked confused. 'But she has come back to you again, after all these years. And when I spoke to her, she seemed to think…'

'What she understands to be true is in some ways different from what I have come to believe.' He turned his head to her, and there was a look of obvious puzzlement on his face. 'At one time I would have liked nothing better than to meet her in church and unite our futures. But in the years since she turned me down in favour of Harry?' He shrugged. 'Much time has passed. I still find her beautiful, and very desirable—for, while I am circumspect, I am not blind to her charms. I enjoy her company, and I value her friendship above all things. But I seriously doubt, should we marry, that I will be a more satisfactory husband than the one she already has. Once the novelty began to pale she would find many aspects of my character are wanting. And for my part? She broke my heart most thoroughly the first time she chose another. But I doubt when she leaves me this time that it will cause similar damage.'

'How utterly perfect!' Rosalind reached out and pulled his boots onto the floor, forcing him to sit up.

'Oh, really?' He was eyeing her suspiciously. 'And just why would you say that?'

She sat down on the couch beside him, in the space his legs had occupied, trying to disguise her obvious relief. 'I will explain shortly, if you can but answer a few more questions to my satisfaction. If you do not want her, then why did you take her back?'

He scratched his head. 'I am not sure. But I suspect that force of habit brought her to me, and force of habit keeps me at her side.'

'That does not sound very romantic.'

'I thought at first that it was lust. A desire to taste the pleasures that I was once denied.' He gave her a significant look. 'But our relationship has not yet progressed to such a stage, and I find myself most content with things as they are.'

'You two are not…? You do not…?' Rosalind took her most worldly tone with him, and hoped he could not tell that she lacked the understanding to ask the rest of the question. For she was unsure just what *should* be happening if the relationship had 'progressed'. But she had wondered, all the same.

'We are not, and we do not.' He was staring at her in surprise now. 'Are you seeking vicarious pleasure in the details of Elise's infidelity? For you are most curious on the subject.'

'Not really.' She gave him a critical appraisal in return. 'I think it is quite horrid that she left Harry, and even worse that you took her in. But if it was all for an ember of true love that smouldered for years, though untended, it would give me some measure of understanding. And I would find it in my heart to forgive her.'

'But not me?' he asked.

'I would suspect you of being an unrepentant rogue, Tremaine, as I do in any case. For you seem ready to ruin my brother's marriage not because you love deeply, but because you are too lazy to send Elise home.'

He flinched at her gibe. 'It will probably spoil your low opinion of me, but here is the real reason I encouraged her to remain in London. I recognise a friend in dire need, and I want to help her. She is lost, Miss

Morley. She will find her way right again, I am sure. But until that time better that she be lost with me than with some other man who does not understand the situation and chooses to take advantage of her weakness.'

'You are carrying on a public affair with my sister-in-law for her own good?'

Tremaine smiled. 'And now please explain it to your brother for me. I am sure he will be relieved to hear it.'

'I think Harry doubts your good intentions.'

His smile widened to a grin. 'I know he does. I think he invited me down here for the express purpose of keeping me away from Elise during the holiday. To the susceptible, Christmas can be a rather romantic season. I believe we both know what can happen in the proximity of wine and mistletoe.'

He looked at the ceiling and whistled, while she glared steadfastly towards the floor.

'Do you know how he attempted to trick me into this visit? By offering to divorce his wife if I won his silly bet. He probably thought I could not resist the challenge of besting him. Little did he suspect that I would tell Elise all, and she would insist on coming as well. It must gall him no end to see the two of us here.'

Rosalind cleared her throat. 'I think you would be surprised at how much he might know on that matter. But pray continue.'

Tremaine laughed. 'For my part, were I a jealous man, I would be enraged at the amount of energy my supposed intended spends in trying to attract her husband's attention by courting mine. She means to go back to him, and he is dying to have her back. There is nothing more to be said on the matter.'

'I will agree with that,' said Rosalind. 'For I have never met a couple better suited, no matter what they might think.'

He nodded. 'We agree that they belong together. And she does want to come home to him, since he did not come to London and get her. So be damned to Harry's machinations for the holidays. I have devised a plan of my own.'

'Really?' Someone else with a plan? She could not decide if she should meet the news with eagerness or dread.

'Harry's scheme, whatever it might be, requires my eagerness to win his wife away from him. In this he does not have my co-operation. I have kept her safe from interlopers for two months now, but it is time she returned home. I was hoping to find my host, lose the bet, and make a hasty escape before Elise realised what had happened. In no time, I would have been back in London. And she would have been back here with Harry, where she belongs.'

She shook her head. 'Until such time as Harry loaned her a coach so that she could leave him again. Which he will do, the moment she asks. It will do no good at all if you leave only to have Elise following in your wake.'

Tremaine grimaced in disgust. 'Why on earth would Harry lend her a coach? I have brought her as far as Lincolnshire. If he lacks the sense to hold on to her once he has her again then you can hardly expect me to do more.'

Rosalind replied, 'Elise's main argument with the

man seems to be that he is too agreeable. And he has admitted to me that he would deny her nothing. If she wished to leave, he would not stop her.'

'Damn Harry and his agreeable nature,' he said. 'In any case, the snow is keeping me from the execution of my plan, since it required a rapid getaway and that appears to be impossible.' He stared at her for a moment. 'But finding you here adds an interesting ripple to the proceedings. Considering our history together, and the results that came of it, I thought perhaps…'

'That I would allow you to dishonour me again to precipitate another falling-out with Elise?' She gave him a sceptical glare. 'While I cannot fault you for the deviousness of it, I do not see what good it would do. You might have escaped marriage to me once, but I expect Harry would call you out if you refused me now.'

He glared at her. 'Very well, Miss Morley. You have proved my plans to be non-starters. I shall fall back on my last resort, of taking all my meals in this room and avoiding both the lord and the lady of the house until I can leave. Unless you have a better idea?' The challenge hung in the air.

She smiled back. 'I was hoping you would ask. For I have a far superior plan.' Or rather Harry had, if she could get Tremaine to agree with it. It would be quite hopeless if he meant to hide in the library the whole visit.

He favoured her with a dry expression, and reached for his teacup to take a fortifying sip. 'Do you, now?'

'Of course. You admit you are concerned with Elise's welfare. And, while I wish her well, I am more worried about Harry. If we are in agreement that what they need for mutual happiness is each other, then it makes sense that we pool our resources and work together to solve their difficulties.'

'Because we have had such good luck together in the past?'

She sniffed in disapproval. 'I would not be expecting you to do anything more than you have done already. Pay courteous attention to Elise. Be her confidant, her escort, her friend. But to do that you must come out of this room, participate in the activities I have planned, and see that she does as well. Your mere presence may be enough to goad Harry to action on the matter, if he is the one who must apologise.'

'That is exactly what I fear.' Tremaine shuddered theatrically. 'Although Harry seems to be a mild-mannered chap, I've found in the past that this type of fellow can be the most dangerous, when finally "goaded to action". If your plan involves me meeting with violence at the hands of an irate husband...'

'I doubt it will come to that.'

'You doubt? Miss Morley, that is hardly encouraging.' He spread his hands in front of him, as though admiring a portrait. 'I can see it all now. You and the other guests look on in approval as Harry beats me to a bloody pulp. And then, Elise falls into his arms. While I wish them all the best, I fail to see the advantages to me in this scenario.'

'Do not be ridiculous, sir. I doubt Harry is capable of such a level of violence.' She considered. 'Although, if you could see your way clear to letting him plant you a facer...'

'No, I could not,' He stared at her in curiosity. 'Tell me, Miss Morley, are all your ideas this daft, or only those plans that concern me?'

'There is nothing the least bit daft about it. It is no more foolish than taking a lover in an effort to get her to return to her husband.' She stared back at him. 'You will pardon me for saying it, but if that is the projected result of an affair with you, it does not speak well of your romantic abilities.'

'I have the utmost confidence in my "romantic abilities". But if you doubt them, I would be only too happy to demonstrate.'

She cleared her throat. 'Not necessary, Tremaine. But, since you are concerned for your safety, we will find a way to make Harry jealous that involves no personal harm to you. Is that satisfactory?'

'Why must we make him jealous at all? If I stay clear of him, and we allow time to pass and nature to take its course…'

'Spoken as a true city-dweller, Tremaine. If you had ever taken the time to observe nature, you would have found that it moves with incredible slowness. The majestic glaciers are called to mind. So deliberate as to show no movement at all. And as cold as that idea.'

He shook his head. 'Spoken by someone who has never seen the ruins of Pompeii. They are a far better example of what happens when natural passions are allowed their sway. Death and destruction for all who stand in the way. Which is why I prefer to keep my distance.'

'You have seen them?' she asked eagerly.

'Harry and Elise? Of course. And I suspect that, although they do not show it outright—'

'No. The ruins of Pompeii.'

He stopped, confused by the sudden turn in the conversation. 'Of course. I took the Grand Tour. It is not so unusual.'

She leaned forward on the couch. 'Were they as amazing as some have said?'

'Well, yes. I suppose. I did not give it much thought at the time.'

She groaned in frustration. 'I have spent my whole life sequestered in the country, drawing the same water-colours of the same spring flowers, year after year. And you have seen the world. But you did not think on it.'

'You are sequestered in the country because you cannot be trusted out of sight of home,' he snapped.

'Because of one mistake. With you.' She pointed a finger. 'But I notice you are to be trusted to go wherever you like.'

'That is because I am a man. You are a girl. It is an entirely different thing.'

'Please cease referring to me as a girl. I am fully grown, and have been for some time.' She glared up at him. 'My diminutive stature has nothing to do with youth, and should not render me less than worthy—despite what Elise might have to say on the subject of what constitutes a good match.'

He was staring at her with a dazed expression. 'Indeed. You are quite tall enough, I am sure. And what does Elise have to do with it?'

'She was speaking on the subject of her marriage to Harry,' Rosalind admitted. 'I still find it very hard to understand, but she seemed to think it important that Harry was tall.'

Tremaine furrowed his brow, and took another sip from his cup. 'That makes no sense. He is no taller than I, certainly. Perhaps even a little shorter.'

'But just right in the eyes of Elise, I assure you. She made a point of assuring me that physically he is a magnificent specimen, and that they are very well suited.'

Tremaine choked on his tea.

'Is something the matter?'

'Not at all. It is just I think you have misunderstood her.'

'Whatever else could she mean?'

He was looking at her in a most unusual way. 'Perhaps at another time we can discuss that matter in more detail. But for now, do not concern yourself with it. I suspect it means that there are parts of married life that she is eager to resume. And that I have brought her home not a moment too soon. We need not concern ourselves with Harry's good qualities. If we wish success, we would be better served to improve on his deficiencies. And, much as I dislike the risks involved, we must do what is necessary to make him reclaim his wife's affection.'

Rosalind smiled at his use of the word 'we'. Perhaps they were working towards the same end, after all. 'My thoughts exactly.'

He returned her smile. 'Well, then. What does she want from him that we can help her achieve?'

'I know from experience that Harry can be the most

frustrating of men.' She frowned. 'If he does not wish you to know, it is very hard to divine what it is that he is thinking. Hence our current predicament. I have no doubt that he adores Elise. But she cannot see it, even after all these years.'

Tremaine frowned in return. 'Can she not see what is obvious to the rest of us?'

'I think she wishes him to be more demonstrative.'

'Which will be damned difficult, you will pardon the expression, with her hanging upon my arm. If he has never made any attempt to dislodge her from it, I fail to see what I could do to change things.'

She patted him on the arm in question. 'You have hit on the problem exactly. She wishes him to *do* something about you.'

Tremaine ran a hand over his brow. 'And I would rather he did not. Is there anything else?'

'She wishes he would talk to her so that she could better understand him.'

He furrowed his brow. 'They have passed the last five years in silence? That cannot be. I would swear that I have heard him utter words in her presence. Is it a difficulty of language? For I have found Elise's comprehension of English to be almost flawless.'

Rosalind closed her eyes for a moment, attempting to gather strength. 'She wishes him to speak about important matters.'

'Matters of state, perhaps? How odd. She has shown no interest in them when speaking to me.'

Rosalind burst forth in impatience. 'This has nothing

to do with English lessons or a sudden interest in politics, Tremaine. Elise wishes Harry to speak openly about matters that are important to *her*.'

'Oh.' He slumped in defeat. 'Then it is quite hopeless. For he would have no idea what that would be. The minds of women are a depth that we gentlemen have not been able to plumb, I'm afraid.'

'Don't be an idiot,' she snapped. 'There is nothing so terribly difficult to understand about women, if you make an effort. We two are conversing well enough, aren't we? You do not require the assistance of a guide to understand me?'

He paused for a moment and answered politely, 'Of course not. But you are more direct in your communication than Elise.'

She smiled graciously, preparing to blush and accept the compliment.

Then he said, 'Almost masculine.' He paused again. 'And why do you persist in calling me just Tremaine, and not Mister? If you prefer, you may call me Nicholas.'

'I do not.' She stood up and moved away from him. 'Nor do I think your behaviour proves you worthy of an honorific. Tremaine will do. And you may continue to call me Miss Morley. And now that we have got that out of the way, are we in agreement about the matter of Elise and Harry? Will you help me?'

'Since it is likely to be the only way you will allow me any peace? Yes, I will help you, Miss Morley. Now, go about your business and let me return to my nap.'

Chapter Nine

Harry sighed in satisfaction as he climbed the stairs towards his bed. The day had gone well enough, he supposed. The house had buzzed with activity. Wherever he went he had found people playing at cards or games, eating, drinking and merrymaking, with Rosalind presiding over all with an air of hospitable exasperation. The only faces that had seemed to be absent from the mix were those of Tremaine and his wife.

The thought troubled him, for he suspected that they might be together, wherever they were, enjoying each other's company. And it would be too obvious of him to pound upon his wife's door and admit that he wished to know if she was alone.

He almost sighed in relief as he saw her in the window seat at the top of the stairs. She was just where she might have been if there had been no trouble between them, sitting in her favourite place and looking out onto the snow falling into the moonlit park below.

He stepped up beside her, speaking quietly so as not to disturb her mood. 'Beautiful, is it not?'

'Yes.' She sighed. But it was a happy, contented sigh, and it made him smile.

'I expect it will make tomorrow's trip into the trees a difficult one.'

'You still mean to go?' She looked at him in obvious surprise.

'Of course. It will be the morning of Christmas Eve. We went out into the woods together often enough that I have come to think of it as a family tradition. Would you like to accompany me?'

She looked excited at the prospect, and then dropped her gaze and shook her head. 'I doubt that would be a good idea.'

He laughed. 'It is not as if we are planning an assignation. Only a sign of friendship. If we cannot be lovers we can at least be friends, can't we?'

'Friends?' The word sounded hollow and empty coming from her. She was making no attempt to show the world that she was happy with their situation.

It gave him hope, and he continued. 'Yes. We can have a truce. If you wish Tremaine to be your lover, then why can I not occupy the position he has vacated and be your trusted friend?'

'You wish to be my friend?' Now she looked truly puzzled.

'If I can be nothing else. Let us go out tomorrow, as we have done in the past. We will take Tremaine with us, so that he can share in the fun. If he is what you want, then I wish to see him well settled in my place before I let you go. Tomorrow I will pass the torch.'

'You will?' If she wanted her freedom, his offer should give her a sense of relief. But there was nothing in her tone to indicate it.

'Yes. I had not planned on your visit, but now that you are here it is a good thing. We cannot settle what is between us with you in London and me in the country. If you wish an end to things, then it is better if we deal with them face to face, without acrimony. Only then will you truly be free.' He let the words sink in. 'You do wish to be free of me, do you not?'

'Yes…'

There was definitely doubt in her voice. He clung to that split second of hesitation as the happiest sound he had heard in months.

'Very well, then. If there is nothing I can do that will make Tremaine lose the bet, on Twelfth Night I will honour my word and begin divorce proceedings. For above all I wish you to be happy. Merry Christmas, Elise.'

'Thank you.'

She whispered it, and sounded so very sad that it was all he could do to keep from putting his arms around her and drawing her close, whispering back that he would never let her go.

'Let us go to bed, then, for it will be an early morning.'

She stood and walked with him, towards their rooms.

Would it be so wrong to take her hand and pull her along after him to his door? Although her manner said that she might not be totally opposed to the idea, neither was there proof that she would be totally in favour of it. It would be best if he waited until he had a better idea of what she truly wanted.

He put his hands behind his back and cleared his throat. 'About our disagreement of yesterday, over the arrangement of the rooms. After we had gone to bed, I realised how it must look to you. And I apologise if you took it as an effort to control your behaviour. You have made it clear enough to me that it is no longer any business of mine what occurs in your bedroom. If there is a reason that you might wish to lock the connecting door, I will allow you your privacy.'

'For what reason would I wish privacy?' She sounded confused by the idea. Perhaps even after two months Tremaine was an idle threat to their marriage. She shrugged as though nothing could occur to her, and gave a tired laugh. 'In any case, what good would it do to lock the door against you? You have the key.'

He held his hands open in front of him. 'I have all the keys, Elise. I could open the door of any room in which you slept. You must have realised that when you came home. But do you really think me such a villain that I mean to storm into your room without your permission and force myself upon you?'

She caught her breath and her eyes darkened. For a moment his threat held definite appeal.

Then he cleared his throat and continued, 'Am I really the sort who would take you until you admitted that there was no place in the world that you belonged but in my arms and in my bed?'

She froze for a moment, and then glared at him. 'No, Harry, you are not. On more careful consideration, I think that I have nothing to worry about. Goodnight.'

And, perhaps it was his imagination, but the way she carried herself could best be described as stomping off to her room. When the door shut, he suspected that the slam could be heard all over the house.

The next morning Harry was up well before dawn, had taken breakfast and dressed in clothes suitable for the weather before going to roust Tremaine. He could not help but smile as he pounded smartly on the door to the poor man's bedroom. He could hear rustling, stumbling noises, and a low curse before the door in front of him creaked open.

Tremaine stood before him, bleary-eyed and still in his nightshirt. 'Eh?'

'Time to get up, old man.'

Tremaine squinted into the hall and croaked, 'Is there a problem?'

'No problem at all. Did I forget to tell you last night? So sorry. But you *must* be a part of today's proceedings. Elise is expecting you.'

'Then come for me in daylight.'

'No, no. What we are about must be done at dawn. And on the morn of Christmas Eve. There is no better time. Pull on some clothes, man. Warm ones. Your true love is awaiting you in the hall.'

At the mention of Elise Tremaine's eyes seemed to widen a bit. Then he stared back at Harry, as though trying to gauge his intentions. At last he sighed with resignation, and muttered something that sounded rather like, 'Damn Rosalind.' Then he said, 'A moment.' And then he shut the door.

'A moment' proved to be the better part of a half an hour. Tremaine appeared at the door again, no happier, but reasonably well dressed for Harry's purposes, in a fine coat of light wool and soft, low shoes. He stepped into the hall and shut the door behind him. It was only then that he noticed the axe in Harry's hands. 'What the devil—?'

Harry nudged him with the handle and gave him a mad grin. 'You'll see. You'll see soon enough.'

Tremaine swallowed. 'That is what I fear.'

'Downstairs.' He gestured Tremaine ahead of him, and watched the cautious way the man passed him. There was a tenseness in his shoulders, as though his back was attempting to climb out of his coat while his head was crawling into it. His neck seemed to have disappeared entirely. He did not relax until he saw Elise, pacing on the slate at the foot of the stairs, probably assuming that Harry would not cut him down dead in front of a lady.

'There you are.' Elise was trying to display a mixture of irritation and trepidation at what was about to occur, but she could not manage to disguise the same childlike excitement that she had shown whenever they had done this in the past. It made Harry happy to look at her. 'I was not sure if you would still hold to the practice.'

Harry smiled. 'Perhaps if you had not come home I might have forgone it. But if you are under this roof then

Christmas will be every bit as full as you would wish it to be. And if we are to do it at all, then we must bring Tremaine, so he will know what is to be expected of him next year.'

If she meant to rescue the poor man, she gave no indication of it. Instead, she nodded with approval. 'Let us go, then.'

'Go where?' Tremaine had found his voice at last.

'Outside, of course. To cut the Yule Log.'

'Oh, I say. You can't mean…'

'A massive oak. I have just the thing picked out.' He turned back to his wife, ignoring the stricken look on Tremaine's face. 'You will approve, I'm sure, Elise. The thing is huge. Sure to burn for days, and with enough wood for two fireplaces.'

'Really?' She was smiling at Harry as though he had offered to wrap her in diamonds. Any annoyance at the chill he would take tramping about the grounds in a foot of fresh snow was replaced by the warm glow of her presence.

But the Christmas spirit did not seem to be reaching Tremaine. He grumbled, 'Surely you have servants to do this?'

Harry shook his head. 'I could never expect them to do such. It is tradition that we choose one ourselves. Elise is very particular about the choice, and she enjoys the walk. I could not begrudge her the experience.'

Elise looked at Tremaine in disapproval. 'You are not dressed for the weather.'

'Here—we can fix that.' Harry removed his own

scarf and wrapped it twice around Tremaine's neck, pulling until it constricted. 'There. All better. Let us proceed.' He opened the front door wide and shepherded them through.

Elise took to it as he had known she would. Though she might claim to adore the city, she needed space and fresh air to keep her happy. She strode out into the morning, with the first glints of sunlight hitting the fresh snow, twirled and looked back at them, her face shining brighter than any star. 'Isn't it magnificent?'

Harry nodded in agreement. As he looked at her, he felt his own throat close in a way that had nothing to do with the tightness of a scarf. She was so beautiful standing there, with the dawn touching her blonde hair. And he thought, *You used to be mine*. He chased the thought away. He would make her come home again. For if he had lost her for ever he might just as well march out into the snow, lie down and wait for the end.

He looked around him—anywhere but at Elise. For until he had mastered his emotions he could not bear to look in her face. And he saw she was right: with a fresh coating of snow over everything, and frost and icicles clinging to the trees, it was a most beautiful morning indeed.

Tremaine merely grunted.

'This way.' Harry pointed to the left, up a low hill at the side of the house. 'In the copse of trees where we used to picnic.' He set off at a brisk pace.

Elise followed him easily in her stout boots and heavy wool skirt. 'You do not mean to take the tree where we…' She was remembering their last picnic in the oak grove, and her cheeks were going pink in a way that had nothing to do with the cold.

He cleared his throat. 'Not that one, precisely. But very nearby. This tree is dying, and we will have to take it soon in any case. Why should it not serve a noble purpose?'

Behind them he could hear Tremaine, stumbling and sliding and cursing his way up the hill. He was falling further behind as Elise drew abreast of Harry.

She said softly, 'I am still amazed that you are willing to do this after what has gone on between us. Although you always complied with my wishes, you complained about the bother of it in years past.'

He appeared pleased, and looked at the ground. 'Perhaps I did. But I found, though I meant to leave it off, that the habit was ingrained. Although I complained to you, perhaps I enjoyed it more than I knew.' He glanced back over his shoulder. 'In future you will have Tremaine to complain over it, when he takes my place. But for myself I mean to spend a quiet hour on a winter morning, watching the sun come up.'

She smiled at him in approval, and then blushed and looked away. He glanced back again, so that she could not see his answering smile, and called, 'Keep up, Tremaine, or you shall miss the best part.'

The tree he had chosen had been carefully notched by a servant, so that most of the work was done and it would fall correctly. In truth, there was so little left to do that it was fortunate the thing had not fallen on its own in the storm. A few blows of the axe would give the impression to his lady love of manly competence without undue exertion.

He stepped around to the far side and swung the axe into the wood. It struck with a satisfying clunk that made Tremaine flinch. 'See? We strike thusly.' Harry swung again, and felt the unaccustomed labour jar the bones of his arms. After several Christmases just like this, at least he was prepared for the shock. It was much better than it had been the first time his wife had suggested the activity. 'It takes only a few strokes to do the job.' He smiled at his adversary again. 'Step away from that side, sir. For the tree is likely to come down when I least expect it.' He took a short pause, turned so that Elise could not see the expression on his face, and stared at Tremaine, not bothering to smile. 'I would hate for an accident to befall you.'

Tremaine fairly leapt out of the way, standing safely behind him. The man was terrified of him.

Harry grinned to himself and swung again. 'It is a dangerous business, using an axe.' *Clunk*. 'No end of things can go wrong. Should the handle slip in my hands, for example.' *Clunk*.

He glanced up at his wife's friend, who had gone bone-white with cold and fear. Harry offered him the axe. 'Here. You must try. For I expect Elise will wish you to learn the ways of this.'

Tremaine muttered low, under his breath, 'If you think next year will find me chopping wood for the holiday, you are both quite mad. I have no property in the country, nor do I plan to acquire one. And I seriously doubt that I will be motivated to march through Hyde Park with a weapon in my hands, doing damage to the landscaping.'

'Oh, Nicholas,' Elise laughed. 'What a droll idea.'

But Tremaine took the axe from Harry's hands, and looked relieved to have disarmed him. Harry stepped back as the other man took a mighty swing at the oak, overbalanced, and fell on his seat in the snow.

'Hmm. It does not seem that you have the hang of it yet. Best let me finish it after all.' He retrieved the axe, and a few more chops and a stout push was all it took. There was a loud cracking noise, and he put out an arm to shield Elise. Tremaine scrambled to safety, away from the falling tree.

It crashed to the ground and they stared at the thing for a moment—Tremaine in disgust, and Elise with obvious satisfaction. Then Tremaine said, 'I suppose now you will tell me that we must drag it back to the house?'

Elise giggled, and Harry said, 'Oh, no. Of course not. This is still much too green to burn. This is the log for next year's festivity. Some people save the cutting for Candlemas, but we have always done it on Christmas Eve morn. And this year it is my gift to you, Tremaine. You will need it next year, when you celebrate Christmas with Elise.' He gestured to the enormous tree on the ground before them. 'You can take the whole thing back with you when you return to London. The servants will take care of it in good time. They are just now bringing in last year's log. We shall see it when we go back to the house.'

'Mad.' Tremaine stared at them in amazement. 'You are both quite mad.' Then he turned from them and stalked back to the house, sliding ahead of them on the downward slope.

Harry looked after him. 'I do not think Tremaine appreciates my gift.'

Elise looked after him as well, trying to look stern, although a smile was playing around her lips. 'That was horrible of you, you know. To drag the poor man out in weather like this. And so early in the morning. He abhors mornings.'

Harry tried to focus on the snow-covered back of the retreating man. Not on the beautiful woman at his side and what her smile might tell him about her intimate knowledge of Nicholas Tremaine's morning routine. 'A pity. For it is the most beautiful time of day. You still enjoy mornings, do you not? Or have your ways changed now that you are not with me?'

'I still enjoy them,' she admitted. 'Although they are not so nice in the city as they are here. It is the best time to ride, though. For many are still sleeping from the night's revelry, and the park is nearly empty.'

'Oh.' He tried not to imagine what a handsome couple his wife and Tremaine would make on horseback in Rotten Row.

'But the city is quite empty at Christmas. And I will admit it would have been lonely to remain there.' She hesitated. 'I must thank you for inviting…Tremaine.'

She had remembered, too late, that she had not been included in the invitation. There was an awkward pause.

'I am glad that you chose to accompany him,' Harry said firmly. 'For I would not wish you to be alone. And I hope Christmas will be very much as you remember it.' He glanced down the hill towards the house. 'You have brought many changes to Anneslea since we married.'

'Really?' She looked surprised, as though she did not realise the merriment she'd brought with her when she'd come into his life. 'Was not Christmas a joyous time when you were a boy?'

He shrugged. 'Much like any other day. When I was small my father was often ill, and there was little cause for celebration. My stepfather, Morley, did not hold with foolishness on a holy day. And once I came here, to stay with Grandfather?' He shrugged again. 'It was a very quiet festival. There was dinner, of course. And gifts.' They had arrived back at the house. A footman grinned as he opened the front door, and they entered the front hall to the smells of pine and spices and an air of suppressed excitement. He looked around him. 'But it was nothing like this. Thank you.' His voice very nearly cracked on the words.

'You're welcome, Harry.' Her eyes were very round, and misty blue in the morning light. Then she looked away from him quickly, letting a servant take her outer clothes and enquiring about tea, which was already poured in the library, just as it had been in years past. It was still early, but any guests who had risen would be in the dining room taking breakfast. For a time it would be just the two of them, alone together.

In the library, she glanced around the room with a

critical eye. And Harry noted with some satisfaction that she seemed unconcerned by the presence of only two cups on the tea tray. Apparently, after his disgrace in the woods, she did not care that Tremaine would be left to fend for himself.

'Do you mean to have Rosalind here for Christmas from now on?' she said softly.

'It depends, I suppose, on whether Morley allows it. But I do not know what I would have done without her help this year.'

Elise looked up from her cup, her eyes still wide with sympathy. 'Does she know that the family recipes as they are written are not accurate?'

'Eh?'

'Rosalind. There are changes in the Christmas recipes, and she should remember to remind Cook.'

Harry waved a dismissive hand. 'I expect she will manage as best she can. It will be all right.'

'Perhaps I should help her.'

'No,' Harry said, worried that her sudden interest in the menu was likely to take her away from him again. 'There is no need, I'm sure. No one will notice if things are not quite up to standard.'

She stared at him. 'Really, Harry. You have no idea how difficult a house party can be.'

He looked warmly at her. 'Only because you made it look so easy, my sweet. But you need not bother.' He gave a slight sigh. 'I will want you here tonight, of course. When it is time to light the Yule Log. For it is still very much a part of you, since you helped me to choose it. And I've still got a piece of last year's log, so that we may light the new one properly.'

Her agitation seemed to fade, and she smiled a little, remembering.

'If we have any regrets from the old year we can throw them on the fire,' he announced. 'Next year we shall start anew.'

She set her teacup down with a click. 'And behave as if none of this has happened?'

He sighed. 'Is it really necessary to retread the same ground? If you are ready to come home, then I see no reason to refer to any of this again.'

'If I am ready to come home?'

He had spoken too soon, and ruined all that had gone before. For the coldness had returned to her voice, and she was straightening up the tea things and preparing to leave him.

'Perhaps I should go to my room and dress for the day. If you will excuse me?'

He followed her to the door and in a last act of desperation held up a hand to stop her as she crossed the threshold, touching her arm and pointing above them. 'Mistletoe.'

She frowned. 'You can't be serious.'

'Not even for old times' sake?'

'Certainly not.' She reached up and caught the thing by a twig. She pulled it down, then threw it to the floor at his feet.

He stared at it, unsure whether to be angry or sad. 'Pity. I would have quite enjoyed it. I think it is your kiss

I miss the most. But there are so many things about you that I miss it is hard to tell.'

'Miss me?' She laughed. 'This is the first I have heard of it. It seems to me that you are managing quite well without me, Harry.'

'It bothers you, then, that I have put Rosalind in charge?'

'Not particularly.'

'But something has made you unhappy again. Are you ready to discuss why you are here?' he asked.

'Whatever do you mean?'

'You have come back to me, Elise, just as I knew you would. It was no real surprise, seeing you. I had a devil of a time persuading Tremaine to take the invitation, but I knew if he came you would not be able to stay away. And I was right.' He looked at her, searching her expression for some evidence that she was weakening again.

'It should not be so terribly strange that I would wish to return with him. I lived here for several years, and associate many happy memories with the place.'

Harry sighed. 'Do you really? When you left I thought you never wished to see the place again. Or was it just the owner you wished to avoid? Because you must have known I'd be here as well.'

'I hold you no ill will,' she insisted, staring at him through narrowed eyes and proving her words a lie. 'And, since you have not said otherwise, I assume you agree that our separation is for the best.'

'You wished to part, not I. Do not mistake my unwillingness to beg for you to return as agreement.' And then his desire to hold her got the better of him, and he stepped even closer. 'There is very little separation between us at this moment.' He grabbed her wrist and pulled her to him, so her body rested tight against him.

'That is none of my doing and all of yours.' But she did not push him away.

He calmed himself so as not to alarm her. Then he put his mouth to her ear and whispered, so softly that only she could hear, 'Kiss me, Elise. Just one more time. I will enjoy it, and you will as well. I would make sure of the fact.' He felt her tremble and knew that he was right. When his lips met hers he would make her forget all about her argument with him. She would think of nothing but how he made her feel, and that would be the end of their troubles.

'I did not come here because I missed your kisses.' She pulled away from him, and the small rejection stung worse than all the others combined.

'And yet you were the one to come home.'

'For a brief visit. There are things in my room…'

'Things?' He laughed, for he had been sure that she would come up with a better lie than that when they finally had a chance to speak. 'If that is all you wanted, then you could have saved me a small amount of personal pride had you come alone, in January, rather than trailing after Tremaine when the house is full of guests.'

'I am not trailing after him,' she snapped.

Harry took a deep breath, for it would not do to lose his temper with her. 'It is all right,' he responded. 'I've grown quite used to it, really.'

But clearly it was not all right to her. He had misspoken again, and she was working herself into a rage. 'You did not expect me to live for ever alone, once we parted?'

'That is not what I mean, and you know it. I knew when you finally left me that you would go straight to Tremaine for comfort. I have expected it for many years.'

Anger and indignation flashed hot in her eyes, as though she could pretend the truth was not an obvious thing and her leaving had been all *his* fault. 'When I *finally* left you? What cause did I ever give you to doubt me?'

'It was never a question of doubt, Elise.' He tried to keep his tone matter-of-fact, for there was no point in fuelling her anger with his. 'I have always known that I was your second choice.'

'How utterly ridiculous,' she snapped. 'I married you, didn't I? Are you saying you doubted my innocence?'

'I am saying nothing of the kind. I am saying that I was not your first choice when you wed. You might have accepted my offer, but Tremaine offered for you first. You might have chosen me, but you always regretted that it could not have been Nicholas. I have had to live with the fact for five years, Elise.' He struggled to hide the hurt in his tone, and instead his voice sounded bitter. 'I had hoped that you would put him behind you once you were married. I would not have offered for you otherwise. But I realised almost from the beginning that it was not to be the case.'

'You realised?'

There was something in the sound of her voice that was almost like an accusation, and he could feel his carefully managed control slipping away. 'It did not take you long to make up with the man. Less than a year. The quarrel that parted you would have mended easily had you been willing to wait. It was really most annoying to listen to you complain, at the end, about *my* lack of devotion. For you have been so clearly devoted to another. Did you expect me to remain for ever the benighted fool who had married you? In the face of your continued indifference? In time one learns to harden one's heart, Elise.'

He was almost shouting by the time he'd finished. And then he laughed again, at the shocked expression on her face. 'Although what you expect by accompanying your lover to our home for Christmas I cannot imagine. Did you hope to create a dramatic scene for the diversion of my guests? Is it not bad enough that you have finally worked up the courage to be unfaithful to me? Must you parade it in front of me as well?' He shook his head, and his voice returned to normal. 'I never in all these years felt you to be so cruel. Perhaps I did not know you as well as I thought.'

Which was foolish, for he had known all along that that was what she would do. He had wanted her to come with Tremaine, had planned for the eventuality. And now he was angry to the point of shouting because his plans had come to fruition. It made no sense at all.

But it was too late to call back the words, or to explain that he wished to discuss things with her in a rational manner. Elise's cheeks had grown hot with anger and shame, but no words were issuing from her lips, and she was staring at him as though she no longer knew him.

As he waited for her response, a part of him wanted to beg her forgiveness, forestall her reaction. But why should he take all the blame when she was the one who had left? It was long past time for her turn to be hurt and frustrated and embarrassed.

It did him no good to feel sure that he was in the right on this. Instead of vindication, he was suddenly sick with the taste of truth. He had spoken too much of it, all in one go, and it sat in his stomach like an excess of Christmas dinner.

Did she expect him to swallow his pride as well, before she was willing to come home? If the silence went on much longer she would see him on his knees, begging her to return.

Then she spoke, and her voice was cool and even. 'So I finally know, after all this time, what you really think of me. It is most gratifying that our separation has given you the ability to speak your mind. And I find I have nothing to add to it.'

Then she turned and walked from the room, leaving him all over again. He stared down at the mistletoe at his feet, and then kicked it savagely aside, before gathering enough composure to meet his guests for breakfast.

Elise walked back towards her room, numb with shock. She could hear Harry turn and walk in the opposite direction, towards the dining room. She was glad of it, for if he spoke one more word to her she would burst into tears and not care who saw her. After all her complaints over not knowing her husband's true feelings, he had finally given them to her. And she found that she liked him better as he had been.

What had happened to the man she'd married? The amiable fellow who had tolerated her behaviour without question? In two months he'd been replaced by an angry stranger who looked at her with hard eyes and a mouth set in bitter disapproval. It was as though he was meeting her for the first time, and was thoroughly disappointed with what he saw.

Why had she come here? It had seemed like a sensible decision at the time. Either she would prove to herself and everyone else that she had put her marriage behind her, or she would make it up with Harry and go back to her old life. She had hoped that she would come back to the house and understand why he had married her in the first place. He would prove that he needed her, even if there were no children, and she would see that her fears were foolishness, and learn to accept his natural reserve as an aspect of his character, not a reflection upon her person.

For a moment she had been sure it was true. He had spoken so fondly of the changes she'd made in his life. And then had proved that he did not need her to preserve them. The last thing she had expected was to find him getting on with things without her help.

And, even worse, that he would come out and admit that there had been a problem from the first, just as she had suspected. Worse yet, it did not sound as if she could easily gain his forgiveness, and the love she wanted. He had spoken as though he had no hope for a closer relationship with her. He had offered for her never expecting to receive her love, or to give his in return. But they could have drifted along in peace and pleasantry had she not chosen to rile him in an effort to fix things.

Rosalind was approaching from the other end of the hall, and Elise reached out to her in desperation. 'I need to talk to you. There is a problem.'

Rosalind replied, 'If it is about the eggs I must argue that they are not at all my fault. I hardly think if one makes a simple suggestion to Cook that a touch more seasoning would be appreciated, that it should result in so much pepper as to make the whole tray inedible. Lord Gilroy took a large portion and grew so red in the face that I feared apoplexy. I—'

Elise grabbed her sister-in-law by the wrist and pulled her into the drawing room. 'It is not about the eggs.'

'What else has gone wrong, then? It is so early in the day that there cannot be more.'

'It is your brother. He is angry with me.'

Rosalind smiled with satisfaction. 'And you have no trouble recognising the fact? That is wonderful news. For it means you are beginning to solve your difficulties.'

'It is not wonderful. It is really quite horrible. He thinks I am faithless.'

Rosalind stared at her and made a face. 'Did you think that taking a lover would assure him of your fidelity? I know things are different in Bavaria, Elise. But they can't be as different as all that.'

'Nicholas is only a friend, nothing more.' She squeezed Rosalind's arm. 'You must believe me. I would never be untrue to Harry.'

Rosalind disengaged her arm and said, 'While I have no trouble believing you, it is what Harry thinks that matters.'

'If Harry were really bothered he should have said something before now.' She realised too late how defensive she sounded—and how guilty.

Rosalind was looking at her in annoyance. 'You have said yourself that Harry does not speak about anything that bothers him. Did you think that this would be different?'

'Perhaps I was trying to make him jealous.' It was difficult to say the words, for they proved that she had known what she was doing was wrong.

Rosalind nodded. 'You were lonely. And by his silence Harry made it easy for you to stray. He is lucky the situation is not worse than it is.'

Elise let out a small sigh of relief. At least Rosalind did not hold her weakness too much against her. 'I wanted Harry to notice me. But now that he has, what am I to do? I would send Nicholas away, but with the weather he cannot get to the end of the drive, much less back to London.' And then she remembered the offer she had made to get him to bring her home. 'And I will have to apologise to Nicholas as well, for I fear I have given him the wrong idea of my feelings.'

Rosalind stared at her, offering no help.

Elise continued. 'We are all stuck here together, the

house is full of strangers, and if we argue everyone in London will hear of it. What am I to do?'

Rosalind replied with a helpless shrug. 'I assumed you would not have come here if you did not have some idea how to proceed once you had talked to Harry. Did you not have a plan? Everyone seems to be full of them nowadays. It is quite the thing.'

'I was so angry with him I did not think.'

'And he was not angry enough. And now you are less angry, and he is more so.' Rosalind nodded. 'In no time at all balance shall be achieved and you shall both be equally annoyed.' She said it as though this were supposed to be good news, and wiped her hands on her skirts.

Elise shook her head. 'But I do not wish to be annoyed with Harry. I wish us to be happy together. If I return to find that we are both still cross, leaving will have been an exercise in futility.'

Rosalind stepped past her towards the hall, gaining speed as she went. 'There is nothing more I can do for you at the moment. I must run to the entry hall and decorate the Yule Log, so that tonight we can throw the whole thing into the fire and burn those same decorations to ashes. I am sure I will be in a much better mood to discuss futile behaviour, after that is done.'

Chapter Ten

Rosalind hurried down the hallway, taking sips from the cup of tea in her hand. It was tepid. But since she had not managed lunch, it was all she was likely to have until supper, and it would have to do. Since the moment she had arisen there had been something that needed doing, or fixing, or seeing to. Harry's friends seemed to think that the food was either overcooked or raw, they found their rooms too hot or too cold, and the servants could not manage to please any of them without constant supervision.

After watching her decorate the Christmas tree, she had nurtured hopes that Elise would see the chaos, take control of the house, and set things to right again. But after one conversation with Harry the woman could not manage to do anything more useful than wring her hands.

It was most distressing.

As Rosalind passed the open door of the library she noticed that the mistletoe was no longer in its place. Was there something wrong with the thing that it could not seem to stay fixed to the door? Was the nail loose? Tremaine had placed it quite securely yesterday. What had happened now?

She searched the floor and found it had not fallen, as she'd expected, onto the doorstep, but had pitched up against the wall, several feet away. Someone must have kicked it by mistake, for it did appear somewhat the worse for wear. She glared at it, as though blaming it as a troublemaker, then shook it roughly and gave it a half-hearted toss in the direction of the hook above her.

It hung for a moment, and then dropped back into her teacup, splashing the contents onto her bodice. Unlike yesterday, there was no sound of muffled laughter. But she took a chance before acting further.

'Tremaine, I need you. Get up from that couch and be of use.'

There was a sigh from the other side of the room. 'How did you know I was here?'

'I have been everywhere else in the house, for one reason or another, and I have not seen you all day. So, by process of elimination, you must be hiding in the library—just as you promised you would *not*.'

'And what in God's name do you mean to involve me in now? I have had quite enough of the festivities, and the fun, as you call it, has barely begun. Do you know what your brother attempted this morning?'

'Whatever it was, he has managed to annoy Elise no end.'

'Annoy her?' Tremaine's angry face peered from

behind the couch. 'When I left them they were as happy as lovebirds. It seems she was not bothered by the sight of her husband threatening me with an axe, or attempting to freeze me to death. And I have ruined my best pair of shoes by walking through the snow. My valet is beyond consolation.'

'As I have told you before, Tremaine, Harry means you no real harm. He is only teasing you because seeing you in a foul temper amuses him. My brother thinks that you have a lack of Christmas spirit, and I'm afraid I must agree with him.'

Nicholas punched the couch cushions in disgust. 'I do not deny the fact. And, since Harry has sufficient spirit for two men, he pretends that he wishes to share it with me.'

She looked down at the dripping mistletoe in her hand, gave it another shake to remove the tea, and reached for the doorframe again. 'If you would be so kind as to take it, then you could save some of us a world of effort. I can be every bit as persistent as my brother, if you give me reason. And if you try to avoid my scheduled activities, I will find a way to force your participation in them. It would be easier for both of us if you could at least pretend to enjoy them.'

He stood and walked slowly towards her. 'I will participate, Miss Morley. But you far overstep the bounds of our limited acquaintance if you think you can make me enjoy the fact. I am a proper gentleman of the ton. And as such I live by certain rules. Conversation should flow freely, but truth should be kept to an absolute minimum. In the Christmas season truth runs as freely as wine.' He made a sour face. 'But the wine is endlessly seasoned with cloves. And therefore undrinkable.'

'So you have an aversion to truth? And cloves? I can do little about the cloves, for they are all-pervasive, but I suppose spontaneous honesty is reason enough to avoid the holiday. Harry and Elise are proving that even if the truth is spoken it is oft misinterpreted. And then there is the very devil to pay. He has finally admitted that he is angry with her.' Rosalind looked heavenward for understanding. 'And yet, she is surprised.'

Tremaine shook his head in pity. 'He'd have been better to hold his tongue. When it comes to women, if you admit to nothing you will have less to apologise for later.'

'I find the fault is with her. One should never ask a man to reveal the contents of his mind if one does not already know what they are.' Rosalind smiled. 'But until they have fought they cannot make up. Some progress has been made. And the game I have chosen for tonight will be perfect to rejoin the two of them. They will be back in each other's arms and laughing together in a matter of minutes. I suspect, once that has happened, the temptation will be great to stay where they are. But you must help fill out the room so that it doesn't look too suspicious.' She looked him up and down. 'You need do nothing more strenuous than take up space. In less than an hour you will be back on that couch, and none the worse for it.' She tapped the mistletoe against her teacup, awaiting his response.

He yawned, as though to prove that taking up space

was near the limit of his endurance. And then he said, 'How can I resist you when you put it so appealingly? Here, now. Will you stop fooling with that accursed thing.' Her tapping had turned into a nervous rattling of china, and with surprising alacrity he snatched the kissing ball out of her hand and put it in place on the hook, above her head. And then he stood perfectly still, totally alert, looking down at her. His mouth turned into a curious smile.

She felt the bump as her back met the doorframe, for she'd scrambled out of reach of his arm without even re-alising it.

And then he laughed. 'You are much more cautious than you once were.'

'And you are no less prone to flirt. But, since I know you wish to return to London alone, I see no point in in-dulging you.' She took another step, which brought her back into the hall and well out of harm's way. 'I will expect to see you in the drawing room this evening, Tremaine. And we will see if you are still so interested in fun and games when my brother is present to chaperone me.'

After a hearty Christmas Eve dinner, Harry gathered the guests in the drawing room for the lighting of the Yule Log. Elise was pleased to see that the trunk of the ash they had chosen the previous year was large enough to fill the fireplace from end to end.

Rosalind had spent a good portion of the afternoon draping it with garlands of holly and ivy, tied on with red bows, until it was almost too pretty to burn. And she had sighed dramatically as she directed the servants to put it on the grate.

Harry produced a charred piece of last year's log and doused it liberally with brandy before thrusting it into the embers and watching it flare to life.

The crowd gave an appreciative 'Ahh' and several people stepped closer to offer toasts.

When Harry felt ceremony had been properly served, he touched the old log to the new and held it until the decorations upon the new log caught. Then he threw his torch into the fireplace.

'There you are, my friends. The Yule Log. May it burn long and joyfully. If you have any regrets of the previous year, now is your chance to throw them upon the fire and start anew.' He looked significantly at Elise as he reached into a basket of kindling and tossed a handful of pine needles upon the fire, watching them flare.

Elise stared at the basket of needles, and at the crowd around them. Did he mean her to do penance, in front of all these people? But what good would it do to stand in front of the guests and wordlessly declare herself a failure as a wife? Even if she could prove herself sorry for her indiscretion with Nicholas, there was so much she could not change. Without a miracle, next year was likely to be as barren as this had been.

When she did nothing, he gave a moment's thought and added a second handful of needles to the fire. Then he smiled, changing easily back into the jovial host. 'Come, everybody—wassail and mince pies!' He made a few steps in the direction of the refreshment table, until he was sure that the guests were well on their way, then turned back to face Elise on the opposite side of the fire.

'Elise. A word, please, in the study.' Harry beckoned to her to follow him and left the drawing room, walking down the corridor and away from the crowd. His smile was as pleasant as it had always been, with none of the rancour it had held that morning. But his tone was that of a husband who took it for granted that a command would be obeyed.

It rankled her to see him falling right back into the pattern of the last five years. Even though she no longer lived with him, he was acting as though there was nothing strange between them, and ordering her from room to room while pretending that she was free as a bird and could do as she liked.

She hesitated. If she wished to come home, then she must learn not to fight him over little things. But if he did not want her back, then what was the point of obeying? At last she sighed, and nodded, and followed him to the study, letting him shut the door behind her.

He turned and faced her, and he must have seen the anger growing in her—and the shame. For a moment he seemed at a loss for words. He held his hands out in front of him and opened his mouth. Then closed it again, and put his hands behind his back, pensive. At last he said, 'I notice that you did not throw anything onto the fire tonight. Am I to take it that you have no regrets?'

'Of course I have regrets,' she said. 'But do you think a handful of burned pine needles and dead silence is a sufficient apology?'

He shrugged. 'Sometimes, when one does not know what to say, it is better to keep silent.'

'But not always.' She looked earnestly at him. 'It is possible, when one cares deeply about another person, to forgive harsh words said in the heat of the moment.'

He frowned and stared at the ground. 'But not always.' He dipped a hand in to his pocket, removing a jewellery box. 'I have your Christmas gift.' He offered it to her.

'Harry…' And now she was at a loss for words, but her mind was crying, *Tell me you didn't.* Their marriage was in a shambles, and he meant to gloss it all over with another necklace. At last she said, 'This is not necessary.'

He gave her another empty smile. 'Gifts rarely are. It defeats the point, when one has ample means but denies necessities to someone all year, to mete them out at Christmas, pretending that they are gifts. That is miserliness in the guise of generosity.'

She pushed the box back to him. 'I mean that it was not necessary for you to buy me a present. I do not wish it.'

'How do you know? You do not know what is inside.' He held it out to her again.

'It is not the contents of the box that concern me. I do not wish another gift from you, Harry.'

For a moment she thought she saw pain in his eyes, before he hid it in sarcasm. 'And yet you have no trouble with my paying for your apartment or settling your bills? You take things from me every day, Elise.'

He was deliberately misunderstanding her, so she struck back at him. 'If it bothers you so, then set me free. Then I would not take another thing from you, Harry.'

He nodded. 'Because you prefer Tremaine, now that he can afford to buy you the things you need?'

'His inheritance has nothing to do with my leaving you.'

'It was merely a fortunate coincidence that six months after his uncle died you went to London to be with him? You barely allowed him enough time to mourn before you returned to his side.'

She started in surprise. It had not occurred to her when she had left how that might look to the casual observer. Or, worse yet, to her husband. 'If you think I left you because of Tremaine, then you do not understand the problem at all.'

'I understand the problem well enough. I have a wife who prefers the company of another.'

'If you wish to see it that way then there is little I can do to change your mind,' she snapped. 'But in truth you have a wife who left because she was tired of being held at a distance. I can understand, Harry, if you are not happy with me. Or if you do not wish to take me into your confidence. But if you do not want me, must you blame me for seeking companionship elsewhere?'

'I do not want you?' He laughed. 'You do not want *me*, more like. Has Tremaine shown you the letter? I assume that is why you are both here? So that he can win his bet and you can gloat over it.'

'That letter was foolishness itself. Do you think our marriage is some kind of joke? And it was most cruel of you to make me a part of it. I did not think you capable of such base behaviour.'

His eyes held the hooded look they had sometimes, and he looked away from her briefly before saying, 'You would be surprised what I am capable of when it comes to you, Elise. But my cruel trick succeeded in making you angry enough to return home for Christmas.'

She moaned in exasperation. 'Really, Harry. If all you wanted was a visit at Christmas, then you had but to come to London and ask me.'

He thrust the jewel box back into his pocket and glared into the fire. 'And the answer would have been no. Or you would have insisted that we discuss a divorce.'

It surprised her to see him looking so sullen. And without intending it, her tone became softer. 'At least we would have been talking again, and the matter of our future could have been decided one way or another. But you felt the need to trick me into doing what you wished instead of asking me outright, and taking the risk that my answer might not be to your liking.' She stared at him, willing him to understand. 'If you do not see the wrong in that, then perhaps you will never understand why I am unhappy with you.'

He grabbed a poker and jabbed at the logs in the grate. 'I understand you well enough to know that you were eager to come back to me for an argument. But I do not think you returned home to climb the hill with me at dawn and watch the sun rise, as you did this morning.'

She swallowed for a moment as the memory of that simple pleasure returned to her. 'You are right. And thank you for that. There is much we need to talk about, Harry. But it has been a long time since we have done something just for pleasure's sake. It felt good to put our differences aside for a few moments.' She hesitated. 'I enjoyed it very much.'

He set the poker aside, wiped his hands on a handkerchief, and then patted the box in his pocket, smiling. 'Then you will enjoy this as well.'

A lump of bitterness formed in her throat at the thought of the jewel box again. 'I brought nothing for you in exchange, you know.'

His voice dropped low. 'There is only one thing I want from you.' He stepped towards her and reached out, taking her hand in his. 'That is for you to return home to me, and for things to go back to the way they were.'

'I would not want to return to what we had, Harry,' she said, surprised that he had not seemed to notice the emptiness they'd shared. 'You cannot continue to pretend that nothing was wrong any more than you can buy my co-operation with jewellery.'

He shook his head in amazement, as though he really did not see a problem. 'I am not attempting to buy you, Elise. I should not need to. We are married, after all. You have been mine for five years.'

His words shocked her back to anger. 'So I am already bought and paid for? Is that the way you see me?'

'What a daft idea. I never said so,' he answered.

'Perhaps because you speak so rarely.'

'Then I will speak now, if you are willing to listen,' he said, and smiled. But for a moment, before the affability returned to his face, she saw frustration underneath. 'I did not mean that I had bought you. I meant that I should not have to buy you now. Do you expect me to outdo Tremaine in some way, to win you back? I had hoped that when we married your choice was fixed. But now I am not so sure.'

She threw her hands into the air. 'I have been gone from your house for two months, Harry. And your best response, after all this time, is that you are "not so sure" I am gone.'

He scoffed. 'You did not expect me to take this division between us seriously, did you? It would serve you right if I went ahead with the divorce you seek and left you to marry Tremaine. But I have forgiven you for it. Now, let us put aside this silly quarrel. I will give you your Christmas present, and we can return to the main room and explain to Tremaine that his presence is no longer required.'

He offered the box to her again, and she knocked it from his hand onto the floor. 'It does not matter to me, Harry, if you have "forgiven" me for leaving. For if you think so little of me, and take our marriage for granted in such a way, how can I ever forgive you?' And with that she stormed from the room.

In the drawing room, Rosalind grabbed Nick by the arm, almost jostling the cup of wassail from his hand.

'Dear God, woman,' he drawled. 'Can I not enjoy a moment's peace?'

'The guests are getting restless. We must start the games soon. Harry has gone off somewhere.' Her eyes darted to the open doorway. 'And Elise appears to be in a state and is headed for her room. Stop her!' She gave him a shove towards the open door that spilled even more of his punch. 'I will find my brother.'

Nick stumbled out into the hall and hurried to catch up with Elise. 'Darling, where are you headed at such an alarming pace? The night is young, and I long for your company.'

She turned on him with a glare, and responded in a torrent of unintelligible German.

He grinned. 'I gather you have been talking to your husband?'

'That man. If I spend one more moment in his company I swear I shall go mad.'

He gestured to the drawing room. 'Then spend a moment with me. I have brought you a cup of wassail.' He held his cup out to her.

She took it, and stared down at it. 'This cup is empty, Nicholas.'

He slipped an arm around her waist, guiding her back to the party. 'Perhaps it is only waiting to be filled. Optimism, Elise. We need optimism at times like this. Twelfth Night will be here soon enough, and then we shall go back to London and I will help you to forget all about this.' He gave her waist a little squeeze.

She blinked, as though just remembering what she had promised him. 'That will be wonderful, Nicholas. I can hardly wait.' But she said it with a sickly smile that proved she had not been living for the moment they would become one. 'I believe I might need a cup of punch after all.'

'I thought you might.' He shepherded her to the refreshments and she downed a cup of wassail, hardly stopping for breath. It was not flattering to see that the thought of intimacy with him required so much fortification. Alcohol could not help but make Harry more appealing to her, so he reached for the ladle and helped her to a second cup.

'I have found another who is willing to play,' Rosalind announced from the doorway. She was ignoring Harry's lack of enthusiasm as she hauled him back into the room by his elbow. 'The more people we have, the more fun it shall be.'

As they passed, Harry stared at Nick's hand, which was still resting on his wife's waist while he plied her with liquor. Harry shot him a look of undisguised loathing before turning to his sister. 'Yes, Rosalind. I think we should all like a diversion.'

'And what exactly is this game we are all so eager to play?' Nick asked dryly.

'Blind Man's Bluff,' Rosalind said. 'And, Harry, as host you must go first.'

Nick thought to remind her that it was rarely polite to put guests last, but he could see the stubborn glint in Rosalind's eye and elected not to challenge her.

'I will blindfold you, and you must identify your guests.' She was tying a handkerchief around Harry's face, and spinning him so that he lost all direction.

Guests who were not interested in playing moved to the corners of the room. Elise looked to the exit with longing, and then to Harry, as though trying to decide between the two.

But Rosalind hurried to close the door, and put her back to it, making the decision for her. 'Quiet, everyone, let Harry try to find you.'

Nick swore silently, and nudged Elise towards the centre of the room and into the game. With Rosalind blocking the door, his escape was thwarted as well. If Harry's eyes were covered, there was little he could do to affect the man. It would have been an excellent opportunity to get away. He shot Rosalind a murderous look.

She shrugged and cocked her head towards the other players, as though telling him to pay attention to the game.

While Nick was distracted by her, Harry lumbered past him, on his blind side, and stamped mercilessly on his toe. 'Eh—what was that?' He stumbled, turned back as though to find Tremaine, and then veered left at the last minute, catching another guest by the shoulders. 'Let me see.' He patted at the man, placing his hands on an ample stomach. 'Cammerville. I do not need eyes to tell it is you.'

The gentleman laughed and sat down.

'That's one down.' Harry swung his arm out wide through the open air and laid hands on a young lady, reaching carefully to touch her hair. 'And the younger of the Misses Gilroy, I believe. For there are your pretty curls.' Then he marched purposefully towards Elise, who took a deep breath and froze like a rabbit, waiting to be caught.

Nick hoped that the game they were really playing would be over once Harry had caught his wife. Elise looked more resigned than happy to be playing, but at least she was no longer as angry as she had been in the hall. But Harry stopped at the last moment and turned, moving across the room again, away from his wife.

Elise put her hands on her hips and glared at his back in disgust.

On his way to wherever he thought he was going, Harry managed to catch himself on a small table and tip it, sending a carafe of wine cascading down the leg of Nick's best buff trousers.

He stifled an oath and mopped at the stain with his handkerchief.

Rosalind glared at him, making frantic gestures that he should hold his tongue and keep to the spirit of the game.

'I have upset something,' announced Harry, grinning without remorse.

Rosalind reached him from behind and spun him, giving him a forceful shove to send him back towards Elise.

Harry lurched again in the direction of his wife, only to catch another woman by the shoulders. 'And this is the elder Miss Gilroy. For I have danced with you before, and recall you as being most slim and just this tall.' The girl dissolved into a shower of giggles.

Elise's countenance darkened with the clouds of a returning storm. As Harry made another pass through the room, instead of avoiding him she stepped in front of him, so that he could not help but run into her.

He swung his arms wide again, turned suddenly, and reached high instead of low, catching Tremaine by the throat. 'What's this, then? Have I caught the turkey for tomorrow's dinner?'

He gave a warning squeeze, and Nick gagged slightly.

'Oh, no. Not a turkey at all. It is Tremaine. I recognise that artfully tied cravat. You're out of the running, old man. Sit down.' He released his throat, spun him around and gave a sharp push to his shoulders that sent him stumbling towards the sofa. 'And stay out of my way.'

The other people in the room laughed knowingly.

He turned again, 'How many is that, then? Almost everyone? But there must be someone left.' He walked deliberately past his own wife again.

Elise was getting angrier by the minute, and was now actively trying to be found—repeatedly stepping into his path, only to be avoided as he seized and identified someone else.

Nick was near enough to Rosalind to hear her fervent whispering. 'Don't toy with her, Harry. Do not toy with her. She does not appreciate it.'

But either Harry did not hear or did not care. He was still pretending that he did not know the location of his wife. He groped in the empty air to the right of her, and when she moved into his path he turned again. It was plain to all there that he was deliberately avoiding her.

'Where is she?'

Several guests laughed, and a young girl called out, 'Behind you. Look behind you.'

At last, Elise could control her temper no longer. 'If you seriously wish to find her, she will be in her bedroom. With the door locked.' Elise gave her husband an angry shove, then marched past him and through the drawing room door.

The room went silent, waiting to see what would happen next. When Harry yanked off the blindfold he looked, for a moment, as though he were torn between staying and following her. And then he smoothed his hair and let out a hearty laugh, to prove that there was nothing seriously wrong.

The guests relaxed and laughed with him.

Rosalind caught Nick before he could leave the room to find Elise. He frowned at her. 'You need some practice, I think, in your tying of the blindfold. Your brother could see us all, clear as day.'

She let out an exasperated puff of air. 'Of course he could. It would make little sense for him to have wandered around blind.'

'That is the point of the game, is it not?'

'When you are in a room with your wife and her lover it is never a good idea to be blind.'

'He has pretended blindness on the subject long enough,' said Nick, with a growing understanding of Harry's predicament.

'But now it is long past time for him to stop pretending.' She glared in the direction of her brother. 'I am so angry with Harry that I can hardly speak. He must have known what I was about by tying the handkerchief the way I did. I gave him an excellent opportunity and he wasted it. But if I question him on it, he will claim that he knows his wife better than I. And she will return to him in her own good time and there is little else to be done about it.'

'You gave him no choice but to act as he did, Rosalind. I had my doubts, when he welcomed me into his home, but the man does have his pride. He wants his wife back, but he does not want to be forced to admit the fact in front of an audience.'

'And why ever not? Admitting that you love your wife is nothing to be ashamed of.'

Nick shook his head. 'Perhaps not. But to solve this problem someone must be willing to sacrifice their pride. And each one is still hoping that it can be the other.'

'It might be easier for us to reconcile them were they not so perfectly suited in their bullheadedness.'

He glared at her. 'It might also be easier if you would include me in the plans that you are making. At least a small warning would have been welcome just now. The man positively mauled me, and I had to stand there and take it in good humour.'

'It serves you right,' she said with vehemence. 'You are quite horrible, you know.'

'I am no worse than I have ever been.'

'And no better than you should be. Harry is right in one thing, Tremaine. You need to change your ways. And, while it pains me to see Harry and Elise struggling with pride, I have no compunction in sacrificing yours. If this season gives you a chance to do penance, then so be it. You may start afresh in the New Year.'

'What if one suspects that no matter what one does the next year will be no different from the last?' He shook his head. 'I find it no cause for celebration.'

'Only if you are unhappy with your life,' she said. 'I

thought you claimed to be content. If so, another year of the same will not bother you.'

Damn her for making him think on it. For as he did he realised that he was far too bored to claim contentment. 'And you are so content in yours, then?' He gave her a sour smile.

She lifted her chin. 'My view of the future is somewhat more optimistic than yours. I do not worry myself over the things I cannot change, and apply myself diligently to those things that I can. I view the New Year as a promise that things do not always have to be the same.' She held out a hand. 'While the book is closing on 1813, there is no telling what 1814 will bring us. You might be a better man.'

Nick stood too close to her, and was satisfied to see the flash in her eyes that proved she was not so immune to his charms as she pretended. 'Are you still convinced there is something wrong with me as I am now?'

Instead of responding playfully to his comment, she looked at him in all seriousness and said, 'Yes, there is. You wonder how it is that you manage to be in such trouble with Harry, and why your life does not change from year to year. But you have only your own behaviour to blame for it.' She glanced towards the hall, in the direction of the absent Elise. 'I saw the two of you together when I brought Harry into the room. And I saw the look you gave her as she left. Do not tell me that you were not about to follow her. It is more than difficult, trying to get the two of them to co-operate and reconcile. If you can muster enough sense to set her free, then it will be much easier for all of us.'

Chapter Eleven

The next day, Nick was lying on his back on the library sofa, struggling to enjoy the peace and quiet of Christmas afternoon. The roads to the village were better, but still suspect. So the party had forgone church and let Harry lead them in morning prayer in the dining room. After luncheon, the servants had hitched up sleighs, and Harry had taken the majority of his guests to go ice skating on a nearby stream. Others had retired to their rooms. There had been no sign at all of Elise since she had taken to her room the previous evening.

He felt a touch of guilt over that point. But jollying her back into good spirits would mean he must forfeit the afternoon, which was going just as he preferred it: dozing with a full stomach, in air scented faintly with pine and punch, and none of the frenetic eagerness to make fun where none was needed. Nor did he wish to give Rosalind Morley fuel for her spurious argument that he did not know how to let well enough alone when it came to his ex-intended. If Elise needed cheering, then perhaps it was time for her husband to do the job.

It had occurred to him that if he wished any real peace, it would be a far better idea to stay in his own bedroom than to stretch out in a common area, where he was likely to be interrupted at any moment. But he had rejected the idea for the illogical reason that it would give him too *much* privacy. Rosalind would not think to look for him if he rested in his room. And he had to admit that he was growing to expect a disruptive visit from the sweet Miss Morley as part of his daily routine. He had promised to stay out of her way, and he had meant to be true to his word. It was no fault of his that she insisted upon searching him out.

His mind ran over and over their conversation of the previous evening. She seemed to think that he was still to blame for the troubles between Harry and Elise, even though he was doing everything in his power to rejoin them. Had he not brought her home? Was he not doing his best to stay clear of them while they sorted out their difficulties?

And had he not immediately fallen back into his role of devoted admirer the minute he'd seen Elise's unhappiness? Damn it all, he did not want to lie with her any more than she wanted his attentions. But the suggestion of it had been enough of a distraction to coax her back to the punch bowl.

Now, despite nagging doubts about the wisdom of it, he would leave Elise to have her sulk. He would be sure to point the fact out when Miss Morley put in an appearance with whatever scheme she was currently hatching. There was no telling what chaos she was likely to bring with her when she came today. He smiled. Although she was a most annoying young lady, at least she did not bore him.

Nick glanced at his watch, and was surprised to see it was almost three. Several hours had passed in relative silence, and he should have been able to settle his mind and get the sleep he'd been craving. Although the library sofa was much more comfortable than the miserable mattress his host had allotted him, he could not seem to find peace.

He looked over the back of the couch at the mistletoe, still hanging in its proper place above the door. On impulse he rose and removed it from the hook, dropping it on the floor under a table. Then he went back to his place by the fire and pretended to sleep.

Rosalind came into the room a short time later, but took no notice of the missing decoration. Instead, she strode directly to his hiding place, coming round to the front of the couch to slap at the sole of his boot. 'Wake up, Tremaine. I have plans for you.'

He pretended to splutter to consciousness, looked up at her, and hurriedly closed his eyes again. 'Then I am most assuredly still asleep. Please leave me in peace.'

'There is much work to be done if you wish to go home alone.'

'Far more than that, I wish to go home alive. And the best way to assure my safety is to stay right here, far away from Harry. The man laid hands on me yesterday. He cannot be trusted.'

'You are being silly again. It was an innocent game.'

When she scolded him, her curls bounced in a most amusing fashion, and he had to force himself not to smile at her. 'The game was innocent enough. But I do not trust some of the players any further than I can throw them.' No more than he trusted Rosalind. He suspected that she had other reasons for wishing him to play.

'You have nothing to fear from Harry. I have known the man almost a quarter of a century. Although he might threaten, he would never do you bodily harm.'

He laughed. 'When you reach that advanced age, little one, and make such claims, then I shall take your word.'

She glared down at him. 'Twenty-five is not an advanced age, and it is most unflattering of you to call it so. The fact that I am near to it does not put me so far beyond the pale.'

Four-and-twenty? But she could barely be eighteen now. He was convinced of it. He looked at her more closely. But hadn't he thought the same thing when he had met her the first time? And that had been years ago. If she was twenty-four, then… He counted upon his fingers.

His silence must have unnerved her, for she said, 'Do not fall asleep again, Tremaine. The festivities have not been so strenuous as to require rest in midday. And if you mean to imply that my conversation bores you to unconsciousness, I swear I shall box your ears.'

He gave a little cough. 'Twenty-four?'

'Twenty-five next month.'

'But you are…'

She gritted her teeth. 'Older than Elise. Just barely. And still single. But I look much younger and always have. Or were you about to say *tiny*? For if you mean to comment on my lack of height as well as my advanced age then you will have nothing more to fear from Harry. I will do more damage to you than he ever shall.'

For a moment, he could swear that he was looking at the same gamine he had found in the hallway at the Grenvilles' ball, five Christmases ago. The only change in her was the cynical glint in her eyes and the determined set to her mouth. 'You look no different than you did when I first met you.'

She put her hands on her hips. 'Considering how well our first meeting went, I hardly know what you mean by that. But I shall assume you mean to compliment me. I hope you are not so cruel as to torment me with my appearance? There is little I can do to change it.'

'I thought you much younger when we first met. You were standing in the doorway of the ballroom, behind a potted palm, watching everyone else dance.'

She smirked. 'You remember that now, do you?'

'I never forgot it.'

'But when my father caught us kissing you announced, "I have never seen this girl before in my life." I assumed that we were keeping to the established lie and pretending that our dance had never occurred.'

'It was only an hour before we kissed. So technically I had not met you before. Not before that night, at any rate.'

'Technically?' She nodded sceptically. 'My father

assumed that I had kissed a man without even taking the time to learn his name. It was very awkward for me.'

'But when we danced,' he said haltingly, 'you told me that you were not yet out.'

'I'd have made my come-out in spring, if Father had allowed me to remain in London. Twenty would have been a bit later than the other girls, of course. But not too late.' There was a wistful note in her voice, and she took a moment to crush it before continuing in a normal, businesslike tone, 'But a come-out is not necessary for a happy life. Only so much foolishness.'

'You were nineteen?'

'As were you, once.' There was another long pause as she came to understand him. 'You mean when we first met? Well, yes. Of course I was. You did not think I had escaped from the schoolroom to accost you? It was only my father's stubbornness, not my age that left me lurking outside the ballroom instead of dancing with the others.'

'But you were nineteen,' he repeated numbly.

'The night we met?' She shrugged. 'It did not matter. My father has very strict ideas on what is proper and improper for young ladies. Girls who are not out should not dance, no matter their age.'

As he remembered that night, he knew there had been girls much younger at the party, giggling in corners, begging for gentlemen to stand up with them and being no end of a nuisance—just as there were in the house today. He had assumed Rosalind to be one of them. But she had been of marriageable age, and yet still denied the pleasure of adult company. Her actions made more sense.

'That was rather strict of him.'

'Perhaps. But there was little to be done about it.'

'And you say you had not tasted wine unwatered?'

She stared at him, as if daring him to doubt her. 'I had not. If you were to speak to my father on the subject, I still have not.' She made a face. 'He does not approve of strong spirits. He drinks his wine with water as well, and forgoes brandy entirely. He says that consumption of alcohol by gentlewomen is most improper.' She smiled. 'It is fortunate for me that I am the one who does the pouring in our household. For, while he trusts me to follow his wishes, he really has no idea about the contents of my glass.'

He tried to imagine what it would be like to have to forgo wine with a meal and could not comprehend it. It was as if she had been trapped in childhood, with no escape on the horizon. 'And he still does not allow you to travel to the city, even after years of good behaviour?'

'I am not encouraged to leave the house at all. He sent me to Harry, of course, because my brother was in need. But I suspect that says more about his disapproval of Elise than anything else.' Rosalind made another stern face. 'He has much to say on the subject of foreigners and their strange ways, and he is none too secret about the satisfaction he feels at Harry's marital difficulties. He will expect a full report of them when I return home. Which will be very soon, should he get wind of the festivities I have organised. I do not care to hear what he will say when he finds out that I have been stringing holly on a Yule Log.'

'How utterly absurd,' Nick replied. 'It is an innocent enough diversion, and most enjoyable.' If one could manage to ignore the nuisance of going into the woods and focus on the blazing fire in the evening. He gave a nod to her. 'And I must say, the thing was most attractively decorated, before Harry set it to light.'

Rosalind looked amused. 'Are you a defender of Christmas now, Saint Nicholas?'

'I do not defend Christmas so much as believe that small pleasures are not a threat to character or a black mark upon the soul.'

'On that point you and Harry agree. It is one of the reasons I see so little of Harry, for he cannot abide my father's treatment of his mother, nor of me. And Father has very little good to say about him.' She sighed. 'But my father means well by it, although he may seem harsh to others. It has done me no real harm. And I must admit, I bring much of his censure on myself. For I have a tendency to small rebellions, and can be just as stubborn as Harry when I've a mind.'

It made Nick unaccountably angry to see her resigned to her future, caring for a man who was obviously impossible to please. And the idea that she had to moderate a temperament which he found quite refreshing, irritated him even more. He said, 'If a wild bird is caged long enough, even for its own protection, it will beat its wings against the bars. If it does itself an injury, whose fault is it? The bird's or the one who caged it?'

'If you are attempting to draw some parallel between me and the bird, then I wish you would refrain from it.

The fault would lie with the bird. For, while such creatures are lovely to look at, they are seldom held up as
an example of wisdom and good sense.'

She was standing close enough to him that the smell
of her perfume blended with the pine boughs on the
mantel and the other inescapable smells of Christmas,
turning the simple floral scent she wore into something
much more complex and sensual. It was just as tempting
as he remembered it, and just as hard to ignore. He
wondered if it had been the same for her. For all along
she had been old enough to understand temptation, but
lacking the experience to avoid it. He smiled in
sympathy. 'It seems I have done you an injustice, Miss
Morley. For this explanation of your behaviour on the
night we met puts the event in a whole new light.'

'I thought we had agreed not to speak of that again,'
she muttered, and tried to turn away.

He put a finger under her chin and urged her to look
up at his face. 'After you were forced to apologise repeatedly for something which was no real fault of
yours? What you were doing was not so unusual,
compared with other girls of your age. If you lacked seasoning or sense, it was because your family did not train
you to know what was expected of you. They thought
that they could confine you until the last possible
moment and then thrust you into the light, where you
would exhibit flawless behaviour with no practice.
When you failed, it was more their fault than yours.' He
hung his head. 'And mine as well. I might have behaved
quite differently had I known the circumstances

involved. And I do not remember at any time giving you the apology that you deserve in response.'

She swallowed. 'It is not necessary.'

'I beg to differ.' He moved so that he was standing before her, and said, 'Give me your hand.'

She was obviously trying to come up with a response that would make things easier between them, but none was forthcoming.

So he reached, and took her hand in both of his. 'I am sorry for what occurred that night,' he said. 'The fact that you were behaving without caution did not require me to respond in kind. If anything, I should have been more circumspect, not less. You have been punished inordinately for it, although I have always deserved the majority of the guilt. Please forgive me.'

He was staring into her eyes, and it made things difficult. For it reminded him of the way she'd looked at him that night, and how it had made him feel, and why it had been so easy to throw caution to the winds and kiss her when he had known he had no right to.

But this time she managed to look away from him, instead of drawing nearer. 'Of course,' she said, and then she closed her eyes and dropped her head, as though praying that humility would be sufficient to bring this awkward scene to a close.

He brought her hand to his lips and held it there. Her skin was soft against his, and he lingered over it for longer than a simple apology would warrant, imagining what it might be like to kiss her palm, her wrist, and all the rest of the white skin leading to her lips. And then he smiled, remembering that this was what had caused the problem five years ago. The suspicion that all parts of Rosalind Morley were eminently kissable, and his sudden, irresistible compulsion to test the theory.

And now she was looking up at him again, over her outstretched hand, as though the kiss were causing her pain when he suspected that it was an excess of pleasure that was the problem. Should he take another liberty with her, she would yield—just as she had the last time. And he would probably run away from her—just as he had been running his whole life, from any situation that smacked of responsibility.

And so he released her, smiling. 'There. I hope it is settled at last. There is nothing wrong with you, Rosalind Morley. Nothing at all. Never mind what your father says, or what others might think of you. You are perfect just as you are.'

It occurred to him, in an idle, confusing way, that it would take a lifetime to catalogue the things about her that were perfectly suited to his temperament.

'Thank you.' Her voice sounded hoarse, as though it were difficult for her to speak. He wished that she would call him Tremaine, and return some sharp rebuke that would put things back to normal between them. But instead she murmured, 'I must go. To see about…something. And you must come as well. I…' She touched her hand to her forehead, trying to remember, and then looked into his eyes again and went very still.

Her vision cleared and she muttered, 'Apples. That is it. We are bobbing for apples. Harry is there. I have managed to get Elise to come out of her room, but she is looking very cross with him, and threatening to go back to bed with a megrim.'

'So I must let your brother drown me to put her into good humour again?'

'If you would be so kind.'

She held out her hand to him, and he was more than ready to follow wherever she might lead. But when he smiled at her, she looked so worried that he put on his most perturbed expression and yawned. 'The least you could do is deny it, you know. If you wish me to behave, you will do much better with flattery than you do with the truth.'

'If I flatter you, it might cause your head to swell more than it already has.' She gave him her usually cynical smile. 'I dare not risk it, Tremaine. Come on, then. We can finish this business by New Year if we apply ourselves to it.'

Chapter Twelve

Rosalind pushed him into the hallway ahead of her, announcing, 'I have found him.'

Harry beamed in triumph. 'And about time. Do not think that you can avoid the party, Tremaine. It is hardly keeping in the spirit of the bet if you do not try.'

Nick sighed, and prepared for a dunking. 'Very well, then. What have I to do to get you to leave me alone?'

'Play our little game.' Harry led him into the hall and gestured expansively towards the centre of the room. 'We have all had a turn, and the other guests are eager to see how you fare.'

True to his word, there was a large crowd gathered around a basin of water, and the air smelled of apples. The daughter of a lord was holding a fruit in her hand and shaking the water from her pretty blonde locks, and everyone was laughing heartily and congratulating her on her success.

There were calls of encouragement from the crowd, accompanied by drunken laughter.

Tremaine approached the pan of water with caution, and looked down at the abused fruit floating there. He stalled. 'And I am to…?' He looked down into the water again.

'Put your face in, grab an apple and bite.' Harry was grinning.

He knew that Harry would never be so foolish as to kill him in front of witnesses. The worst that would happen would be a wet head. Embarrassing, of course. But not so terrible, really. It would be over in a minute. Nick stepped up to the basin, bent awkwardly at the waist, and placed his face near the water.

He dutifully chased one of the remaining apples around the edge of the pan, while Harry stood behind him, pretending to offer encouragement.

'You have nothing to be afraid of.'

Harry was laughing at him, the miserable bastard. But he could hear Elise laughing too, so he soldiered on.

'The water is not so very deep. You will not drown,' Harry said. And then he whispered, directly into Nick's ear, 'I'm right behind you.'

Nick leaned too close to the water, trying to escape him, and took a quantity of it up his nose. He gasped and shot upright again, coughing, to the laughter of the crowd around him.

Harry clapped him smartly on the back to clear his lungs. 'There, there. You have it all wrong. You are not to drink the water. You are to eat the apple. Try again.'

He glared at Harry and stared at Rosalind. 'This is part of your brilliant plan, is it?'

She gave him a frustrated smile, and said, 'Take your turn and let others have a chance.' She rolled her eyes and cast a significant glance at Elise.

'Very well. But if anything untoward occurs I will hold you responsible, even in the afterlife.'

'Tremaine, do not be an ass.' She pushed past her brother, took him by the back of the neck, and pushed his face down into the water.

This time he had the good sense to hold his breath, and came up dripping, with an apple in his mouth. To complete the humiliation of it, Elise was leading the crowd who laughed at his discomposure.

'That was not so bad, was it?' Rosalind grabbed him by the collar and pulled him out of the way of the next player. Then she took the apple from his mouth and offered him linen to dry his face.

'Did I perform to your satisfaction?' he asked, tipping his head to drain the water from his ear.

'You were most amusing. Elise is laughing again— at you, and in front of Harry. That cannot but help put him in a good mood.' She took a bite from the apple that he had caught.

He watched her slender fingers caressing the fruit, her red lips, so memorably kissable, touching the place where he had bitten, the delicate workings of her pale throat as she chewed and swallowed. And suddenly he knew how Adam must have felt when Eve came to him with a wild scheme that he knew would end in disaster.

He had agreed, because how could he have refused her, even if it meant the ruin of all?

'It will not be long, I think, before Harry decides his pride is not so very important.' She looked speculatively at Elise. 'Then perhaps I shall be able to turn the rest of the party over to his wife.'

'And when she is back as mistress of this house what shall you do?' he whispered. 'Do you mean to see Pompeii, then? Once you have your freedom?'

The apple froze, halfway to her mouth, and she gave him a blank stare. 'What do I mean to do? Harry is right, Tremaine. You are an idiot. Harry will send me home after the holidays. I will return to Shropshire and my needlework, my jelly-making and my good works.'

He snorted at the idea. 'Do you miss home so much?'

'I do not miss home in the slightest. But where else am I to go?' She took another bite of the apple.

He watched her lick a drop of apple juice from her lip, and fought down the desire to suggest some good works she might try that had nothing to do with making jelly. 'Now that you have left your father's house, you might enjoy travelling. For you seem to have a taste for adventure.'

She laughed. 'Tell me, sir, when you are in the city, what do you drive?'

He thought for a moment. 'At this time I have several carriages. A curricle, of course, and a high-perch phaeton as well. Pulled by the finest pair of matched blacks in London.'

She gave a little moan of pleasure, and then looked

him square in the eye. 'We have a pony cart, which Father allows me to drive to the market in Clun. But only when the weather is fine and no one else is free to take me. The rest of the time I must walk.' She pulled a stern face, probably mimicking her father. 'But never alone. My father warns against the dangers present for young ladies travelling alone. But what they are I have no idea.' She gave a dry sigh. 'A trip to Pompeii might have seemed a lark to you, but it would be no more likely for me than a trip to the moon.'

Rosalind was making her future sound quite grim, so he rushed to reassure her—and himself—that it needn't be so. 'Do not fear, little one. Some day you will find a man who will take you to Italy.' Although he found that thought to be strangely annoying.

She spun the apple core on its stem, looking for a place to set it. 'I do not understand why everyone is so convinced that I cannot find a husband. As it so happens, I find them frequently enough. And then I find them wanting. I have had three proposals, just this year. All fine, upstanding men, who were willing to offer me a life no different from the one I have: full of restrictions and cautions and common sense. It appears being a wife is little different from being a daughter, and so I will have none of it. In this, at least, I am in full agreement with Elise. If a husband does not offer the love and respect I truly desire, and means to treat me no better than an overgrown child or an inanimate object, then it is better to do without.'

This took him aback. 'You have refused suitors?'

'Yes, I have. The rest of the world does not find me so repellent as you must, Tremaine.'

Here he was supposed to offer a compliment. But his glib tongue failed him, and the best he could manage was, 'I would hardly say you were repellent.'

She gave him a tired look and batted her lashes. 'I shall cherish your sweet words on my journey back to Shropshire.'

'But there must be some other alternative. Another place you could go…' He racked his brain for a better answer.

She set the apple core on the tray of a passing servant, and took back the linen she had given him to wipe her hands on it. 'There is not. The fact of the matter is this: I have no other female relatives, and a father who wishes help with his parish. When I am finished here I will go where everyone expects me to go. Where I am needed.' She tipped her head to the side. 'Although I must say the parish would be better off if my father was encouraged to marry the widow who comes to see to the cleaning of the church. She is a very organised woman, and a skilled housekeeper. He is very fond of her. They would make an excellent match.'

'If this woman is so well suited to your father, then why does he not offer for her?'

'Because then what would become of me? While the widow is suited to my father, I do not like her at all. And two women under the same roof would be one too many, when those women are not in harmony. Any progress my father has made in finding a new wife will be thwarted by my return home.'

He could not be sure, but he thought for a moment she glanced at him in a most strange way, and the pause before her next words was a touch longer than normal.

'Unless there is any reason that I should not go back to Shropshire.'

'When your brother is finished with you he means to send you back to your father, with no care for your future?' The thought rankled, for it was most sweet to see this girl doing everything in her power to help the brother who cared so little for her.

'When he presented the idea of a house party, he offered me my pick of the bachelor guests to prevent my flight.' She glanced around the room and frowned. 'Of course since he neglected to invite any single gentlemen, it has done me no good to entertain them. I have never seen so many happily married men, so many wives and children.' She gave another sidelong glance at Tremaine. 'You are the only unattached man in the house.'

'That was most unfair of him,' Tremaine agreed. 'But do not worry. I am sure when you least expect it you will find someone to suit your tastes.'

'The men who seek me out are hoping for a moderation in my character.' She glanced in the direction of Elise. 'Someone more like my sister-in-law, who has grown in the last few years from a naïve and somewhat awkward girl into a polished lady. I, on the other hand, am very much as you found me when we first met:

wilful, short-tempered, and prone to acting in haste and following with regret.'

He suppressed a smile. 'I will admit your personality is more volatile than Elise's.'

She shrugged. 'When the men of England come to value volatility over grace and candour over artifice, then I shall have my pick of them. Now, if you will excuse me, I should see to the other guests.' She walked across the room to Elise, and said something that made the other woman laugh.

He took a moment to admire the two women together, and had to admit they had little in common. Elise's cool beauty was paired with an equally cool wit. The sort that made a man long to melt the icy exterior and find the warm heart beneath. And Rosalind? Her kisses were as tart as Elise's were sweet. And her skin and hair tasted of cinnamon and pepper.

He stopped and blinked. It had been years, and yet he could remember everything about that single kiss as though he had stolen it moments ago. With each new sight of her, the past had come flooding back, sharper than ever. She smelled the same, her skin was just as soft, and her face held the same mix of devilment and innocence.

He glanced across the room at Elise, and tried to remember the kisses that he had shared with her the year they'd met. There had been months of dancing, laughter, and a few passionate stolen moments alone. But it was all a vaguely pleasant blur, and not nearly so clear as their time spent in friendship since. Try as he might, he could not sort the incidents of his engagement, supposedly the happiest time of his life, from his time spent with the dozens of other pretty girls he had known before and since.

But he could still remember every moment of the hour he had spent with Rosalind Morley. The way he had felt when he'd looked at her. The way she'd felt in his arms. And how he had known it would be wrong to kiss her and done it anyway. She had positively glowed with an unsuppressed fire, and he had been helpless to resist.

A sensible man would have pulled her out from under the mistletoe that night and sent her home to her father before anything untoward happened. It would have been far better to douse the fiery spirit, even if it had turned her tart wits to bitterness. Only a fool would have leapt into the flames and laughed as he burned.

A fool, or a man in love.

He turned away quickly and took a sip of his drink, hoping for a soothing distraction. But the spices in the mulled wine heated his blood rather than cooled it. Love at first sight. What an utterly prosaic notion. It lacked the sophistication of lust or the banal thrill of debauchery. It was gauche. Naïve. A simplistic explanation for a natural physical response to finding a beautiful young girl alone and willing, and taking advantage of the opportunity to kiss her senseless.

And running away had been a natural response as well. He had given little thought to what the girl might have felt over it. She would have given the incident too much significance, since she had nothing to compare it with. He knew better. That brief intimacy, and his resulting obsession with it, was a result of too much whimsy in a season given over to such behaviour. To avoid such revelry in the future was the best way to keep one's head and prevent further mistakes.

He had ignored the vague feeling that his perfectly acceptable engagement to Elise was a misalliance of the worst sort. And the faint sense of relief he'd felt when Elise had rejected him. The feeling that he was very lucky to be free of it. His subsequent inability to find anyone to suit him better was merely selectiveness on his part. It did not mean that he'd given his heart away on a whim, several Christmases ago, and lacked the courage to find the girl and retrieve it.

He shook his head. This was not an epiphany. This was temporary insanity—brought on by too many parlour games, too much punch, and a severe lack of oxygen from too many nights packed in tight at the fireside next to people who were happier in their lives than he. One did not make life-altering decisions based on a brief acquaintance with a girl, no matter how delectable she might be. And, even worse, one should not make them in the presence of mistletoe.

Should he manage to get clear of his attachment to Elise, if he wished for the change to be permanent he should run and keep running. It would be even wiser to give a wide berth to Harry Pennyngton and all of his extended family.

He took another sip of wine.

But where would be the fun in that?

His sip became a gulp, and he choked and spluttered on it, gasping to catch his breath.

A hand hit him sharply between the shoulderblades, to help him clear his lungs. And then hit him again out of sheer spite.

'Anneslea,' he gasped.

'None other.' Harry was grinning at him again, revelling in Nick's distress. 'First I see you nearly drown in the apple bucket, and now in a single glass of wine? It is a good thing I am here to take care of you. Heaven knows what might happen if you were left on your own.'

There was probably a double meaning in his words, just as there always was. But suddenly Nick found it impossible to care. He took in a great gulp of air, reached out and took Harry by the shoulders to steady himself, and announced, 'I am a faithless cad.'

Harry clapped him on the back again. But this time it was in camaraderie. 'You have realised it at last, have you? Good for you, sir. And a Merry Christmas to you.' Then he disengaged himself and headed back to the apple barrel.

Nick stared after Harry, wondering if the man had interpreted that as an apology, or just a random statement of fact. Apparently, he had come to some level of self-awareness. But what was to be done about it? If he ran to Rosalind with the news, he was not positive that his discovery would be welcome. And even if it was, he did not dare risk breaking her heart again until he was sure how things would come out.

But if all went as planned, Elise would be home for

good in a few short days, and Rosalind would be faced with a return trip to Shropshire. If he could bide his time until then, Rosalind might be open to possibilities that might prevent her homecoming.

He grinned to himself. Even if she had doubts about a future with him, it would take only a closed door, some mistletoe, and a few moments' persuasion to convince her of the advantage in total surrender.

Elise stared down at the apples floating in the basin and forced a bright smile. Her head still ached, and her eyes felt swollen and sandy from crying. But she had promised herself there would be no more sulking in her room. After last night's outburst it would not do to let the guests see that she was upset.

Of course her husband's continual rejection of her during the game had hurt her. He had known all the girls in the room by touch, and had joked and laughed with them. In his study, he had claimed to want her back. But he had shown no sign of it a moment later. And now she must smile and chat with the women he had hugged as though nothing was wrong.

She focused her attention on the apples and dipped her face into the water, deep enough so that it lapped at her cheeks, cooling the fire in them. And if, while submerged, she imagined either of the Misses Gilroy, plunged headfirst into the same water until their hair dripped and their gowns were ruined? Then at least no one could see it in her face.

She caught an apple easily in her teeth, and rose to

laughter and applause. She set the fruit on the small table beside the basin, and turned to find Harry right behind her, holding out a towel.

He grinned at her. 'Very good, my dear. Very good indeed.' And she noticed his eyes shift away from her face, lower, to the neckline of her gown.

She could feel a drop of water sliding slowly down her skin, ready to disappear into the hollow between her breasts. Was it this that was drawing his attention? She took the towel from him. And then, as though she were flirting with a stranger, she offered him a languid hand. He took it, and led her away from the apples.

She dabbed carefully at her face with the towel, taking care to leave the single drop of water quavering on the swell of her breast. When they reached a quiet corner of the room she paused and looked up, to catch him staring again. For a moment, she expected him to give her a guilty smile to acknowledge that he was behaving improperly, and fix his gaze upon her face. For this was her husband, not Nicholas or some other gentleman of the ton.

But, although he must know that she had caught him, he continued to stare at her body as though the passage of the water were of the utmost importance to him. He wet his lips like a man parched from too long without a drink, and gave a small sigh of longing as it disappeared from sight. When he met her gaze again, his eyes were a dark, smoky green. And for a moment she was sure that honour, pride and propriety meant nothing to him. Even though they were in a crowded hall, if she gave the slightest of nods he would bury his face between her breasts, find that drop and kiss it away.

She felt a thrill of desire, just as she always did when Harry looked at her with that strange intensity. But this time it was heightened by abstinence, and the fact that he was admiring her so obviously, in so public a place. If he had been brazen before she'd left she would have scolded him. Told him to wait for evening, until they were upstairs. And he would have laughed and complied with her wishes, banking his desire until they were safely behind bedroom doors.

But he had been behaving quite unpredictably of late. It was possible she might never again see that look in his eyes. And suddenly dread mixed with desire, and she knew that it was of the utmost importance to hold his interest.

So she played the coquette, just as she would with a gentleman whose affections were not guaranteed. She touched the skin of her throat with one hand, spreading the fingers until they gave the briefest caress to the track the water had followed, and then traced the neckline of her gown. 'It is surprisingly warm in the house today, is it not?'

'Indeed.' His reply was innocent enough, but his eyes followed the progress of her hand.

'The water was most refreshing.' She smiled at him, gazing through her lashes. 'I am surprised that you have not taken a turn.'

'Alas, I have no skill in apple-bobbing. But there are other games I prefer.' His voice was a purr, and the invitation it held was clear.

Would it be success or failure to give in to desire, just for a night? It would not solve their problems, but at least she would be sure that he still wanted her. 'But so many games require a partner. It is most frustrating to find oneself unmatched when one wishes to play.'

'Very,' he agreed.

She bit her lip and pretended to hesitate. 'You seemed quite taken with the young ladies of the Gilroy family during yesterday's game. Perhaps either of them would suit?' She waited for the assurance that he would much prefer someone else.

Instead, he said, 'It is an interesting idea. They are both lovely girls—well-formed, fair of face. And on the whole I find them both to be good company. Too young, of course. Although their mother remarked, after you had left the room, that Lord Gilroy always retires early. I suspect she is also in search of a partner.' And he glanced away from her, to Lady Gilroy, who was wearing a dress cut far too low for daytime, and bending over the apple barrel to call attention to the fact.

He looked back to Elise, and she could feel the jealous colour rising in her face, spoiling her efforts to appear coy and detached. 'It is no business of mine,' she snapped. 'I am sure it does not matter who you choose to partner you.'

He sighed. 'You are wrong, of course. I'm sure it would hurt some people very much.'

Me. It would hurt me. Even the thought that Lady Gilroy was interested caused an ache in her heart. It was even worse than seeing Harry's innocent flirting with her daughters. But she must remember where she was, and the number of prying eyes around her. For she had a shameless urge to grab him by the arm and plead with him to assure her she had nothing to fear.

He continued. 'Think of Lord Gilroy, knowing that his wife is eager to give her attentions to another. It is most difficult to suffer in silence.'

Suffering. He was right to call it that. For now, with each minute they were apart, she would know that he was free, and she would worry that he might choose to exercise that freedom. It did not matter that he did not care for her, nor that there were other women who would be a better wife than she had been. She was overcome with a desperate, selfish desire to have her old life back.

Harry was staring across the room in the general direction of Lord Gilroy. 'I suppose it is easier to let people think he does not care than to appear a tired old fool who cannot keep his wife satisfied.'

Oh, God. Perhaps it meant nothing. Perhaps he was only speaking of Gilroy, and not of himself. If it mattered to him, why had he not spoken? If he truly cared for her, then every smile that she'd given to Nicholas, every dance, every shared laugh, would have been like a knife in her husband's heart.

'Harry?' Her voice was shaking, as were her knees. In fact it felt as if her whole body were trembling, afraid of the answers to the questions she must ask him.

'Darling?' He reached out and took her hand again, gave it a squeeze of encouragement.

'Anneslea!' Lord Cammerville was tottering over to

them, smiling broadly and gesturing with his glass. 'So good to see you with your lovely wife at your side again.'

Harry gave a slight bow of pride.

Elise smiled as well, letting the curses flow in her mind. Why had the fat old toad chosen *now* to interrupt them?

'And how have you managed to keep that delightful sister so well hidden from society? You are truly fortunate to be surrounded by such beauty.'

'Hardly surrounded, Cammerville. This is the first time I've been able to enjoy the company of both of them for an extended period. Rosalind's father, the Reverend Morley, has very little faith in my ability to watch out for the girl, even though it is long past time for him to let her fly the coop.'

Elise turned her wrath upon the absent Morley. 'He is very foolish. There can be no better place for her than with you if she wishes an introduction to polite society.'

Harry gave a surprised smile in response to her small compliment. 'If you asked her father's opinion, I doubt it would be the same. I was eight when he married my mother, and he still looks on me as a wilful schoolboy with a decadent upbringing that has permanently flawed my character. Didn't think much of my late father or his family, I'm afraid. Couldn't abide Grandfather, who was Anneslea before me.'

Cammerville laughed knowingly. 'Tried to cane the title out of you, did he?'

Harry winced, and laughed in response.

'He beat you?' Elise stared at him in surprise. For he had never mentioned any such thing.

'Spare the rod and spoil the child,' Cammerville answered.

Harry nodded. 'And Morley was a firm believer in biblical retribution—especially when it concerned the sin of pride.'

'Why did you not tell me?' It was the wrong time to ask him, in a room full of people. But suddenly it was urgent that she know.

He considered for a moment. 'Have I not? Hmm. I thought I had.' He shrugged in apology. 'I find I am happier if I do not think on him much. As I am sure he is content not to think of me.'

'Is that why you left home so early? Rosalind said that you found it easier to stay at Anneslea with the old Earl. And that she hardly saw you at all until after she was grown-up.' She reached out and touched his sleeve.

He smiled at her in reassurance. 'That is the way we like to remember the facts, yes. I came to live with my Grandfather Pennyngton because Lincolnshire was closer to my school than our home in Shropshire. It was much easier to come here for holidays.' He shrugged again. 'But I suspect that if we measured the distance it would have been a much shorter trip to the rectory, and on roads that were better and less affected by weather. The truth of the matter was Morley would not have me at home, and I had no desire to return. Nothing my mother could say would sway him.'

'That was most unfair of him.'

'I cannot say I blame him overly. By the time I was thirteen I was nearly as tall as he was.' He gave Cam-

merville a knowing wink. 'The day came when I dis-
agreed with his parental advice. So I snatched the stick
from his hand and broke it over his back.'

Cammerville laughed so hard that tears ran from his
eyes, and Harry laughed as well.

'You struck him?' Elise looked at him in continued
amazement.

He must fear that she was angry with him for keeping
secrets, for he hurried to say, 'I doubt that Rosalind has
heard that story either. It is one of the many things that
we do not discuss in my family. Nor do we dwell on the
fact that Morley threw me, bag and baggage, from his
house. But that is the real reason I ended up with my
father's family.'

'That is horrible.' She looked back and forth between
his smile and Cammerville's obvious amusement, and her
lip trembled in sympathy for the little boy he had been.

Harry reached out and laid a comforting hand on her
shoulder, as though surprised by her strong reaction to
something that had been over and done with for almost
twenty years. 'It was not so terrible. It was quite possible
that I earned the punishment he gave me. After Father
died I was well on the way to having an uncontrollable
temper. Grandfather took me in and put me right. He
taught me that one does not need to rage to accomplish
what one desires. One can do as much by patience as
one ever can with temper.'

'Perhaps you learned too well,' she murmured. 'But it
was better, if Morley beat you, that you remained away.'

'And in time I demonstrated my improved character

to him, and he allowed me home to visit Rosalind.' He frowned. 'Of course it was too late to heal some wounds. I only saw my mother once before she died.'

'He separated you from your mother?' Her voice was an anguished bleat, and Cammerville laughed at her tender heart.

Harry blinked, and absently brushed a lock of hair out of his eyes. 'It had to happen eventually, once I went away to school. The miserable old goat brought the whole family up here for Christmas, after I was of age. Of course, he turned around in only a day and rushed them all home again. But I had a very nice dinner with mother and Morley that evening.' He put his arm around her shoulders and gave her a cautious hug. 'It was fine, really. And over very long ago. Nothing to be so distressed about.'

'Oh, Harry.' Now she was both tearful and slightly disgusted with him. And he was giving her such a puzzled look, as though he knew he had done something wrong but had no idea what it might be. Like a lost little boy.

She stamped her foot, trying to drive the sob back down her throat, and whimpered, 'Excuse me, Lord Cammerville.' Then she seized the towel from Harry's hand and hurried towards the door.

Behind her, she could hear Cammerville's explosive, 'Women, eh? They are an eternal mystery. Is it too early for a brandy, do you think?'

And Harry's response. 'Let us find Rosalind and see where she is hiding it. I feel strangely in need of cheer.'

Elise hurried into the hall before the tears could overtake her. Of all the times for her husband to open up and reveal his soul it would have to be when they were chatting with one of his more ridiculous friends, in a room full of people. Lord Cammerville must have thought her quite foolish to be near to crying over a story that they thought was nothing more than a common fact of boyhood.

But not to her. Never had she seen her father raise a hand to Carl. Nor had her brother reason to respond in anger to punishment. And the sight of Harry running a hand through his hair like a lost child, telling her how one mistake had cost him his mother…

She gulped back another sob.

'Here, now, what is the matter?' Nicholas reached out and seized her by the arms, arresting her flight. 'Crying in a common hallway? What is the cause?' He looked happier than she had seen him in months, but his expression changed quickly to concern.

'I have done something terrible.'

He looked doubtful. 'Surely not?'

'I have left my husband.'

'Not again.' He drew away from her in alarm.

'No. Before. When I left him to come to you, Nicholas.' And she took him by the arms, trying to get him to listen. 'I teased him, and it hurt. And then I left him when he needed me.'

'And you have noticed this now?' Nicholas shook his head in amazement. 'Very well. And what do you mean to do about it?'

'I do not know. You are a man. Tell me. What can I say to him that will make it all better?'

'Say to him?' Nick responded with his most rakish smile. He put his hands on her shoulders and looked deep into her eyes. 'Oh, darling, I doubt you need say anything at all to have a man at your feet. You have but to wait until the guests are safely asleep, and open your bedroom door. You will not need words after that.'

There was the sound of masculine throat-clearing, and an inarticulate noise of female distress. And then her husband and his sister walked past them, down the hall.

Harry looked his usual calm, collected self. But Rosalind was nearly overcome with emotion, her eyes darting from Elise, to Nicholas and back, trying to choose whom she should scold first.

When she slowed, Harry took her by the arm and pulled her along, refusing to let her stop. But as they passed he gave Nicholas an arch look that made the man carefully release Elise's arms, as though he were taking his finger off the trigger of a primed pistol. Then Harry smiled to his sister, and said, 'The brandy, Rosalind. Remember the brandy. We shall find a glass for you as well. Your father will not approve, but so be it.'

Chapter Thirteen

Rosalind's foul mood continued unabated through dinner, despite the small glass of brandy Harry had given her to calm her nerves. While he'd said it was flattering to have a sister so devoted to one's happiness as to be reduced to spluttering rage by the scene of one's wife and her lover in a position that could be considered by some as compromising, he'd assured her it was hardly a reason to ruin Christmas dinner.

His assurances that it did not require action had been met with frustrated cries of, 'Oh, Harry,' and elaborate threats on her part to chase down Tremaine and make him pay bitterly for his lack of manners.

A rumour from the cook that the evening's goose was past its prime and too tough to eat had driven the scene temporarily from her mind, and Harry had made a mental note to reward the kitchen staff generously on Boxing Day for the timely distraction. He had smiled to himself in satisfaction and poured another brandy. For, after seeing the tears in his wife's eyes over his tragic childhood, he doubted that Tremaine, annoying though he might be, was making as much progress as it appeared.

After a dinner of goose that had been more than tender enough for his taste, Rosalind stood and announced, 'Tonight, for those who are interested, we shall have dancing in the ballroom. Come and join us once you have finished your port.'

Harry followed her out of the dining room and down the hall to the ballroom. 'If you can still manage a ball, darling, you are a magician.'

'And how so?' Her gaze was defiant, her smile frozen and resolute.

'There are no musicians,' he said reasonably. 'They did not arrive today—probably because of the bad weather. I am certain we can forgo the dancing and no one will mind.'

'It is not the first problem I have had with this party of yours,' she said through gritted teeth. 'And I doubt it will be the last. But if we cancel the dancing then I will have to find a better activity to pass the evening, and I can think of none. Besides, the room has already been decorated and the refreshments prepared. The servants have moved the pianoforte to the ballroom, and I am more than capable of playing something that the guests can dance to.'

'But if you are playing then you cannot dance yourself,' he pointed out.

'It is only polite that I sit out in any case.' Her voice was cold reason. 'It is slightly different than I feared, but I was marginally correct. Your numbers are unbalanced, and in favour of the women. Several families have brought daughters, and there are no partners for them. Better that I allow the others to dance in my place.'

'But no one expects you to forgo the pleasure all evening,' he said. 'You do not have to play for the whole time.'

'Really it is no problem. I enjoy playing. And I will have the opportunity to sit down while doing it.' The look in her eye said if the party knew what was good for it, they would dance and be glad of it, because she did not wish to be crossed.

Harry put on his most fraternal smile. 'But you also enjoy dancing, do you not? I can remember the way you stood on my boots and let me waltz you around the drawing room.'

She gave him a pained look. 'Twenty years ago, perhaps. Then, it was not so important to have a partner.'

He clutched at his heart. 'I am no partner? You wound me, Rosalind.'

'You are my brother,' she said firmly. 'And if you are the only unpartnered man in the room I suppose it is not improper that we dance. But it would be far more pleasant for me if you stand up as a courtesy to the daughters of your guests than with me out of pity.' For a moment she did sound a bit pitiable. But then she snapped, 'If you cannot manage that, then perhaps you should dance with your wife. It is what you want to do, after all. It does no good to pretend otherwise. But for myself? I prefer to remain at the keyboard. Thank you very much.'

Guests had begun to filter into the room behind them, and she sat down and began to play a tune so brisk that they could not resist standing up to dance.

Harry did as she'd bade him and offered his hand to a blushing girl of sixteen. He was gratified to see the look on her face, as though the room could hardly contain her joy at being asked. When they stood out, he had an opportunity to view the others in the room.

His wife was standing up with Tremaine, of course. They made a most handsome couple, as they always had. Their steps were flawless, their smiles knowing. It was painful to see them together, so he smiled even wider and raised a glass of champagne in toast to them.

Rosalind sat at the piano, playing a seemingly endless progression of happy melodies. To look at her was to suspect that the instrument in front of her had done her an injury, and that she wished to punish it with enthusiastic play. Her eyes never wavered from the empty music stand in front of her, even though she was playing it all from memory, and her hands hammered away at the keys with an almost mechanical perfection. She seemed to focus inward, and there was no sign that the sights she saw were happy ones.

And suddenly Harry felt the fear that if something was not done he would see her in the same place next year, and the year after, ageing at the piano stool, the lines in her face growing deeper and her expression more distant as the world laughed and went on without her.

So he smiled his best host's smile, remarked to all within earshot that it was a capital entertainment, and encouraged them to help themselves to refreshment when the music paused. If they thought him a naïve cuckold, so be it. Perhaps after this holiday they would have no reason to. But, no matter what became of him, he would not allow Rosalind to become the sad old maid who kept his house.

He turned to the girl beside him, pointed to Rosalind, and enquired if she played as well.

'Not so well, sir. But I have lessons. And my piano master says I am his most proficient pupil.'

'I would see my sister stand up for a set. But first I must find someone to replace her at the instrument. Can you help me?'

The girl was radiant at the thought.

Very good, then. He was only being a good host by making the offer.

He went to Rosalind. 'Dear sister, I have a favour to ask of you.'

She sighed, but did not pause in her playing. 'Another favour? Am I not busy enough for you, Harry?'

He laughed. 'Too busy, I think. Templeton's daughter was remarking at what a fine instrument this appears to be, and it seems she is a musician. But obviously not much of a dancer, for she trod upon my toes on several occasions. If she is thus with the other guests it might benefit all to have her play for a time and rest from dancing. If you could give up your seat to her, I would be most grateful.'

Rosalind considered for but a moment. 'It would be for the best—if she does not seem to mind.'

'Very good. Have a glass of champagne, and I will see her settled here.

He installed the Templeton girl at the piano, then watched as his sister visited the refreshment table and became occupied with haranguing the servants about the dwindling supply of wine. When he was sure she would take no notice of him, he swallowed his distaste, refreshed his smile with another sip of wine, and strode into the room to find a partner for Rosalind.

'Tremaine—a word, if you please?'

It was always a pleasure to see the way the man cringed when Harry addressed him directly, as though snivelling and subservience were sufficient apology for all he had done.

'Harry?' He took a deep sip from his glass.

'I need a favour from you.'

'From me?' Now the man was totally flummoxed. And then suspicious. His eyes narrowed. 'What can I do for you?'

Jump off the nearest cliff. Harry pushed the idea to the back of his mind, readjusted his smile, and said, 'I need a dancing partner. Not for me, of course.' He gave a self-deprecating laugh. 'For m' sister. She will not stand up from the damn piano if she must stand with me. And you are the only man in the room who could pass, in dim light, for eligible.'

Tremaine looked past his usual partner towards Rosalind, who had seated herself next to a potted palm, almost out of sight of the crowd. His face took on a curious cast in the flickering light of the candles. 'And she does love dancing,' he said. His voice was distant, as though lost in memory.

Harry wondered if he needed to repeat his request, and then the man next to him seemed to regain focus.

'Of course,' he said. 'You are right. She should not be forced to sit out the whole evening because of some misplaced sense of duty to her guests.'

'Make her think it is your idea, for I doubt she will do it for me. She was most cross that I even suggested she dance before.'

'Yes. Yes, of course.' And Tremaine strode across the room and passed by Elise as though she did not even exist.

Elise raised her eyes to follow him, and nodded with approval when she saw him go to Rosalind.

Tremaine smiled his cynical London smile and bowed to Rosalind, offering his hand.

Rosalind shook her head, gave him an outraged glare, and replied with something tart and equally cynical, which must have amused him. He laughed, and then repeated his offer, with a deeper bow and hands held open in front of him.

She tossed her head, and made a great show of getting up, against her better judgement, to take his hand and let him lead her into the room. But Harry could see the faint flush of guilty pleasure on her face, and the exasperated curve to the lips that had replaced her stoic lack of expression.

Harry went to stand next to the girl at the piano, who was looking nervous now that the attention was to be on her. 'Something simple to start, I think. You can manage a waltz, can you not? They are slow, and the beat is steady.'

The girl nodded and began.

When Rosalind realised what was about to occur, alarm flashed across her face, and the pink in her cheeks was replaced by white. She hissed something to her partner, stepped away from him, and made to sit down.

But Harry watched as Tremaine caught her hand easily in his and pulled her back into the dance, giving another slight bow before putting his arms about her.

She still hesitated for a moment, and then looked down at the floor and coloured again, as though she would be anywhere in the world but where she was. But as the dancing began she relaxed. Her small body settled into the circle of his arms like a sparrow seeking warmth in the winter.

For his part, Tremaine stood close enough to her that she could not see his face. He gazed over her head and past her, into the room. And wherever he was it was not in the present. His eyes were looking somewhere very far away, some place that gave him both great happiness and great pain, for there was more sincere emotion in his eyes than Harry had ever seen. The man was in torment, and yet there was a faint smile on his lips.

For a moment Harry sympathised.

As the couple danced it was not with the easy, perfectly matched grace of Tremaine and Elise, but as one person. Their steps were not flawless, but their mistakes matched their successes, and the false notes in the music did nothing to hinder them.

And then the dancing was over, and Rosalind pulled away from him and rushed from the room.

After a moment's hesitation Tremaine went after her, his urbane lope failing to disguise the speed of his response.

Harry sighed. That answered that. It would be even more complicated than he had hoped. But it was just as he had always feared, and he could not pretend surprise.

Chapter Fourteen

Elise watched the couple on the dance floor too, trying to disguise her ill ease. They were an unusual pair, for Nicholas was a head too tall to dance easily with Rosalind. But they were attractively matched in colouring. And of a similar temperament. If circumstance had been different, and Elise had been hostess at Harry's side, she would have seated the two together at meals just to see what became of it. It was disturbing that the idea held such appeal. For it showed her how easy it would be to forget the man who had stood by her side for so long, and had so graciously escorted her back to this house, although he must have known what it might mean.

She watched the dancers take another turn, and saw the expression upon Nick's face. The most incorrigible rogue in London looked the picture of restraint—and none too happy about it. For a moment Elise flattered herself that it was for her benefit, to show his loyalty. But only for a moment. She knew the man too well for that. He must want the girl in his arms most desperately to make such a great effort not to want her.

And as he turned again she could see Rosalind. It was as though the girl were dancing to her favourite tune on the edge of a cliff—for she was clearly struggling not to enjoy the waltz, nor her contact with the man who danced with her.

So that was the way it was to be. It pained Elise to think that she had not matched the two long ago, for Rosalind needed a way to escape from her father, and Nick needed a steady hand to hold his. She shook her head at her own folly. Rather than help him she had stood in his way, making it more difficult for him to leave her. How great a fool she was, to realise it now that things had grown so complicated.

But perhaps it would be easier if Tremaine wished a parting as much as she did. At least she would not be obliged to break his heart before returning to Harry. For, after their conversation of the afternoon, she was sure she meant to return—if he would still have her.

She frowned. Had she gained anything by her two months away? She suspected that once she was back in his house, Harry would cease his complaints about her loyalty and drop easily back into the role of affectionate but distant husband. She must learn to tolerate his silences without complaint now he had shown her the reason for them. And she would not trouble him any more with Nicholas, or any other foolish flirtations.

Although Harry had not run to fetch her from London, he had at least admitted, aloud, that he wanted her back. And she knew she wanted to be with him, perhaps even more than she had before. If he was willing to overlook their barren union, then she should count her blessings. Most men would not have bothered to disguise their dissatisfaction with her, or to mask their disappointment in false smiles and silence. Perhaps she should learn to view Harry's self-restraint as a gift.

She saw Nicholas whisper something to his partner, and the girl started like a frightened fawn. Then she broke from him and left the room.

For a moment Elise thought to go after her, but she saw Nick glance once around the room to see if the other guests had noticed. Then he followed in the girl's wake.

'I wonder what has got into Rosalind?' Harry had come to stand by her side.

'She is probably overcome with the burden you have forced on her with this party. It was most unfair of you to saddle her with it at so little notice.' Elise gave him a mildly disapproving look, and then smiled to prove it a joke.

He smiled and answered back, 'Perhaps it is unfair to my sister to say so, but you would not have had the trouble she has. I have seen you rise to greater challenges than this without faltering. Should we go and see to her, do you think?' He paused dramatically. 'But wait. I saw Tremaine go after her. So I needn't worry. He is very good at taking care of women in distress, is he not?' His expression was supremely innocent, but he was obviously trying to make her jealous.

'I have always found him so,' she answered with an equally blasé look, ignoring the bait. If he did not wish to question her directly about what he had witnessed in the hall, then did she really need to explain it? And then she remembered how he had been in the afternoon. And she responded in kind, 'Sometimes things are not as they appear.'

He glanced at her, as though surprised at her acknowledgement. And then he gave a small sigh, of fatigue or relief, and said, 'So I assumed.'

The girl at the piano began another waltz, and he bowed to her, holding out a hand. 'Will you favour me with a dance?'

When she hesitated, he added, 'You need not read too much into it. It is only a waltz. I trust Tremaine will not mind if I borrow you for a few moments?'

He was working very hard to appear neutral, but she could see the challenge in his eyes.

So she answered it. 'It does not matter to me what Nicholas thinks.' And she took his hand and let him lead her onto the floor.

It felt so good to be back in his arms again that she had to struggle for a moment to keep herself from saying it aloud. Would it be too much, too soon, to admit tonight that she wished to come home? Though a truce had been declared for Christmas Day, she was not sure it would last. And it would serve her right if he wished to toy with her a bit, as punishment for leaving, before accepting her apology.

Her hopes rose when he said, in a carefully polite

tone, 'It is good to dance with you again. Yet another of the many things I've missed since you have gone.'

He was willing to make the first move, to make things easier for her. She leaned back to get a better look into his face, surprised at his choice of words. 'Oh, Harry. You loathed dancing.'

He laughed and shook his head. 'Not true. I made a great show of loathing it. Because I so liked the things you were willing to do to coax me into it.'

She blushed at the memory of long nights spent in his arms after various balls, and he laughed again.

'But now I must take what pleasures you will allow, with no more foolish dissembling to gain ground.' He squeezed her hand, and tightened his fingers on her waist as he spun her around the floor.

She relaxed and let him lead her, enjoying the feel of his strength. Tonight she would do as Nicholas had suggested and open the connecting door between their rooms. And everything would return to the way it was.

'I shall know better,' he said, 'when next I seek a wife.'

She stumbled against him. He was teasing her again. Or did he mean it? She tried to match his tone as she responded, 'Do you have plans of that nature?'

'It all depends on what the future holds for us. I shall know if Tremaine is serious about keeping you by his actions this holiday. If he is true to his word, then we shall see about the divorce.' He paused for a moment. 'If you still wish for it, that is.'

Here was her chance to admit that her feelings on the subject had changed. She approached the subject elliptically, as he had. 'I understand,' she said, 'that the courts of England are not likely to be co-operative in the matter of a divorce. Once the bonds between two people are set they are not to be easily broken.'

'That is probably for the best,' he answered. 'But there should be some regard to the happiness of the individuals involved. It would not be good to force someone to remain if they were truly unhappy.'

And she had been miserable.

That was why she had left. She had loved him dearly, and still did, but it had not been enough to make a happy marriage. If she came back to him, perhaps for a while she could pretend that his silence didn't matter to her. She would forgo the companionship of other men so as not to arouse his jealousy, and she would learn to speak around the things that were most important to her, so as not to upset the delicate balance between them. But if it was to be just the two of them, alone until death?

'We are not likely to have any children,' she blurted, unable to avoid the truth a moment longer.

He tensed. 'Are they necessary for a happy union?'

'I assumed, when you offered for me, that they must be a primary concern to you. There is the title to consider, after all.'

'Well, yes, of course.' He glanced around them. 'I just choose not to discuss it in the middle of a crowded ballroom.'

She all but forgot the promise she had made to herself to be patient with his reticence. Once she came home she might never get a second chance to say what she needed to. 'No, Harry. You choose not to speak of it at all. You have left me to guess your opinions on the matter.'

'We are speaking of it now, aren't we?' He lowered his voice, hoping that she would follow suit.

She looked from her husband to the people around them. 'I know. It is the wrong venue, if we do not want our problems known to all of London. But at least I know that you cannot walk away in the middle, before you have heard what I mean to say.' She took a deep breath. 'In daylight, you treat me like a child if I wish to discuss matters of importance. But at night it is clear that you know I'm a grown woman, for you do not wish to talk at all. You visit me regularly enough. But I assume that you are hoping for a result from those visits. It must be gravely disappointing to you.'

She felt his spine stiffen. And suddenly it was as though she were dancing with a block of wood. 'I was under the impression that you enjoyed sharing a bed with me.'

'I never said I did not.'

He began to relax again, and his fingers tightened on her waist in a way that offered a return to intimacy should she be inclined.

She continued. 'But, pleasurable or not, I am beginning to think that nothing will come of it.'

'Nothing?' He grew stiff and cold again. 'And I suppose you think you will do better with someone else? Is this one more way that you believe Tremaine to be my superior?'

'I did not say that.' For she was not the one that needed an heir.

'But neither are you denying it.' He stopped dancing

and released her. 'Go to him, then, and see if it is better. It is obvious that I have nothing that you want. And I certainly cannot buy you children.' Then he turned and left her alone on the floor.

Rosalind leaned against the closed door of the library and felt the breath come out of her in a great, choking sob. She had done an excellent job controlling her emotions, in regard to Tremaine. And now it was all collapsing. It had taken years to convince herself that her first response to him had been the result of alcohol and inexperience. She had been sure that if she met him again she would find him no different from a hundred other town bucks. He would be no more handsome, no quicker to take advantage of a foolish girl, than if he were a man of better character.

But in comparison to the other men of her experience he was still perfection: sharp-witted, urbane and funny. And at such moments as he chose to turn his attention upon her he was no easier to resist than he had been that first day. And when they danced…

It was not fair. It simply was not. To be in the arms of a man one barely knew and feel convinced that one was home at last, finally in the place where one belonged. To feel all the wrongness and confusion of the rest of her life vanish like a bad dream. And to know that when the music ended she would find that she had confused dreams and reality again. Nicholas Tremaine was the fantasy. Not all the rest.

If she could have a moment alone to gather her wits

she would return to the ballroom as though nothing strange had happened. She would claim any redness of the eyes as brought about by cinders from the Yule Log.

'Rosalind? Open the door, please. We need to talk.'

She glared at the wood, as though she could see through it to the man on the other side. 'I think we have talked more than enough, Tremaine. I have nothing to say to you at the moment.'

'I need to know that you are all right before I return to the dancing.'

'I am fine. Thank you. You may go.'

'Rosalind! Open this door.' He was speaking more loudly than necessary, perhaps so that he could be heard clearly through the oak.

She rubbed at the tears on her cheeks. 'Don't be an ass. I am perfectly all right. Go back to the dancing, and to your…your…usual partner.' The words came in little gasps. Even without opening the door it would be obvious to him that she was crying. She winced at having revealed herself so clearly.

'Now, Rosalind.' His tone had changed to coaxing. 'What you think you saw in the hall today—it was nothing.'

'Nothing?' she parroted back. 'Tell that to Harry, for he says much the same thing. But I am not blind, nor foolish, nor too young to know better. I can recognise "nothing" when I see it. "Nothing" is what we share. But you and Elise have "something".'

'Barely anything, really. We are old friends, just as I have told you. Exceptionally close, of course.'

'Everyone knows about your "close" friendship, Tremaine. As apparently they always have. Nothing has changed in all these years. Everyone here can talk of nothing else.' She tried not to think of that first foolish Christmas, when she had had no idea of the truth. And how much easier it had been to know only half the facts.

He cleared his throat. 'It is not quite as it once was. When I first met you, Elise and I had an understanding, and I was not free. Now? Now we have a different sort of understanding. And until I can sort it out I cannot call my future my own.'

'Your future is no concern of mine, Tremaine. Nor do I wish to speak of how it once was. Frankly, I would rather forget the whole thing. I wish it had never happened.'

There was a long pause. 'And is that why you ran from the room after we danced? Because it reminded you of the first time we waltzed? I remember it well.' His voice had gone soft again, quiet and full of seduction. 'You were spying on the other dancers. I put a finger to your lips, to let you know that what we were doing was to be secret, and I pulled you out of the doorway and waltzed you around the corridor.'

She remembered the finger on her lips, and the feel of his arms. And how, when she had been confused by the steps, he had held her so close that he could lift her feet from the ground and do the dancing for both of them, until she had dissolved into giggles. And then the giggles had changed to something much warmer, almost frightening. He had set her back down on her feet rather suddenly, and put a safe space between them to continue the dance. She wrapped her arms tightly around her own shoulders, trying to focus on the disaster that had ended the evening and not on how wonderful the dancing had been. But she would always remember her first waltz as a special thing, no matter what had come later.

His voice was quieter, more urgent. 'And I distinctly remember thinking, Ah, my dear, if only you were older…'

She dropped her arms to her sides. 'Really? Well, I am quite old enough now. And it makes no difference. Elise still leads you about like a puppy, and you still dawdle behind, sniffing after any available female. And if any of them get too close, you have Elise and your poor broken heart as an excuse to remain unmarried. Do not think you can play that game with me, Tremaine, for I know how badly it will end.'

'Rosalind.' He said it softly, and she waited for what might come next.

When nothing did, she said, 'Go back to the ballroom, Tremaine. And leave me in peace. Just as I wish you had done five years ago.'

There was another pause, before she heard the sound of his footsteps retreating down the corridor to the ballroom. She crept further into the room and went to sit on the sofa, where she had so often found Tremaine. She laid her hand upon the cushion, imagining that there was still some warmth there. Why did everything have to be so complicated, so unfair? She was quite sure that of the four of them she was the least to blame for the mess they were in. Why was *she* the one who was being punished? For she suspected that, despite what he might feel for her, in the end she would be no closer to Nicholas Tremaine than she had ever been. He was everything that she longed for and always had been. But for the fact that he did not want her, he would be perfect.

The door of the library opened and Elise stalked into the room, showing no respect for her privacy. She dropped down on the couch beside Rosalind and stared into the fire. 'I do not understand your brother in the slightest.'

Rosalind glared at her, wishing with all her heart that she would go away and take her close friend with her. 'Then you are truly suited. For neither does he understand you.'

'Harry claims to want me back. But now that I am here we do nothing but argue.'

'You were doing that before, were you not?'

'I was arguing. But he did not respond. And now?' She shrugged. 'It seems I can do nothing to please him. He misunderstands me at every turn, and I cannot convince him that I do not prefer the company of Nicholas.'

'Perhaps because he finds you in Tremaine's arms in a public hallway begging you to give in to his desires?'

Elise stared at her in confusion, and then said, 'Today? That is not at all what was going on.'

Rosalind cast a jaundiced eye upon her. 'And did you tell Harry that?'

'I told him that things were not as they appeared.'

'Small comfort. You will not unbend sufficiently to put his mind at rest, but you still think all your problems are caused by what he does or does not say?'

'You do not understand,' Elise argued. 'He becomes even angrier when I speak the truth.'

'Well, let me be forthcoming, since you set such a high price on honesty,' Rosalind snapped. 'You were unhappy before you left because you did not know his mind, but now that you know it you are still not satisfied. Perhaps you are the one who cannot be pleased, Elise.'

Elise shook her head. 'That is because he is not being logical. One moment he wants me, the next he tells me he would marry again. He tortures Nicholas, but tells me to go back to him. He wants our life to be just the way it was before I left. But if I must lie to him, and tell him all is well, then what good will it be to either of us?'

'Before he was trying to hide the truth, to keep the peace. But now that he must face facts, he is as angry and stubborn as you are.'

'Me?'

'Yes. You. You refuse to admit that you were happy, just as much as he refuses to admit his unhappiness. And if neither of you can manage a happy medium?' Rosalind sighed. 'Then I expect you will continue to make those around you even more miserable than you make yourselves.'

'We are making other people miserable?' Elise gave her a blank look. 'I fail to see how. Everyone here seems to be having a delightful time.'

Rosalind stood up and threw her hands in the air. 'I stand corrected. All is well, and everyone who matters is perfectly happy. And, since that is the case, I need not concern myself with the situation. I am going to my room.' She stalked to the door of the library. 'And it will serve you all right if I do not come out until Easter.' With that she stamped out of the room, allowing herself the luxury of both a muttered curse and a slam of the door.

Elise waited until she was sure that her sister-in-law had gone well away, and then followed slowly up the stairs to her own room. Was it only a few hours ago that she had been convinced her problems were almost over? And now Harry was angry with her and Rosalind even angrier. Only Nicholas was still her friend. But it was most unwise to rely on him any longer if he wished to be free. Rosalind was right: she was making everyone around her miserable.

Elise sighed in defeat. The sooner she learned to hold her temper and her tongue, the better it would be for all concerned. She would go to her husband, take all the blame onto herself, and beg him to take her back. Perhaps she would never have the sort of marriage she wanted, but anything would be better than the chaos around her now, and the aching loneliness she had felt when Harry had left her on the dance floor.

She sent her maid away and undressed hurriedly, leaving the clothes in a pile on the floor. She rummaged in the wardrobe for the dressing gown she had worn on her first night with Harry. Would he remember it after all this time? Perhaps not. But if Nicholas was right it would not matter overmuch. Once she had come back to his bed Harry would cease to be angry with her. And if she could lie in his arms each night, the days would not be so bad.

She wrapped her bare body in the silk and went to the connecting door. For a moment she was afraid to touch the knob. What would she do if he had locked it against her? But it turned as easily as it always had, and she opened the door and entered her husband's room.

To find it dark and empty. The candles had not been lit. The fire was banked low in the grate. And the bed was cold and still neatly made.

She hesitated again, and then went to it, climbing in and crawling beneath the covers to wait for Harry. The night wore on, and the linen was cold against her skin. So she pulled her wrapper tight around her, curled into a ball and slept, shivering through fitful dreams.

She awoke at dawn, still alone.

Chapter Fifteen

The next day, Rosalind felt even worse than she had after storming off to her room. She'd spent the night staring up at the ceiling, thinking of all the things that had gone wrong and all the ways the people in her life had failed her. And after a few fitful hours of sleep she had woken to find that her problems were not just a bad dream. The house was just as she'd remembered it: full of people she did not want to see ever again, and manned by servants who were just as slow and disobedient as ever. But, since it was Boxing Day, she was obliged to thank them for the fact, and respond to the lack of service with light duties and generosity.

After a cold breakfast she went down to the library, to take it all out on Tremaine. He was lounging in his usual place by the fire, eyes closed and feet up, as though the struggle of tying his own cravat had caused him to collapse in exhaustion.

She pushed his boots from their place of elevated

comfort. When they hit the carpet she glared down and kicked them for good measure. 'Get up this instant. You are required in the drawing room.'

He sighed. 'For what possible reason could you need me? Are there not enough drunken fools available to bend to your will? I swear, I still have the blue devils from last night.'

So the tenderness while they had danced was to be explained by an excess of champagne? She said, in a voice that she hoped was painfully loud, 'Then it is about time you learned moderation. A headache is no more than you deserve. Now, get up.'

He draped an elegant hand over his brow. 'Do you show such cruelty to all your guests, Miss Morley? Or do you reserve it especially for me? If I were in my right mind I'd return to London immediately.'

'Do not think you can fool me with idle threats. The roads have been clear for several days, but you are still lying about on this couch, insisting that you will leave at any moment. If you mean to go, then stand up and do it.'

'Very well, then. I admit it. I intend to stay for the duration of this farce, until I can see Elise safely back into the arms of her loving husband.'

She glared down at him. 'As always, I cannot fault you for your devotion to Elise. Let us hope, once she is settled and you are long gone from this place, that you can find some other woman who is worthy of such un-wavering affection. But for now you will have to content yourself with my company, and I need your help.'

He gave an elaborate sigh, to prove that her words

had little effect upon him. 'Very well. I am your humble servant, Miss Morley. What do you require of me now?'

'Elise is out of temper with Harry again. She looks as if she has not slept a wink. Harry is little better. He appeared at breakfast still in his evening clothes, smelling of brandy.'

'And what am I to do with that? Make possets and sing lullabies?'

Rosalind smothered the desire to kick him again, and to keep kicking him until she had made her feelings known. She took a deep breath and said, 'We are having charades. Elise adores the game, and I'm sure she will play to show the world that nothing is wrong. Harry means to remain in whatever room has the punch bowl, so he is easily controlled. I have prepared clues to remind them of the happiness that is married bliss. The game will either leave them in the mood for reconciliation or murder. At this point I do not really care which. Either would solve my problem.'

'And what do *I* have to do with all of this?'

She narrowed her eyes. 'You need merely be as you are—incorrigible, irritable and unbearable. Harry cannot help but shine by comparison.'

He sat up and glared back at her. 'You have no idea what it means to know of your confidence in me. You have decided I'm unbearable, have you?'

She lifted her chin and said, with all honesty, 'Yes. I have.'

'I was dragged here against my better judgement. For reasons that have nothing to do with the sincere celebration of the holiday and everything to do with schemes concocted by you and your brother. I am forced to be the bad example so that everyone else may shine. And yet you find fault with my behaviour?' He had gone white around the lips, and was looking at her with a curious, hard expression, almost as though she had hurt his non-existent feelings.

She shifted uncomfortably from foot to foot, and for a moment she was tempted to retreat. But then her anger at him got the better of her, and she retorted, 'You talk as though you are the injured party in all this. I am sorry, Nicholas, but you are not. In my experience, you are just as I have described you. You are wilful, self-serving, and have no thought to the comfort of anyone but yourself. Because of this, you are finally getting what you deserve.'

He stood up and came near to her. When he spoke, his voice was so soft that only she could hear it. 'You have a very limited experience where it concerns me.'

She shook her head. 'I have more than enough.'

He stared at her for a long moment, as though there was something he wished to say. Or perhaps he was awaiting a sign from her.

She glared all the harder, and deepened her frown.

At last, he said, 'In your eyes I will always be a monster who ruined you and then abandoned you. Very well, then. Let us play-act. And I shall be the villain, since you have cast the parts.'

He stepped past her and stalked to the door. On his way he stopped, looked down at the floor, and scooped up the tattered ball of mistletoe, which was out of place again. Then he turned back, glared at her, and threw the thing into the library fire.

Nick preceded Rosalind into the drawing room and took a place at the back of the room, arms folded. The little chit had all but told him that he was repellent to her, and now expected him to do her bidding like a common lackey. Rosalind Morley had never been anything but trouble to him from the first moment he had laid eyes on her—cutting up his peace, altering his plans, and disappearing in body but remaining stuck in his mind like a burr, a constant irritant to his comfort. He had wondered on occasion what had become of her after they had first parted. In moments of weakness he had even thought about enquiring after her, before common sense had regained the upper hand. If a single dance with her had turned into his life's most fateful kiss, there was no telling what a casual meeting or a friendly letter might become.

And his fears had proved true. For after only a few days in her company his life had been turned upside down. There she stood at the front of the room, with a false smile on her face, acting for all the world as if she did not even notice him. Which was a total falsehood. He could feel when they were together that she was attracted to him, and he had a good mind to go up there and drag her back to the library, to give her a demonstration of the flaws in his character. No matter what she might claim, once the door was closed it would take only a few moments to prove that her character was no better than his. And afterwards he would have her out of his system and could go back to London in peace.

At the front of the room, Rosalind continued to explain the rules in an excessively cheerful voice that gave the lie to everything he had just seen. 'First we must choose who is to guess and who is to help with the clues.' She scanned the crowd. 'I must stay here, since I already know the answer, but I will need two helpers.'

Elise came to her side immediately, and looked hopefully across the room to Harry.

Harry began to rise unsteadily from his chair. Very well, the two would play nicely together, just as Rosalind wished. But that did not mean that Nick had to waste his time watching over them. He began a subtle retreat towards the door, hoping that Rosalind had forgotten her original plan after his outburst in the library.

But she was ignoring Harry, and had turned her attention to the doorway. 'Mr Tremaine. You as well, I think.'

So she still meant to involve him in this? He turned back into the room and saw the dark look on Harry's face before the man collapsed back into his seat with an easy and devious smile. Whatever Rosalind had planned, the results were not likely to be as she expected. Nick strode to the front of the room, conscious of all eyes upon him.

'The rules are simple,' Rosalind announced to the group gathered before her. 'I have a riddle, and the answer is a three-syllable word. If you cannot guess the word from the riddle, we will act out the parts to help you. Here is the riddle:

Vows are spoken, True love's token, Can't be broken.'

She passed a folded piece of paper to Elise, and then to Tremaine.

Elise frowned.

Nick read it, then stared at Rosalind. 'This is a four-syllable word. Not three.'

She gritted her teeth. 'It does not matter.'

'I think it does if you mean people to guess the answer.'

She glared at him. 'And if I do not care for them to guess too quickly,' she whispered, so that Elise could not hear, 'it does not matter at all.'

She had that wild look in her eye again, that she normally used on mistletoe. And she was turning it on him. He glared back at her. 'You are right, it does not matter.'

'Here, Elise,' Rosalind said, smiling too brightly. 'You must take the first clue.'

Elise read the clue again and stepped forward. She stooped to lift an imaginary object and then remove from the ground another, which appeared to be a key. She made a great show of placing it in a non-existent lock and opening an invisible door to step through. There were the expected calls of, 'Doorknob,' 'Enter,' and Harry's muttered, 'Leave.'

'Don't be an idiot, Harry,' Rosalind whispered, loud enough so that everyone could hear. 'It is clear that she is coming back.'

'Clear to you, perhaps,' he responded, looking more sullen than Nick had seen him all week.

Elise frowned in his general direction, and then went back to her play-acting. She pretended to look back over the threshold and notice something on the ground, to go back to it and stare down and carefully wipe her shoes.

Whereupon Harry announced, in a clear voice, 'Husband.'

Elise's glare was incandescent, and to stop the outburst that she knew was coming Rosalind announced, 'I should think it is obvious. The answer is—'

Nick put his hand over her mouth, stopping the word. 'You cannot make the riddle and give us the answer,' he announced, giving everyone a false grin. 'Where would be the fun in that?'

'Door,' announced someone in the crowd.

Elise pointed to her feet.

'Feet.'

'Shoes.'

'Dirt.'

'Mmmmmmm,' said Rosalind, around the edges of his fingers.

At last someone shouted, 'Mat.' And he could feel Rosalind, sagging in relief against his hand. He released her.

She looked out at the other guests and announced, 'And now the next word. Tremaine, you must do this one.'

He gave a deep sigh and turned to face the crowd, making a great dumb show of pouring wine from a bottle into a glass. He drank from his imaginary glass, then held it up to the light to admire it, held it out to the crowd and deliberately ran his finger along the rim.

'Wine.'

'Drink.'

'Drunkard,' shouted Harry. 'Inebriate. Wastrel.'

Rosalind put her hands on her hips. 'It is not the person you are supposed to look at, Harry. It is the thing in his hand.'

'Philanderer,' Harry supplied, ignoring her guidance.

Nick took an involuntary step towards him, before regaining his temper and pointing to the imaginary glass in his hand.

'It starts with an R,' Rosalind supplied, and gave an encouraging look to the audience.

'Rascal. Reprobate,' Harry answered. 'Rake.'

'Now, see here…' Nick threw down his imaginary glass and balled his fists.

Rosalind muttered, 'Rim,' under her hand, until a member of the audience took the hint and shouted it.

Nick stalked back to where she was sitting. 'I have had quite enough of this. I wish a resolution to these issues as much as you do. But if it means that I must stand before the entire room while your brother attacks my character for the amusement of the other guests—'

She answered, making no attempt to whisper, 'Oh, really, Tremaine. Stop protesting and play the game. After all, you did steal the man's wife.'

'He did not steal me,' Elise announced. 'I went willingly.'

Tremaine and Rosalind turned to her and whispered in unison, 'This is none of your affair.'

She held up her hands and said, 'Very well, then.' And took a step back.

'Elise is right,' Tremaine muttered back. 'The current

problems are none of my doing and all of theirs. I am an innocent bystander.'

'Innocent? Oh, that is rich, sir. The picture of you as an innocent!'

'And now I suppose we are talking of what occurred the night we met? As I remember there were two involved, and not just one. And if that event had not transpired, then today it would be Harry attempting to steal Elise away from *me*.' He stopped. Perhaps that was exactly what would have occurred. For he could much more easily imagine Harry stealing Elise than he could imagine himself exerting the effort to take her away.

'As if Harry would ever do such a thing. Look at him.' Rosalind held out a hand. 'He is the picture of innocence.'

They paused in their whispered argument to look out at Harry, who smiled and offered a wave.

'And there you go again with your twisted notions of guilt and innocence.' Nick looked at Harry again. The man appeared to be harmless, just as he always had. But, from the first, there had been a resolute glint in his eye that did not match the mild exterior.

'He is wondering what we are arguing about.' Rosalind flashed a bright, false smile in the direction of Harry, and nudged Nick until he did the same. 'So, let us go back to the game for now. We will continue this discussion when there are not so many people present.' There was something in her tone that said they would be doing just that, as soon as the guests were out of earshot.

He nodded in agreement and thrust the last clue to Elise. 'Here, take this.'

'I think it is Rosalind's turn,' Elise responded meekly.

'Take it,' Rosalind said with finality, transferring her anger to Elise. 'The last clue.' Rosalind gestured to Elise as she walked to the front of the room.

'I certainly hope so,' Nick replied, then looked at the other guests. 'But it is a two-syllable word.'

Rosalind slapped his arm. 'I said it does not matter.'

'And I beg to differ.'

'Shh.' Elise stared at them, hands on hips, as though she were viewing a pair of unruly children, and they fell to silence.

Elise mimed reaching into her pocket and removing something.

'Handkerchief?' someone supplied.

Tremaine glared into the crowd. 'And how many syllables might that be?'

Elise held the object up between her fingers, then made a great show of opening it and reaching inside.

'Bag?'

'Reticule?'

'Purse.'

She gave an approving nod, and then removed something from it and counted objects out into her hand.

'Coins.'

'Pounds.'

'Notes.'

'Money!' shouted Harry, rising from his chair. 'No surprise that this clue should come from you, Elise. For it is the only thing you care about, is it not?'

Elise's hands dropped to her sides and her eyes narrowed. 'Harry, you know that is not true.'

His chin lifted. 'And I say it is. When I offered for you, your eyes fairly lit as I told you my income. And what were we arguing about the day you left? Now that Tremaine has come into his inheritance you are no longer at my side but at his.'

There was a fascinated murmur from the crowd around them, as though they were finally getting the Christmas entertainment they had hoped for when accepting the invitation.

'You still think this is all about money, then?' Elise laughed. 'And so you *would* like to think. For it removes any blame in this from you, Harry. You, who spent all these years trying to buy my affection. If you had been less quick to give of your pocket and more willing to share of yourself, then we would not be having this argument.'

He stood up. 'I have given you everything I can, Elise.'

'And I say you have not. For Nicholas is the one who has given me love.'

'Because it cost him nothing.'

Nick took another step towards Harry. 'First I was a drunkard, then a rake. And now I'm cheap, am I?'

Rosalind pulled on his arm to draw him out of the line of fire.

Elise stepped towards her husband. 'Even though I chose another, he has given me love and faithfulness and honesty.'

'Ha!' cried Rosalind, unable to contain herself. 'If you knew—'

'Not now.' Nick pulled her back. 'It will not help, Rosalind, I swear to you.'

Elise ignored the interruption. 'But for one misstep. And that was years ago.' She turned back to him and said, as an afterthought, 'It was a mistake ever doubting you, Nicholas.'

'No, it wasn't,' whispered Rosalind.

But Elise had returned her attention to Harry. 'And an even bigger mistake to marry *you*.' She swept from the room.

Harry dropped back into his seat, shocked into silence.

Nick turned to Rosalind, gesturing wide to encompass the mess she had made of things. 'There. See what you have done with your little game? She wants nothing to do with him now he has insulted her. I must go and see if I can mend the damage you have caused.'

She reached for his arm. 'That is the last thing you should do, Tremaine. Let them work this out for themselves. For it is your meddling that is the cause of half their problems.'

He laughed and pulled away from her. 'You dare to accuse me of meddling in the affairs of others, after the games you have had us playing? You have done more than I to tinker with something you do not understand. And a fine pass it has brought us all to.'

He was following Elise out through the door, even if his mind was telling him Rosalind was right. He would be better off to wash his hands of the whole affair.

'Go, then,' Rosalind shouted. 'Follow her, if her happiness means so much. Follow her, just as you always do. I hope it brings you what you deserve.'

The words struck him in the back like blows, but his feet did not slow their pace. She was right. The last thing he should be doing was following another man's wife down the hall to offer her comfort. If she was so in need of it then it was her husband who should provide it, not some other man.

And it was not as if Harry would deny her. He had been quick enough to sense her distress when he offered for her, and it had been plain to see from the man's enraptured expression after the wedding that his offer had had nothing to do with seizing an advantageous opportunity, and everything to do with his hopeless love for Elise.

If Nick had had the sense to keep himself out of their way the couple would have been able to solve their problem on their own. But here he was, still insinuating himself into a situation he had no real desire to join.

He stopped at the open door to the library and turned to make his retreat. But it was too late. Elise had caught sight of him. She gave a watery moan of, 'Nicholas,' and held a limp hand out to him.

And, as he had always done, he sighed and went to her.

'I swear what he said is not true,' she sobbed. 'It was never about your money. Or even about his. Perhaps at first it made a difference. It was nice that an earl had offered for me. And I thought, Oh, Nicholas shall be so jealous, when I accepted. For he could give me much more than you could back then. But mostly I was afraid that no one would want me at all.'

Nick nodded and sat beside her, putting an arm around her shaking shoulders.

'But once we were married it changed. He was so good to me, and so kind. I could not help having tender feelings for him. I felt very guilty about it at first. For it seemed like a final betrayal of what we had together. And that is why I have worked so hard to see that we remained friends.'

'And I have always been your friend in return.' He gave her a small hug. 'For I did not wish you to think you had been abandoned, just because your future did not lie with me.'

'But now?' She shook her head. 'I wonder if it has all been a mistake. Does he really care about me at all?'

'I am sure he does.' But why was the ninny tarrying? If he wished to keep his wife he must come and tell her so. 'Perhaps he is not good with words.'

'He was good enough with them back in the drawing room.' He could feel her tense. 'I think he has finally given me the truth of it, just as I wanted him to. But why did it have to happen in front of all those people? He thought me a fortune-hunter, and in secret he regrets marrying me. He is wrong. But I love him enough to want him to be happy, and to have a wife he respects. And a family. And that is why I cannot go back.'

Nick held her as she composed herself, and silently damned her husband to seven types of hell. If he could not come and force some sense into his wife, then at least he might have given Nick more powerful ammunition to defend him. For after the debacle in the drawing room, her assessment of her marriage appeared to be accurate.

'He cannot mind your spending too much. Even while you are away he supports you, does he not?'

'He is obligated. And I have accepted it because I could not think of another way. But I certainly cannot take his money after what he has said.' She paused, and then drew closer. 'Whatever might happen in the future, I cannot live as a burden on Harry any longer.' She paused again. 'Nicholas, do you remember our discussion before we came to this house, and my promise to you?'

'Vaguely.' He felt a wave of disquiet.

'When I said that if you did this for me there would be no more barriers between us?'

'Yes.' *No.* At least he did not wish to remember what he was sure she must be talking about.

'I may never be free by the laws of the land, but my heart has no home.' She paused again. 'It is yours if you still want it.'

After all these years, how could he tell her that he did not? She had expectations of him, just as surely as if he had offered for her. If her husband would not have her, then it was his responsibility to take on her care. Even if they did not marry, he could offer some sort of formal arrangement that would give her security. It would make her little better than a mistress in the eyes of society, but that could not be helped. Perhaps if they left London they could leave the scandal behind as well. But wherever he lived, it would mean that he could have nothing to do with Harry Pennyngton's sister, for the sake of all concerned.

'Of course, darling,' he said, closing his eyes and accepting the inevitable.

And he felt the relief in her, for she must have suspected by now that he did not want her either. He did not have the heart to tell her she was right.

She looked up at him, obviously expecting something. 'Is this not worthy of a kiss?'

'Of course,' he said absently, and kissed her.

She was still looking at him in the same strange way. 'A real kiss, Nicholas.'

'That was not?' He tried to remember what he had done.

She was smiling sadly. 'It appeared to be. But it was an attempt to save my feelings wrapped up in a pretty package. Can you not kiss me as though you mean it?'

'Now?' There was an embarrassing squeak in his voice that undid all his efforts at urbane sophistication. Kiss her as if he meant it? Now was as good a time as any. It was long past time. For how could one tell the person that the world had decided was one's own true love that one longed for freedom to marry another?

'Yes, Nicholas.' Her lashes were trembling, and there was a hitch in her voice. 'I can never go back to Harry. It is quite impossible. But that does not mean that I must be alone for the rest of my life. On my darkest days, I feared that there was some deficiency in me that rendered me unworthy of true love. Perhaps there was some flaw in my character that had left me without heart. At such times it has been a great comfort knowing that your love remained true after all these years. I would tell myself, If my husband does not want me, then at least there will always be Nicholas.'

He closed his eyes, trying to look as if he was gratefully accepting the compliment that all but sealed his doom. Did she not recognise the difference between love and flattery when it was right before her? It was not possible that Harry was devoid of the emotion that she was so convinced *he* held for her in abundance.

She held out her arms to him and closed her eyes, looking no happier than he felt.

What had that imbecile Harry hoped to prove by behaving as he had in the drawing room just now? And why would he not swallow his pride and come and get his wife this instant? Tremaine had a good mind to find the fellow and punch him in the nose.

He stared at the woman in front of him, stalling for time. 'Perhaps it would be better to wait until we are back in London.'

She searched his expression, trying to read the meaning in it. Then she leaned forward and touched the lapel of his coat, and dropped her gaze so that he could not see her expression. 'If we are to do it at all, there is no reason to delay. I cannot wait for ever in expectation that things will change between my husband and myself. It will soon be a new year, Nicholas, time to put the past behind me. And I think things will be easier between us once we have jumped this particular hurdle.'

'Oh.' His hand shifted on her shoulder, and he could not help giving it a brotherly pat. It wasn't terribly flattering to have the act of physical love viewed as a hurdle. If she would admit the truth to herself, she would see that she wanted this even less than he did.

'Yes. I am certain of it.' But her voice didn't sound the least bit certain, and he feared there were tears at the edge of it.

'If you are sure, then,' he said, and waited for her to come to her senses.

And then she stopped talking and came into his arms, all trembling beauty. That was the way it had always been with Elise. Almost too beautiful to resist, even though she had never been right for him. Her body pressed tight to his, soft and yielding, and her face tipped up to give him easy access for his kiss. Perhaps she was correct, and giving in to lust was all it would take to clear his head of romantic nonsense. So he tried to kiss her in the way she wished to be kissed, as though it mattered, and made every effort to drum up the old passion he had felt for her so long ago.

Her response to him was just as devoid of true desire as his was to her. After a time she pulled away from him and looked up, disappointment and awareness written plainly on her face. When she spoke, her voice was annoyingly clear of emotion. 'This is not working at all as I expected.'

'No,' he answered in relief. 'It is not.'

'I suppose it is too much to hope that you are feeling more than I am on this matter?'

'I am sorry, but I am not. If there were anything, Elise, I would tell you. But do not think that I am disguising my true feelings for you to save your marriage.

I will be your friend for ever, but I do not love you in the way you desire.'

She pulled away from him, stood up. And as she walked towards the door she looked sad, but strangely relieved. 'All this time I have been so afraid that I was supposed to be with you. And now? Things are not as I expected at all.'

He nodded, following her. 'I will admit to being somewhat surprised on that point as well. When you came back, I thought perhaps… But, no. I have suspected for some time now that it was not meant to be.'

She sighed in annoyance. 'And when did you mean to share this knowledge with me? For if you meant to take advantage of the situation, Nicholas Tremaine, I swear…'

He held up his hands in surrender. 'I do not know why everyone expects the worst from me, for I am utterly blameless in this. It is not as if I sought you out.'

'You have flirted with me all these years, Nicholas.'

'You and everyone else, darling. I am incorrigible. You have told me so on many occasions. And you never for a moment took me seriously. It is only since the trouble between you and Harry that you have given me real consideration. Frankly, I found it to be rather alarming, and most out of character for you. But I thought, as your oldest and dearest friend, that if you meant to do something foolish you might as well do it with me.'

'You thought you would spare me pain by entering into a dalliance with me?'

He smiled. 'Better me than another. I never claimed to be a noble man, Elise. I am a rake, pure and simple.

But I sought to be the lesser of two evils, and I think, after a fashion, that I have succeeded. Never mind what the world thinks has occurred. We have done nothing that your husband will not forgive.'

Her face darkened. 'And what makes you think that my husband cares to forgive me?'

Damn his tongue for speaking of Harry too soon. He did not wish, at this delicate juncture, to spoil progress towards reconciliation. 'I am merely saying that should you ever wish to return to him, my conscience is still clear. I have not broken your heart. I have not even truly engaged your affections.'

'Neither has he.'

Tremaine resisted the urge to inform her that a woman whose affections were not fully engaged would not be going to such trouble to exact revenge. 'Even so, if you do not wish to settle for less than a full commitment from your husband, you need hardly settle for less than you deserve from me.'

She considered the situation. 'You think that I should choose another lover, then?'

Once again he felt himself losing control of the situation. 'That is not what I said at a—'

'Tremaine!' Harry's hand fell on his shoulder, heavy as death, and yanked him away from Elise. Then Harry pushed him back to the wall, and stared into his eyes, too close. 'I have had quite enough of your interference in the matter of our marriage. It has been difficult enough to have you sniffing about the edges, waiting for my wife to stray. I have tolerated it for Elise's sake. But if you mean to cast her off and pass her on to some other man? You are a heartless cad, sir. You are filling my wife's head with nonsense, and you are to stop it this instant.' His face had the same amiable smile it always had, but this time the tone of his voice was menacing. 'Or I will be forced to take action.'

'Ha!' Elise's response was a shrill laugh. 'You will take action, now, will you? After all this time?'

Nick could feel the fists of the man holding him begin to tense on the lapels of his jacket. 'Elise,' he said in warning. 'Do not goad the man.'

Elise ignored him, as it had always been her nature to do. 'I have been gone for months, Harry. And I have been with Nicholas all that time.'

'But not any more,' Nick announced, hoping that it would end the matter.

She smiled with pure malice at her husband. 'I suppose you can imagine what has occurred?'

Judging by the look on Harry's face as he stared at Nick, he was doing just that.

Nick gave him an ineffectual pat on the arm. 'It does no good to let one's imagination run free and create scenarios where none has existed. She's all yours, old man, and always has been.'

'I am not,' Elise insisted. 'I am not some possession of yours, Harry. And if I wish to take one lover, or a dozen, there is no way you can stop me.'

'Oh, really?' Harry was angry enough to strike someone, and since he would never raise his hand to a lady, no matter how vexing she might be, Nick closed his eyes and waited for the punch. Then, just as suddenly as Harry had grabbed him, he pulled him off balance and pushed him out into the hall, slamming the door after him.

Nick hit the wall opposite the door and bounced off it, landing on the floor with a thump. He leaned his back against the wall in relief, and waited for his head to clear. The situation was solved at last. Judging by the look on Harry's face as the door had closed, Elise would be given no more opportunities to roam. And even if she did, Nick would be risking life and limb should *he* involve himself in the situation. In any case, she had admitted that he was not the true object of her affections. If she could not manage to solve the problems in her marriage she would not come back to him again, hoping to regain the past.

Which meant he was free.

What a strange thought. For he had been free all these years, hadn't he? There was no wife to tie him down. Since his break from Elise he had sampled all the pleasures available to an unattached man in the city. He had indulged whims to the point of boredom, and was more than ready to give them up and settle down. But there had been something holding him back from seeking an end to his solitude.

In the background there had always been Elise—unattainable and yet his constant companion. For even when she had married he had grown used to the idea that he was in some way still responsible for her happiness. He had feared that while she might tolerate his mistresses and small infatuations, and laugh at his penchant for opera dancers and actresses, any serious attachment of his to another would break her heart.

But if she was returning to her husband, this time it would be in soul as well as body. He stared at the closed door in front of him, then rose to his feet, surprised at the lightness of his heart. He would always be her friend. But it was as if some bond had snapped, a tie that had held him so long it had felt more like security than restriction. As though he had been staring at a brick wall so intently he no longer knew if he was outside or inside of it.

And now there was nothing to prevent him from doing what he suspected he had wished to do from the very first.

Chapter Sixteeen

Rosalind stopped to retie a bow on the Christmas tree, only to be rewarded by a shower of needles on the rug beneath. After Harry's embarrassing outburst, and the disappearance, one by one, of the key players in the domestic drama, the audience had escaped to the dining room for luncheon and gossip.

She was in no mood to hear the scene reworked by curious strangers, so had remained behind with the pretence of refreshing the decorations. She kicked the needles into a small pile at the base of the tree, only to see more fall onto the cleared spot of carpeting. The silly pine had no right to die on her so quickly. How was she to keep the candles lit even for one more night with the tree in this condition? Well, they could carve 'Happy New Year' on her tombstone if they were burned in their beds because of the decorations.

Not that she was likely to remain here much longer. If things had progressed as she thought, Harry had finally come to his senses and she would be back in her own bed in Shropshire long before Candlemas. And Tremaine was still full of excuses, and no closer to offering for her than he had been all those long years ago.

She walked to the drawing room door and stretched and strained until she had pulled down the mistletoe ball. Without thinking, she began to shred the leaves in her hands. What had possessed her to hang the things all through the house, so she could not get a moment's reprieve from them? Damn all mistletoe, anyway. She was likely to see everyone else in the house put it to good use, but gain nothing by it herself.

She could hear steps in the hall, clicking on the marble at the far end. Tremaine, she thought, for there was the distinctive tap of his fine leather boots. But he was coming indecorously fast. What had started out at a measured pace on the marble was growing faster with each step. She ducked her head out into the hallway to see if she had guessed correctly.

At the sight of her, he sped up. And when he reached the rug that began at the entry hall, it was at a dead run.

She looked both ways, searching for the cause of the disturbance. 'What is it? Is something amiss? Do I need—?'

In a moment he was upon her, pushing her back into the room, closing the door and yanking the destroyed plant from her hand. Then he pinned her against the doorframe, his hand twisted in her hair, the mistletoe crushing beneath it, and his lips came down to hers with surprising force.

It was just as wonderful as she remembered it from the first time they'd kissed: the smell of him, the feel of his hands, the warmth of his body near to hers. She opened her mouth, as he had taught her then, to find the taste of his tongue against hers was deliciously the same.

If she was not careful, the end result would be the same as well. He would kiss her, and then he would leave. So, no matter how much she was enjoying it, she gathered her will and pulled away from him, trying to appear shocked. 'Tremaine, what the devil are you doing?' she managed, before he overpowered her weak resistance and stopped her speech with another kiss.

Actually, there was no question of what he was doing. He was driving her mad, just as he had when she was young and foolish. She could feel her pulse racing to keep up with her heart, and felt the kiss from her mouth to the tips of her toes, and every place in between. It did not matter any more than it had the first time that this was wrong. She wanted it anyway.

He pulled away far enough to speak. 'What I am doing, darling, is settling once and for all the location of the mistletoe. You have been standing under it for days, a continual source of temptation. I feel I have done an admirable job of ignoring the fact. But no longer.'

She struggled in his grasp, shocked to find that his other hand had settled tight around her waist, holding her to him in a way that was much more intimate than the brief meeting in their past. The situation was getting quickly out of hand. 'I did not think it mattered to you.'

'And I find I can think of nothing else.' When he

realised that he was frightening her, he relaxed for a moment, smoothed her hair with his hand and looked into her eyes. There was a softness in his expression, a tenderness that she had not seen since the day they had first met. Then he smiled, and was just as wicked as he ever was. He kissed her again, into her open mouth, before she could remember to stop him, thrusting with his tongue, harder and harder, until she gave up all pretence of resistance and ran her hands through his hair and over his body, shocking herself with the need to touch and be touched.

'I suppose,' she said breathlessly when he paused again, 'that when someone catches us here you will insist that this is all my doing, just as you did before.' She regained some small measure of composure and pushed at his hands, trying to free herself from his grip. But as she struggled against him she suspected that, despite the trouble it would cause, total surrender was utterly superior to freedom.

'On the contrary. This time, if you wish, you may claim yourself the innocent victim of my animal lust.' And he kissed her again, dominating her easily, to prove that any attempt to escape him was quite futile.

'Really?' She smiled, delighted, and stopped fighting. His head dipped to nuzzle her neck. 'I have never been an innocent victim of anything before.'

He laughed against her skin. 'I thought not. I expect once we are married you shall prove even more difficult to handle than Elise would have been.'

Married? She did her best to frown at him, for it

would not do to appear too eager after all the time she had waited for this. 'I expect you are right. If, that is, I decide to marry you. You have not offered as yet, nor have I accepted.'

'I have owed you a proposal for over five years. I assumed your answer would be yes.'

'Never assume,' she said, a little breathlessly. 'I would rather die an old maid than spend another Christmas as I've spent this one—as someone's dutiful wife, cooking geese and tending to the ivy.'

He reached out and took her fingers, bringing them to his lips, drawing them into his mouth to suck upon the tips until she gasped. 'If you marry me, your hands will never touch another Yule Log.' He held them out, admiring the fingers and kissing each one in turn. 'But they would look very attractive wrapped around the reins of a curricle in Hyde Park.'

Her eyes sparkled. 'You would let me drive?'

He smiled back. 'We must see if you have the nerve for it. And you would have to be very good to me, of course. But if you indulge my every whim, how can I deny you yours? We will discuss that later.' He tucked a sprig of mistletoe into his pocket and kissed her again, until she was quite breathless.

'Later?' She caught at his hand as it reached to touch her breast. 'You are being quite wicked enough now, Tremaine.'

'Not hardly,' he answered back, then kissed her once more until she let him caress her. 'You have led a most sheltered life, Miss Morley. And you are utterly unprepared to deal with a reprobate such as myself. But I will be only too happy to educate you in the ways of the world. For instance, I'm sure you will agree that this is much more shocking than a few kisses under the mistletoe.' And his hand slipped beneath the neckline of her gown.

His fingers found her nipple and began to draw slow circles about it. He was right. Judging by the way it was making her feel, it was much worse than kissing. 'You mustn't,' she whispered, and then arched her back to give him better access. 'If someone finds us...'

He pinched her. 'Then I shall be forced to marry you immediately.' He sighed. 'Which is just what I mean to do in any case. I cannot wait another moment. I must have you, darling. And I cannot very well remain under this roof and do what I wish to do with you. I have just left off trying to seduce Harry's wife, and now I mean to ruin his sister? I must show some respect for the poor man. It is Christmas, after all. He deserves to be rid of me. And absconding with his hostess in the middle of a house party is a fitting gift, considering what kind of host he has been to me.' Then he smiled. 'But I have not given you a gift either, have I?' And his other hand slipped beneath her skirts.

'Tremaine, whatever are you doing?'

'You will know soon enough, love.' And she felt his hand caress the bare skin of her leg above her stocking. 'Now, speak. Will you have me?'

She had wanted nothing more for as long as she could remember. But she was afraid he would stop trying to persuade her if she gave in too easily. Was it the knowledge that he was touching her so intimately, or the touch itself that was so compelling? She smoothed down her skirt, to hide what his hand was doing, and tried to appear uninterested. 'I doubt my father will approve of you.'

'Then we shall not tell him until it is too late to matter.'

His fingers travelled up, until they could go no further, and then gave a gentle caress that caused her to gasp in shock. She decided it was definitely the touch that was affecting her, for he had increased the speed of his stroking and was driving her mad with it. His fingers played in a gentle rhythm against her body, reaching places that she had never thought to touch, and creating a jumble of new sensations that made it much easier to feel than to think.

She could barely hear him as he said, 'Now that the roads are clear, it's Gretna for us, my love. And then to bed.'

'I have never…never…never been to Scotland,' she gasped, and grabbed his shoulders for support, trying and failing to hold on to common sense as the feelings built in her.

'Then it will be a day of firsts for you.'

He held her in place against the wall, one hand tightening upon her breast and the other teasing between her legs. She was not sure what was happening, but she knew at any moment that she would have no choice but to say yes, most emphatically, to anything he might ask.

So she closed her eyes and leaned her head back against the wall. With her last strength she whispered,

'Show me Pompeii, Tremaine, and I am yours for ever.' And then she gave herself over to him, and dissolved in pleasure at his touch, accepting his proposal repeatedly and with surprising enthusiasm.

He laughed and kissed her throat. 'Tomorrow, if you ask for it, I will give you the world. But tonight, Vesuvius is nothing compared to what you shall have.'

Chapter Seventeen

Elise had heard Nicholas's body strike the wall with some considerable force. It had surprised her, for although she knew Harry was strong enough, he was not usually given to displays of brute strength. But now, as he turned back to face her, she began to wonder if she had ever known him at all.

It was not yet noon, his clothing was a mess, and he smelled of brandy. His face had not seen a razor that morning, and a slight stubble emphasised the squared set of his jaw. Everything about him seemed larger, more intimidating than she remembered, and he was advancing on her in a way that might have seemed threatening if she hadn't known that it was only Harry Pennyngton. But then he reached her, and before she quite knew what was happening he had taken her in his arms and crushed her body to his in a kiss she could almost describe as ruthless.

'Harry, whatever are you doing?'

'What I should have done months ago,' he said through gritted teeth. 'We are going to settle what is between us once and for all.'

'I thought it was settled,' she said.

'For you, perhaps. Since dear old Harry has allowed you to do whatever you want, in the vain hope that you will grow tired of wandering and come home. But I am done with patience.'

'If you think that I am so easy to control as all that, you had best think again, Harry.' She squirmed in his arms, expecting him to release her, but instead he held her tighter, until she gasped with pleasure.

'Easy to control?' He released her then, and she swayed against him. 'You are more trouble than any two wives. I am sure that the sultans of Arabia do not have the challenges in dealing with an entire harem that I have with you.'

'If I am so much trouble, you had best divorce me and save yourself the bother.' She started towards the door.

But he was past her in a flash, and pushed her back into the library ahead of him. Then he stepped in after her and slammed the door. 'On the contrary, my dear. I have no intention of letting you go. Especially if you mean to throw Tremaine aside and take another lover.'

She stopped and stared at him. 'Whatever difference should it make to you, who I choose to be unfaithful with?'

'I have always known, should you choose to leave me, that it would be for Tremaine. For you have wondered from the first if your decision in marrying me was a wise one. But now that you have had a chance to compare us, I hope that I appear more favourably in your mind.'

'Harry,' she groaned, 'that is the most cold-blooded thing I have ever heard. If you are willing to stand aside and allow me a lover for purposes of comparison, then it proves you don't love me in the slightest.'

'Not a lover, Elise. Only Tremaine. He has been as regular a feature in our marriage as a dog, lying beside the fireplace. Lord knows, I have often had to kick the blighter out of the way to regain your attentions. But it is my good fortune that he has as much initiative as an old dog as well.'

'I beg your pardon?' she said indignantly. 'Nicholas Tremaine is a notorious rake, with a very passionate nature.'

Harry scoffed. 'And no threat at all to our marriage. If he were half the man you claimed he'd never have let me take you away. Failing that, he'd have hounded you day and night, until you could no longer resist the temptation and allowed him into your bed. Instead, I have borne his half-hearted flirtation with you in good humour, knowing that it would lead to nothing. That in the end you went to him, and not the other way round, should tell you everything you need to know about his grand passion for you.'

The words hit close to home, and she felt like a fool for not noticing earlier. But at least Harry did not seem jealous any more. And then, as though unable to resist, she taunted him again. 'If what you say is true, and he does not have a burning desire for me, then I am sure there is someone who does.'

Harry's eyes narrowed. 'Oh, Elise, I have no doubt of it. But if you think you will be allowed to seek any further than this room for such a man you are sorely mistaken.'

He was finally angry enough to show her the truth that she wanted to see, and his words sent desire pulsing to the centre of her being. She pushed him again. 'Seek in this room a man with sufficient passion to hold my attention? If you had sufficient passion, Harry, I would not be looking elsewhere.'

If she had hoped for a reaction there was none apparent. His smile was the same vaguely placid one that he often wore. But there was a strange light in his eyes that had not been there when last she'd looked.

'Very well, then. If you wish a demonstration of the depth of my feelings…'

Before she realised what he had done, he'd locked the door behind her, torn the key from the hole and pitched it into the fireplace.

She stared into the embers, and she thought she could see the metal as it heated to glowing. 'Harry, what the devil are you doing?'

'Making it impossible for you to leave the room before we have finished our discussion. I imagine the fire shall be almost out by the time I am finished with you, and then you will be able to retrieve the key and open the door.' He said it in a way that made her think discussion was the last thing on his mind, and she felt another thrill go through her—one that she had been missing for over two months.

'Now, let me describe to you how I am feeling.'

And then she felt the desire start to fade, for it seemed they were only going to have another silly argument. 'You are going to tell me *now* how you feel? After five years of nothing, you have told me more than enough of your feelings in the last few days. Must I hear more of them? For I have had quite enough.' But when she looked at him, staring into his eyes, she wondered if that was true.

'Really?'

'You have made it quite clear that I have lost your trust. And I am sorry, Harry. I know I've given you cause to doubt me. But until recently I did not think it mattered to you how I behaved. I am sorry. There—I have said it. Though we did comfortably well together, proximity has not made us into lovers. You deserve more. As do I.'

'More comfort than I have given you?' he sneered. 'My pockets are deep, Elise, but they are not bottomless.'

She slapped at his shoulder. 'I cannot make you understand, and I am tired of trying. I do not wish you to buy me a new dress, or a diamond, or even a larger residence, so that I can live in luxury without you. If you want, you can take it all back. Sell every last jewel and turn me out on the streets in my shift. I do not care a jot for any of it if I cannot have a marriage that is more than remuneration for services rendered.'

'Am I to understand that you wish a meeting of hearts, and not just an equitable living arrangement?' He smiled.

'Exactly.' She was relieved that at last he understood her. But she found it strangely disappointing that it might mean he'd let her go.

'What utter nonsense.'

'Harry, it is not nonsense at all. It is what I have longed for all my life.' She reached out a hand to push his shoulder, to move him out of her way. But he caught it easily, sliding his palm over hers, wrapping his fingers around it and squeezing tightly, rubbing the ball of his thumb slowly over the pulse-point beating on her wrist.

'But, Elise, what kind of a fool would I be to give my heart to you now, knowing that you have ignored it for so many years?'

'Me?'

'When I sought to court you, as smitten as any young buck in London, you all but ignored me. You struggled to hide your disappointment when you married me. Since that time, you have been everything a man could desire in a wife. I have had all I could want save one thing.'

She thought of the children that should be gracing their home, and felt a moment's pain.

'You have not loved me.'

She started.

'And so I have kept my distance as well. For there is nothing more pathetic than a man so lost in love that his wife leads him like an ape on a string for the amusement of the ton. But now, after you have left me, you expect me to show you the depths of my feelings and risk ridicule or indifference?'

It was as if he was throwing her own thoughts back at her, and she found she had no way to answer for them. There must be something she could say that would make it all right between them, but for the life of her she could not think of the words.

When he realised that a response would not be forth-coming, he sighed. 'Very well, then.'

She feared that she had lost him with her hesitation. And then he kissed her.

The strength of her reaction came as a shock, and she wondered how she had ever become convinced that he was taking her for granted with the casual affection he displayed. He seemed to put no effort into arousing her. But he had managed it all the same. Where Nicholas Tremaine's kisses had been skilled enough, but not particularly passionate, Harry's lacked grace in their eagerness to bring her pleasure. In the months they had spent apart he had forgotten none of what she enjoyed, and now he was using all of his accumulated knowledge against her, until she caught fire in his arms.

He was kissing her with every last ounce of desire, his tongue sliding past her teeth and his lips devouring hers. And it no longer mattered what he had said, or not said, whether he loved her, hated her, or cared neither way. She could not help it that a small moan of pleasure escaped her lips, and then a somewhat louder moan of disappointment when he pulled away from her.

His voice was low and husky when he spoke. 'Do you still doubt the state of my heart after all we have been to each other?'

He had brought her close to climax with the force of his kiss. So she gathered her breath and whispered, 'The fact that you are a skilled lover does little to tell me your true feelings.'

He allowed himself a satisfied grin. 'So I am a skilled lover, am I?'

She was near to panting with eagerness as she said, 'I am sure there are many as talented as you, who care only for the pleasure to be gained from the act of love and not the woman they share it with.'

'Really?'

'Nicholas, for instance—'

And his lips came down upon hers again, stopping her in mid-sentence. This kiss was rougher, and more demanding, and his hands held her tight to his body as he rubbed his hips against hers. He was hard and ready for her. When he felt her growing soft and weak in response, near ready to give in, he pulled away from her again.

'There will be no more talk of Tremaine, Elise. For I do not care what he thinks when alone with a woman. I can speak only for myself when I say that it is much more pleasurable when one has the love of one's partner. And if, after tonight, I have not gained yours, then there will be no point in our continuing. If you do not love me with your whole heart, then I do not want you back.'

He would not take her back? She was struck by the shock of the idea. For she had believed for so long that he did not love her, it was a surprise to think he had feared the same.

'You want my love?' she asked softly.

He buried his face in her neck, inhaling the scent of her. 'As I have wanted it from the first day we met. I still remember the first time I saw you, standing in a doorway at some party or other. I cannot remember anything else about that night but you. You wore blue satin, and it matched the colour of your eyes. I had to force my way through a crowd of suitors to gain your hand for a dance.'

'That was a long time ago,' she murmured, trying to ignore the feeling of his lips on her throat so that she could hear his words over the singing in her blood.

'Barely an instant. You are no less beautiful. You were so bright—glowing like a diamond.'

She tried to remember the last time he had spoken to her thus, with anything more than polite approval. 'I did not know you had noticed my appearance.'

He raised his head to look into her eyes. 'Every hour of every day. Just to look at you was a pleasure, and still is. But you belonged to someone else, and I thought there was no hope. Can you blame me, then, for using Tremaine's downfall to my advantage?'

She pulled away and looked at him in surprise. 'And how did you do so? For we were parted before you offered.'

For a moment the old Harry was back, hesitant, guarded, evasive. 'The anonymous note you received? Telling of his perfidy? It was from me.'

The shock of it shook her to her very core. 'You lied to me?'

'It was the truth. The girl involved was Rosalind. As much her fault as his. But he was not blameless, for it was his flirting that led her to disaster.'

'Rosalind?' And suddenly the pieces of Elise's life began to fall together. The strange behaviour of her sister-in-law, and the even stranger behaviour of Tremaine.

'I should have called the bastard out instead of keeping what he did a secret. But Morley wished the thing covered up, and rushed her back out of town. And then I saw my opportunity to hurt him, and to have you as well. I sent the note, and I would do it again in a heartbeat.' He squared his jaw in defiance. 'If you believe I won you through unfair means, then so be it. I would have done anything to part the two of you. That the man was too decent to dishonour my sister further and tell you the truth came as a great relief to me. For I realised too late that I had jeopardised her reputation further by hinting at the facts. But he was not honourable enough to marry her, and he deserved some punishment for it—not the reward of your love as well.'

'You deliberately ruined my engagement?' He had changed her life to suit his own desires, tricked her into his bed and pleasured her until she was helpless to resist. The thought should have enraged her. But the rush of emotion she felt was closer to lust than anger.

'I was mad with wanting you.' And then he added, as if it should mitigate what he had done, 'You would not have suited. Tremaine is too shallow, and would not give you the safety and security of home that you desire. You would have discovered it yourself eventually, to your own regret, if I had not intervened.' He frowned. 'But if I had known that I would never be free of the man, and that you would still be pining for him five years later, perhaps I would not have bothered.'

'I have not been pining for him,' she snapped. 'I have made every effort to be a good wife to you, just as you deserved.'

He snorted. 'I got what I deserved, all right. A woman beautiful, passionate, and in mourning for the man she had given up. But willing to do her duty to the husband she never wanted. I am not sorry for what I did to get you. I would do it again to have even a day with you in my arms, though your heart was divided. But, believe me, I paid the price.' He looked at her again, his eyes strange and sad. 'For I will always wonder what it would have been like had you loved me first.'

As he spoke, it sounded as though something was over. Which was strange, because perhaps nothing had ended at all.

'I cannot tell you what might have been,' she said. 'I only know that my future does not lie with Tremaine, no matter the past.'

Harry looked at her with a slow, hot smile that made her insides melt.

'And what do you mean to do tomorrow?' He pulled her a little closer, and her body shocked her with remembrance.

'Tomorrow?'

'Yes, tomorrow. If you mean to leave both me and Tremaine, and find another lover, it will have to wait for morning. I have plans for you tonight.'

'Harry, it is barely noon.' Her breath came out in a

little squeak. It surprised her, for it sounded almost as if she was frightened by her mild milquetoast of a husband.

'I am well aware of the fact. For now, it is you and me and the library fire, my love. And, by God, if you go out through that door tomorrow morning, I will see to it that you remember what you have left.' Then he pushed her back to the door and kissed her so hard that she thought her lips must bruise.

'Harry,' she gasped, when he allowed her a moment to breathe.

'Indeed.' He was after the hooks on her gown, pulling until she felt them give.

'Stop it this instant. This is my best dress.'

'I will buy you another.' She heard the faint pop of seams and the rip of lace and silk as he pushed the dress down to her waist and ran his tongue along the tops of her breasts, where they peeked over her stays, before setting to work on the laces at her back.

She slapped at his hands, trying to slow his progress, for desire was rising in her again. 'At least let us go upstairs to my room.'

His hands froze, and he looked up from his work. 'If you like your bedroom so well, then I will allow you to return to it. Tomorrow. But today I mean to have you, here and now, in whatever way I care to.'

She swallowed, and felt her knees go weak as another wave hit her. She let out a shaky sigh before saying, 'Suppose someone discovers us?'

'The door is locked.' He plunged a hand beneath her skirts and stroked between her legs, and then laughed in triumph because there was no way for her to hide the evidence of her desire.

'But they might hear.'

He stroked again, and slipped a finger into her, making her moan. 'I expect they will.' And he settled his mouth over a nipple and thrust again with his hand, harder and faster, until she shuddered and groaned his name.

He raised his head to look at her, critically, but with a small smile playing about his lips. 'There. That is how I prefer you. Unable to argue with me.'

It was difficult to argue when her body was crying for more. But, since he was growing more passionate with each objection she raised, she found the strength to disagree. 'Do not think you can persuade me so easily, Harry Pennyngton. I have no intention of giving you your way in this. Unlock the door and let me go.'

'She has found her tongue again,' he murmured. 'A sharp tongue, but a pretty mouth.' And he kissed her again, biting at her lips and taking what little sense she had left. Then he scooped her legs out from under her and carried her into the room.

She kicked. 'Put me down this instant.'

He dropped her onto the chaise longue and stood over her, undoing his cravat. 'You are down. Stay where you are while I get out of these blasted clothes. And know this: if you run, I will catch you.'

As she watched him undress, her heart was pounding so that she feared she would dissolve into ecstasy before he had even touched her. 'If you do not stop this instant I shall scream.'

He was grinning now. 'I certainly hope so—eventually.' He threw his jacket down beside her and pulled his shirt over his head. 'Our guests will find it the most diverting entertainment of the year, but it will not dissuade me from what I mean to do.'

She propped herself up on her elbows and made to swing her legs onto the floor. But he blocked her, and she kicked at his knee with her slipper. 'Harry, be reasonable.'

He glanced down at her as he stripped off the last of his clothing. 'I have tried for five long years to be reasonable, Elise. And today reason fails me.' Then he knelt on the chair, with his legs straddling her, caught her hands in his and pinned them to the cushion beside her head.

She had to admit that it was difficult, under the circumstances, to maintain a level head. He was poised at the entrance of her body, and she lifted her hips to greet him as he plunged into her.

He gave a long, slow stroke that was so good it made her gasp, then leaned away to look at her, trapped beneath him. 'There—that is more like it.'

'This changes nothing,' she said, but the words came out in short pants as he thrust again.

'You are the one who wishes change, not I.' His breathing was barely laboured, but she could see a sheen of sweat glowing on his body. 'For my part, you are perfect just as you are.'

She groaned. 'You say that now. But when we are clothed you will say nothing at all.'

'How would you know what I say, since you show no desire to be at my side?' His thrusts increased their tempo, bordering on violence, and she could feel the pressure building inside her, ready to break. 'At least when I bed you I know that you are not thinking of another.'

And in truth she could think of nothing at all but him, and what he could do to her. Her body was liquid, hot and wet. Release was moments away. A few more thrusts would send her spinning over the edge. And he knew what he was doing to her, for he had five years' practice in making her respond. He slowed again and began to withdraw. She bucked her hips under him, trying to deepen the penetration.

And then he gritted his teeth in a pained smile, and said, 'Speak my name. Tell me that you want me.'

'Harry,' she whispered.

He gave a single thrust. 'Louder.'

'Harry, please.' She pushed against him, wriggling her hips.

'That's better. Now, tell me there will be no other but me. Tell me, or I swear I will withdraw and leave you unfinished.'

'You can't,' she gasped.

'I can.' And he thrust gently, just enough to keep her on edge.

It was so good that she didn't care what came tomorrow if she could have this moment. 'Not fair,' she panted.

'All's fair in love and war,' he muttered against her throat, and thrust into her again.

'Love?' He was filling her senses, and she struggled to remember if he had ever used the word to her, even in jest.

He paused again, and then rocked gently against her until she was trembling under him, dying for release. 'You are the one that wants war, not I. Now, tell me you love me. That you will be mine for always.'

He was moving slowly inside her, awaking every nerve. She struggled to reach for him, but he held her fast. She whipped her head from side to side, until she found his wrist and rubbed her cheek against it, groaning. 'I am yours, heart and mind and body. Always. Please…' And she felt her body clench at the words, and then go to pieces in spasms of rapture.

He felt it too, and laughed, then fixed his mouth on hers and smothered her screams of pleasure as he pounded into her body. He fell shaking against her, helpless with the strength of his own release.

When she could catch her breath, she whispered, 'I do love you, Harry. Truly.'

In response, he released a surprisingly shaky sigh and whispered back, 'At last. I despaired of ever hearing you admit it. I have loved you to distraction since the first moment I saw you.'

'You have?' She could not keep the wonder from her voice.

'Indeed.'

'You never said so.'

He laughed. 'I thought I had made it abundantly clear when we came together.'

'I knew you were happy with me in that way,' she whispered.

He groaned. 'Delighted. Ecstatic. Delirious.'

'But I thought perhaps a good marriage should be more.'

'A good marriage is whatever we choose it to be, my darling,' he whispered back, and kissed her again. 'And while ours happens to be a very satisfying physical relationship, I feel it *is* more than that. Do you know how I have missed you since you have been in London? The sound of your voice, the sight of you each morning at breakfast, the little things you did to bring joy to my life every single day. My only regret has been that I gained you through trickery. I was afraid that some day you might discover the truth and I would lose you. It seemed as though I was for ever on guard, lest in some impulsive moment I revealed too much. But you left me anyway. The secrecy was for naught.'

He looked worried now that he had told her. Could that have been the great mystery all along? That he had loved her past all honour, since the very first? She felt the thrill of it go through her. And then she relaxed against him for what seemed like the first time. For why did she need to be wary of losing a man who wanted her with such uncontrollable passion? She noticed the way his arm drew her tight, as it always did after they made love, as though he would never let her go. Perhaps it had always been thus and she had never noticed.

She turned her face to him and kissed his chest. 'It was very wicked of you,' she said. 'But I think I can forgive it after all this time.'

He broke into a grin, then, and hugged her again.

She blinked. 'If you can forgive me for Tremaine. I did not understand how you felt.'

He stroked her hair. 'If you have come back to me, then what does the past matter?' He looked away from her then, and said, as though it did not matter, 'Of course it made me very jealous.'

She poked him in the ribs. 'You worked very hard at hiding it until just recently. I did not think you cared a jot for how I behaved.'

'I told myself that he would take no greater liberties than he had already, even when you were free. But if I was wrong…' He paused again, and said with difficulty, 'I understand how much you long for children. But I have not been able to give them to you.' He paused and touched her belly. 'If there is any reason why you might need to return to him, or any likelihood of an occurrence that we might need to explain, then it would be best if you told me sooner and not later.'

She could feel the tenseness between his shoulder-blades as he waited for her answer. But his grip on her did not loosen. It stayed as protective and gentle as ever, even as he discussed the possibility of raising another man's bastard. She looked up at him, and for the first time she was sure, beyond a doubt, that he loved her.

'Harry,' she whispered, and hugged him back. 'You have nothing to fear. There has never been anyone but you. Nor will there be.' She frowned, and then pushed forward with her own greatest fear. 'There will be no surprises of that kind because of my time away. But what if there are to be no surprises at all? Even after I come home? We have been together for years, Harry, and nothing has happened. It has been so long.' And she waited, afraid that he would turn from her again.

He smiled, and it was sad, and then he gathered her close to him again. 'It has. But we are not too old yet, I think. And if we are not blessed then we will have to content ourselves with the future God has sent us. In any case, there is not another woman in the world I would wish at my side.'

He reached for his jacket and pulled it over them, to try to keep back the chill. It was hopeless, for the narrow tails did little to cover their bare legs, and they struggled with it, tangling together until she was laughing again. Then he reached into a pocket and withdrew the box he had offered her before.

'Look what I still have for you. Will you accept your gift from me now? You have given me what I want.' He kissed down the side of her neck. 'Let me give this to you.'

Her laughter disappeared at the sight of the box. He had made her laugh. Made her believe in him again. But here he was with another jewellery box, likely to stop talking and spoil it all. 'Must you?'

He shook his head and smiled softly. 'You do not want more jewels? I fear I do not understand women at all. I certainly do not understand you, darling, although if you open this box you will see that I am trying to do better.' He hesitated. 'But, before you do, let me assure you that the thing you read in the paper was nothing. I swear. There is no problem with money that will not fix itself, given time. Do not think that the value of this gift implies a lack of funds.'

She leaned back to examine his face, and was surprised to see the trepidation there. It did seem that he was unusually worried about her response.

'Do not be silly, Harry. It is not the value of the gift that matters to me. It never has been. As I have told you, time and time again, I do not wish any more jewellery from you. But if you mean to give me the thing, and I can no longer avoid it, then let us get it over with.' She steeled herself and reached for the box.

He was obviously rethinking the wisdom of his gift, for he pulled it away from her at the last minute. 'We will see how serious you are when you say that. For the contents of this box are really nothing at all. Nothing more than foolishness. But when I made it for you I did not think how it might appear…'

'You *made* it for me?' Surely she had not heard him correctly.

But he nodded, and coloured like an embarrassed schoolboy. 'We will go to London and get you a real gift once the guests have gone…'

'We most certainly will not,' she said, and snatched the box from his hands, popping open the lid.

Inside, lying on a bed of velvet, as though it came from the finest jeweller in London, was a tiny straw heart, threaded through with the same ribbon she had used for the Christmas ornaments.

He poked it with a finger. 'I fear I am not much good at braiding, although I have seen you do it often enough.

I worked for the better part of an afternoon, and the results are still quite sad. But I wanted to give you my heart on a string for Christmas. You have always had it, you know. But I did not truly miss it until you were gone. I am empty without you.'

She kissed him then, with an enthusiasm that took him quite by surprise. She was crushing the box between them, and further mangling his gift, not caring in the least whether it was crooked, or crude, as long as it came from her darling Harry.

He pulled away, catching his breath. 'It is all right, then?'

'It is the most perfect thing I have ever seen.' She picked up the ribbon and held it out to him. 'Put it on me—for I mean to wear it until Twelfth Night.'

He was embarrassed again. 'Not in front of the guests, surely?'

'Until you wish to take it off me again.' She gave him an inviting smile and rubbed her bare leg against his. He sighed happily in response, and took the necklace from her.

There was a knock at the door.

Which they ignored.

His hands were at the back of her neck, fumbling with the ribbon, but his lips were on her throat, warming the place where the straw was lying. She snuggled back into the wool of his jacket, squirming against him to distract him, until he had to start all over again and give her even more kisses while he re-tied the bow.

The knock came again—this time more insistent. And a polite clearing of the throat which, if it was to be heard through the heavy oak door, must have been as loud as a normal man's shout. It was followed by the butler's soft, 'Your lordship? I would not normally trouble you, sir. Under the circumstances… But this is urgent.'

Elise wondered what it could possibly be that should be deemed that important, and hoped it was nothing Rosalind had done. For one more evening the house must run itself, without her help.

Harry rolled his eyes and gave an exasperated groan. He answered, 'A moment, please.' Then he slipped out from under the jacket and covered her up again, struggling into trousers and shirt, going barefoot to the door. He tried the knob, and then remembered the key, still hot in the coals. 'Do you have your keys, Benton?' he muttered. 'You must open the door from your side. I will explain later. Or perhaps not.'

A moment later, there was a rattling of the lock, and the door opened far enough for the butler to proffer a piece of paper.

Harry took it, unfolded the thing, and read in silence for a moment before exploding with an oath. 'Damn the man. Damn him to hell. For that is where I will send him once I catch him. I cannot believe the audacity.'

'What is it, dear? Who do you mean to send to hell?' She could not help but smile when she looked at him.

'Your lover.' He glared down at her. 'I dare say you will be none too happy with him either. Tremaine has run off to Scotland. And he has taken my sister. I swear, Elise, this is outside of enough.' He slapped the note in his hand. '"Dear Harry—" And whenever have I been the least bit *dear* to the blighter? "—I wish you well in this happiest of seasons." Ha! "May it bring you a happy reunion with our beloved Elise." Our beloved? The nerve of the man... "Since my services are no longer needed, I must away. And since you no longer need Rosalind as hostess she means to join me. We travel north to Gretna Green, and then to warmer climes. Do not expect to hear from us until spring, for Rosalind craves more adventure than Shropshire can offer, and I do not wish to deny her. Merry Christmas. Your new brother, Tremaine."'

Harry shook the paper again, and then crumpled it in his fist. 'The bastard has stolen my sister.'

'Your half-sister,' Elise reminded him. 'Who, lest you have forgotten, is well of age, and should have married long before now.'

'But to Tremaine?' Harry made a face as though he was tasting something foul. 'Tremaine.' He shook his head and mouthed the name to himself again. 'Why must it be him?'

'I think that should be plain enough. They love each other.'

'Well, of course,' he spluttered. 'I have known that for years. But I thought he would at least have the decency to court her as he should, make an offer and wait for the banns to be read. Instead he has rushed my little sister over the border like some lust-crazed animal. And he has done it while she was in my care. What am I going to tell Morley? I suspect when he hears of this he will burst from apoplexy.' Harry considered for a moment. 'Which means that some good has come of it, I suppose.' He stared down at Elise. 'You are taking this surprisingly well.' And he smiled at her, in joy and relief, and forgot all about Rosalind.

Elise supposed she was. After all they had been through perhaps she *should* feel something other than joy at the prospect of Tremaine happily married to someone else. But she could not.

'It was time for Nicholas to marry as well. He is a dear man, but he can be a bit of a nuisance. Now that there is someone to watch out for him, his character will be much improved.' She leaned on her elbow and stared at her husband, the love of her life, and fingered the heart at her throat. She gave a theatrical sigh. 'While I cannot begrudge your sister her happiness, I confess that it makes me feel somewhat undesirable.'

'Never,' he breathed. 'Not while I live.'

She held out her arms to him as he walked back to her. 'Show me.'

* * * * *

A REGENCY
CHRISTMAS CAROL

With thanks and apologies to Charles Dickens. And a question. Why did the spirits do it 'all in one night' when Marley is so specific about needing three? That's always confused me.

Chapter One

December 1811

Barbara Lampett ran down the lane at the edge of the village of Fiddleton, feeling the crunch of icy mud beneath her feet and the stitch in her side from the cold air in her lungs. Lately it seemed that she was always running after something or other. She wondered if the lack of decorum on her part was the first sign of a life spun out of control.

It was really no fault of her own. Had she the choice, she'd have been in a seat by the parlour fire, staring out at the changing weather and pitying those forced to go about in it. But Father paid little heed to his own discomfort when he was in one of his moods, much less that of others.

And she could hardly expect her mother to go. Mother's volatile nature would add warmth to the day, but it would do nothing to cool her father's zeal. Nor was Mother young and strong enough to face the crowd that surrounded him when he spoke, or to extricate him from the hubbub he created.

The new mill lay almost two miles from the centre of the village. It was too short a distance to harness a carriage, but longer than a pleasant walk—especially on such a chill December day as this. Barbara found some consolation that the ground was frozen. She had decided to forgo pattens in favour of speed, but she did not wish to ruin the soft boots she wore by walking through mud.

And much mud there would have been if not for the cold. Ground that had once been green and lush was now worn down to the soil, with the comings and goings of wagons and goods, and the tramp of growing mobs that came to protest at the gates of the new buildings of Mr Joseph Stratford.

A crowd gathered here now. Another of the demonstrations that had been occurring almost daily thanks to her father's speeches. Mixed amongst the angry weavers were the curious townsfolk. They did not seem to care either way for the plight of the workers, but they enjoyed a good row and came to the gatherings as a form of entertainment.

There was a sudden blast of wind and she wrapped her shawl more tightly about her, unable to fight the feeling of dread that came with the exhilaration. While it pleased her to see the people attracted to her father's words, the path he was leading them down was a dangerous one and his actions dangerously unwise. With each passing day he seemed to grow more reckless, speaking from the heart and not the head. He could not seem to understand what his comments would do to the local populous.

But she could feel them, caught in the crowd as she was, buffeted by the bodies of angry and fearful men. There was a growing energy in the mob. Some day a chance word or a particularly virulent speech would push them too far. Then they would boil over into real violence.

When the wind blew from the east you could still smell the burned-out wreckage of the old mill, where so many of these men had been employed. That owner had paid dearly for his plans at renovation, seeing his livelihood destroyed and his family threatened until he had given up and quit the area. That had left the protestors with no work at all, and even angrier than they had been before.

It seemed the new master would be cagier. When he'd built his new mill, like the pig in the old story, he had used bricks. It loomed before her, a blight on the horizon. Every element was an insult to the community and proof that the person who had built it lacked sensitivity for his neighbours. It was large and squat and altogether too new. He had not built in the wreckage of Mackay's Mill, which might have given the people hope of a return to normality. Instead he'd placed it closer to the grand old house where he currently lived. It was not exactly in the front park of the manor, but plainly on the estate, and in a place by the river that the Clairemonts had allowed all in the village to use as common greensward when they'd lived there. It was obvious that Mr Stratford had thought of nothing but his own convenience in choosing this site.

Though he showed no signs of recognising the impropriety of the location, he'd built a fence around a place that had once been the home of picnics and fêtes, trampling the freshness to hard-packed mud. Barbara was convinced it demonstrated on some deep and silent level that the master of it knew he was in the wrong and expected to receive trouble for it. The wrought-iron border surrounding the yard separated it from the people most likely to be angry: the ones whose jobs had been taken by the new mechanised looms.

She pushed her way through the crowd to the place where her father stood at the foot of the stone gatepost, rallying the men to action. Though recent misfortune had addled his wits, it had done nothing to dull the fire in his eye or the clarity in his voice. While his sentiments might be unwise, there was nothing incoherent in the nature of his words.

'The Orders in Council have already depressed your trade to the point where there is no living to be made by an honest man—no way to sell your cloth to America and other friends of France.'

'Aye!'

There were shouts and mutters, and the brandishing of torches and axe handles in the crowd. Barbara's heart gave an uneasy skip at the thought of what might happen should any man think to bring a firearm into the already volatile situation. She was sure that the mill owner towards whom the ire was directed sat in the closed black carriage just behind the gates. From there he could listen to every word. Perhaps he was even noting the name of the speaker and any others preparing to act against him.

But her father cared nothing for it, and went on with his speech. 'The new looms mean less work for those of you left and more jobs falling to inexperienced girls, while their fathers and brothers sit idle, dreaming of days past when a respectable trade could be plied in this country.'

The mutterings in answer were louder now, and punctuated with shouts and a forward surge of bodies, making the gates rattle in response to the weight of the crowd.

'Will you allow the change that will take the bread from your children's mouths? Or will you stand?'

She waved her arms furiously at her father, trying to stall what was likely to occur. The government had been willing to use troops to put down such small rebellions, treating their own people as they would Boney's army. If her father incited the men to frame-breaking and violence they would be answered with violence in return. Mr Stratford might be as bad as her father claimed, but he was not the timid man Mackay had been. He would meet strife with strife, and send for a battalion to shoot the organisers.

'Father!' she shouted, trying to catch his attention. But the workers towered around her, and her voice was swallowed up by the din. Before she could speak a calming word the first shot rang out—not from the crowd, but from the door of the carriage in front of them. Even though it was fired into the air, the mob drew back a pace like a great animal, startled and cringing. Barbara was carried along with it, relieved all were safe and yet further from her goal.

The carriage door opened and Stratford appeared, leaping to the ground before his worried footman could help him and springing to the same stone post where her father stood. He climbed easily up the back of it until he stood at the top and towered over her father and the other men. He held what looked like a duelling pistol in his right hand. With his left he drew back his coat, so the crowd could see its mate was tucked into his belt. He looked like a corsair—nimble, fearless and ready for battle. Barbara could easily imagine him with a blade between his teeth, rushing the crowd.

She was just as sure that he would be the sort to take no prisoners. Though he was a handsome man, in a dark and hungry sort of way, there was nothing in his sharp features that bespoke a merciful nature. His grey eyes were hard and observant. His mouth, which might be capable of a sensual smile, was twisted in a sneer. Her father thought him the very devil, set upon the ruin of all around them.

But if devil he was then he was a handsome devil as well. Although she could think of a hundred reasons she should not notice it, she thought him a most attractive man. She schooled herself not to stare up with admiration, as she had caught herself doing on those few times she'd seen him in the village.

Perhaps she should have found him less impressive, for that sneer on his face quite spoiled the evenness of his features. While she had thought the position he took on the wall made him look taller than average, he hardly needed the advantage. He stood well over six feet. Today he was a fearsome thing, and nothing for a young lady to gawk at.

To match his physical presence he had the sort of forceful personality that seemed to incite strong emotion in friends as well as enemies. And, frightening though he might be, Barbara was sure that once she was focused on him she would not be able to look away.

'Who will be the first through the fence, then?' Stratford shouted down at the crowd. 'I swear to you, that man will lose his life along with his livelihood.'

The workers shrank back another pace, huddling against each other as though seeking warmth in the cold.

The man on the post laughed down at them. 'I thought as much. All bluff and bluster when there is no risk to you, and cowardice when there is.'

Her father turned, shouting up at him. 'It is you who are the coward, sir. Vain and proud as well. You hide behind your gates with your idle threats, unwilling to walk among the common man and feel his pain, his hunger, his desperation.'

Stratford glared back at him. 'I do not have to walk among you to know about you. I can go to the ruins of Mackay's place—a mill that you destroyed—to see the reason for your poverty. If you could, you would burn my factory as well—before I've even managed to open it. And then you'd complain that I'd treated you unjustly. I tell you now, since you have so conveniently gathered here, that I will not listen to your complaints until you begin making sense.'

It was unfair of him to compare this gathering to the burning of Mackay's place. Most of the men here had taken no part in that, rushing to save their workplace and not destroy it. The matter was much more complicated than Stratford made out. He was too new here to know and unwilling to listen, just as her father had said. Barbara pushed against the men around her, trying to work her way to the front again so that she might be heard.

Just as she thought she might reach her objective a man's boot caught in the hem of her gown and she started to fall forwards under the crush. She felt a rush of panic as she realised that no one around her was noticing as she fell. They had forgotten their fear of the second gun and were advancing to disprove Stratford's claims of cowardice.

She called out again, hoping that her father might hear and help her. But his back was to her as he shook a fist to threaten Stratford. He was too preoccupied to notice what was happening. In a moment she would be knocked to her knees. Then she would be dragged under, as though sinking beneath a human wave, and stamped into the mud in the trample of hobnailed boots.

'Ay-up!' She felt a sudden change, and the crowd parted around her. A hand caught her by the shoulder and yanked her to her feet with a rip of cloth. There was a shout as loud and ringing as her father's. But it came from close at her side, easily besting the noise of the crowd. 'Mind what you are doing, you great oafs. You may say what you like to me, but mind that there is a lady present. Have a care for her, at least. Perhaps I judge you unworthy of employment because you behave no better than animals.'

Then she was back on her feet, and the support was gone from her arm. She felt the crowd swirl around her again as her rescuer retreated. But for a moment there was a subdued quality to the actions of the mob, as though their frenzy had been defused by shame.

And the man who had saved her was back at the front of the group again, pushing past her father and climbing back onto the pillar that held the gate. She had thought Mr Stratford an intimidating figure even while behind the gates. But it was even more startling to have been so close to him, even for a moment. He had used his strength to force others out of the way, and his agility to be down to the ground and back up the fence before the mob had realised that he had been in their grasp. He was staring down at them again, his expression more disgusted than angry, as though they had proved to him that he was correct in his scorn.

'Go home to your families, if you care so much about them. A new year is coming, and a new age with it. You had best get used to it. When Stratford Mill is open in a month there will be work for those of you willing to put aside this nonsense and tend to your shuttles again. But if you rise against me I will see the lot of you transported and run it with your daughters. They will cost me less and have the sense to keep their tongues.' He reached towards his belt, and the group before him gasped. He withdrew not a pistol, but a purse, showering the coins into the crowd.

'A Merry Christmas to you all!' he shouted, his laugh both triumphant and bitter as he watched the threat dissolve as the crowd scrambled for the money. 'Do not bother to come here again. As long as I breathe, I will not be stopped. If you destroy the machinery I will get more, until you wear yourselves out with breaking it. Take my money and go back to your homes. I have summoned the constable. If you are here when he arrives you will spend Christmas Day in a cell, longing for your families. Now, be off.'

It shamed her to watch the men of the village too

busy on the ground to notice this new threat. They were a proud bunch. In better times they would have thrown the coins back in the face of this stranger rather than accept his charity and his scorn. But the recent economic troubles had left most of the village without work and in need of any money they might find to make any kind of a Christmas—merry or otherwise—for their families.

Her father's rallying cries were lost in the scuffle as men scrabbled in the dirt for pennies. Barbara pushed through them easily this time, until she could lay her hand upon her father's arm. 'Come away,' she whispered. 'Now. Before this goes any further. You can speak another day.'

It seemed the mood had left him, passing out of his body like a possessing spirit, leaving him quiet and somewhat puzzled, as though he did not quite know how he had come to be standing here in front of so many people. He would come away with little struggle, and she would have him home before the law arrived. All would be well. Until the next time.

Directly above her, and removed from the chaos, Joseph Stratford observed—distant and passionless, as though he did not know or care for the pain he was causing. When she looked at him all her father's anger and frustration seemed to rush into her. If the Lord had bothered to imbue her with reason, then why could he have not made her a man, so that other men might listen to her?

She turned and shouted up at the dark man who thought himself so superior to his fellows. 'You blame the men around me. But you should be ashamed of yourself as well. You stand over us, thinking yourself a god. You are mocking a level of hardship that you cannot possibly understand. You act as if you are made of the same rough wood and cold metal gears that fill your factory. If I could see the contents of your heart it would be nothing but clockwork, and fuelled by the coal running in your veins.'

Just for a moment she thought she saw a change in his face, a slight widening of the eyes as though her words had struck home. And then he gave a mirthless, soundless laugh, little more than a lifting and dropping of the shoulders. 'And a Merry Christmas to you as well, my dear.' Then he turned and stepped easily from his perch, dropping to the ground, though it must have been nearly eight feet, and strolling back to his carriage and his nervous grooms and coachman. They came cautiously forwards to open the gates so that the carriage could get through. They needn't have worried, for the men who had blocked the way had turned for home in embarrassed silence as soon as the money on the ground had been collected.

She pulled her father to the side of the road so that the horses could pass. But there was the signalling tap of a cane against the side of the box as the vehicle drew abreast of them, and the driver brought it to a stop so that Stratford could lean out of the window and look at them.

'This is not the end of it, Stratford,' her father said in a quieter voice. Now that the crowd was gone he sounded capable of lucid argument, and quite his old self.

'I did not think it was, Lampett,' Stratford replied, smiling coldly down at her father, staring into his eyes like a fighter measuring the reach of his opponent before striking.

'I will not let you treat these people—my people—like so many strings on your loom. They are men, not goods. They should be respected as such.'

'When they behave like men I will give them respect. And not before. Now, go. You have lost your audience, and your child is shivering in the cold.'

I am not a child. She was full four and twenty. Not that it mattered. But she *was* shivering—both from fear and the weather. The slight made her stand a little straighter, and fight the shudders until she could appear as collected and unmoved as her enemy was.

It did not seem to bother Joseph Stratford in the least that the weight of the entire town was against him. They had broken his frames once already and sabotaged the building of the mill at every turn. Still he persevered. Barbara wished she could respond in kind with that careless, untouchable indifference.

The envy bothered her. Perhaps—just a little—she appreciated the man's sense of purpose. However misguided it might be. When she looked at him she had no doubt that he would succeed. While her father was all fire, he flared and burned out quickly. But Stratford was like stone, unchanging and unmoved. It would take more than a flash of anger to move a man like him once he had set himself to a goal.

She looked again at him and reminded herself that he was proud as well. That sin would be his downfall if nothing else was. He could not succeed if he reduced all men to enemies and herself to a faceless, valueless child.

As she watched the two men, locked eye to eye in a silent battle, she was relieved that her father did not own a firearm. Though she thought she could trust Mr Stratford—just barely—not to shoot without provocation, there was no telling what her father might do when his blood was up and his thinking even less clear than usual. She reached out for her father's arm again, ready to guide him home. 'Come. Let us go back. There is nothing more that you can do today. If he has truly called for the constable, I do not wish to see you caught up in it.'

He shook off the embrace with a grunt and stepped back, giving an angry shrug as the carriage moved again, travelling up the road to the manor house. 'It would serve him right if I was arrested. Then the world would see him for the sort of man he is: one who would throw an old man into jail to prove himself in the right.'

There was no point in explaining that the only lesson

anyone was likely to see was that Stratford sat in a
mansion at a fine dinner, while Lampett sat hungry in
a cell. 'But it would make me most unhappy, Father,'
she said as sweetly as possible. 'And Mother as well.
If we can have nothing else for Christmas, can we not
have a few days of peace?'

'I will be peaceful when there is reason to be,' her
father acceded. 'I doubt, as long as that man breathes,
we will see that state again.'

Chapter Two

Joseph Stratford rode home alone in comfortable, if somewhat pensive, silence. The conclusion to today's outing had been satisfactory, at least for now. The crowd had dispersed without any real violence. But if Bernard Lampett continued stirring, the town was likely to rise against him. Before that happened sterner measures would need to be taken.

In his mind, he composed the letter he would send to the commander of the troops garrisoned in York. It was drastic, but necessary. If one or two of them were hauled off in chains it might convince the rest of the error of their ways.

His carriage pulled up the circular drive of Clairemont Manor and deposited him at the door—so close that the chill of the season barely touched him on his way into the house. He smiled. How different this was from his past. Until last year he'd frequently had to make do on foot. But in the twelve months his investments had turned. Even with the money he'd laid out for the new mill he was living in a luxury that he would not have dreamed possible in his wildest Christmas wishes.

Joseph handed hat, gloves and overcoat to the nearest footman and strode into the parlour to take the cup of tea waiting for him by the second-best chair near the fire. As he passed the closest seat he gave a gentle kick at the boot of the man occupying it, to get Robert Breton to shift his feet out of the way.

Breton opened a sleepy eye and sat up. 'Trouble at the mill?'

'When is there not?' He lifted his cup in a mock salute and Breton accepted it graciously, as though *he* owned the house and the right to the chair he usurped. While Joe might aspire to knock away at his own rough edges, affect the indolent slouch and copy the London accent and the facile gestures, he would never be more than false coin compared to this second son of an earl. Bob had been born to play lord of the manor, just as Joe had been born to work. He might own the house, but it was Bob's birthright to be at ease there.

And that was what made him so damned useful—both as a friend and an investor. The Honourable Robert Breton opened doors that the name Joseph Stratford never would, and his presence in negotiations removed some of the stink of trade when Joseph was trying to prise capital from the hands of his rich and idle friends.

Joseph took another sip of his tea. 'Lampett has been giving mad speeches again—raising the population to violence. Lord knows why Mackay did not run him off before now, instead of allowing himself to be scared away. He might have nipped the insurrection in the bud, and his business would still be standing.'

Breton shrugged. 'Anne tells me that Lampett was not always thus. There was some accident when the men fought the mill fire. He has not been right in the head since.'

'More's the pity for him and his family,' Joe replied. 'If he does not leave off harassing me he will be the maddest man in Australia by spring.'

'Anne seems quite fond of him,' Breton said. 'Until they closed the school he was a teacher in the village and a respected member of the community.'

Joseph reminded himself to speak to Anne on the subject himself, if only so that he might say he had. It did not seem right that one's best friend got on better with one's prospective fiancée than one did oneself. But Bob and Anne enjoyed each other's company—perhaps because Bob was able to converse comfortably on subjects other than the price of yard goods and the man hours needed to produce them.

'If Anne respects him, then she has not seen him lately. From what I have observed he is not fit company for a lady. There was a girl at the riot today who must have been his daughter, trying to drag him home and out of trouble. She came near to being trampled by the crowd and Lampett did not notice the danger to her. I rescued her myself, and did not get so much as a thank-you from either of them.'

'Was this before or after you threatened to have the father arrested?' Breton asked dryly.

'In between threats, I think.' Stratford grinned.

Breton shook his head. 'And you wonder why you are not loved.'

'They will all love me well enough once the mill is open and they are back to work.'

'If there is work to be had,' Breton said. 'The Orders in Council limit the places you can sell your wares. As long as America is a friend of France, there is little you can do.'

'They will be repealed,' Joseph said firmly.

'And what if they are not?'

'They will be. They must be. The merchants are near at breaking point now. The law must change or we are all ruined.' Joseph smiled with reassurance, trying to imbue confidence in his faint-hearted friend. 'It will not do to hesitate. We cannot err on the side of caution in this darkest time. If we wish for great profit we must be more sure, more daring, more active than the others. A busy mill and a full warehouse are the way to greatest success. When the moment comes it will come on us suddenly. Like the handmaidens at the wedding, we must be ready for change.'

Breton shook his head in wonder. 'When you tell me this I have no trouble believing.'

'Then take the message to heart and share it with your friends.' Joseph glanced out of the window at weather that was slate grey and yet lacking the snow he wished for. 'When we have them here for Christmas I will wrap them tight in a web of good wine and good cheer. Then you shall explain the situation, as I have to you. Once they are persuaded, I will stick my hand into their pockets and remove the money needed for expansion.'

Breton laughed. 'You make me feel like a spider, waiting for so many fat flies to ride up from London.'

'But that is not the case at all, my dear fellow. I am the spider. You are the bait—if spiders use such a thing. Without you, they will not come.'

'We will be lucky if they come at all. Here in Yorkshire you are quite far out of the common way, Stratford.'

'And you are the son of the Earl of Lepford. There must be a few in London, particularly those with eligible daughters, who would be eager to spend a holiday in your august presence.'

'Second son,' Breton corrected. 'No title to offer them. But I am rich, at least. In much part I can thank you for that.'

'Be sure to inform your guests of the fact, should the opportunity present itself.'

Breton made a face. 'Talking of money at a Christmas house party is just not done. They will not like it if they get wind of your scheme, Joe.'

'That is why you will do it subtly—as you always do, Bob. They will hardly know what has happened. You may apologise to them for my lack of manners and let them plunder my cellars to the last bottle. Talk behind your hand about me, if you wish. Dance the pretty girls around the parlour while I am left to their fathers. They will think me common at the start. But by the time I leave I will have their cheques in my pocket. To one in business, Christmas must be a day like any other. If your friends wish to invest in this new venture they will see a substantial return to make their next Christmas a jolly one.'

The door opened, and the housekeeper, Mrs Davy, entered, with an apology for the interruption and a footman carrying a large armful of greenery. As he began swagging bows from the mantel, Joseph stood and quizzed the woman, ticking things off the list in his head as he was satisfied that they had been taken care of.

'Everything must be in perfect order,' he said firmly. 'While nearly every mill owner in the district has had some problems with frame-breakers and followers of Ludd, it would reflect poorly on me if my guests see a lack of control over my own household. I cannot fault the cleaning you have done, for I would swear you've scrubbed the house with diamonds it sparkles so.'

The housekeeper bobbed her head in thanks, and showed a bit of a blush. But his praise was no less than the truth. Everywhere he went he could smell the beeswax that had been worked into the oak panelling 'til it reflected the light from multitudes of candles and fires with a soft golden glow.

'And the larder has been stocked as well, I trust?'

'It was difficult,' Mrs Davy said modestly. 'There was little to be had in the shops.'

'You sent to London, as I requested?'

She nodded.

'There is no shortage of food in the city, nor shortage of people with money to buy it. My friends from the South will not understand the problems here, and nor do they wish to be enlightened of them. If they come all this way to visit me, I mean to see that their bellies are filled and their hearts light.' He grinned in anticipation. 'And their purses emptier at the end of the trip.'

The housekeeper's smile was firm, if somewhat disapproving. 'They shall eat like lords.' She passed him the menus she had prepared. 'If you will but select the meals, Mr Stratford.'

Given the bounty she presented, it was impossible to make a choice. He frowned. 'There must be goose, of course, for those who favour it. But I would prefer roast beef—and lots of it. With pudding to sop up the gravy. Swedes, peas, sprouts.' He pointed from one paper to the other. 'Roasted potatoes. Chestnuts to roast beside the Yule Log. And plum pudding, Christmas cake, cheese…'

'But which, sir?' the housekeeper asked.

'All of them, I should think. Enough so that no one

will want, no matter what their preference. It is better to have too much than too little, is it not?'

'If we have too much, sir, it will go to waste.' From the way she pursed her lips he could tell that he was offending her to the bottom of her frugal Northern heart.

'If it does, I can afford the loss. A show of economy in front of these investors will be seen as a lack of confidence. And that is something I will not be thought guilty of.' He paced past her, down the great hall, watching the servants tidying, examining ceilings and frames with a critical eye and nodding with approval when he found not a speck of dust. 'All is in order. And, as just demonstrated, you have seen to the greenery.'

'There are still several rooms to be decorated,' she admitted. 'But some must be saved for the kissing boughs.'

'Tear down some of the ivy on the south wall. There is still some green left in it, and the windows are choked to point that I can barely see without lighting candles at noon. With that, you should be able to deck the whole of the inside of the house. Clip the holly hedge as well. Trim it back and bring it in.' He gave a vague sweep of his hand. 'Have them search the woods for mistletoe. I want it all. Every last bit of the house smelling of fir and fresh air. Guests will begin to arrive tomorrow, and we must be all in readiness for them.'

'Yes, sir.'

From behind him, Breton laughed. 'You are quite

the taskmaster, Stratford. Lord help the workers in your mill if this is the way you behave towards them.'

'I mean to master you as well, Bob. I will expect you to get up from your chair to help lead the games.'

Breton looked stricken at the prospect. 'Me, Stratford?'

'Of course. They are your friends. You will know what it takes to entertain them.'

'I don't think it is my place.' The man was almost physically backing away from the task. 'You are the host, after all.'

'I am that in name only,' Joseph insisted. 'I can manage to pay the piper, of course. But in God's name, man, do not expect me to dance to the tune. There has been little time for that in my life, and I never got the knack of it. I fear I am much better with machines than with people.'

'But I...' Breton shook his head. 'I am not the best person to stand at the head of the set for you.'

'At best, all they want from me is a hearty meal and a full punchbowl. At worst, they are coming to gawk at what a common mess I am likely to make of a grand old house. They would do without me if they could. For I am—' he made a pious face '—*in trade*. Too humble by half for the people who have invested in me. But the money draws them like flies. Everyone wants their little bit of sugar, Bob. We will provide it for them. Though they sneer into their cups as they drink my wine, they will not be too proud to swallow it.'

'But must I be a part of it? If they do not want you, then surely...?'

'You are one of them,' Joe said firmly. 'I will never be. I am lucky to have won over Clairemont, and will have his daughter to dance with, of course. If she means to accept my suit then she had best get used to being seen with me. The rest of the ladies I leave to you.'

'And what am I to do with them?' For all his town bronze, Bob could be obtuse when he wished to be.

'Smile at them. Flatter them. Keep their glasses filled. You could do worse than following my example and taking a wife, you know. Oaksley has three daughters, from what I understand. Perhaps one of them will do for you.'

There was also the daughter of that firebrand in the village. She had not been invited to the festivities. It would show a considerable lack of wisdom to have that man and his family here, to undermine his success. But she would be a fine match for Bob. She was both pretty and intelligent, and a gentleman's daughter as well. She was more respectable than he himself would have aspired to be just a few short years ago. Miss Lampett would be perfect for his friend in every way. Although now that the opportunity presented itself to suggest a meeting, Joseph found himself strangely unwilling to voice his thoughts.

'I have no intention of marrying,' Bob said firmly. 'Not now. Not ever.'

'Then take advantage of some more earthly

pleasures,' Joseph said, oddly relieved. 'There will be enough of that as well, I am sure. I've heard that Lindhurst's wife rarely finds her own room after a night of revels. I hope I do not have to explain the rest for you. Avail yourself of my hospitality as well. Eat, drink and be merry.'

For tomorrow we die.

Joseph shuddered. He was sure he had not finished the quote. But he'd heard the words so clearly in his head that he'd have sworn they'd been intoned aloud, and in a voice that was not his.

'Stratford?' Bob was staring at him as though worried.

'Nothing. A funny turn, that's all.' He smiled in reassurance for, though he liked the idea of socialising with strangers no better than Bob, he could not let his nerve fail him. 'As I was saying. I expect you here and making merry for the whole of the week. I mean to keep my nose to the grindstone, of course. But we have made a success of this venture, and you should be allowed to take some pleasure in it. There is more to come in the New Year. Now is the time to play.'

Chapter Three

〜〜〜✦〜〜〜

That evening, as ever, Joseph's trip to his own bedroom was a little disquieting. Much as he knew that he owned the house, he did not really feel it suited him. It was beautiful, of course. But at night, when the servants had settled in their quarters and it was mostly him alone, he walked the wide corridors to reassure himself that it existed outside of his boyhood fantasies of success.

The place was too large, too strange and too old. It would not do to let anyone—not even Breton—know how ill at ease he was, or that this late-night walk was a continual reminder of how far from his birth and true station he had come.

It was not as if a pile of stones could come to life and cast him out. It was his, from cellar to attic. He had paid for it and had got a good price. But when it was dark and quiet, like this, Clairemont Manor felt—for want of a better word—haunted. Not that he believed in such things. In an age of machines there was hardly room for spirits. Clinging to childish notions and common superstition bespoke a lack of confidence that he would not allow himself.

With a wife and children in it, the house would fill with life and he would have no time for foolish fancies. But since the wife he was in the process of acquiring rightly belonged here, it sometimes felt as though he was trying to appease them rather than banish them. Setting Anne Clairemont at the foot of the table would restore the balance that had been lost. It had been her father's house, whether he'd been able to afford to keep it or not. Returning a member of the family to the estate, even if it *was* a female, might pacify some of the ill feelings he had created in the area. It fell in nicely with his plans for the business. There was nothing superstitious about it.

It was a pity the girl was so pale and lifeless. Had he the freedom to choose a woman to suit himself, it would certainly not be her. He'd have sought someone with a bit more spirit, not some brainless thing willing to auction herself to the highest bidder just to please her father.

He'd have wanted—

He stopped in his tracks, smiling to himself at the memory. He'd have wanted one more like the girl he'd seen in the crowd today. Fearless, that one was. Just like her father, that barmy Bernard Lampett who led the rebellion against him. What was the girl's name?

Barbara, he thought, making a note to enquire and be sure. She did not seem totally in sympathy with her father, from the way she'd tried to drag him away. But neither did she support Joseph, having made it quite clear that she disapproved of him. Barbara Lampett knew her own mind, that was certain. And she had no fear of showing the world what she thought of it.

But it wasn't her sharp tongue that fascinated him. She was shorter than Anne, curved where Anne was straight, and pink where his prospective fiancée was pale. When he'd been close to her, he'd seen a few freckles on her turned-up nose, and handfuls of brown curls trying to escape from her plain bonnet.

But it was her eyes that had drawn him in. Her gaze had been cool and direct, like blue ice, cutting into him in a way that simple anger could not. She judged him. It made him doubt himself. For could any cause be wholly in the right if it might result in harm to such a lovely thing as a Barbara Lampett, tramping her casually into the dirt? While he was sure he bore a greater share of the right than the men who stood against him, the truth of what might have happened to her, had he not intervened, weighed heavy on his conscience.

And so tonight he walked the halls more slowly than usual, thinking dark thoughts and counting the many rooms as though they were rosary beads. If the servants had noticed this ritual, they were too polite or well trained to comment. But he found himself taking the same path each night before retiring, as though he were touring someone else's great house and marvelling at their wealth. Reception room the first, library, breakfast room, dining room, private salon, stairs, reception room the second, card room, music room, ballroom. And then a climb to the second floor: red bedroom, blue bedroom, master bedroom... There was a third floor as well, and servants' rooms, larders, kitchens and possibly some small and useful places he had not bothered to investigate.

It was a sharp contrast to his childhood. When it had been but one room they'd lived in there had been no reason to count. As his father's business had grown, so had the rooms. A three-room flat. A five-room cottage. A house. They had risen from poverty in the days long before the war, when trade was unobstructed and money easier. But the successes had been small, and the work hard and unpleasant. He had hated it.

He had broken from it, rebuilt the work in his own image. And now he lived in the grandest house in the county—and was not happy here either. Perhaps that was his curse: to hurry through life reaching for the next great thing, whether it be invention or business. Each time he succeeded he would be sure that this time he had gained enough to please himself. Then the success would pale and he would seek more.

The thought left him chilled, and he felt the unease that seemed to stalk him through these halls. He remembered again the eyes of Barbara Lampett, who could see through him to his clockwork heart. It made him

want to grab her and prove that his blood flowed just as
hot as other men's, and perhaps a little warmer for the
sight of her. If the girl were the daughter of any other
man in the village he'd have at least attempted a flirtation. But she was too young and too much of a lady to
understand the discreet dalliance he had in mind. Even
if she was of a more liberal nature it would not do to
have her thinking that sharing her charms might lead
him to show mercy on her father.

While he might consider offering a bijou, or some
other bit of shiny to a pretty girl, something about Barbara Lampett's freckled nose and the sweet stubbornness of her jaw convinced him that she was likely to
bargain for the one thing that he was not willing to
share: clemency for the man who plotted his undoing.

He shook his head, rejecting the notion of her as the
long-case clock in the hall struck twelve and he opened
the door to his room. To be sure he would not weaken,
it was best to leave all thoughts of her here in the corridor, far away from his cold and empty bed.

'Boy.'

Joseph started at the sound of a voice where there
should have been nothing but the crackle of the fire and
perhaps the sounds of his valet laying out a nightshirt.
The opulence of the room, the richness of its hangings
and upholstery, always seemed to mute even the most
raucous sound.

But the current voice cut through the tranquillity
and grated on the nerves. The familiar Yorkshire accent

managed to both soothe and annoy. The volume of it was so loud that it echoed in the space and pressed against him—like a hand on his shoulder that could at any moment change from a caress to a shove.

He looked for the only possible if extremely unlikely source, and found it at the end of the bed. For there stood a man he'd thought of frequently but had not seen for seven years. Not since the man's death.

'Hello, Father.' It was foolish to speak to a figment of his imagination, but the figure in the corner of his bedroom seemed so real that it felt rude not to address it.

It must be his distracted mind playing this trick. Death had not changed his da in the least. Joseph had assumed that going on to his divine reward would have softened him in some way. But it appeared that the afterlife was as difficult as life had been. Jacob Stratford was just as grim and sullen as he'd been when he walked the earth.

'What brings you back? As if I have to ask myself... It was that second glass of brandy, on top of the hubbub at the mill.' When he'd rescued the Lampett girl he'd been literally rubbing shoulders with the same sort of man as the one who had raised him. The brutal commonality of them had attached itself to his person like dust, sticking in his mind and appearing now, as he neared sleep.

'That's what you think, is it?' The ghost gave a disapproving grunt. 'I see you have not changed a bit from the time you were a boy.' Then he ladled his speech thick with the burr that Joseph had heard when he was in the midst of the crowd around his mill. 'Th'art daft as a brush, though th' live like a lord.'

'And I will say worse of you,' Joseph replied, careful to let none of his old accent creep back into his speech. No matter what his father might say of him, he had changed for the better and he would not go back. 'You are a stubborn, ignorant dictator. Two drinks is hardly a sign of debauchery. And I live in a great house because I can afford to. It is not as if I am become some noble who has a line of unpaid credit with the vintner. I pay cash.' He'd been told by Bob that the habit was horribly unfashionable, and a sign of his base birth, but he could not seem to break himself of it. It felt good to lie down knowing that, though he might need investors for the business, he had no personal debts.

Although why his rest was now uneasy he could not tell. The bad dream staring him down from the end of the bed must be a sign that all was not right in his world.

His father snorted in disgust. 'No matter what I tried to teach, you've proved that buying and selling is all you learned. You know nothing of art, of craft or the men behind the work.'

'If the men behind the work are anything like you, then I think I've had enough of a lesson, thank you. You may go as well.' He made an effort to wake and cast off the dream. To be having this conversation at all was proof that he was sleeping. To rouse from slumber would divest the vision of the last of its power.

His father gave a tug on his spectral forelock. 'Well, then, Your Lordship, I am put in my place. I hope by now you know that you don't fit with the posh sort that you suck up to. You are as much of a dog to be kicked from their path as I am to you.'

'Probably true,' Joseph admitted. There was no point in lying about that, even to himself. Though the gentry might be forced to mix with those in trade, there was nothing to make them enjoy it. 'But if I am a dog, then I am a young pup with many years ahead of me. Their time is ending, just as yours did. In the day that is coming men of vision will be rewarded.'

'At the expense of others,' his father replied.

'Others can seize this opportunity and profit as well, if they wish to,' Joe snapped back. 'It is not my responsibility to see to the welfare of every man on the planet. They had best look out for themselves.'

'That is no better than I expected from you,' his father replied. 'And not good enough. Believe me, boy, I can see from this side of the veil that it is not nearly enough. It is no pleasant thing to die with regrets, to have unfinished business when your life is spent and to know that you have failed in the one thing you should have profited at: the care of another human life.'

The statement made the speaker uncomfortably real. It was most unlike anything in Joseph's own mind. It sounded almost like an apology. And never would he have put those words in his father's mouth—no matter how much he might have wished to hear them. If things went as planned Joseph would be a father soon enough. It would not take much effort on his part to do a better job of it than his father had done with him.

'You would know better than I on that, I am sure. As of this time, I have no one under my care. I answer only to myself, and I am happy with that.' Surreptitiously he made a fist and dug his nails into his palm, pinching the skin to let the pain start him awake.

'Boy, you are wrong.'

'So you always told me, Father. Although why I should dream of your voice now, I do not know. I have only to wake up and look around me to prove that I am doing quite well for myself.' Although, thinking on it, he could not seem to recall having fallen asleep in the first place. But it was the only explanation for this. He was not in the habit of conversing with ghosts.

He was sound asleep in this bed and having a dream. No. He was having a nightmare. If he could not manage to wake, he must try to go to a deep, untroubled rest where his father would not follow. To encourage the change he sat upon the edge of the bed and began to undress himself. While it seemed strange to do so during a dream, he could think of no other way to set things right.

As he leaned forwards to pull off his boots his father stepped closer and brought with him the smell of the grave—damp earth, a faint whiff of decomposition and the chill of a cold and lifeless thing made even colder by the season. 'Do not think to ignore me. You do so at your peril.'

'Do I, now?' Joseph could not help it and stole a glance up at the spirit—if that was what it was. And he wondered when he had ever had a dream this real. He could smell and feel, as well as hear and see. He had to struggle to keep himself from reaching out to touch the shroud that the man in front of him carried like a mantle draped over his bony arm. He stared at the ghost, willing it to disappear. 'I ignored you in life as best I could. Because of it I gave you enough money to die in comfort, instead of bent over a loom. But that was years ago. Go back to where you have been and leave me in peace.'

'You do not have peace, if you would be honest and see the truth. Just as it always was when you were a boy, you are careless. You have not attended to both the warp and the weft. The tension is uneven. You have done much, and done it quickly with your fancy machines. But your work is without shape.'

Joseph glared into the hollow eyes before him, too angry at the slight to stay silent. 'I bore enough of that needless criticism from you when you lived—trying to teach me to weave when it was clear I had no skill for it. The last piece of work you will ever see me make on an old-fashioned loom was the shroud I buried you in. I wove it on your old machine with my own hands. I made it out of wool in respect for custom and your trade. If you have come to me to complain of the quality, then go back to your grave without it. As for my current life—there is no basis for this criticism. I can measure my success by my surroundings. This Christmas I will have a house full to the brim with guests and a table creaking with bounty. I have a new mill. When it opens I will be able to afford to fill the warehouse with goods, ready to ship when the sanctions are lifted.'

The ghost shook his head, as though all the achievement was nothing, and waved the shroud before him. 'Shapeless. Tear it out. Tear it out before it is too late. Your grain is off, boy.'

Joseph finished with his undressing and pulled a nightshirt over his head. Then he lay down on the bed with his arms stiff at his sides, fighting to keep from stuffing his fingers in his ears. He could hear the old man's death rattle of a breath, along with the same repeated criticisms that had tortured him all through his failed apprenticeship.

Then he thought of the girl who had been clinging to Bernard Lampett's arm in front of the mill. Her difficulties with her father had raised these memories in him. He felt a sympathy with her. And, for all his convictions that there could be no mercy shown, he would not rest easy until he had found a peaceful solution.

He looked at the shade of his father again, half hoping that it had evaporated now that he'd found the probable cause. But it was still there, as stern and disapproving as ever he had been. 'If you are my own guilty conscience, the least you could have done,' Joseph said, 'was come to me in the form of Barbara Lampett. And I'd be much more likely to listen if you told me plainly what you wanted.'

The ghost looked at him as though he was both stupid and a disappointment. It was a familiar look. 'It will not go well for you if you persist in talking nonsense. I came here hoping to spare you what is soon to come. My time is wasted, for you are as stubborn as you were right up 'til the day I died.'

'You? Spare me?' Joseph laughed. 'When did you ever wish to spare me anything? It was I who saved myself, and none other. I used my own brain and my own hands to make sure that I did not live as you did. And I succeeded at it.'

The ghost looked troubled, but only briefly. 'My goal is not to make you into myself. I was a hard man in life. A good craftsman, but a poor father.'

'Thank you for admitting the fact now that it is years too late,' Joseph snapped, annoyed that his mind would choose his precious free hours to remind him of things he preferred to forget.

'I bear the punishment of my errors even now. But my goal was to make you something more.' The ghost pointed with a pale, long-fingered hand that in life had been nimble with a shuttle. 'Here you are—proof that my job was not done. You are less than you should be. You are certainly less than you must be. That is why you must tear out what you have done. Tear out the work and start again, while you are able. It is not too late to go back. Find the mistake and fix it. Start again, before tomorrow night, or face another visitor.'

'I have no intention of destroying the work of a lifetime to please some niggling voice in my own mind that will be gone in the morning.' He pulled up the coverlet and waved a hand. 'Now, go, sir. Come again as some more interesting dream. You do not frighten me, though I will be glad to see you gone. Bring the girl instead.'

He smiled at the thought. If he could choose a bedtime fantasy, she was better than most. Then he pulled the sheet over his head and rolled away from the figure, trying to ignore the strange green glow that seemed to seep through his closed eyelids. What sort of dream remained even after one ceased to look at it?

One that could still speak, apparently. His father's voice came from just above him, unbothered by his ignoring of it. It was louder now, and Joseph had his first moment's fright, thinking if he pulled the blankets away he might find himself inches away from a corpse—close enough to choke on the smell of rotting flesh and see the waxy vacancy of a dead man's eyes.

'Very well, then. It is as was feared. You will not listen to me. Be warned, boy. If you have a brain, you will heed before Christmas Eve. From here, I can see what is coming, and I would not wish that—even on you.'

'Thank you so much, Father, for such a cold comfort.' Joseph snuggled down into the pillow.

'There will be three before Christmas. Look for the first when the clock chimes one tomorrow. If you have any sense you will heed them, before it is too late.'

Joseph laughed into the bedclothes. 'You mean to ruin my sleep between here and Christmas, I suppose? And destroy every last pleasure I take in this holiday. Only *you* would be trying to visit me with dire predictions on this of all weeks. Come back after Twelfth Night and perhaps I shall care.'

'Sir?'

Joseph opened his eyes.

The voice was not that of his father but of his valet, who sounded rather worried. 'Were you speaking to me, Mr Stratford? For I did not quite catch…'

When he pulled back the covers the candles were still lit and there was no sign of the eldritch glow he had been trying to shut out, nor the figure that had cast it. 'No, Hobson. It was only a dream. I was talking in my sleep, I think.' It must have been that. He had come back to his room and dozed, spinning a wild fancy without even bothering to blow out the light.

His valet was standing in a litter of clothes, looking around him with disapproval. 'If you were tired, you had but to ring and I would have come immediately to assist you.' Hobson picked the jacquard waistcoat from off the floor, smoothing the wrinkles from it and hanging it in the wardrobe.

'I was not tired,' Joseph insisted. Although he must have been. Why had he been dreaming? Though he could remember each piece of clothing as he'd dropped it on the floor, he could not seem to manage to remember falling asleep at any point—dressed or otherwise.

'Then might I bring you a warm drink before bed? A brandy? A posset? In keeping with the season, Cook has mulled some wine.'

'No, thank you. No spirits before bed, I think.' At least not like the one he'd had already.

There will be three.

He looked to the valet. 'Did you say something just now?'

'I offered wine…' The man was looking at him as though he was drunk.

'Because I thought I heard…' Of course he was sure that he had not heard Hobson speak. It had been his father's voice for certain, come back to repeat his warning. Although, looking around the room, he could see no sign of a spectre. 'Did you hear a voice?'

The valet was looking behind him, about the empty room. Then he looked back at his master, struggling to keep the worry from his face. 'No, sir. Just the two of us conversing.'

Joseph gave a laugh to mask the awkward moment. 'I must be more tired than I thought. Pay me no mind. And no wine tonight, please. A few hours' untroubled rest is all I need.'

But if there were to be another evening such as this one he doubted that serenity would be a quality it possessed.

Chapter Four

In the little corner of the Lampett kitchen set aside as a still room, Barbara inhaled deeply and sighed. After the ruckus of yesterday it was comforting to be home again, immersed in the sights and scents and sounds of Christmas preparation. There were mince pies cooling on a shelf beside the pudding bowl, and the makings for a good bowl of punch set aside against any guests they might have between now and Twelfth Night. Before her she'd arranged what fragrant ingredients she could find—dried rose petals and lavender, cloves, the saved rinds of the year's oranges and handfuls of pine needles to refill pomanders and refresh sachets in recently tidied closets and drawers.

She glanced down at her apron, pleased to see that there were few marks on it to reveal the labours of the day. Everything spoke of order, cleanliness and control. She smiled. All was as it should be, and as she liked it.

Suddenly the back door burst open and her mother rushed into the room, dropping the empty market basket and looking hurriedly around her.

Barbara stood, fearing the worst. 'What has happened?'

'Your father? Is he here with you?'

'No. He was in the parlour, reading his paper. I've heard nothing unusual.' Barbara rushed to the kitchen door, opening it and staring into the empty front room.

'On the way to the village I passed Mrs Betts. She had seen him heading towards the mill. He was carrying the axe.'

Barbara stripped off her apron, pushing past her mother to grab a shawl and bonnet from pegs by the door. 'I will go. You stay here. Do not worry. Whatever he is up to, I will put a stop to it before any real damage is done.'

There could be little question as to what he meant to do if he had taken a tool of destruction. The papers were full of reports from other villages of the frame-breakers—followers of Ned Ludd got out of hand—destroying machinery. And of mill owners dead in their beds or at their factories by violence. While there was much that annoyed her about Mr Stratford, he hardly deserved death.

It might go hard for her family if her father was left unchecked. He could well lose his freedom over this—or his life. She thought of the pistol in Stratford's hand the previous day. His first shot had been fired into the air. If he felt himself sufficiently threatened he might aim lower, and her father would be the one to suffer for it.

She ran down the path from the Lampett cottage, forgoing the road and heading cross-country over the patch of moor that separated the mill from the village. She splashed through the shallow stream, feeling the icy water seeping into her shoes and chilling her feet near to freezing, making her stumble as she came up the bank. The thorns in the thicket tore at her skirts and her hem was muddy, the dress practically ruined.

It was a risky journey. But if she wished to catch her father before he did harm she must trust that the ground was solid enough that she would not be sucked down into the peat before she reached her destination. Even the smallest delay might cost her dearly.

When she reached the front gate to Stratford's mill she found it chained and locked. She wondered if Mr Stratford had left it thus, or if her father had gone through and then locked it behind him, the better to do his mischief in privacy. For a moment she imagined Joseph Stratford, working unawares in the office as an assailant crept stealthily up behind him, axe raised…

She threw herself at the wrought-iron bars, crying out a warning, shaking them and feeling no movement under her hands. And then she was climbing, using the crossbars and the masonry of the wall to help her up. Mr Stratford had made it look simple when he had climbed to face the crowd. But he had not done so in a sodden dress and petticoats. She struggled under the weight of them, stumbling as she reached the top. What she'd hoped would be a leap to the ground on the inside was more of a stagger and a fall, and she felt something in her ankle twist and give as she landed.

It slowed her, but she did not stop, limping the last of the way to the wide back entrance. She passed through the open dock, where the vans and carts would bring materials and take away the finished goods, through the high-ceilinged storeroom waiting to hold the finished bolts of cloth. She passed the boiler room and the office and counting house, which were quiet and empty, and continued on to the floor of the factory proper, with its row upon row of orderly machinery, still new and smelling of green wood and machine oil.

From the far side of the big room she heard voices. Her father's was raised in threat. Mr Stratford's firm baritone answered him. The two men stood facing each other by the wreckage of a loom. Her father's axe was raised, and the look in his eyes was wild.

Stratford must have been disturbed in working with the machinery. He was coatless, the collar of his shirt open and its sleeves rolled up and out of the way, with a leather apron tied around his waist and smudged with grease. In one hand he held a hammer. Though his arm was lowered, Barbara could see the tensed muscles that told her he would use it in defence when her father rushed him.

'Hello?' she called out. 'What are you doing, Father? I have come to take you home for dinner.'

'Go home yourself, gel, for you do not need to see what is like to occur.' Father's voice was coarse, half-mad and dismissive. There was nothing left of the soft, rather pedantic tone she knew and loved.

'Your father is right, Miss Lampett. It is unnecessary for you to remain. Let we gentlemen work this out between us.' Stratford sounded calm and reassuring, though the smile he shot in her direction was tight with worry. His eyes never left the man in front of him. 'You will see your father directly.'

'Perhaps I will,' she answered. 'In jail or at his funeral. That is how this is likely to end if I allow it to continue.' She hobbled forwards and stepped between them. And between axe and hammer as well, trusting that neither was so angry as to try and strike around her.

'Miss Lampett,' Stratford said sharply. 'What have you done to yourself? Observe, sir, she is limping. Assist me and we will help her to a chair.' He sounded sincerely worried. But she detected another note in his voice as well, as though he was seizing on a welcome distraction.

'My Lord, Barbara, he is right. What have you done to yourself now?'

Her father dropped his axe immediately, forgetting his plans, and came to take her arm. Sometimes these violent spells passed as quickly as they came. This one had faded the moment he had recognised her injury.

Stratford had her other elbow, but she noticed the handle of his hammer protruding from an apron pocket, still close by should he need a weapon.

'I fell when climbing down from the gate. I am sure it is nothing serious.' Though the pain was not bad, and she could easily have managed for herself, she exaggerated the limp and let the two men work together to bear her forwards towards a chair.

'The front gate?' Stratford said in surprise. 'That is nearly eight feet tall.'

Her father laughed, as though lost in a happier time. 'My Barb always was a spirited one as a youngster. Constantly climbing into trees and taking the short way back to the ground. It is a good thing that the Lampett heads are hard, or we'd have lost her by now. Sit down, Barbara, and let me have a look at your foot.'

She took the seat they had pressed her to, and her father knelt at her feet and pulled off her muddy boot, probing gently at the foot to search for breaks.

She sat patiently and watched as Stratford's expression changed from concern to interest at the sight of her stocking-clad leg. Then he hurriedly looked away, embarrassed that he'd been caught staring. He gave her a rueful smile and a half-shrug, as if to say he could hardly be blamed for looking at something so attractive, and then offered a benign, 'I hope it is nothing serious.'

'A mild sprain, nothing more,' her father assured

him. For a change, his tone was as placid as it had ever
been. He was the simple schoolmaster, the kind father
she remembered and still knew, but a man the world
rarely saw. She wanted to shout into the face of the mill
owner to make him notice the change.

*This is who he is. This is who we all are. We are not
your enemies. We need you, just as you need us. If only
you were to listen you might know us. You might like
us.*

'Would it help for her to sit with her foot on a cushion
for a bit?' Mr Stratford responded as he was addressed,
behaving as though she had twisted an ankle during a
picnic, and not while haring to her father's rescue. 'My
carriage is waiting at the back gate, just around the
corner of the building.'

'That will not be necessary,' she said. This had hardly
begun as a social call, though both men now seemed
ready to treat it as such. While she doubted her father
capable of guile, she did not know if this new and gen-
tler Stratford was the truth. What proof did she have
that they were not being led into a trap so that he could
call the authorities? Even if he did not, at any time her
father might recollect who had made the offer and turn
again to the wild man she had found a few moments
ago.

'A ride would be most welcome,' her father said, loud
enough to drown out her objections. His axe still lay,
forgotten, on the floor behind them. For now he was

willing to accept the hospitality of a man he'd been angry enough to threaten only a moment ago.

'Then, with your permission, Mr Lampett, and with apologies to you, miss, for the liberty...' Joseph Stratford pulled off his apron, tossed it aside, then reached around her and lifted her easily off the stool and into his arms.

While it was a relief to see how easily he'd managed her father, it was rather annoying to see how easily he could manage her as well. He was carrying her through the factory as though she weighed nothing. And she was allowing him to do it—without protest. The worst of it was, she rather liked the sensation. She could feel far too much of his body through the fabric of his shirt, and her face was close enough to his bare skin to smell the blending of soap and sweat and cologne that was unique to him. Such overt masculinity should have repelled her. Instead she found herself wishing she could press her face into the hollow of his throat. At least she might lay her head against his shoulder, feigning a swoon.

That would be utter nonsense. She was not the sort to swoon under any circumstances, and she would not play at it now. Though she *did* allow herself to slip an arm around his neck under the guise of steadying herself. His arms were wrapped tightly, protectively, around her already, and such extra support was not really necessary. But it gave her the opportunity to feel more of him, and to bring her body even closer to his as he moved.

'It seems I am always to be rescuing you, Miss

Lampett,' he said into her ear, so quietly that her father could not overhear.

'You needn't have bothered,' she whispered back. 'I am shamming.'

'As you were when the crowd knocked you down yesterday?'

Then he spoke louder, and directly to her father. 'If you would precede us, sir? I do not wish to risk upsetting the lady with too rough a gait. Tell the coachman of our difficulties. Perhaps he can find an extra cushion and a lap robe so that Miss Lampett will be comfortable on the journey.'

'Very good.'

As her father hurried ahead, Stratford stopped to kick the axe he had been wielding into a darkened corner. 'Though you may not want my help, I think it is quite necessary today, for the safety of all concerned, that we play this to the very hilt.' He started again towards the carriage at a stately pace, stopping only long enough at the door to lean against it and push it shut behind him. 'Do you really wish to protest good health and risk your father remembering and using his weapon?'

She shifted a little in his grasp, feeling quite ridiculous to be treated as some sort of porcelain doll. 'Of course not. But I do not wish you to make a habit of swooping in to care for me when I am quite capable of seeing to my own needs.'

'Your independence is duly noted and admired,' he said. Then he dipped his head a little, so he could catch her scent. 'Though I find your infirmity has advantages as well.'

She slapped hard at his arm. 'You are incorrigible.'

'You are not the first to have told me so. And here we are.' He said the last louder, for the benefit of her father, to signal that their intimate conversation was at an end.

She frowned. Stratford could easily have ridden the distance between the manor and here, or perhaps even walked. To bring a full equipage and servants to wait after him while he worked was just the sort of excess she had come to expect from him—and just the sort of thing that was angering the locals. Or it could mean that he had a sensible fear of being set upon, should he travel alone and vulnerable along a road that might be lined with enemies.

He set her down briefly, only to lift her again, up into the body of the carriage, settling her beside her father on a totally unnecessary mound of cushions, her injured ankle stretched out before her to rest on the seat at Stratford's side.

The carriage was new, as was everything he owned, and practically shining with it. The upholstery was a deep burgundy leather, soft and well padded. There were heavy robes for her legs to keep out the cold, and a pan of coals to warm the foot that still rested on the floor. The other was tucked up securely, the stocking-clad toes dangerously close to the gentleman there. The foot was chilled, and she resisted the urge to press it against his leg to steal some warmth.

Stratford had noticed it. He stared down for a moment, and then, as unobtrusively as possible, he tossed the tail of his coat over it and shifted his weight to be nearer.

Barbara warmed instantly—from the contact with his body and the embarrassment accompanying it. It was a practical solution, of course. But she would be the talk of the town if anyone heard of it. And by the smug smile on his face Joseph Stratford knew it, and was enjoying her discomfiture.

Then he signalled the driver and they set off, with barely a sway to tell her of the moment. It was by far the richest and most comfortable trip she'd taken, and she had to struggle not to enjoy it. Her subdued pleasure turned to suspicion, for at another signal to the driver they proceeded through the unlocked gates down the road towards Clairemont Manor.

'This is not the way to our home,' she said, stating the obvious.

'My house is nearer. You can both come for tea. I will send you home once I am assured that you are warmed and refreshed, and that no harm has come to you while on my property.'

'That is most kind of you,' her father said.

It was not at all kind. It was annoying. And she was sure that there must be some sort of ulterior motive to his sudden solicitousness.

But when she opened her mouth to say so, her father went on. 'There are not many who are such good neighbours. And are you new here, Mr...?' He struggled for a name. 'I am sorry. My memory is not what it once was.'

Barbara coloured, part relieved and part ashamed. She needn't worry that her father was likely to turn violent again, for it was clear that he had lost the thread of things and forgotten all about Mr Stratford while concerned for her ankle. But what was she to do now? Should she remind him that his host was the same man who, according to her father's own words, treated his workers 'like chattel to be cast off in pursuit of Mammon'? Or should she continue to let him display his mental confusion in front of his enemy and become an object of scorn and pity?

Stratford seemed unbothered, and responded with the barest of pauses. 'We have met only briefly, and I do not fault you for not recalling. I am Joseph Stratford, and I have taken residence of Clairemont Manor now that the family has relocated closer to the village.'

Her father gave a nod in response, still not associating the man across from them with the evil mill owner he despised.

'Would you do me the honour of an introduction to your daughter, sir?'

As her father presented her to this supposed stranger with all necessary formality, she thought she detected a slight twitch at the corners of Stratford's mouth. If he meant to make sport at the expense of her father's failed memory she would find a way to pay him out. But, after the briefest lapse, he was straight-faced and respectful again, enquiring after her father's work and commiserating with him on the closing of the little school where he had taught, and his recent difficulties in finding another occupation.

Mr Stratford had changed much since the last time she'd seen him brandishing a pistol and taunting the crowd. Though she could not say she liked him, she'd felt an illogical thrill at the power of him then, and the masterful way he had come to her aid. Now she was left with time to admire him as he conversed with her father, displaying intelligence and a thoughtful nature that had not been in evidence before. She found herself wishing that things could be different from the way they were and that this might be their first meeting. If she could look on him with fresh eyes, knowing none of his behaviour in the recent past, it might be possible to trust him. But she could not help thinking that this display of good manners was as false as her sprained ankle.

He had let the groom help him on with his coat again before they had taken off, and she could see that it was the height of London fashion, tailored to perfection and designed to give a gentlemanly outline to the work-broadened shoulders she had felt as he carried her. He was clean-shaven. But his hair was a trifle too long, as though he could not be bothered to spare the few extra minutes that the cutting of it would take. A lock of it fell into his eyes as he nodded at something her father had said, and he brushed it out of his face with an impatient flick of his hand. Though she could not call them graceful, his movements were precise. She could imagine that these were hands better at tending machinery than creating art, more efficient than gentle.

He made conversation with her father in an accent carefully smoothed to remind the listener of London, though she doubted that his tongue had been born to it. He spoke nothing of himself or his own past. But in the questions that drew her father to conversation Barbara heard the occasional lilt or drawl that was the true Joseph Stratford. He was a Northerner. But for some reason he did not like to show it.

She looked away before he could catch her staring. Even if he was nothing more than a tradesman masquerading as gentry, he deserved more courtesy than she was giving him. They were drawing up the long drive towards the great house where she had played as a child. That was before Mary had died, of course, and before her sister Anne had grown into such a great and unapproachable lady. Had the manor changed as well? she wondered. Were the places she'd hidden under chairs and behind statues the same or different? Although she wished the circumstances had been different, she very much wanted to see the place—just once more.

She could feel the eyes of the other man on her, watching her reaction to the house. So she worked to relax her posture and not stare so, or appear eager for a visit to it. It was little better than staring directly at him to admire his property as though she coveted or desired the luxury he took for granted.

'I had a friend who lived here once,' she blurted, to explain her interest.

'And perhaps you will again,' he replied easily.

She looked up sharply into a face that was all bland innocence. The carriage pulled up before the great front entry, and as it stopped he signalled for the door to be opened, allowing her father to exit first so that he might help her on the steps.

For a moment they were alone again, and he touched her hand and smiled. 'There is no reason for us to be enemies,' he said.

'Nor any particular reason for friendship,' she reminded him, drawing her hand away.

'I think it is too soon for either of us to tell,' he announced, ignoring her animosity.

The process of entering the house was much the same as their setting off from the mill had been, with him carrying her while she protested, her shoeless foot waving in the air. There was a flurry of alarm amongst the servants, many of whom recognised her and her father.

'Put me down now,' she insisted. 'Talk of this will reach the village. It will be the ruin of me.'

'If it is, your father is right here to set them straight.' He was smiling again, as though he knew how likely it was that her father would have no real memory of the event, for good or ill.

'I would prefer that no explanation be needed,' she said.

'And I would prefer that people think me less of an ogre,' Stratford replied. 'I will not have you limping about my house while I offer no assistance. Then it will get round that I let you suffer as a punishment to your father.'

For her own sake, and to preserve her reputation, he explained in a loud voice for the benefit of the staff that Miss Lampett had fallen, and he did not wish to risk further injury until she had rested her foot. But as he did so his hands tightened on her body, to prove to Barbara that he was enjoying the experience at her expense.

'You may put me down, and I will take my chances,' she said, glancing at a parlour maid who stood, wide-eyed, taking in the sight. 'I feel quite all right now.'

He pretended that he had not heard, and called for tea to be brought to the library, carrying her down the wide hall and depositing her on a couch by the fire.

How had Mr Stratford known, she wondered, the calming effect that the presence of books had on her father? Though he seemed to have more difficulty with people since the accident, the printed word still gave him great comfort. The Clairemont Manor library was the largest in the area and the best possible place to cement her father's recovery.

As the servants prepared tea, her father stood and

ran a hand along the rows of leather-bound volumes. Stratford studied the behaviour and then invited him to help himself to whatever he liked, lamenting that business gave him little time to enjoy the books there.

Her father gave a grateful nod and fell quickly to silence, ignoring the cup that had been poured for him, and the plate of sandwiches, in favour of the Roman history in his hand.

Stratford gave her a wry smile. 'While your father is preoccupied, would you enjoy a brief walk down the corridor? If your ankle is better, as you claim, a spot of exercise will assure me that it is safe to send you home.'

She wanted to snap that she did not need him seeing to her safety. She had not wanted to come here at all. And now that she was here she would go home when she was ready, and not at his bidding. But it would be shaming to discuss her father's rude behaviour while she shared a room with him, so it was best that she allow herself to be drawn away.

'That would be lovely,' she lied.

He went to fetch her boot and helped her with the lacing of it, commenting that the lack of swelling was an encouraging sign. Behind a placid smile, she gritted her teeth against the contact of his fingers against her foot and ankle. He was very gentle, as though he cared enough not to cause injury to a weakened joint. But she suspected the occasional fleeting touches she felt against her stocking were not the least bit accidental.

He was touching her for his own pleasure. Much as she did not wish to, she found it wickedly exciting.

Then he rose and went ahead to open the door for her, standing respectfully to the side so that she might pass. She forced herself to stifle the unquiet feeling that it gave her to have him at her back—even for a moment.

It was possible that this latest offer masked something much darker. Perhaps he had designs upon her virtue. For, this close, she could not deny the virile air that he seemed to carry about with him, and the sense that he had a man's needs and would not scruple to act upon them. She gave a small shudder, barely enough to be noticeable.

'Is the house too cold for you?' he prompted. 'If so, I could have a servant build up the fire, or perhaps bring you a wrap…'

'No, I am fine. I suspect that I took a slight chill on the moors.'

'Your clothing is still damp from the fall. And I took you away from the tea I had promised.' He frowned. 'But I wished to speak alone with you for a moment, so that you might know I bear you no ill will because of recent events.' He rubbed his brow, as though tired. 'One can hardly be held responsible for the actions of one's parent. I myself have a troublesome father.'

He stopped.

'Had,' he corrected. 'I *had* a difficult father. He is dead now. For a moment I had quite forgotten.'

'I am sorry for your loss,' she said politely. 'I assume the passing is a recent one, if you still forget it?'

He looked away, as though embarrassed. 'Almost seven years, actually. It is just that he has been on my mind of late. He was a weaver, you see.'

'You are the son of a weaver?' she said.

'Is that so surprising?' There was a cant to his head, a jutting of the chin as though he were ready to respond to a challenge. 'With all your father's fine talk of supporting the workers, I did not think to find you snobbish, Miss Lampett.'

'I am not snobbish,' she retorted. 'It merely surprises me that my father would need to tell a weaver's son the damage automation does to the livelihoods of the men here.'

'What you call damage, Miss Lampett, I call freedom. The ability to do more work in less time means the workers do not need to toil from first light to last. Perhaps they will have time for education, and those books your father finds so precious.'

'The workers who are put from their places by these machines will have more time as well. And no money. Time is no blessing when there is no food on the table.'

He snorted. 'The reason they are without work this Christmas has nothing to do with me. Was it not they and their like who burned the last mill to the ground and ran off the mill owner and his family? Now they complain that they have no source of income.'

'When men are desperate enough, they resort to desperate actions,' she said. 'The owner, Mr Mackay, was a harsh man who cared little for those he employed, taking them on and casting them off like chattel. It is little wonder that their spirits broke.'

'And I am sure that it did not help to have your father raising the rabble and inciting them to mischief.' He looked at her with narrowed eyes.

'That is a lie,' she snapped. 'He had nothing to do with that argument. He did not support either side, and worked to moderate the cruelty of the one with the need of the other.'

Stratford scoffed. 'He saves his rage for me, then, who has not been here long enough to prove myself cruel or kind?'

'He was not always as you see him,' she argued. 'A recent accident has addled his wits. Until that night he was the mildest of gentlemen, much as you see him now. But of late, when he takes an idea into his head, he can become quite agitated.' When he recalled the scene she had come upon at the mill, just a short time ago, he must know that 'agitated' was an understatement. 'Mother and I do not know what to do about it.'

'You had best do something,' Stratford said. 'He appears to be getting worse and not better. If you had not come along today…' He paused. 'Your arrival prevented anyone from coming to harm, at least for now.'

From his tone, it did not seem that he feared for his own life. 'Are you threatening my father, Mr Stratford?'

'Not without cause, I assure you. He is a violent man.

If necessary I will call in the law to stop him. That would be a shame if it is as you say—that the rage in him is a thing which he cannot control. But you must see that the results are likely to be all the same whether they proceed from malice, madness or politics.'

'Just what do you propose we do? Lock him up?'

'If necessary,' Stratford said, with no real feeling. 'At least that will prevent me from having him transported.'

'You would do that, wouldn't you?' With his understanding behaviour, and his offers of tea and books, she had allowed herself to believe—just for a moment—that he was capable of understanding. And that if she confided in him he might use his ingenuity to come up with a solution to her family's problems. But he was proving to be just as hard as she'd thought him when she'd seen him taunting the mob of weavers. 'You have no heart at all to make such threats at Christmas.'

Joseph Stratford shrugged. 'I fail to see what the date on the calendar has to do with it. The mill will open in January, whether your father likes it or not. But there is much work I must do, and plans that must be secured between then and now. I will not allow him to ruin the schemes already in progress with his wild accusations and threats of violence. Is that understood, Miss Lampett?'

'You do not wish our coarseness and our poverty to offend the fancy guests you are inviting from London,' she said with scorn. Everyone in the village had heard the rumours of strangers coming to the manor for the holiday, and would be speculating about their feasting and dancing while eating their meagre dinners in Fiddleton. 'And you have the nerve to request that I chain my father in our cottage like a mad dog, so that he will not trouble you and your friends with the discomfort of your workers?' She was sounding like her father at the beginning of some rabble-rousing rant. And she was foolish enough to be doing it while alone with a man who solved his problems with a loaded pistol.

'There was a time when I was little better than they are now,' he snapped.

'Then you must have forgotten it, to let the people suffer so.'

'Forgotten?' He stepped closer, his eyes hard and angry. 'There is nothing romantic about the life of a labourer. Only a woman who has known no real work would struggle so hard to preserve the rights of others to die young from overwork.' He reached out suddenly and seized her hands, turning them over to rub his fingers over the palms. 'As I thought. Soft and smooth. A lady's hands.'

'There is no shame in being a lady,' she said, with as much dignity as she could manage. She did not try to pull away. He could easily manage to hold her if he wanted to. And if he did not respond to her struggle the slight fear she felt at the nearness of him would turn into panic.

His fingers closed on hers, and his eyes seemed to go dark. 'But neither is there any pride in being poor.

It is nice, is it not, to go to a soft bed with a full belly? To have hands as smooth as silk?' His thumbs were stroking her, and the little roughness of them seemed to remind her just how soft she was. There was something both soothing and exciting about the feel of his fingers moving against hers, the way they twined, untwined and twined again.

'That does not mean that we should not feel sympathy for those less fortunate than ourselves.' He was standing a little too close to be proper, and her protest sounded breathless and excited.

'Less fortunate, eh? Less in some ways, more in others. Without the machines they are fighting I would be no different than they are now—scrabbling to make a living instead of holding the hands of a beautiful lady in my own great house.'

It was not his house at all. He had taken it—just as he had taken her hands. 'I did not give you leave to do so,' she reminded him.

'You gave me no leave to carry you before either,' he said. 'But I wanted to, and so I did. You felt very good in my arms.' He pulled her even closer, until her skirts were brushing against the legs of his trousers. She did not move, even though he had freed her hands. 'It is fortunate for me that you are prone to pity a poor working man. Perhaps you will share some of that sweet sympathy with me.' He ran a finger down her cheek, as though to measure its softness.

She stood very still indeed, not wishing him to see

how near she was to trembling. If she cried out it would draw the house down upon them and bring this meeting to a sudden end. But her words had failed her, and she could manage no clever quip that would make him think her sophisticated. Nor could she raise a maidenly insistence that he revolted her. He did not. His touch was gentle, and it made her forget all that had come before.

He seemed to forget as well, for his voice was softer, deeper and slower. 'Your father broke one of my looms today. But it will be replaced, and I will say nothing of how the destruction happened.'

'Thank you,' she whispered, wetting her lips.

'If you wish to make a proper apology, I would like something more.' His head dipped forwards, slowly, and his lips were nearing hers.

Although she knew what was about to happen she stayed still and closed her eyes. His lips were touching hers, moving lightly over them. It was as it had been when he had touched her ankle and held her hands. She could feel everything in the world in that single light touch. Her whole body felt warm and alive. Hairs rose on her arms and neck—not from the chill but as though they were eager to be soothed back to smoothness by roving hands.

She kissed him back, moving her lips on his as he had on hers. His mouth was rough, and imperfect. One corner of his smile was slightly higher than the other, and she touched it with the tip of her tongue, felt the dimple beside it deepen in surprise.

In response, he gave a playful lick against her upper lip, daring her. Her body's response was an immediate tightening, and she pressed herself against him, opening her mouth. And what had been wonderful became amazing.

He encircled her, and his arms made a warm, safe place for their exploration—just as they had when he'd carried her. The slow stroking of hands and tongue seemed to open her to more sensations, and the tingling of her body assured her of the rightness of it, the perfection and the bliss. Although she knew all the places on her body that he must not touch, she was eager to feel his fingers there, and perhaps his tongue.

Just the idea made her tremble with eagerness, with embarrassment, and the knowledge that had seemed quite innocent was near to blazing out of control. And it was not only his doing. Even now she had taken his tongue into her mouth, and it was she who held it captive there, closing her lips upon it.

She could tell by his sigh of pleasure that he enjoyed what she'd done. But his only other response was to go still against her. His passivity coaxed her to experiment, raking his tongue with her teeth and circling it with her own, urging him to react.

He had trapped her into being the aggressor. At the realisation, she pulled away suddenly. He let her go, staring down at her in mock surprise, touching his own lips gingerly, as though they might be hot enough to burn his fingers.

'Stop that immediately,' she said.

He smiled. 'You have stopped it quickly enough for both of us. And now I suppose you wish me to apologise for the way *you* kissed *me*?'

'Only if you wish me to think you any sort of gentleman,' she said, feeling ridiculous.

'But I am not a gentleman,' he said with a shrug. 'Isn't that half the problem between us? I sit here, a trumped-up worker, in a house that should belong to my betters, had they not lost it through monetary foolishness. My presence in this house upsets the natural order of things. My touching you...'

'That is not the problem at all,' she snapped. 'I do not care who you are.'

'If you do not care who I am, it was highly indiscriminate of you to allow me the kiss. And even worse that you returned it.'

'You are twisting my words,' she said. 'I meant that it should not have happened at all. Not with any man. But especially not with you.'

'I don't know,' he said with an ironic laugh. 'I might be the best choice for such dalliance. If you complain to your father, I would be obligated to do right by you. Then my house and my fortune would be yours. You might trap me with your considerable charms and force me to marry you.'

'But to do that I would have to admit to Father that you had touched me, Mr Stratford. I think we can safely say that such a circumstance will never happen. Not for all the money in the world, and Clairemont Manor thrown into the mix. Now, please return me to the library.'

He smiled in triumph, as though that had been his end all along. 'Very well, then. Let us go back to your father, and both of you can be gone. I trust that now we have spoken on the subject I will see no more of you, or be forced to endure any more of your father's tirades? For, while I can see that there is more than a little madness to them, they cannot be allowed to continue. If arms are raised against me and the opening of the mill disrupted, or my equipment damaged further, I will be forced to take action. While I am sure that neither of us wants it, you must see that I do not intend to be displaced now that I am so near to success.'

He turned and led her back towards the library. As he opened the door he made idle comments about the furnishings and art, as though they had just returned from a tour of his home. It was all the more galling to know that some of the things he said were inaccurate, proving that he knew little more about the things he owned than how to pay for them. He really was no better than he had said: a man ignorant in all but one thing. He had made a fine profit by it. But what did that matter if it had left him coarse and cruel?

As they entered, her father looked up as though he had forgotten how he had come to be there. 'I think it is time that we were going, Father,' she said firmly. 'We have abused Mr Stratford's hospitality for quite long enough.'

Her father looked with longing at the book in his hands.

Joseph Stratford responded without missing a beat. 'I hate to take you from your reading, sir. Please accept the volume as my gift to you. You are welcome to come here whenever you like and avail yourself of these works. It pleases me greatly to see them in the hands of one who enjoys them.'

Because you have no use for them, you illiterate lout, she thought. She responded with a smile that was almost too bright, 'How thoughtful of you, Mr Stratford.'

Her father agreed. 'Books are a precious commodity in the area, and it is rare that we get anything new from London that is not a newspaper or a fashion plate.' He wrinkled his nose at the inadequacy of such fare to a man of letters.

Stratford nodded in sympathy. 'Then we will see what can be done to correct the deficiency. If there is anything you desire from my library, send word. I will have it delivered to you. And now it appears that your daughter is properly recovered. If I may offer you a ride back to the village?'

Her father stood, and the men chatted as they walked to the door as though they were old friends. In a scant hour Bernard Lampett had quite recovered from his fit of rage, and Mr Stratford was behaving as though the incidents in the mill and in the hall had not occurred.

If he remembered them at all, he appeared untouched by them.

But in the space of that same hour Barbara felt irrevocably changed, and less sure of herself than she had ever been.

Chapter Five

Later that evening the guests began to arrive, and Joseph was relieved to have no time to think of Barbara Lampett. Even when he should have focused his energy elsewhere, he could feel the memory of her and her sweet lips always in the background. It had been madness to take her out into the hall. He had known that he could not fully trust himself around her. When they were alone he should have limited himself to urging her to moderate her father's actions. But he'd had the foolish urge to show her his house, so that she might see the extent of his success. There might even have been some notion of catching her under a kissing bough and stealing one small and quite harmless kiss. He had been eager to impress her, and had behaved in a way that was both foolish and immature.

All of it had got tangled together in an argument, ending with a brief and heated display of shared emotion. It had been as pleasant as it had inappropriate. While such little indiscretions happened all the time, ladies like Barbara Lampett did not like to think themselves capable of them. She would not wish to be reminded, nor to risk a repeat display. He would not see her again.

And that was that.

He turned his attention to more important matters. After the rejections in today's post, it appeared that his house would be barely half-full for Christmas. There had been several frosty refusals to the offer of a trumped-up tradesman's hospitality. But it would not matter. Even one or two would be plenty—if they were rich enough and could be interested in his plans.

As promised, he let Bob take the lead in introductions and in the planning of activities, doing his best to respond in a way that was not rough or gauche. His casual offer that tomorrow's skating on the millpond might end with cakes and punch served in the empty warehouse was accepted graciously—once the ladies were assured that it was quite clean and that no actual work was being done. While they were there he would arrange a tour of the tidy rows of machinery. Breton would make mention of the successes they'd shared with the production and sale of such looms to others. The seed would be planted.

Before they returned to London one or two of the men would come to Bob, as they always did after such gatherings, making offhand remarks about risk and reward. A discreet parlay would be arranged in which no money would change hands. There would be merely a vague promise of it, for such people did not carry chequebooks with them. They carried cards and wrote letters of introduction to bankers, who stayed in the background where they belonged. But if they offered, they would deliver. Honour was involved. A true gentleman's word was as good as a banknote.

He frowned as the last of his guests took themselves off to bed, leaving him free for a few hours of rest. He was tired tonight, after last night's uneasy rest. Dinner had tired him as well. It was like speaking another language, dealing with the gentry and their need to seem idle even while doing business. So much easier to deal with the likes of mad Lampett. Though he was of a changeable nature, he would at least speak what was left of his mind.

For plain speaking, Lampett's lovely daughter was better than ten of the milk-and-water misses he was likely to see this week. Even Anne Clairemont, whose family had put in a brief appearance this evening, had looked puzzled by the conversation, and nervous at the prospect of a little skating on a properly frozen pond. He would not have faulted her if she had politely excused herself from it. But she had looked from her father to him, blinked twice and then forced a smile and declared it a wonderful notion.

Miss Lampett, in a similar situation, would have likely announced to the assembly that the whole trip was a thinly disguised attempt at business and refused to take any part in it. For some reason the imagined scene did not bother him. He could just as easily imagine drawing her out in the hall to remonstrate with her, only to have the conversation degenerate into another heated kiss.

When his valet had left him for the night he settled back into the pillows and pulled the blankets up to his chin, closing his eyes and thinking of that kiss. He really shouldn't have taken it. It had been improper and unfair of him to take advantage of her innocence. But he would do it again if he had the chance. That and more...

He awoke hungry. It made no sense. The clock was only striking one, and dinner had been a feast, stretching late into the evening. He had partaken of it with enthusiasm. But it was gone from him now, leaving his guts empty and gnawing on themselves in the darkness.

He had not known want like this since he'd become master of his own life. This was the kind of nagging hunger he'd felt as a child, going to bed with an empty belly and knowing that there would be nothing to fill it again tomorrow. It was a kind of bleak want that existed in the body like an arm or a leg: something that one carried with one from moment to moment, place to place, always there and impossible to cast off.

But it was easily rectified now. He had but to sit up in bed and ring for a footman. He would explain the need and have it filled. It would mean getting some poor maid out of her bed to do for him. But what was the point of having servants if one could not make unreasonable demands upon them?

When he opened his eyes, the room was strange. Not his own bedroom at all, but a different, emptier room, filled with a strange, directionless golden haze.

From the corner of the room there was a sigh.

Joseph sat bolt upright now, searching for the source of the sound. And with it he found the origin of the glow. A man sat in the corner—a Cavalier, in a long well-curled wig and heavy-skirted coat. The light seemed to rise from the gold braid upon it, diffusing into a corona around him.

This man was a stranger, and yet strangely familiar. He looked around the room and sighed again. He glanced across at Joseph and gave a pitying shake of his head. 'When I was summoned here, I must admit I expected better. These are not the surroundings to which I am accustomed. But I suppose if there is no problem, then there is no need…' The Cavalier gave another heavy sigh.

'Just what do you mean by that?' snapped Joseph, rubbing his eyes. 'I grew up in a room not unlike this one, and…'

As a matter of fact he'd grown up in a room exactly like this one. Its appearance was softened somewhat, by the glow of the phantom and by his own fading memories, but it was the same room. It was where he'd felt the hunger that plagued him now, which was still as sharp and real as ever it had been.

'I belong at the manor and have been sent to fetch you back to it,' the man said bluntly. 'Although even that is no treat. For I must tell you the place under your governance is not as nice as it once was.'

'Now, see here,' Joseph said, sitting up in his bed only to realise that it was not the thing he'd lain down on but a narrow bunk, with a rush mattress and thin blankets that could not keep the cold from his feet. 'You need not take me back, for I did not go anywhere. I am still there, fast asleep and dreaming.' This time he gave himself a hard pinch on the back of the hand, not caring if the spirit before him saw it.

'I was told that this had been explained to you. Three visitors would come. We would show you your errors. You would learn or not learn, as was your nature…' He droned in an uninterested way that said he did not care what Joseph learned, so long as he did it quickly and with as little bother as possible.

Joseph glared at the spirit, annoyed that it was still before him. 'I was told by my father. Who is dead and therefore should not be telling me anything. While he said there would be three, he did not say three of what. If there was any truth in it he might as well have said four, thus counting himself.'

'Do not think you can reason like a Jesuit to get yourself out of a situation that you yourself have created.' The Cavalier sighed again, and flicked a lace handkerchief in front of his nose as though offended by the stench of such humble surroundings. 'Be silent and I will explain. And then we might be done with this vision and go back to the house.'

'But you are not real,' Joseph argued. It was most annoying to be lectured at by one's own imagination. And then he placed the identity of the thing sitting before him. 'You are Sir Cedric Clairemont, and nothing more than a portrait hanging in the gallery on the second floor. This room is the place where I was born. I am blending memories in a dream.'

Sir Cedric gave a resigned glare in his direction, and sighed again as though facing a difficult child. 'Let me put this plainly, so that you might understand it. I would say I am as real as you, but that would lack truth. I was real. Now I am a spirit, as is your father. As are the two that will come after. By the end of it you will know where you were, where you are and what you will become.'

'I know all these things for myself, without your help. I will not be frightened into a change of plans by some notion created out of a second helping of trifle after a roast pork dinner.'

'Touch me,' commanded the spirit.

He did look almost real enough to touch, and just the same as he did in his portrait. But from what memory had Joseph created the man's voice, which was a slightly nasal tenor? Or his mannerisms as he swaggered forwards with his stick and looked down at Joseph with amused superiority? This man was not some ghost from a painting, but so real that he felt he could reach out and…

Joseph drew his hand back quickly, suddenly aware of the gesture he'd been making—which had looked almost like supplication.

The ghost stared at him with impatience. Then he brought the swagger stick down upon Joseph's head with a thud.

'Ow!'

'Is that real enough for you, Stratford? Or must I hit you again? Now, get out of the bed and take my hand— or I will give you a thumping you will remember in the morning.'

The idea was ludicrous. It was one thing to have a vivid dream. Quite another for that nightmare to fetch you a knock to the nob then demand that you get out of bed and walk into it.

'Certainly not.' Joseph rubbed at the spot where he'd been struck. 'Raise that stick to me again and, dream or not, I will answer you blow for blow.'

Sir Cedric smiled ironically. 'Very well, then. If you wish to remain here I can show you images of your childhood. Although why you would wish to see them, I am unsure. They are most unpleasant.'

As though a candle had been lit, a corner of the room brightened and Joseph felt increasing dread. It was the corner that had held the loom.

'Tighten the warp.' He heard the slap and felt the impact of it on the side of his head, even though it had landed some many years before on the ear of the young boy who sat there.

'S…sorry, Father.' The young Joseph fumbled with the shuttle.

The man who stood over him could barely contain his impatience. 'Sorry will not do when there is an order as big as this one. I cannot work the night through to finish it. You must do your share. Sloppy work that must be unravelled again the next day is no help at all. It is worse than useless. Not only must I do my own part, I must stand over you and see to it that you do yours. You are worse than useless.'

'I was too small,' Joseph retorted, springing from the bed and flexing his muscles with a longing to strike back. 'My arms were too short to do the job. All the bullying in the world would have made no difference.'

'He cannot hear you,' the ghost said calmly. 'For the moment you live in my world, as much a spectre to him as he is to you.'

'It was Christmas. And it was not fair,' Joseph said, trying to keep the childish petulance from his voice.

'Life seldom is.'

'I made it fair,' Joseph argued. 'My new loom is wider, but so simple that a child can manage it.' The weavers of Fiddleton and all the other places that employed a Stratford loom would not be beating their children at Christmas over unfinished work.

But the ghost at his side said nothing, as though Joseph had done no kindness with the improvement. He held out his hand again. 'Do you need further reminders of your past?'

Without thinking, Joseph shook his head. The past was clear enough in his own mind without them. It had been hard and hungry and he was glad to be rid of it. 'I made my father eat his words before the end,' Joseph said coldly. 'He died in warmth and comfort, in a bed I bought for him, and *not* slaving in someone else's mill.'

'Take my hand and come away.' Sir Cedric sounded almost sympathetic, his voice softer, gently prodding Joseph to action.

Joseph turned his back on the vision and reached for the arm of the spectre, laying his hand beside the ghostly white one on the stick he held. The fingers were unearthly cold, and smooth as marble, but very definitely real to him in a way that the man and boy in the corner were not. 'Very well, then. Whatever you are, take me back to the manor and my own bed.'

There was a feeling of rushing, and of fog upon his face, the sound of the howling winds upon the moors. Then he was back in his own home, walking down the main corridor towards the receiving rooms in bare feet and a nightshirt.

'What the devil?' He yanked upon Sir Cedric's arm, trying to turn him towards the stairs. 'I said my bedroom, you lunatic. If my guests see me wandering the house in my nightclothes, they will think I've gone mad. All my plans will be undone.'

If this was a ghost that escorted him, the least it

could do was to be insubstantial. But Sir Cedric was as cold and immovable as stone. Now that they were joined Joseph could not seem to pull his hand away. He was being forced to follow into the busiest part of the house, which was brightly lit and brimming with activity, though it had been empty when he'd retired.

'Don't be an idiot, Stratford. Did I not tell you that I am a spirit of the past, and that you might pass unseen through it?' The ghost sniffed the air. 'This is the Christmas of 1800, if I have led us right. It is the same night when we saw you clouted on the ear. Well past my time, but the holiday is much as I remember it from my own days as lord here, and celebrated as it has always been. The doors are open to the people of Fiddleton. Tenants and villagers, noble friends and neighbours mix here to the joy of all.'

The ghost gave a single tap of his stick and the ball-room doors before them opened wide. The same golden glow Joseph had seen before spilled through them and out into the hall, as if to welcome them in.

This is how it should be.

The thought caught him almost off guard, as though the sight of this long-past Christmas was the missing piece in a puzzle. The rooms were the same, the smells of Christmas food very nearly so. But it was the people that made the difference.

Even in mirth, his current guests were polite and guarded. The men considering business looked at him as though calculating gain and loss. Anne's family treated him with an awkward combination of deference and contempt. A few others avoided him, acting as though the wrong kind of mirth on their part would admit that they did not mind his company and would result in some life-changing social disaster.

But the very air was different in this place. It was not simply the quaint fashion of the clothes or the courtliness of the dancing. There was a look in their eyes: a confidence in the future, a joyful twinkle. As though there was no question that the future would be as happy as the past had been. But they were not bending, more than ten years on, under the weight of a never-ending war, or the feeling that their very livelihood might slip from their fingers because of the decisions made by men of power and wealth. They were dancing, singing and drinking together, unabashed. The spirit was infectious, and Joseph could not help but smile in response to the sight.

There was a pause in the music and he heard the laughter of young girls—saw a pair, still in the schoolroom, winding about the furniture in a game of tag.

'Do you not wish they would stop?' the ghost prodded gently. 'It is most tiresome, is it not? All the noise and the bustle?'

'No. It is wonderful.' For all the quiet dignity of the party he was throwing, there was something lost. It lacked the life of this odd gathering so bent on merriment. He could see village folk amongst them—the grocer, the miller and younger versions of the same weavers who had threatened only yesterday to break the frames in his factory. But now they danced with the rest, as though they were a part of the household.

He cast a questioning glance at the ghost.

'It is the annual Tenants' Ball,' Sir Cedric supplied. 'Held each Christmas night—until the last owner could no longer keep the spirit of the season or afford the house.'

'Perhaps if he had been a wiser steward of his money and not spent it on frivolities such as this he would still reside here.' But his own conscience told him that was an unfair charge. The celebration *he* was throwing was far more elaborate than this, and not a tenth as happy.

'He seems successful enough there, doesn't he?' Sir Cedric raised his stick and pointed towards the corner, where stood Anne's father, Mr Clairemont, looking happier and less careworn than he had done since Joseph had known him. And there was Mrs Clairemont, who showed a change even more drastic. Eleven years ago she had been a gracefully aging beauty. Now she was grey, pinched and nervous.

'Whatever the reason, the Clairemonts are gone from here and none of your concern. I hear the house is held by a harsher master now.' The ghost gave him a look one part disappointment and one part disapproval, followed by another heavy sigh.

'I am harsh because I did not invite the whole village for Christmas dinner?' Joseph waved a hand at the assembly. 'How was I expected to know of this? It is not as if I was born of this area. The cottage we began the night in was miles from here. Clairemont said nothing of this responsibility when he sold me the house.'

'And you are so tragically robbed of speech that you could not enquire.' The ghost nodded in mock sympathy.

Now the lord of the manor was offering baskets to the families that had come, shaking hands and slapping backs as though every last man was an old friend. If the Clairemonts were still in the house, it must mean that the woman he now meant to marry was somewhere in the throng—and no older than the girls at play. He searched for the pair he had seen and dismissed earlier, but there were so many children, and they seemed to swarm out of doorways and hiding places, tearing down the halls, heedless of the other guests.

Then he spied Anne. Even now he could not quite manage to think of her as 'his' Anne. The unfamiliarity of her youth made it no easier. This little girl was as unlike her in manner as she was like in face. In childhood there had been none of the sombre grace that the woman carried now. She was a mischievous imp who did not care that her hair ribbons had come untied so long as she was not caught by the one who followed.

And the other, following close on her heels, was just alike. A twin? Or very nearly so? For the girls were very similar in looks. If they were not birthed together, then no more than a year could have separated them.

'Mary! Anne! Wait for me.' A third girl appeared,

as though out of nowhere, seemingly forgotten as the game of hide-and-seek went on without her. When he turned to the sound of her voice he saw a hanging on the wall that had concealed her still rustling back into place.

Focused as she was on the two who had passed, she did not see him until it was too late, striking his legs with a surprisingly solid thump. 'Excuse me, sir.'

As he reached out a hand to steady her, her little face turned up to his. Barbara Lampett. It must be her. For there was the same turned-up nose. And those were her blue eyes, as bright and searching as a beacon, with the curiosity of unvarnished youth. No one had told her not to stare, or taught her to cloak the energy of her spirit in courtesies and false manners.

He felt the same connection he had at the riot, and again in this very hall. But this was different. Tonight she knew nothing about him. She'd had no chance to form an opinion, no reason to think him anything less than a gentleman. She had no cause to dislike him. She was smiling at him with those same pursed lips that had shown such disapproval this afternoon.

The thought staggered him. Seeing her here, as she had been, he very much wished that he might have met the girl full-grown tonight, and had even the smallest opportunity to let the woman she had become see him as anything else than an enemy.

He steadied her, and stepped out of her way. 'No harm done, Miss Lampett. Go and find your friends.'

But the other girls had come back for her, grabbing her hands and pulling her away, paying no heed to him.

'Barbara, what are you waiting for? Come.'

Then she was gone from him, with one passing look and a tip of her head, as though she could not quite make out his purpose in standing in the hall, staring.

'Who is the man in the nightshirt?' she said to the nearest girl, looking back at him again.

'What man?' Her friends looked back, through him.

'I… Never mind.' Barbara smiled and looked away again, as though the memory of him was already fading.

'She saw me?' he said in wonder, looking down at his own hand as though he could still feel the muslin of her gown under his fingers.

'It seems so,' said the ghost, barely interested. 'There are those who see the world around them plainly, and those who don't. Miss Lampett is more perceptive than most.'

Joseph thought again of her ill opinion of him. That was hardly a sign of keen perception. Her animosity seemed to be shared by most of the community.

'And some others can learn to see properly if they are shown,' the ghost added.

'You are speaking of me, I suppose?' Joseph answered.

'You do seem to be most singularly blind to your surroundings.'

'I see it more as an ability to avoid distractions and to focus on the future.'

'Really?' It was more a question than a statement. 'The future is not my purview. There is another…' The ghost stopped for a moment and gave a slight shudder. 'You will see soon enough how clear a view of the future you hold. But for now I bring you to the past so that you might learn from it. Do not forget it, my boy.'

'Stratford! What the devil? Joseph, get up immediately. What are you about, sleeping in a common hallway?'

Joseph started awake, focusing in confusion for a moment on a man's legs, before looking up into the worried face of Breton. 'Hallway?' he echoed in puzzlement, struggling to remember the details of the previous evening. It had begun normally enough. But now…

He looked around him. He was slumped on the floor in the hall, in front of the ballroom, still clad in his nightclothes. He stood up quickly, glancing around to make sure they were alone. 'Did anyone…?'

'See you? Dear God, I hope not. I am sure we will hear of it if they have. But you must consider yourself fortunate that I am an early riser and can help you out of this fix. What happened?'

'I am not sure. I must have roamed in my sleep. I had a very vivid dream.' And vivid it must have been. He could see the bruise on his hand where he had pinched himself. And feel a small knot on his skull where he had been rapped by the Cavalier's beribboned walking stick.

'Well, you look like the very devil. Grey as a paving stone and just as cold.'

Joseph turned behind him to the curtain that hung on the wall and swept it aside, to reveal a small alcove with a stone bench just large enough to hide a pair of lovers. Or a girl playing at hide-and-seek.

'I did not know of this before now,' he said numbly to his friend. 'But I dreamed it was here.'

Breton was staring at him as though he were as barmy as Bernard Lampett. 'If you wish to search the house for priests' holes, it might be best to continue when fully dressed.'

'Perhaps so.' He frowned. 'But I am surprised I had not noticed this before.'

His friend took him by the arm, tugging him towards the back stairs. 'That is little shock to me. It has nothing to do with the running of the mill. That is all you seem to care about lately.'

'Unfair,' Joseph charged. 'I care about many things. It is not as if I am made of clockwork, you know.' Who had told him he was?

They mounted the steps and Breton hurried him towards his room, his valet and his clothing. 'Sometimes I wonder. But, if you have them, tell me of these other interests. I defy you to name one.'

Now that he was pressed, Joseph could not seem to think of any. Unless he could count Lampett's fractious daughter as an interest. If the spirit of Sir Cedric had taught him anything, it was of his desire to see another of the smiles she had worn as a child.

In response to his silence Bob gave a snort of disgust. When he spoke, the amusement in his voice had been replaced with sincere annoyance. 'That was where you should have announced your excitement at your impending engagement. Have you forgotten that as well?'

'Of course I have not forgotten.' But he had responded too late to be believable.

'I might just as well have included it as part of your business. It is little more than that to you, isn't it?'

'Little more to her as well,' Joseph said, a little defensively. 'Her father wishes her back living in this house. This is the most efficient way to accomplish it.'

Breton pushed him towards his room. 'Once she is here, you will notice her as little as you do your own furnishings—or that hole in the wall you found so fascinating. And that is a pity. Anne is a lovely girl, and deserving of better.'

There was that prickling of his conscience again, and the echoing warning of his father to unravel his plans and start fresh. Perhaps that was what he'd meant. His other business plans were sensible enough. He hardly needed a wife to cement his place. But he could think of no honourable way to back out of the arrangement he had made with Clairemont.

'There is nothing to be done about it now,' Joseph said with exasperation. 'We are as good as promised to each other. Everyone knows I mean to make the announcement on Christmas Eve. I cannot cry off, even if I might like to. The scandal to the girl would be greater than any that might befall me.'

'Then the least you can do,' Breton said more softly, 'is to recognise that you have won a prize, and treat the girl as such. For if I find that you are neglecting her, or making her unhappy, I will be forced to act.'

Joseph looked at his friend as if for the first time. Bob, who had been ever loyal, friendly and trusting, was acting as strangely as though he had been receiving nightly revelations as well. He looked angry. It was disquieting.

'Very well, then,' Joseph answered, searching his friend's expression for some understandable reason for this change. 'I will take your words to heart. Although it will not be a love match, I will make sure that she does not suffer for my neglect.'

His friend sighed. 'I suppose it is as much as I can expect from you. But see that you remember your words.'

And mine as well.

The echo of a voice from the portrait gallery caused him to start nervously.

His friend gave him another suspicious look. 'Is there something wrong, Joe?'

'Nothing,' he said hurriedly. 'You are right. I have been working too hard. I have not slept well for two nights. And I am neglecting Anne. Today I will change.

I promise. But for now I must dress. I will see you in the breakfast room shortly.' He backed hurriedly into his bedroom and shut the door before the conversation could grow any more awkward.

He would make a change—if only to avoid another night like the one he'd just had. Although, with the minimal direction his nightly ghosts had given him, God only knew what that change was supposed to be.

Chapter Six

'**W**ill that be all, Miss Lampett?'

Barbara checked carefully through the list she'd set for herself to finish the Christmas shopping. A matching skein of wool to complete the warm socks she was knitting for Father, and the new fashion plates that her mother would enjoy, along with enough lace to make her a collar. 'I can think of nothing more.'

'Do you want this sent round to the house, Miss Lampett?' The girl behind the counter looked at her expectantly.

There was plenty of space left in her market basket on top of the groceries: three oranges, one for each of them, and a pound of wheat for her father's favourite frumenty. The roast she'd got from the butcher sat in the bottom of the basket, wrapped tightly in brown paper so that it would not spoil the rest. The poor bit of meat was leaner than she'd wished for. But then so was the butcher. What with the war, and the general poverty of the area, Christmas itself would be sparse for many people, and she had best be grateful that her family had the money to purchase a feast.

Barbara counted the remaining coins in her purse, calculating the pennies needed to reward the boy at the end of his journey. 'No, thank you. It is a fine day, and not far. I will carry this myself.'

The shop girl gave her a doubtful look and wrapped the package carefully, placing it on top of the others.

Barbara hefted the basket off the counter, feeling the weight shift. It was heavy now. In a mile it would be like lead on the end of her arm. Her muscles would ache with carrying it. But she smiled in gratitude, to show the girl that it was all right, and pulled it to her side, turning to go.

'Allow me, Miss Lampett.' Without warning, Joseph Stratford was there at her side, as suddenly as he had been two days past in front of the mill. He had a grip on the basket handle, and had pulled it from her without waiting for her to give him leave.

'That will not be necessary,' she said, trying not to sound breathless from the shock of the sudden contact. It was strange enough to see him in the village, shopping amongst the peasants in the middle of a work day. But it was doubly disconcerting to have him here, close to her again, after the intimacy of yesterday.

'Perhaps you do not think it necessary,' he agreed. 'But I would not be able to stand aside and watch you struggle with it. You had best take my assistance, for both our sakes.'

'I would prefer not.'

'But I would not be able to sleep, knowing I had left a lady to carry such a burden.' He smiled at her in a way that might have been charming had she not known so much of the source. 'I can hardly sleep as it is.'

The charm faded for a moment, and she saw shadows under his eyes that had not been there two days ago. Maybe her father was weakening him, after all. She reminded herself that he deserved any suffering he felt, and gave him a false smile in return. 'Heaven forefend that you are uneasy in your rest, sir.' She reached again for the basket, but he pulled it just out of reach.

'Come. You and your packages will have a ride home in my carriage.'

'It is a short distance,' she argued.

'The weather is turning. Come with me, and you will stay warm and dry.'

'My reputation…'

'Will be unharmed,' he finished, glancing at the people around him for confirmation. 'I mean you no mischief. I will take you directly home. It is on my way.' He looked around with a glare, cowing the shop girl and the other customers. 'No one will cast aspersions if I attempt to do you good. They can see plain enough that you are resisting, but I am giving no quarter. Come along, Miss Lampett.'

Then he and her basket were ahead of her, out of

the door and walking towards the large and entirely unnecessary carriage. She had no choice but to trail after.

As she passed, his groom jumped to attention, rushing to take the basket, get the stair down and hold the door as he helped her up. Across from her, Joseph Stratford leaned back into the seats as though he was ascending to a throne.

Then he smiled at her, satisfied. 'There. As you can see, you are perfectly safe, and still in clear view of those in the street. I am all the way over here—properly out of reach of you. There will be no such incident as there was the last time we were alone together.'

'I had no doubt of that, Mr Stratford. I would die first.'

He laughed at her for her primness. 'You are a most ungrateful chit, Miss Lampett. One kiss did you no permanent harm. And, if you will remember the altercation outside the mill two days past, you must admit I have shown concern for your welfare. If I was as awful as you pretend, I would have let the mob trample you.'

'You would not have.' He'd moved with such speed to get to her side that she was sure it had been all but involuntary.

He looked surprised. 'You give me credit for that much compassion, at least. Thank you for it.'

The silence that came after served to remind her just how unequal things had become, and just how unfair she was being to him—even if she did not particularly like the man. 'I deserve no thanks, Mr Stratford. I owe them to you. At least for that day. I am perfectly aware that if you did not save my life, you at least spared me serious injury.'

'You're welcome.' He seemed almost embarrassed that she had noticed the debt she owed.

'But now you are giving me a ride, when I told you I did not wish one. After yesterday...'

'Can you not accept this in the spirit with which it was given?' he asked with a smile. 'It is foul outside, but it appeared that you wished to forgo even the help of a delivery boy and struggle home by yourself. There was no reason for it.'

He looked at her sideways for a moment, and then out of the window, as though his next comment was of no consequence.

'Perhaps I remember what it was like to count pennies as though they were pounds, and do without the smallest luxuries.'

He had guessed her reason for walking? 'Then I also apologise for the comment I made in our last conversation, accusing you of being unsympathetic to those in need.'

He was frowning now, and hardly seemed to speak to her. 'You were right in part, at least. I had meant, when that time passed, to remember it better. I pledged to myself that I would be of aid to those who were impoverished, as I had been while growing up. It seems I have forgotten.'

'Do not think to make my family an object of pity to salve your stinging conscience,' she snapped. 'If you wish to offer charity, there are others that need more of it.' Then she looked out of the window as well. She felt bad to have spoken thus, for it was very ungrateful of her. He seemed able to put her in the worst temper with the slightest comment. But then, he could arouse other emotions as well.

Her cheeks coloured as she thought again of the kiss. When she'd accepted this ride, had there been some small part of her that had hoped he would attempt to do it again? Was that what made her angry now? She was a fool if she thought that his offer had been anything other than common courtesy. She meant nothing to him. Nor did the kiss.

'It is hardly charity to offer another person a ride on a cold and rainy day,' he said gently. 'I'll wager you'd have accepted if the offer had come from Anne Clairemont or her mother.'

'That would not have been likely,' she said.

'Why not? You were friends with the Clairemont girls as a child, were you not?'

She turned and looked at him sharply. 'What gave you that idea?'

His gaze flicked away for a moment. 'You mentioned it as we were driving towards the house yesterday.'

'I said I'd had a friend there. But you said "girls" just now. I did not mention Mary.'

'Perhaps Anne did,' he said, still not looking at her. 'Mary was her sister, then?'

The idea that Anne might have mentioned her seemed highly unlikely. Something about the calculated way he spoke made her suspect he fished for information and was piecing the truth together with each slip Barbara made. 'Mary has been dead for quite some time,' she said, praying that would be the end of the conversation.

'What happened to her?'

'There was nothing mysterious about her death. She took ill, faded and died. If you wish to know more you had best ask your fiancée, Miss Clairemont.'

'I have not offered as of yet.'

'But you will. The whole village knows that the festivities you have organised are meant to celebrate your engagement to her.'

'Do they, now?' His voice had dropped briefly, as though he was talking to himself. 'I did not know that the world was sure of plans that I myself have not spoken.'

Were they not true? Anne seemed sure enough of them, as was her father. But Stratford's response gave Barbara reason to fear for them. It would be most embarrassing should they have misunderstood this man's intent so completely and allowed themselves to be used to further his business. 'I am sorry. Perhaps I was mistaken.'

'Perhaps you were.' He was looking at her rather

intently now, as though trying to divine her opinion on the subject.

She reminded herself that she had none. Perhaps she was a little relieved that he was not riding with her or kissing her while planning to marry Anne. She had no wish to hurt that family again by seeming too interested in Mr Stratford. Nor did she want to do anything that might encourage him to become interested in her if he was otherwise engaged.

But his eyes, when seen this close, were the stormy shade of grey that presaged a violent change in the weather. The slight stubble on his chin only emphasised the squareness of his jaw. Now that she had noticed it she found it hard to look away.

He broke the gaze. 'Then again, perhaps you were not mistaken about my engagement. I have not yet made a decision regarding my future, or that of Miss Anne Clairemont.'

She looked down at her feet, embarrassed for having thought anything at all other than cursory gratitude that she was not walking in the rain. 'Either way, it is rude of you to discuss it with me. And, I might add, it does not concern me whatever you do. You might marry whoever you like and it will not matter to me in the slightest.'

'It is good to know that. Not that I planned to seek your approval.' This was more playful than censorious, and delivered with a strangely seductive smile, as if to say it was in his power to make it matter, should he so choose. 'But why do you say that the Clairemonts would not offer you a ride if you needed one? They seem like nice enough people, from what I know of them.'

Perhaps enough time had passed that they were better. Barbara was not sure of the mood in the Clairemont household. But she would rather cut her tongue out than ask Anne, for fear the answer she might receive would open old hurts afresh. She gave a firm smile. 'It is an old family quarrel, and nothing of importance. I would not seek to bother them if I did not have to.'

'But I would like to hear of it, all the same.'

'You will not hear it from me,' she said, shifting uncomfortably in her seat. 'You are new to Fiddleton, Mr Stratford, and might not know the ways of small villages. When one lives one's life with the same people from birth, it sometimes happens that one makes a mistake that cannot be corrected and that will follow one almost to the grave.'

'Are you speaking of the Clairemonts, then? What mistakes could you have made to render you less than perfect in the eyes of this village? From where I sit, I see a most charming young woman—and well mannered.' He smiled. 'Although not always so to me.'

'You do not always deserve it, sir.'

'True enough,' he agreed. 'But you are kind to others, modest, clearly devoted to your family. And beautiful as well.'

'Though too old to be still unmarried,' she finished for him, sure he must be thinking it. 'The verdict has already been rendered as to my worth in that regard. I have learned to accept it.'

'Then we are of a kind,' he said. 'Although I am the worse of the two of us. I have just got here, and I have made myself universally hated. But I do not let it bother me. I do not care a whit for the opinions of the locals. I am who I am, and they had best get used to it.' He looked her up and down again. 'If they think less of you, for some foolish reason or other, I cannot give their views much credence.'

Between the kiss they had shared and the look he gave her now, she suspected he had got quite the wrong idea about it all. He was hoping that there had been a man involved in her downfall. But their trip was almost over, and he had offered no further insult, so it was hardly worth correcting him. As long as they were not alone again he would give her no trouble.

But his disregard for his own reputation bothered her. 'Perhaps you *should* care what people think. There are worse things than social ostracism, you know. Mill owners have been accosted in their own homes and on their ways to and from the factories they own.'

'That is why I carry this,' he said, patting the bulge in his pocket and reaching in to draw out the handle of a pistol.

'Are you really going to use it?'

'Do you doubt my bravery?'

'I do not doubt your foolhardiness,' she said. 'It has

but one bullet in it. If there is trouble, there will likely be a gang behind it.'

'Then I will be forced to appeal to the garrison for aid, and it will not go well with them,' he said, as though that settled the matter. 'I do not seek violence, Miss Lampett. But if I feel myself threatened I will resort to it. You need have no doubt of that.'

She imagined the possible consequences with a sinking heart. 'Since the violence you describe is likely to be turned against my father, I believe we have nothing more to say to each other. It is fortunate that we have arrived at my home.'

Stratford glanced out of the window. 'So we have.' He turned and tapped on the door to signal the driver. 'Another turn around the high street, Benjamin. The lady and I are not finished with our discussion.'

'And I have just said we are.' She reached for the door handle, only to fall back into her seat as she felt the carriage turning. 'This is most high-handed of you, Mr Stratford.'

'But, knowing me as you do, you must expect nothing less of me, Miss Lampett.' He smiled again, as though they were doing nothing more serious than dancing around a ballroom. 'The subject we discuss is a serious one. I think I may have found an agreeable solution to several dilemmas at once. But it requires your co-operation, and the chance for us to speak privately for a little while longer—as we are doing now.'

Which explained the ride, she supposed. She should

be relieved that he had not sought her out of any deeper desire for her company. But, strangely, she was not. 'Very well, then. Speak.'

'As you say, in a small village news travels fast. You say that you know of my plans for the Christmas holidays?'

'You are entertaining guests from London. The only people of the village who will be in attendance are the Clairemonts. If it is not an engagement, then I suspect the gathering has something to do with the opening of the mill.'

'Why would you think that?' he asked, surprised.

'Because you are the host of it. Having met you, Mr Stratford, it seems unlikely that the people coming are old friends.'

'Ha!' Rather than being angered by her insult, he seemed amused by it.

She continued. 'Everything you do has to do with your business in some way or other. This Christmas party is like to be the same.' Then she allowed her true feeling of distaste to show. 'It is vulgar in the extreme to use the Lord's birth as a time for doing business, if that is what you mean to do.'

'Whether you have reached your conclusion from local gossip or shrewd deduction, you are correct, Miss Lampett. I am entertaining investors from London.' He gave a slight frown. 'Because, apparently, I think of nothing but business.' He paused for a moment, as though he had forgotten what it was he meant to say. 'I do not have quite so many guests as I had hoped. There were more negative replies in today's post.'

'Probably from gentlemen who understand the impropriety of it,' she said.

He shrugged. 'Or perhaps they do not wish to associate with one who is in trade, even though he offers them the opportunity to do it far from the prying eyes of the *ton*. It does not matter, really. As you have pointed out, they are not my friends. But I need only one—perhaps two—to come, agree and invest. Then, for me, this Christmas will be a happy one.'

It appeared that her father was right about the man, if that was how he measured his happiness. 'There would be far more joy for all should you choose to spend that time in meeting your neighbours, sir. If you could not manage that, then perhaps you could release the Clairemonts from their obligation to attend? For I suspect it will pain them greatly to see their home treated as the London Exchange.'

'It is no longer their home, Miss Lampett. It is mine to do with as I please.'

'But I do not see why you wish to tell me of it. It is no business of mine,' she said, almost leaning out of the window in an effort to put space between them.

'On the contrary. I mean to make it your business. I understand that there has traditionally been a gathering of villagers at the house for Christmas. You have been in attendance at it, with Miss Anne Clairemont and her sister.'

'But that was years ago,' she admitted. 'Not since…' Not since Mary died and the Clairemonts shut up the house at Christmas. But the circumstances were no business of Stratford's.

'You and your family will honour me with your attendance this year as well,' he said. 'I am short of ladies, and there are likely to be several young bucks who would prefer an eligible young partner to dancing with their sisters.'

'On our limited acquaintance, you expect me to sit in attendance on your guests? That is rude beyond measure, sir.'

'Nothing of the kind. I invite you to be one of my guests. There would be no obligation to dance if you did not wish to do so. Though should you meet someone and form an attachment to him it would solve the question of your unmarried state quite nicely. Between your father's trouble, and the problem you have hinted at with local society, it must be difficult for you to be so removed from the company of equals.'

It was. Though she tried to control it, a wistful longing arose in her at the prospect of a chance to put on her nicest gown and dance. 'I do not need your help in that situation,' she said primly. 'I am quite fine on my own.'

'So you keep telling me. But I need *your* help, Miss Lampett,' he said, his hands open before him. 'My business negotiations, whether they are improper or no, are at a delicate juncture. I dare not risk your father giving another angry speech while the investors are here to see it. Nor do I wish to call the law down on him with Christmas dinner.'

'Then I think you would want us quiet at home for the holiday, and not dancing at the manor.'

'On the contrary. I have seen your father's interactions with you. When he is concerned about your welfare, all thoughts of violence go quite out of his head. If you told him that you wished to come to my party he would not disrupt it for fear of spoiling your enjoyment.'

'Even so, I would not trust him for any length of time in the company of strangers.'

'Then I shall send him a selection of books from the library. Old favourites of mine that are sure to occupy his mind for the duration of the week.'

'Old favourites of yours?' she said in surprise. 'You gave me to understand that you had no time for books.'

'Not now, perhaps. But I'd read most of the volumes in the Clairemont library long before my arrival here. In the coming year, when the mill is employed, I hope to have some evenings to myself and might read them again.'

'You said you were a weaver's son,' she said, thinking of her father's recalcitrant students and wondering if she had misunderstood him.

'I did not say I was clever at the trade. I was a horrible weaver, and no amount of teaching could make me better. I was more interested in books than the loom. When Father did allow me to go to school I taught myself, in whatever way I could manage.' He smiled bitterly. 'I fear I was a grave disappointment to him.'

'But why did you remain involved in the trade? Surely there might have been another occupation more suited to your tastes?'

'The life I wanted was forever closed to me, for I was not born a gentleman, Miss Lampett. It appeared that, no matter my lack of skill, I was destined to weave. So I redesigned the loom to make it easier for my clumsy fingers to manage. The machines to be used at the factory are of my own invention.'

Somehow she had imagined him purchasing the frames he used with little knowledge of their workings. But there was real passion in him as he talked of cold and unfeeling machines, and an energy that drew her in like a lodestone. It was only with effort that she noticed the fact that there was no mention of anyone other than himself.

'Is that why the talk of frame-breaking bothers you so? It must be difficult to see your work destroyed.'

He shrugged. 'Not really. Before coming here, my business was mostly in the supplying of other mills. When their looms were damaged by vandals, I made additional money in the repair and replacing of their machinery. While the production of cloth is a risky business, there can be no surer trade right now than the making of a thing that is useful, and very much in demand, but needs to be purchased multiple times when it is ruined. That business was the source of my wealth. Though your father and his friends might seek to see the end of me, like men have been my making.'

'You view the misfortune of others as the source of your success?' she said, amazed at how far removed he was from the people around him.

'So it has been. But enough of me and my business. Tell me what your response to my offer is likely to be.'

'It would be most improper for a single lady to accept an invitation from a gentleman if there is no understanding between them,' she said, wondering what he could be thinking to ask her in this way.

'Of *course*.' He pounded his fist against his leg once, in irritation. Then he gathered himself a little straighter. 'Please accept my apologies. It was forward of me. I will extend a formal invitation, in writing, for your whole family to join in whatever activities take place. There will be nothing to upset your father, I assure you. There will be dinners, dancing, games. I expect that it will be a very jolly time. If your parents do not wish to come, you must come alone—in the company of Miss Anne Clairemont and her family.' He gave her a firm look. 'There will be no trouble on that front. The doors of my house are open to you.'

There was a faint emphasis on the word 'my' to remind her that things had changed. She wondered if he would put the situation to the Clairemonts in the same blunt tone. It almost made her pity them.

But, no matter what he did, it would not be as it had once been. The merriment would not touch the community that it bordered. 'No, thank you,' she said. 'It hardly seems appropriate to celebrate when so many people are unhappy.' They had reached the gate of the cottage again, and she looked longingly in the direction of her home.

'How very pious of you.' He had noticed their destination as well, and tapped to signal the driver. 'It is a lovely day. Let us make another pass of the high street, shall we?'

'Do you mean to hold me prisoner in this carriage until I agree to your scheme?'

He held his hands up in a symbolic gesture of release. 'The thought had occurred to me. But I will let you go home to consider this and see if you do not think it a temporary respite from our troubles. Either way, the mill will open in January. Change is coming and there will be no avoiding it. Once it is open, and at least some of the locals are employed in it, we will find them less likely to raise a hand against me. Until then we must find together a way to stall your father from upsetting my plans—or I will take steps that are pleasant to neither of us.'

The carriage drew smoothly to a stop, and when the door opened he went before her, offering his hand to help her to the ground. Then he signalled for a footman to carry her basket to the house and returned to his seat, closing the shiny black door behind him.

Chapter Seven

When she was through the door of the cottage she saw her father waiting in the front room, arms folded across his chest. Today she did not fear him so much as dread the weight of his displeasure.

'Well?' There was so much disappointment in the one word that Barbara glanced behind her, out of the open door and down the road, thinking that the burden of carrying the weight of her loaded basket could not possibly have equalled this.

She turned back, squared her shoulders and explained. 'Mr Stratford offered me a ride from the shops because the weather was changing.' She gave a little shake of her cloak to show the patter of icy drops that had hit her in the short walk from the carriage to the house. 'He was quite insistent. It seemed that I was likely to create more of a scene by refusing than accepting. So I relented.'

'There was time enough for someone to come from the village and inform me of the fact and be gone again,' her father said suspiciously. 'One would think that a man on foot could not best a team of horses in traversing the distance.'

She cleared her throat. 'Mr Stratford was deep in conversation with me as we neared the house. To continue it, he turned the carriage and we travelled once more around the village.'

'Thus it became a social drive.' Her father shook his head. 'That is a demonstration of the perfidy of the man. It is much like the mill—offered as an olive branch to the people of this community, only so he can snatch it away as they draw near. He took you, just as he took their jobs, and he dangles you like a bauble, just out of reach, and plays with you at his leisure.'

'Hardly, Father. We talked for but a few moments. The carriage remained on the high street and I sat in the window of it. I am sure that many in the community could see me and know that nothing untoward was happening.'

The argument seemed to have no effect on him, for he went on with increasing anger. 'The man is the very devil, Barb. I swear. The *devil*. He is here to ruin the village and all the people in it with his new ideas and his cheap goods. Nothing can come of cheapening the quality of the work, I am sure. It is the veritable road to hell.'

'And nothing to do with the matter at hand,' her

mother added firmly from behind him. She looked past him at her daughter. 'You say that you were seen the whole time? The carriage took no side trips, nor left the sight of the high street?'

'Not at all, Mama.'

'You could not have waited until the rain had passed? Or hurried home before it?'

'I did not want to spare the penny for the boy if I did not have to. The basket was heavy. And Mr Stratford would not take no for an answer.'

Her mother nodded. 'The offer of transport was fortuitous, even if there was an ulterior motive. What did you speak of?'

'His business.' And Mary, of course. They had spoken of her. But it was hardly worth mentioning.

'Then it had nothing to do with you?'

'Just as I suspected. It was an effort to turn you against me, and the village against us. The man is the devil,' her father insisted.

'Enough!' her mother snapped, ignoring her husband again and turning back to Barbara. 'We must deal with the more important matter first. And that should be the honour of our only child, which has not been harmed in the least by the trip, whether it was social or practical.'

'He invited us to the manor for Christmas,' Barbara added. 'He suggested that there might be gentlemen there, and dancing.' She tried to sound matter-of-fact about it, as though it did not matter one way or the other. She did not particularly wish to meet gentlemen.

There was one in particular that she might like to know better, but her father was probably right to call him a persuasive devil who was best avoided.

Still, it had been a long time since she'd danced—with or without demons. Would it really do any harm?

'Dancing at the manor? Of course you should go, then.' Her father's sudden change caught them unawares, as it often did. Though he had been angry only a few moments before, now he was smiling at her. 'You have not been since last Christmas, and you always enjoy it so. Visiting Anne and Mary will do you a world of good.'

She shot a worried glance over his shoulder to her mother, and then said, 'Father, Mary is dead. The Clairemonts no longer live at the manor. There has not been a Christmas celebration there in six years.'

'I know that,' he said quickly, embarrassed at his lapse. 'I only meant that you would be better off dancing at the manor than driving on the high street with Lucifer in a silk waistcoat.' He darkened again, as suddenly as he had brightened. 'A silk waistcoat made by hands that slaved for pennies so that he might ride high and mighty like a prince.' His eyes lit at the sound of his own words. 'I must write this down. It will be the basis of my next speech.'

'You do that, Father.' Barbara hurried to the little desk in the corner, setting out paper, uncapping the ink and trimming the nib of the pen. Then she pulled out his chair and took time to settle him there. It seemed to give him comfort, for he sat down and began writing industriously, staring out of the window before him into the sleet-streaked sky as though the next words were written on it and he could pluck them from the air.

'Come into the kitchen, Barbara. Let us see what you have brought back from the market.' Her mother turned quickly, but not before Barbara could see the trembling of her lip that was the beginning of tears.

'A moment, Mama.' She hurried to the sewing basket, to conceal her mother's Christmas gift. Then she followed her out of the room.

By the time she had reached her in the kitchen her mother was more composed, though clearly worried.

'What are we to do, Mama?' she whispered. 'He is like this more and more.'

'There is little for us *to* do. There is no changing him.' Her mother gave a brief, bitter laugh. 'He changes often enough on his own. Like the tides, he goes to extremes at both ends.'

If he continued thus there would be no chance of him returning to employment, and they would end their days living off the dwindling inheritance her mother had received from her own family. Barbara thought of the pennies in her purse again, and gave quiet thanks to Mr Stratford. Even if he was the devil, he had saved her the bother of a wet walk.

Her mother seemed to be thinking of him as well. 'Tell me about this Christmas invitation you have received. It does seem to be a lone bright spot in the day.'

'I told him it was improper,' Barbara said, frowning. 'For I did not think Father would approve.'

'Your father is lucky to remember from one minute to the next why he hates the man. We will tell him that you are gone to see Mary. For if there are gentlemen there, as he said…' Her mother was thinking forward, hoping for a bright future in which a wealthy stranger would appear with an offer and solve all their problems.

'But I refused,' Barbara said, dashing her hopes.

'Oh,' said her mother, properly disappointed.

'He offered again—including the family. When I told him that there was no way Father could manage such a gathering, he offered a selection of books as Christmas gifts—to keep him home and quiet over the holiday. He said he would send something written, so that I would know he spoke with sincerity.'

'A written invitation to the manor?' Her mother positively glowed with the prospect.

'I doubt he will remember,' Barbara said hurriedly. 'I am sure it was said only in passing, to make conversation. It was just an effort to be social.'

'A most curious effort, then.' Her mother was looking closely at her, trying to determine what she might be concealing. 'He has made no attempts at civility to the rest of the village. And yet he singles you out. A gentleman would know better than to make promises he cannot keep—especially when he is courting another.'

'One can hardly call him a gentleman, Mother. He is in trade. He admitted to me that he was a weaver's son.'

'Really?' Her mother's eyebrows arched. 'You speak like your father, my dear. It is idealistic to set men of business firmly below us and to act as though birth is all. Perhaps realism would be a better path, considering our circumstances. It is possible to be a gentleman and poor as a church mouse, while the weaver's son dines and dances in a manor. The world is changing. While we might not approve of all the changes, we must make the best of them. Let us hope that Mr Stratford is as good as his word.'

And his offer proved true. A short time later, while her father still pondered his latest diatribe, there was a knock on the door. Outside, the same coach that had deposited her waited for the liveried servant who held a properly sealed and decorated invitation and a package of books.

Before her father could say otherwise, her mother had snatched it from the poor man's hand and instructed him to wait upon the response. Then she pushed her husband's work aside and reached for paper and pen.

'As usual, Satan sends his handmaidens in fine garments to tempt the unwary,' her father barked.

The footman looked rather alarmed and peered behind him, unaware that he was the handmaiden in question.

'Nonsense, dear. It is an invitation to the manor. Nothing more. It can do us no harm to accept, surely?'

'Well, then.' Her father beamed. Then he waved a hand at the man who waited. 'My regards to Lord Clairemont, his wife and his daughters. Tell them to be wary, just as they are merry.' Then he opened the first of the books and immediately forgot the source of his discomfiture.

The man gave a hesitant nod, and waited upon the hurriedly scribbled response from her mother before returning to the carriage.

Mother and daughter returned to the kitchen.

'You cannot mean for us to go, Mama,' Barbara whispered. 'Look at Father. There is no way for us to keep the pretence that it will be as it was. And no way to predict, once he is there, what he will say in front of Mr Stratford and his guests. It would be better if we refused politely and stayed home.'

'It would be better if your father and I stayed away. But there is no reason why you cannot go,' her mother said firmly. 'While I like dinner and a ball as well as the next person, I am content to sit here with your father and allow you to get the benefit of an invitation. He said there might be gentlemen?'

'Friends from London.'

'Stratford means to marry Anne. She and her parents will be there to recommend and chaperone you. I am sure, if you wrote to her, she would offer you a space in their carriage so that you needn't walk to the manor.'

'That was what Mr Stratford suggested as well. He said he would speak to them. But I do not think they would like it very much. Perhaps there is another way.' Although Barbara could think of none.

'I will not let you walk to the manor in dancing slippers. Nor will I allow you to refuse this invitation,' her mother said, giving her a stern look. 'I will write to the Clairemonts about it. I will choose my words with care. Perhaps, after six years, you should not blame yourself for something that was no fault of your own, and they should find it in their hearts to forgive you.'

It was not nearly enough time, Barbara was sure. It had been just this morning that she'd met Lady Clairemont walking down the street and seen the way the lady looked sharply in her direction, and then through her. 'Please, Mother, do not.'

'There is no other way. This is an opportunity that you dare not turn down. If there were other suitable men anywhere in the area I might think twice. But if there is a chance of a match amongst Mr Stratford's guests we must seek it out for you. One of your old gowns will have to do. But we can trim it up with the lace you bought this morning and I am sure it will look quite nice.'

'Mother!' Despite her best efforts, her mother had seen into the shopping basket. 'That was intended as a gift.'

'For someone who has less need of it than you,' her mother said, laying a hand on hers, 'it would do my

heart good to know that you are out in society again—
even if it is only for a day or two. I will write the letters,
and then we will see what can be done with the gown.
You must go where you are invited, Barbara, and dance
as though your future depended on it. For it very well
might.'

Chapter Eight

Joseph went to his bed that night in the knowledge that his rest would be well and truly settled. He had managed his guests—impressing the men with his plans for the mill, and charming the ladies without appearing ill-mannered or common. He had skated Miss Anne Clairemont twice around the millpond without falling or precipitating a fall in her. Then he had gone into the village, located Miss Lampett and presented his proposition.

If the ghost, or whatever it had been, had meant to upbraid him on the fate of that poor girl, he had done his best to return her to the society to which she was accustomed. Although why her fate should fall to him, he had no idea.

Perhaps it was because he was the one with the most power to change it. When his future mother-in-law had protested that she would not be seen in the company of 'that girl', he had explained tersely that it would be so because he wished it so, and that was that.

He wondered for a moment what Barbara had done to deserve such frigid and permanent rejection, but concluded it was nothing more than the usual fall from grace involving some young man—possibly a suitor of Anne or the departed Mary. If that was the case Miss Lampett had well and truly atoned for it, after years of modest dress and behaviour.

And more was the pity for it. If the kiss they'd shared had been any indication of her capability for passion, he'd have liked her better had she *not* found her way back to the straight and narrow. He smiled, imagining a more wanton Barbara, and the sort of fun he might have had with her.

The clock in the hall struck two.

'Leave off having impure thoughts about the poor girl, for your work is far from finished.'

Joseph sat bolt upright in bed at the sound of another unfamiliar voice, booming in the confines of the chamber. He had not even risked wine with supper, and had shocked his valet with a request for warm milk before bed. But now he wondered if perhaps it might have been better to forgo the milk and return to a double brandy in an effort to gain a sound and dreamless sleep. 'Who might you be, and what makes you think you can read the contents of my mind?'

'You are young enough, and healthy enough, and smiling at bedtime. If you are not thinking of a young lady then I do not wish to know what it is you *do* think on.'

This night's ghost wore a scarlet coat of a modern cut trimmed in gold braid. His buff trousers pulled tight across his ample belly as he laughed at his own joke. The brass of his buttons was gleaming as bright as the gold leaf upon the coach he must drive. But tonight it seemed to be even brighter than was natural, as was the coachguard's horn he carried in his right hand as further indication of his job.

'As to who I am, you may call me Old Tom, and know that I departed this life just a year ago, along the Great North Road. You would not have had to ask my name had you lived any great time in this country. All know me here. At least those who are not so high and mighty as to have no need of public conveyance.'

Joseph snorted. 'Although I have no real memory of you, I've heard of you—driving drunk and taking your passengers with you to the next life when you upset the coach. I must be running out of ideas. I am reduced to populating my own dreams with little scraps of facts that do not even concern me.'

The driver laughed again. 'You give yourself far too much credit, Joseph Stratford. Even if you think yourself clever with machines, you are rather a dull sort for all that, and not given to colourful imaginings.'

'Dull, indeed.' Joseph rather hoped the ghost was real. If it was not, it was proof that his own imagination was prone to self-loathing and insult. 'If I refuse to believe in spirits it is a sign of a rational mind, not a slow one. For ghosts do not exist.'

'If you do not believe in ghosts, then why are you sleeping in your clothing?' asked the shade, drawing back the bedclothes to reveal Joseph still in shirt, trousers and boots.

'Because I woke this morning near naked in a downstairs hallway. Ghost or not, the situation will not be repeated.'

'Very well, then. You are not dull. More like you are so sharp you'll cut yourself. You are willing to believe anything, no matter how unlikely, so that you don't have to accept what is right before your eyes.' Old Tom glared. 'For your information, I was not drunk on the night I crashed. I did sometimes partake, when a glass was offered. Who would not, with the night air being chill and damp? But that night I was sober as a judge and hurrying to make up time. A biddy at the Cock and Bull had dawdled over her supper and left us to run late.' He leaned closer and added in a conspiratorial tone, 'And she will not leave off nagging and lamenting about the time, even now on the other side. Some people never learn, as you well know.'

The ghost looked him up and down and laid a finger to the side of his nose, as though Joseph should learn something from the comment. Then he went on. 'I was late, and pushing the horses to their limit, when a rabbit darted out from the hedge and right under 'em.

It spooked the leader and he got away from me. Just for a moment. And that was that.'

Joseph swung his feet out of bed and sat up to face the ghost. 'An interesting tale, certainly. But there is no way to prove it, and nor am I likely to try.'

'You would not believe it even if you found the truth,' Old Tom replied in disgust. 'You are cold as ice, Joseph Stratford, and just as solidly set. I gave you too much credit when I arrived. It is just as likely I found you warming your thoughts not with some beautiful lady but with fantasies of machinery and ledger books.'

'So I have been told,' Joseph said with bitterness. 'Yet I have spent a portion of this day seeing to the wants of others, with no chance of personal gain likely to come of it.'

'No gain at all?'

He remembered the way he had phrased his offer to Barbara, as an effort to keep her father safely at home. 'Very little gain. The majority of the good done will benefit others. After last night's visitor, I made a change in my plans and invited Miss Barbara Lampett back to the manor house. There is my proof that I have learned something and rendered tonight's lesson unnecessary. I am making an effort to help the daughter of my enemy.' He gave a wave of his hand. 'And so you may depart.'

'Well, thank you, Yer Lordship,' the ghost said with a sarcastic bob of his head. 'But for your information it is I who will set the time of my departure, and not you. Before I can complete my final journey I have been called back for one task alone to make up for the care-lessness of my end. I mean to do the job properly. When I leave here you will be well and rightly schooled.'

The ghost shuddered for a moment, as though uncomfortable in his surroundings. 'I'd have thought that if called to haunt I could have taken to the road, just as I did in life. Instead they sent me to *this* dreary place, colder than a moor in December.'

Again Joseph was annoyed that his spiritual visitor seemed less than satisfied with surroundings it had taken him half a lifetime to afford. 'This is the finest house in twenty miles, as you should know. The fire is lit, as are the candles. There is tea on the hob and brandy in the flask. Or perhaps you would like a shawl, like an old woman?'

Tom snorted. 'As if I could take pleasure in such, here on the other side. I am quite beyond feelings such as that.' He shuddered again. 'But I can see things you cannot. There is a cold coming off you like mist from a bog.'

He raised a finger to point at Joseph. In an instant the friendly driver was gone, and before him Joseph saw only a tormented spirit with a dire warning.

Then Tom smiled. 'But I have been set to warm you up a bit. A hopeless task that is like to be. Now, come on. We haven't got all night.' The ghost reached out a hand. 'Tonight you will walk with me, and if you are lucky you will learn to see the world as others do. At the least you will see what you are missing when you cannot take your nose from the account books and your feet from the factory floor. You will learn what people think of you. It should do you a world of good. Now, take my hand.'

Joseph's mind warred with itself, but the battle was shorter than it had been on the previous two nights. Whether real or imagined, Tom would not leave until he was ready to. And Joseph did not like being afraid of men—in this world or the next. So he reached out and grabbed the hand that was offered to him.

To touch it was even worse than touching Sir Cedric the previous night. Old Tom's hand was large and doughy, and thick with calluses from handling the reins. But it was freezing cold—like iron lying on the ground in December. The instant Joseph touched it his own fingers went as numb as if they'd died on his hand. And this, more than anything else, made him believe. His father might have been a memory, and Sir Cedric a walking dream. But in his wildest imaginings, he'd have conjured nothing like the feel of this.

He withdrew quickly, and after a stern look from the ghost adjusted his grip to take the spectre by the coat-sleeve instead. That was cold as well, but not unbearably so.

'The first stop is not far,' the ghost assured him, as though aware of his discomfort. 'Just beneath you, as a matter of fact.' Then they seemed to sink through the floorboards until they stood in the first parlour.

Though he'd thought that she had gone home with

her parents, he found Anne sitting in a chair by the fire and weeping as though her heart would break.

'There, there,' he said awkwardly, reaching out a hand to comfort her.

'Have you not yet learned what a pointless gesture that would be?' Old Tom asked. 'While you are with me she will not notice you.'

'Perhaps she will.' Joseph reached out to pat her shoulder, only to feel his hand pass through her as though she was smoke. He looked helplessly at the ghost. 'Last night, it was not always so,' Joseph argued, remembering the young Barbara.

'And tonight it is,' Old Tom said.

Behind them, the door opened. Though he needn't have bothered, Joseph stepped to the side to allow a man to enter the room.

Robert Breton glanced into the hall, as though eager to know that he was not observed, and then shut the door behind him and went quickly to the seated woman and took her hand.

'Bob?' Joseph knew then that he must indeed be invisible, for never had he seen such a look on his friend's face—nor was he likely to. The gaze he favoured Anne with was more than one of sympathy to her plight. It had tenderness, frustration and—dared he think it?—love.

On seeing him there, Anne let her tears burst fresh, like a sudden shower, and her shoulders shook with the effort of silence.

'Tell him,' Breton said. 'I have confronted him on the subject. He will not break off at this late date for your sake. He fears for your reputation even more than you do. If you do not end it for yourself, it is quite hopeless. I will not speak if you say nothing, no matter how much I might wish to. I have said more than enough already. You must be the strong one, Anne.'

'And I never was,' she answered, not looking up. 'Perhaps if Mary was here…'

'Then the lot would have fallen to her. Or it might never have occurred at all. But it does not matter,' Breton said firmly. 'She is dead and gone, much as no one wishes to acknowledge the fact. You cannot rely on her for help. You must be the one to speak, Anne.'

'Speak what? And to whom? To your father? To me?' Joseph took his place on her other side, as though he could make himself heard to the woman through proximity. But she said no more and, realising the futility of it, he looked up at the ghost. 'What do you want? I will give it to you, if I can. I am not totally without a heart, you know.'

'I think you can guess what she wants,' the ghost said. 'And why she does nothing about it.'

'It is not as if I am forcing the union on her. She agreed to it. And what does Bob have to do with any of it?'

'Not a thing, I expect, if it all goes according to your plan. He is a gentleman, is he not?'

'But he is a man first,' Joseph said. 'If he wants the girl for himself, then why does he not say something?'

The coachman laughed in response. 'You make it all sound quite simple. I envy you, living in a world as you do—where there are no doubts and everyone speaks their mind. The woman he loves has chosen another. He has been bested by a richer man. He will step out of the way like a gentleman.'

'But not before warning me to care for her,' Joseph said glumly. Their conversation in the hall that morning made more sense to him now. 'I cannot cry off now that there is an understanding. Unless she finds the courage to speak, we must all make the best of it.' But now that he knew the mind of his would-be fiancée it would be dashed hard to pretend a respect where none existed.

'Is this all, then?' he asked of the ghost.

The ghost smiled in a way that was hard and quite out of character with his jolly demeanour. 'Did you think it was likely to be? Your sins, when added together, total more than just heartlessness to this poor, foolish girl.'

'If you mean to brand me sinner, show me the proof of it so that I may go back to my bed. Take me away from here, for I have seen all you intended me to in this place.' He did not wish to follow the ghostly coachman, and this might still be little more than an unsettling dream, but the sight of his friend and Anne together felt like a violation. If he could not find a way to change things, then the least he could do was allow the two who were suffering a moment's privacy.

'Very well.'

Old Tom stepped forwards, and Joseph along with him. There was a rushing of wind, and in the time it took for his foot to fall he was stepping into another room, in another house. This place reminded him of his visit to his childhood home the previous night, though it was not so grim. It was sparsely furnished, and bare of ornament, but the kitchen where they stood was kept with the sort of earnest tidiness he expected of a home with a living wife and mother. A woman was busy at the hob. Her husband sat at the table, shoulders slumped and head bowed as though in prayer.

'Who might this be?' Joseph asked, for though the man's face was familiar he could not attach a name to it.

'If you had bothered to speak to him, or any other in this community, you would know him already.'

'I know that he was waving a sledgehammer at me when last I saw him, just two days ago,' Joseph said testily. 'It did not put me in the mood for gaining a proper introduction.'

'His name is Jonas Jordan,' replied Old Tom, ignoring his retort. 'He is the most skilled worker in the area, and might be your foreman should you and your mill survive long enough to hire him. And this is his family, preparing for the Christmas you and your kind have made for him.'

The man had not moved from his place, though his wife now gathered the children for their meal, overseeing the washing of hands and the setting of places. There were five of them. The youngest was a babe that was likely still at breast, and the oldest was too young to work.

In this little house, on a narrow side road just off the high street, there were none of the smells he had come to associate with the season—neither burning Yule Log nor sizzling fat and fresh bread. The fire in the grate burned low with the meagre handful of coal that made it, so that the cold crept out into the corners of the room, and the children, who should have been boisterous, huddled together as though they had little energy to do else.

'Mama,' said the second youngest, 'I am hungry.'

Without a word, the woman brought out bowls and set them around the table. The children gathered to take their places. Then she ladled some thin porridge from the pot that sat by the fire, and reached for the jug that sat upon the table. She poured out water rather than milk. The children took it in silence and she looked on, worried. When she reached to set a bowl before her husband he pushed it away, without a sound, until it sat before her.

She watched, her own supper untouched, as the children finished what they had. Then she shared the contents of the last bowl between them. She sat hungry, as did her man.

'It would be more nourishing for the children to have a bowl with a good dollop of cream in it,' Joseph said stupidly, knowing that there would be none of that in this house.

'Perhaps if the lord of the manor had not sold off the herd that once grazed where the new mill stands they might have. It has been the nature, these many years, of the Clairemonts to keep the dairy and to graze the herd. All those who wished might come with jugs and buckets to take their share. But now they must send for milk from the next village. It is one more thing, along with all the rest, that this family cannot afford.'

'So they are starving?' Joseph said, doing his best to harden his heart. 'They were just so before I arrived. It might well be because this very man stood up against the last master and burned his place to the ground.'

'When men are pushed to the edge of reason by circumstances they act without thinking!' The ghost shouted the words at him, as though even a spirit could be pushed beyond endurance. 'Jordan and his family were hungry before. But they ate. He stayed at home with his babes the night the old mill burned. What has happened was no fault of his.'

'Then when the new mill opens he shall have work,' Joseph promised. 'If that is the only reason you visit me, you have no reason to fear. I am bringing employment to the area.'

'For some,' the coachman said.

'For as many as I need,' Joseph answered him. 'If it means so much to them, I will enquire with Clairemont about the dispersal of the herd and decide what can be done to reopen the dairy on different ground. It was never my intention to cut people out of their places or make their children suffer.'

'But neither did you make enquiries into their needs when you came here. I am sure if I asked you to quote figures about your building and your products you would know them, chapter and verse, without even opening a ledger. Yet this man, who will be your good right hand if you let him, might starve and die as a stranger to you.' The ghost's brow furrowed as though he were working a puzzle. 'It is a wonder that the only way you can be made to look clearly at the suffering right before your eyes is to be dragged from your bed by a supernatural emissary.'

The ghost was hauling him forwards, through a closed door towards God only knew what fresh nightmare, and Joseph pulled back, struggling in futility against his grip.

'Very well, then. I see my present clearly,' Joseph shouted back. 'The people I need to work in my mill are starved to the point of hatred. My best friend betrays me. The woman who I would take to wife cannot be bothered to speak a word of truth to my face and set me free of the promise I made to her family. I have seen enough. I will do what I can. Take me back to my room.'

'Not just yet. There is one more you must see.'

Now they were in the home of his nemesis: Lampett.

'Not here,' he said to the ghost. 'I get quite enough

of what I am likely to find here without a ghostly visitation.'

'And what is that?'

'Abuse heaped upon abuse. Violence from the father, and scorn from the daughter.' He thought of the previous evening. 'It is likely she will see me, as she did last night. How will I explain myself to her?'

The ghost crooked a smile. 'She is grown into the sort of woman who is much too sensible to see ghosts. And she has given you more than abuse, if I have heard correctly.'

'You mean the kiss?' Joseph scoffed. 'It was hardly a gift freely given. I took it from her, and then I tricked her into responding.'

'Did she enjoy it?'

'I expect that Eve enjoyed her taste of the apple. But that hardly made hers a wise decision.'

The coachman laughed all the harder. 'You think yourself the devil?'

'They do.'

'Let us see, shall we?'

Just in case, Joseph huddled inside the brassy glow of Old Tom's shadow, thinking that the light would render him invisible if nothing else could. Perhaps this Barbara *was* too sensible for ghosts. But she could see through him easily enough if she chose to do so—just as he could see more of her heart than he wished to.

More of her life as well. He should not want to spy upon her. Her life, her family, her thoughts and words when she was not with him should be no concern of his. But there was a dark undercurrent growing in the curiosity he felt tonight—a possessiveness that was stronger than anything he felt for Anne, or even for his business. Suddenly he was hungry for any detail he might learn of her. Secretly he was glad that the spirit had brought him to her again. Once he had married there would be little chance for any conversation with her. For now, he would rather hear a bitter truth from her lips than the silence he deserved.

To hide his confusion, he examined his surroundings. The Lampett house was nicely though simply kept, and too small to need a servant. There was no sign of strife or need except for the worried look in the eyes of the pretty girl as she stood at the shoulder of the man sitting at a desk by the window.

'Please, Father, take some stew. It is supper, and you must not go without eating.' She set the dinner on his desk, nudging it in the direction of the paper he had been writing upon. Unlike in the last house, there was meat in the bowl she offered, and Joseph could smell fresh bread and mince pies cooling in the kitchen. His mouth watered.

But her father seemed unaffected by the sight and smell of the food. 'Don't want it. There is work to be done. I must stop Stratford before this goes any further.' The man pushed the bowl to the side, and his daughter shot a worried glance in the direction of her mother, who sat by the fire, stitching a piece of blond lace on to a blue muslin gown.

Joseph wished he could offer some reassurance— prove that they had nothing to fear from him, or his mill. When it had opened, and the men were back to work, he might be able to sit at their table as a guest, talking about books with her father and offering polite compliments about the housekeeping of the mother and the prettiness of the daughter. Despite the tension in the air there was a feeling of love and family that was lacking in the manor, just as it had been missing from his childhood.

Then he remembered that he was in the last house in Fiddleton where he might be welcomed as a friend. The disappointment he felt was sharpest when he looked at Barbara. While he was used to hearing her father rail against him, she had much more personal reasons to despise him and he deserved every scornful word.

'Go on, then,' Joseph said, bracing himself. 'Give your opinion of me. When I am with you, you do not have a word of kindness for me other than the few thank-yous I have forced out of you. What do you say when we are apart?' It would hardly be a surprise. She was quite plain about it when they were together. She did not like him in the least. But all the same he tensed, waiting for her words.

'While many of the things he has been doing are wrong, they are not so much evil as they are misguided,' she said, as slowly and carefully as possible. 'I am sure, with time, he will come closer to your way of thinking.'

'Defending him, are you now?' Her father was staring at her, hurt, betrayed and sullen. She was clearly torn by the sight of his agitation.

'Go ahead,' Joseph said softly to her, putting aside his bitterness at the sight of her distress. 'Say what makes this the easiest. It is not as if one more harsh word will hurt me. His mood upsets you. Agreeing with him will calm him down.'

'Yes,' she said suddenly. 'I *will* defend him against your more unreasonable charges. The men in the district need work, Father. You must see that. There must be a mill of some sort, and Mr Stratford has built one where there was nothing. He has done it at great expense and risk to himself. Do the papers not say that it is a bad time to be doing business? He could just as easily have tried his hand at something more profitable. He could have stayed in London. Or built elsewhere.'

'So he brings a few jobs to the Riding?' her father said dismissively. 'He will find another way to make the men starve once it is opened.'

'Perhaps,' Barbara admitted. 'But perhaps not. If we show him reason and kindness and make him feel welcome here he might respond in kind. He does not have to be like Mr Mackay. He might provide a safe and clean work place, and be a benefit to the community. He is an extremely clever man. In talking to him, I find that he is well read and ingenious. If there is anyone who can help the people here, I believe it might be him. You will like him when you know him better. Do you remember the books he sent to you?'

'Yes,' her father said grudgingly, like a child forced to be mannerly.

'They are his favourites, and you like them as well. Might that not be a sign of a kindred spirit? But he must be given a chance to prove it to you.'

Joseph sank to the bench in the corner, quite taken aback by the flood of warmth he heard from her. 'You listened to me, didn't you?' He grinned at the ghost, his own spirit much lighter than it had been. 'It was not all anger on her part. Her chiding had some bluster in it. Perhaps there is some hope for me, after all.'

Old Tom laughed. 'I wonder how your wife will feel about your success with this girl. Since she does not care for you, she will likely be relieved that you seek the affections of another. And you will have this one talked around in no time. If you wished to get her into bed—'

Joseph jumped to his feet, fists balled. 'Do not say another word, sir, about the honour of that lady, or you will answer to me at dawn.'

The ghost observed him with a deathly expression. And, coming from one with such an intimate experience with that state, it was a truly fearsome thing. 'You are a year too late to threaten me, Mr Stratford. Being from beyond the grave gives one the ability to say what one likes without fear of repercussion. So I will tell you that you're only pretending to be a gentleman towards her. You care little enough for people unless they can be of benefit to you. You would bed this girl in a heartbeat if you saw the chance to do it. You would do it even faster if you thought it would give you an advantage over her father.'

Joseph opened his mouth to defend himself, and then closed it again as he realised he had considered doing just that. The fact that he had not acted on the impulse was hardly a point in his favour. As the ghost pointed out, he'd had no opportunity.

Old Tom held up a hand to silence him, for the Lampetts were speaking again.

'Let us talk of something more pleasant.' Her mother interrupted the argument between father and daughter. 'It is almost Christmas, after all.'

'And a time for gifts,' said Barbara, seizing upon the subject. 'Although I do not know how I shall surprise you, Mama, if you keep rummaging through my sewing basket and stealing the contents for other purposes.'

'Never mind what we want. What are we to get for you, my dear?' her father asked, turning back into the doting parent that Joseph had seen the other day. 'You still have not said. And it is too late to send to London for anything special.'

'You know that is not necessary,' the girl said, dropping her head.

'We wish to get you something,' her mother insisted. 'It gives us pleasure to know that you are happy.'

'You should know by now that I am happy just to have the days pass,' Barbara said, staring into the fire. 'It is never an easy time for me.'

'But by now it should be. It has been years, Barbara,' her mother said firmly.

'Almost six,' Barbara said absently.

'It is not as if we expect you to forget.'

'Very good. Because I shall not.'

'Only that it is time to cease punishing yourself for a thing which was none of your fault.'

'There are still those that blame me,' she said, without looking up.

'Fools,' her father grumbled.

'Let us not talk of them, or of the past,' Barbara said quickly, as though eager to avert another dark mood. 'Let us simply say that I am not overly fond of Christmas. I would prefer to celebrate it by knowing that those I love are safe and happy, and not by focusing on my own wants and needs.'

The scene seemed to fade from view again. Joseph could see the players in it, but could no longer hear their words, though he strained to catch some whisper of them. He turned back to Old Tom, frustrated. 'Very well, then. You are right. I have been base and callous in regard to the people of Fiddleton, and this family in particular. But it would help me to understand them better if they were more open about the truth. Six years,' Joseph said, counting on his fingers. 'She would have been eighteen then.' He stared at the ghost of the coachman. 'You were still alive. What happened?'

'I am here to show you the present, not explain the past to you,' the ghost said, a little impatiently. 'If the information is important to you, then you should talk to the girl before you.'

'Did you not just hear her?' Joseph retorted. 'Whatever it is, she will not speak of in front of her own family. How likely is it that she will reveal all when I question her?'

The ghost gave him another sidelong glance. 'I expect it will depend on how you ask her.'

'Stop tormenting me with the idea that I will seduce her,' Joseph said, setting his jaw against the idea. 'It is clear that she has unhappy memories associated with Christmas time. I do not mean to be another of them. If that is what you wished me to learn this night, then let me go.'

In the blink of an eye he was in his bedroom again, standing alone and fully dressed before the fire, and lecturing the mantel clock as it struck three.

'I will not forget,' he said, just in case some wisp of the spirit remained. 'I will be better. You will see. Let this be the last of these nightly visits. For I have had quite enough of them.'

He changed for bed, then—cautiously, as though at any moment he might be interrupted and dragged away again. It was nearly dawn before he closed his eyes.

Chapter Nine

The next evening found Barbara packed as an unwelcome fourth into the Clairemont carriage, trundling through the sodden streets towards the road that led to the manor. The drizzle had continued for most of the day, as though trying to decide minute to minute whether it would be rain or snow. Barbara felt in sympathy with it. Her own heart was as changeable as the weather, still unsure whether it wished to run towards this evening and its host, or away from it.

But Anne seemed unbothered. 'I am sure it will be a delightful time,' she said, with a wan smile. 'There is to be dancing. And cases of champagne. Cook is preparing a fine buffet, and a cold supper at midnight. Joseph has promised a celebration to rival anything in London.'

'Hmmmf,' said her father, and scowled out of the window.

Her mother said nothing at all, unwilling to acknowledge either their destination or the extra passenger they had accrued for the short journey. The Clairemont family had moved to the largest house in Fiddleton proper, with five servants and room enough to keep both a carriage and horses, but it was nothing compared to the manor. Returning to it as guests was obviously a source of irritation that they would conceal only when absolutely necessary.

But Anne seemed to feel less of it, looking from one to the other of them with a kind of desperate enthusiasm, as though she could imagine nothing better than visiting her old home only to leave it again at the end of the evening. 'Joseph says the chestnuts are particularly good this year. He has sampled them already.'

'I imagine he would have,' her father retorted. 'He goes to excess in all other things. If he is not careful he will be prone to gluttony.'

'I doubt it will come to that,' Anne assured him. 'He will not sit still long enough to grow soft. It is more likely that when he is in the throes of work he will need to be reminded to eat.'

Her father muttered something barely audible beyond the word 'trade'.

Anne fell to silence again, and Barbara could almost hear her thoughts. She was wishing that she had not brought up the subject of her prospective fiancé having an occupation at all. It was clearly another sore spot in the conversation.

She looked desperately to Barbara, who said gamely,

'He seems a most solicitous gentleman. When I was struggling in the shop yesterday he offered to transport myself and my basket in his carriage.'

Anne gave an approving nod, as if to say she would not have thought any less of him.

Her mother responded, 'That might just as easily show a fickle nature. What is he doing, offering courtesies to others when he is promised elsewhere?' She narrowed her eyes at Barbara. 'Unless you were angling after a ride?'

Anne sucked in her breath, but Barbara managed to keep her reaction invisible to the other passengers. She knew Lady Clairemont's opinion of her. But she'd hoped to see no obvious demonstration of it tonight.

'Mother,' Anne said quickly, 'I am sure it was nothing of the kind. Though you might not think it so, Joseph has a kind and generous heart. I am not the least bit surprised that he should offer to aid Miss Lampett.'

'Until his ring is on your finger you had best be less generous and more sensible,' her mother informed her. 'This party would be an excellent time to finalise the arrangement between you.'

'I cannot very well demand that he make the announcement,' Anne said, obviously embarrassed by her mother's bluntness.

'But his inviting other young ladies to this ball does not bode well.'

'I think there is someone he wishes me to meet,'

Barbara said hurriedly. 'He was quite clear about there being eligible gentlemen in attendance.'

'Probably that Breton fellow,' Anne's father grunted. 'He's a bit high in the instep for you, my dear. But a bit low... Second son...' His comment trailed off into inaudibility again.

'You have not even met him, Father.' Anne gave Barbara another silent apology. 'He is really very nice. A true gentleman—neither too high nor too low.'

'And no concern of yours, no matter what his birth. He will do for Barbara, here, if that is what Stratford intends for them. But he cannot be much of a man if he lets a business associate make such decisions for him.'

Anne stared out of the window, as though searching for another topic of conversation. 'I hope the weather favours us this evening. It seems likely that the rain will turn to snow.'

'Then we shall be forced to remain at the manor,' her mother said, showing the first signs of cheerfulness. 'I assume that Stratford has taken the master bedroom. But we shall make do in the next best suite, and you shall have your old room back, Anne.'

'Then I hope that travel is not made difficult,' Barbara said, considering the awkwardness of the situation. 'I am quite unprepared to stay the night.'

'Oh.' Lady Clairemont gave a sad little moue that ended in a smile. 'Do not worry upon it, my dear. I am sure there is a maid that can lend you a nightdress, should we be stranded.'

When they had arrived at the manor, the Clairemonts' behaviour grew no warmer. Lord and Lady Clairemont swept into the ballroom as if they still owned it, greeting other guests as though they were old friends. Anne trailed along in their wake, polite and silent.

When Barbara made to follow, Lady Clairemont turned, giving her a cold and very deliberate look. The direct stare seemed to change as she held it, to look past Barbara and then through her, as though she did not exist at all. The cut was so beautifully made that for a moment Barbara longed for a mirror, convinced that it was she who had faded to transparency. With a single look, Lady Clairemont had made it clear to her that, whatever Joseph Stratford might think, Barbara Lampett was an unwelcome guest here. If there were introductions to be made, he had best appear and make them himself, for the Clairemonts planned to pretend she did not exist.

She had to admire the perfection of the revenge Lady Clairemont had devised. The room was full of strangers. And, if she wished to be thought a well-mannered young lady, Barbara could hardly introduce herself to any of them. She would spend her first night in ages as a sort of social ghost, separated by a glass wall of propriety from the merrymaking.

Nor would Anne come to her aid. Though she did not hold the deep animosity for Barbara that her parents did, she lacked the spine to stand against them.

She was sure that Joseph Stratford would help her, if

she could find him. But there was no sign of him, and she assumed that he must be in a card room somewhere, talking business. She could expect little else. To him, that was the only purpose for the gathering. Even if he had meant to be a proper host, it should be Anne standing at his side and not her.

But it was just as well Mr Stratford did not see her. Having taken a moment to admire the other women, she could see that she did not belong amongst them. While her dress had seemed quite nice in the cheval glass at home, it looked dowdy compared to the pale silks and fine embroidered shawls she saw tonight. And the loveliest amongst them was Anne Clairemont. Her net gown was trimmed with tiny pearls, her hair held in place with diamond pins. She glided through the room like a swan: pure white, slender and graceful.

In comparison, Barbara's retrimmed blue gown managed to be both too bright and too plain. Her neck was bare. Her hair was dressed simply, with no jewels to ornament it. Even if Joseph were to see her he would look on her with pity rather than desire. She was little better than a charity case here—just as she had been the last time she saw him. She must learn to face the reality of it and not let the disappointment show. Invited or not, she did not belong here.

She must remember not to call him Joseph—to his face or to others. Anne Clairemont had that right of intimacy. She did not. But she quite liked the sound of the name in her head. After receiving a secret kiss from him, and being alone with him on two occasions, in the privacy of her thoughts she did not need to think of him as Mr Stratford.

To save herself the embarrassment of another cut, Barbara withdrew, pretending to admire the hangings in the ballroom nearest the door and then easing through it to stroll towards the portrait gallery, as though engrossed in the quality of the art. She considered herself fortunate that the manor was so large, and she so familiar with it. She would steal her share of the refreshments and then wander away by herself to relive happier times in her mind.

When she went home she would concoct a story for her mother about the fine food and the dancing, and the courtly gentlemen who had paid her attention. None so specific as to make her expect a call, but she would claim that it had been a delightful night, and that she had enjoyed herself most thoroughly.

A group of gentlemen passed her in the hall, carrying heaped plates of cakes and sandwiches, clearly on the lookout for a quiet place to sit. Lord Clairemont was amongst them. To avoid further awkwardness she withdrew to one of the many hiding places she'd known as a girl—a chair behind a statue of Mars, which had been decorated in a most undignified manner with garlands of holly.

'Has anyone seen our esteemed host this evening?' asked the first, a rather large man with a lurid pink waistcoat.

'Still trying to do business,' the next remarked. 'He would not let me alone before. Stratford is a most persistent fellow.'

'Little else can be expected of his sort,' the other responded pityingly. 'In trade, you know. It seems they can think of nothing else.'

Unlike some, who thought of nothing but filling their bellies. Barbara looked hurriedly down at her empty glass and the plate of crumbs beside it. Of all the sins of which Joseph was guilty, she could not fault his hospitality to his guests. The portions were generous, and any whim would be indulged for one so fortunate to have been invited into his home.

It made the absence of the villagers more keenly felt. She was sure, had he bothered to include them, that he would have rewarded any stranger from the village with the same casual generosity.

It seemed Lord Clairemont viewed the abundance with less charity. 'There is too much of everything here.' He picked a leaf from Mars and flicked it to the floor. 'When Anne is mistress, I trust she will teach him manners. He is rich, of course, but quite common. Did you see what he has done to the ivy on the south side of the house? He has stripped away great patches of it and brought it here.'

'Decorations, man!' Pink Waistcoat laughed. 'It is hardly Christmas without the stuff.'

'But there is a time and a place,' Lord Clairemont said primly. 'One does not go about denuding houses.'

Barbara was in two minds about that. The rooms looked very nice with the fresh greens. And now that some of the troublesome vines had been removed from around the windows she suspected there would be daylight in the library and the ballroom. Both had been gloomy places even by day, and she recalled being quite frightened of them.

'Stratford and your daughter do make a lovely couple,' one of the men remarked grudgingly. 'It seems that birth does not show on one's face.'

'But it is plain enough in his conversation,' Lord Clairemont remarked. 'He goes to the best tailor in London, but he tells people that the fabric for his coat was woven by himself—on his own modern loom.'

'Perhaps we will find him in the parlour, knitting a muffler?' said Pink Waistcoat. The men around him laughed, moving on.

Barbara leaned back against the wall, eyes closed, wishing she had stopped her ears, before hearing a word of that conversation. She was ashamed of herself for eavesdropping, and embarrassed for Joseph as well. How awful must it be for him to be an object of ridicule amongst his guests and a source of amusement in his own home. She felt a rush of kinship with him. Of all the people in the manor tonight, maybe neither of them belonged.

'Playing at hide-and-seek, Miss Lampett? I understand it is a common game here at Christmas.'

Her eyes flew open to find her host, leaning against

the wall at her side, scant inches away, smiling down at her.

'I was doing nothing of the kind. I was simply—' she searched for a plausible explanation '—resting for a moment. The dancing is most strenuous.'

'It must be, for you to grow tired just by watching it. But you have not even done that, have you? I have been in and out of the ballroom all evening, and have not seen you there at all. Explain yourself.'

'Before I stand up to dance I must be asked,' she said. 'And before that there must be introductions.' She smiled politely. 'But I am having a lovely time, reacquainting myself with the house. It is beautiful— especially done up for Christmas. I thank you for your invitation.'

'Rubbish,' he said sharply. 'You came with the Clairemonts, did you not?'

'They were kind enough to give me a ride in their carriage.'

'But they did not make you known to the other guests?'

She could think of no proper answer for this, so she remained silent.

'And I was negligent in my duties as host and let you wander, alone and abandoned.' He swore then, a short colourful vulgarity that she had never heard before. She supposed she should be shocked by it, make some comment about his low birth and stalk off. But he had

had enough of that reaction, she was sure, and she did not have the heart to add her censure to the rest.

He collected himself quickly, and gave a curt bow of apology. 'Come, Miss Lampett. We are going back to the ballroom so that you might dance with me.'

'Really, that is not necessary,' she whispered.

'There you are again, trying to tell me what is needed and what is not.' He grabbed her by the arm and pulled her out from behind the statue. 'You must know by now that it is quite hopeless to stop me once I have an idea in my head.'

'But I must try,' she said, pulling her arm from his grasp, and permitting him to escort her properly. 'I know that your invitation here was little more than a sop to gain my father's silence. But if we dance the Clairemonts are likely to think it was something more.'

'Do not ascribe such dark motives to me,' he said. 'Perhaps I merely thought that you would enjoy the opportunity of socialising and devised an excuse so that you would not refuse my invitation. Instead I see you are wedded to the wall because my future in-laws are unable to behave like the lady and gentleman they purport to be. I do not know what the gripe is between you. But it ends now.'

'This is a waltz,' she said, tripping along at his side as he stalked into the ballroom. 'And I do not know how. Perhaps if we waited…' But it was hopeless. He was tugging her very gently towards the dance floor.

'It is the simplest of all dances, and you will learn

it as we go,' he said, swinging her about to face him. 'People will call me rude and brash and inappropriate. But I am quite used to that already and will not be bothered.'

'And if people think ill of *me* because of it? Dancing so intimately with a man I barely know?' Although she quite liked the sound of the music and the feel of his hand on her waist. She liked even better the look of shock she saw on Lady Clairemont's face as she spun past her.

'I am your host,' he said, giving a gentle push on her hand to guide her. 'You can hardly refuse me. It is Christmas, which is traditionally a time for small latitudes. No one will say a word.'

'Even if they do, they are all from London and I will never see them again.' She sighed in satisfaction.

With his hand upon her ribs, he noticed. 'That was a happy sigh, I trust?'

She gave a hesitant nod. 'I have not had many opportunities to dance. Sometimes it seems as though I went directly from the schoolroom to the shelf, with no stopping between.'

He snorted. 'You? On the shelf? I should say not.'

'I am twenty-four years old,' she said, with a purse of the lips. 'There are few gentlemen in the area. And girls who are younger, prettier, more biddable...'

He laughed again. 'You make those sound like virtues.'

'Are they not?'

'Young and biddable is often synonymous with naive and without a fully moulded character. Easier at first, perhaps. But it would make for a most dull union to marry such a girl.'

Which was strange. Because it was exactly how she would have described the object of his own matrimonial plans, had she been called to compare with her. 'And beauty?' she asked. 'Surely you have no problems with that?'

'At your worst, you are quite pretty enough to suit even the most discriminating men,' he said, looking down at her with an appraising eye. 'Tonight you are looking most charming indeed. If you hear any complaints on the subject you must send the offenders to me.' His fingers flexed on her waist and his hand squeezed hers. Just for a moment his face dipped closer to hers, sharing a conspiratorial smile.

And she thought, with a sudden flash of insight, *If I allow it, he is likely to kiss me again. Right here on the dance floor. Or in a dark corner, when we can be alone.*

She knew, if the opportunity presented itself, that she would let him. She stumbled and broke the moment of intimacy.

He concentrated on the steps, easing her gently back onto the beat until they were steady again, pretending that the mistake was his to put her at her ease.

It made her feel quite awful. She had accused him of all manner of horrible things, directly to his face. She had thought even worse about him. But it was becoming plain that, though his nature seemed brusque, he was quite capable of behaving like a gentleman when he wished to. It was a shame that he was not being treated as such.

Though it was the height of bad manners to repeat what she had heard, neither did she feel right about keeping the truth from him. 'They are all laughing at you, you know. The other guests. Even Anne's family.' Then she realised that it might sound as if she was sabotaging a rival. 'Not Anne, of course. She is much too good for that.'

'Oh, of course not,' he answered back with sarcasm. 'But she and the rest are not too good to accept bread and board from likes of Mr Joseph Stratford. They lack the strength of their convictions. Some of the people I'd hoped to see tonight refused me outright. I have more respect for them. They are incapable of pretence.' There was no tension as he said the words, sweeping her further out on the dance floor, twirling her effortlessly with the other dancers.

'You realise what they are saying about you?'

'Of course,' he said, with a wry smile. 'You did not honestly worry I'd be hurt, did you? What a sensitive creature you must think me, Miss Lampett. I do not shrink from their displeasure, nor do I acknowledge their gossiping. I am willing to stand against your father and his armed mob, my dear. But to my knowledge no one has ever bled to death from the cut direct.'

'Maybe people would not act that way to you if only you were not so...' She could not seem to find a word to describe it.

He sighed and smiled at her. 'I am too much of everything, I fear. But it is hard to explain the novelty of a full larder to one that has always had their fill.' He looked out of the window at the snow falling in the gardens, as though he could see past it into his own future. 'This is nothing compared to what it will some day be. Two years ago it was a few machines. Now it will be a factory. And before I am through? An empire.' He waved a hand towards the hall they had left. 'They may laugh behind their hands, if they like. But the gentleman in the horrid pink waistcoat has promised me ten thousand pounds. And the gentleman beside him another five. Both will see a good rate of return on their investments. Neither of them need fear that I will reveal our association or bother them with my presence in London. It will work well for all of us.'

'That is all that concerns you?'

He nodded. 'If I had chosen to behave properly and stay where I was born I would be on the other side of the gates right now, looking in at the people dancing. Tomorrow I would be standing outside another man's mill, threatening the master with violence, living in fear that the last crust of bread would be ripped from my hand.'

'You have a very grim view of the world, Mr Stratford.'

'And a very accurate one. I was once poor, Miss Lampett. Now I am rich. But I will never clear the stink of poverty from my skin. I accept that.' He grinned. 'But, all the same, I cannot help but revel in the change.'

The dance ended and he walked her to the edge of the floor. As they approached the people standing there she hesitated, laying a hand on his arm to halt him. 'If they think so little of you, then what will they say to me, in last season's gown retrimmed in borrowed lace?'

'They will treat you with the utmost courtesy, I am sure. I will introduce you to Robert Breton, who is a true gentleman with impeccable manners. He will shepherd you about the room to the others. I recommend that once I am gone you comment at my boorish behaviour in forcing you to dance. Your future will be secure.'

She could not help it, and gave a short laugh. 'I would never...'

'I know you would not.' He was looking into her eyes again, and she felt the warmth, the pull. 'Although I am sure you have thought it.'

'No.'

'Do not lie,' he said, giving her hand a squeeze. 'But do not feel that I fault you. You cannot be blamed. My manners are rough. Considering our circumstances, I appreciate that yours are not, and thank you for it.'

Then he led her across the room to his friend, making another formal bow and as proper a presentation as she could have hoped for. In truth, it was a bit too formal, but that was better than the alternative of being forgotten.

In turn, Mr Breton made polite and much more polished conversation, then took her around the room to his friends and acquaintances, making sure that she was properly introduced to each of them. Her dance card for the evening was quickly filled with gentlemen of the *ton*—younger brothers and married men, who had been rousted from the card room to make up for the lack of dancers.

It was pleasant. She relaxed and remembered what it had been like to attend similar parties, before the house had been shut up in mourning and she'd felt the sting of rejection. But this night was different in that she longed to turn and find the eyes of a particular gentleman following her about the room, even though they had danced only once.

Joseph had taken a personal interest in her. It was to be expected, she supposed. He wished her to be at ease, just as he did the other guests. That was all it was. If there had been any proprietorial interest it was a fabrication on her part. His effusive compliments were another sign of his lack of social grace, not a partiality unique to her.

When she looked for him, as she found herself frequently doing, he was giving his attention to Anne, just as he should. The man was engaged to her, or near to it. He wanted nothing more than to see Barbara similarly happy.

As another dance ended, her partner returned her to Mr Breton, who offered her escort on a trip to the refreshment room. As they passed Joseph Stratford, Breton caught her gaze and looked back at his friend with a mixture of frustration and admiration. 'If you foster hopes in that direction you must know that there is an understanding with another young lady.'

'I know that,' she said, trying not to blush at how obvious he must think her. 'I am merely surprised at how kind he has been to me—though he barely knows me, except through Father. And that is…difficult.'

'So I understand,' said Breton. 'You must go home and explain to your father, if you can, that all is not as simple as it seems.' He looked across the room at his friend. 'For all his faults, Stratford is a visionary. We must trust him to know what is right.'

'I cannot say that I approve of his vision,' Barbara said, shaking her head. 'To the villagers, it seems to be nothing more than wanton destruction and change that benefits one man more than any other.'

'Not at all,' Breton insisted. 'I was there when he made the decision to come here. He was poring over a pile of maps, gazettes and indexes. He chose and then rejected several sites. Then he showed me this place. "Here," he said, "is the land, and here are the workers. Here is the river that will bring the finished goods to London and to the ports. Here are the fields, already full of the sheep to give us supplies, and the roads that will bring the coal."' Breton grinned with pride. 'He sees it all as though it were a pile of loose links, waiting to become a chain. Some men can come up with an idea for improvement, but he is one of the few that understands enough to put that change to work.'

'You are a gentleman,' she argued. 'I would think you knew better than to get so closely involved in trade.'

He shrugged. 'At one time, perhaps. I am a second son, and must make the best of my inheritance. I was dubious when he came to me with the idea for an improved loom. But he is very persistent. He would not leave. So I made one quiet investment. He turned my modest income into a fortune. When he suggested an expansion, I decided I would be a fool to refuse him.'

He glanced around at the largely empty dining hall. 'He expected there to be more speculators, since the chance to do business far outside the eyes of the *ton* would be a pleasant one. Joe's cellar is good, and his table groans. The house is as nice as any one might see in London. The beds are soft enough for a lord, certainly. I have no complaints.'

Barbara pursed her lips. 'He spoke to me of this, and he does not seem disappointed. But I wonder what the Clairemonts think of it all.'

'It hardly matters,' Breton supplied with finality. 'It has been demonstrated to me on several occasions that the God-given right to property does not automatically assume the wisdom or skill to keep it. While your friends the Clairemonts could not maintain their position, I am sure you will find Mr Stratford to be more than able. This is the first such fortune he will make in his lifetime, and the first house he shall purchase. While he continues to advance, the Clairemonts of the world shall be left with nothing more than the honour of their names. Genteel poverty is poverty nonetheless, Miss Lampett. Surely you must know that by now?'

The man they had been discussing rounded the corner, coming upon them without warning. He stopped suddenly and stared at the two of them in surprise, and then offered a hurried apology before turning back the way he had come.

'Whatever does he mean by that?' Barbara said in confusion.

Breton glanced up. 'He thinks he has caught us under a kissing bough. Although how we could manage to avoid them I am not sure. Stratford has them hung in nearly every room and doorway, despite the decidedly unromantic nature of this gathering.'

'Surely if there is an engagement to be announced, there must be a trace of romance in the air.' The thought did nothing to lift her spirits, and Mr Breton seemed equally pensive. He was looking up at the garland of mistletoe and ribbons and around at the empty room. 'I suppose we had best make use of it while we are here.' He hardly sounded enthused about the prospect.

Barbara did not wish to show her own lack of desire. 'If you wish, sir. It is Christmas, after all.' She closed her eyes and raised her face to his.

She had hoped it would be the briefest buss—over

quickly and forgotten. But it appeared that he wished for something more memorable, and did not immediately withdraw. Neither did he advance, or show any real enthusiasm for it. It was not exactly unpleasant, but it was most definitely awkward.

There was a gasp of surprise from the doorway, a stifled sob and then the pattering of lady's slippers down the hall. Breton jerked away from her and muttered a curse. 'If you will excuse me, Miss Lampett?' He gave a hurried bow and raced from the room, leaving her alone again.

Chapter Ten

Joseph Stratford practised the words of his proposal quietly to himself in the silence of the library. If he meant to do the deed he had best do it tonight, while there were guests to celebrate it. It was a culmination of sorts—a final proof to his investors of the confidence that the Clairemonts placed in him. It was another step in his entry into society.

In all ways it was an excellent choice. He had selected Anne with clinical precision, just as he had the household decorations. There was no question that she was a beauty, and her manners and breeding were impeccable. Though her father might be cold and abrupt to him, Anne paid just the correct amount of interest, making it clear without seeming inappropriately eager that when he chose to offer the answer would be yes.

His heart was not engaged, of course. Neither was hers. That was for the best. If he sought affection elsewhere she would likely be more relieved than upset. Though he would make every effort to see her happy, as he had promised Bob, he would expend nothing more to try to win a love that was not likely to appear. And if she sought comfort with another? As long as the first son looked like him, what right did he have to care?

He thought of the brief and unpleasant scene he had witnessed a few moments ago: Breton and Barbara standing awkwardly under the kissing bough. That had been his plan when he'd invited her. She should find someone who valued her, and he could think of no better choice than Bob.

But Joseph did not find his success nearly as enjoyable as the one dance he'd shared with her, or the heroic feeling of rescuing her from her hiding place in the portrait gallery. If he was not careful he'd destroy plans that had been months in the making in trying to interpret a few mysterious dreams and appease spirits that were entirely the makings of his own overtired brain. If he was lucky, the girl was even now getting on well with Breton, and he would never have to think of her again.

Anne was her superior in every way, he reminded himself firmly. Barbara's face was as far from patrician as one could imagine. To call her complexion ruddy was unfair, but it had a healthy glow about it—as though she partook freely of the northern air. She was not short, nor stout, though she appeared stunted next to the tall and slender Anne. In all ways she seemed less refined, less delicate, less of a lady.

And his body did not seem to mind that a bit. While Anne might be as lovely as a china doll, china dolls were made to be admired more than touched. They were expensive things, to be cherished, set upon a shelf and forgotten.

Other toys were meant to be played with. When he looked at Barbara Lampett, oh, how he wished for playtime. She made him think of Christmas morning, with gifts waiting to be unwrapped, games to be won, and nights full of pleasant surprises. The likelihood that she would spend her adult life as a spinster caring for her mad father seemed vastly unfair. He wondered yet again what the truth was in her disgrace and banishment from local society. If there was a stain already on her character, perhaps in time…

The door opened suddenly, and he was face to face with his intended. 'Anne,' he said dumbly, taking a moment to wipe his mind clear of its recent speculation.

'Joseph.' She seemed to need a moment's composure as well. He pretended not to notice the deep breath she took, and the fading flush on her cheeks. 'I am sorry. I did not mean to disturb you.'

'It is quite all right. I meant to seek you out just now. If you have a moment…?'

'Of course.'

Now that the time was upon him, he was unsure what the correct emotion was to suit it. Whatever was expected, he was sure that he was not feeling it. There was no tingle of nerves, no pleasant sense of anticipation, no triumph and no relief. He was certainly not feeling the desire he might wish for as she stepped into the room, closing the door behind her and leaving them alone together for the first time in their acquaintance.

She was totally composed again, staring at him with a pleasant, neutral smile, waiting for him to speak. He wondered if he should begin with some inane comment like, *I suppose you wonder why I've asked you here.*

But they both knew damn well the reason. To pretend there was doubt as to the question and its inevitable answer was an annoying ceremony that he could not quite manage.

So he waited until the click of the door latch no longer echoed in the still air of the room, took the few steps to her side, went down on one knee and said, 'Miss Anne Clairemont, would you do me the honour of becoming my wife?'

The words, though they were only a formality, were surprisingly hard to say.

'Thank you. I would be honoured in return.' It was good that he had not expected her to go into raptures. Her expression had not changed one iota from the one she had worn in the ballroom.

He rose. 'I have no ring to offer at this time. After Christmas I will take you to London, where you may choose something suitable that is to your taste.' It would save her being embarrassed at his lack of style, should he choose incorrectly.

'That will not be necessary,' she said, with the same

unfailing smile. 'I am sure Mother will have something appropriate in her jewel case.'

Apparently when he had purchased the house and its contents he had purchased the bride and her ring as well. He stifled a sudden and totally inappropriate desire to laugh.

'Very well, then. Let us meet in the ballroom at—' he checked his watch '—midnight exactly, to make the announcement. Until then…' They had almost three quarters of an hour. If he was wise, he would use the time to get to know his bride in a way that was more physical than social.

He leaned forwards and she closed her eyes, preparing herself to be kissed. He reminded himself to be gentle, though there was hardly a need. She did not seem frightened of him. Their lips met.

She was warm and pliable, and with a small amount of pressure her lips opened and she responded. It was clear that she knew what was expected of her, but she did not behave like a strumpet so much as a woman reconciled to the prospect of intimacy with a stranger. He had the sudden horrible feeling that now the words had been spoken she would permit whatever he might dare, greeting it with the same polite and placid smile.

To say that it was like kissing a statue was unfair. It was more like *being* a statue. Though he could feel the pressure and taste her tongue against his, it was little different from the walks with his ghosts had been, when he had been near the action but not really a part of it.

He broke the kiss. 'Until then I will allow you to refresh yourself. Now, if you will excuse me...?' He gave a brief bow and left her.

He was not fleeing the room, he told himself firmly. Merely returning with alacrity to the ballroom—to see to his other guests, prepare the musicians for the announcement and await his fiancée so that he could take her hand and make the biggest mistake of his life.

She would smile demurely, like the wooden poppet she was. She would colour with the faint blush of excitement that he assumed she was even now painting on her face in the ladies' retiring room. And he would smile, to prove himself aware of his good fortune, and accept the hearty congratulations that he would receive and the endless toasts drunk in their honour.

The very idea made him want to choke.

From the moment that he had kissed her—really kissed her, hoping to feel something of their impending life together—he had known it was a mistake. But by then the words were already spoken and it was too late to call them back.

In an act of supreme cowardice he swerved as he passed the little alcove in the hall, and ducked behind the curtain. He could not hide for ever. But even five minutes of privacy would be a welcome thing.

'Joseph!' Her voice was a hissing whisper that stirred his blood.

He turned in the tight, confining space and found Barbara Lampett hiding there as well. He put his hands to her waist, drawing her close, and though his mind roiled his body forgot that there was anything or anyone outside of this small niche and responded.

'Miss Barbara Lampett. Hiding again? And now, I assume, we are playing sardines?'

'Nothing of the sort,' she snapped.

'Then apparently you do not know what you are playing at,' he said suddenly, jerking her body until it rested against his, and relishing the feeling of being once again in control. Then he took her mouth, because he could not stand to be without her for another moment. She responded as he'd known she would, massaging his tongue with her own, urging him on. The taste of her sent the life rushing back into his body, and a joy so reckless that he knew it must be dangerous. He pulled away.

'Release me and exit from here immediately, or I swear I shall scream.'

Her words were the correct ones for any offended maiden. They had to be said, if only to be ignored. But as she spoke she made no struggle to escape him. Nor was there any fear in her voice. Instead she gripped his arms and leaned into him.

'Scream, then,' he said, half wishing she would. It would solve many of his problems. Anne would surely hear of it, and his engagement would be over before it had begun. But it seemed whatever indiscretion she had taken part in six years ago had left her devoid of outrage, and he was damned glad of the fact.

She took a deep breath, and for a moment he almost thought she might make good on her threat. Then she sighed, as though defeated. 'Just once, will you not do the proper thing? Why must you make this so difficult?'

'Perhaps it is because I do not wish to let you go,' he replied.

'And I lack the strength to resist you.'

'I doubt that very much,' he whispered, touching her lips with his. 'You are stronger than you know. Strong enough to break my will.' Then he brought his mouth back down to hers to give her the kisses he should have given another. And he felt her burst into flame again.

She took a breath, and he took it away again, letting the smell and the taste of her soak in, until it became a part of him to his very bones. His future might be as cold as a northern winter, but if he could have nothing else he would have a woman like this to remember. He thrust his tongue deep into her mouth and she raked it with her teeth, biting almost hard enough to draw blood, pushing her breasts eagerly against his waistcoat and swaying to excite herself.

He broke the kiss and pushed her away, stroking his fingers once down the front of her gown, making her tremble. 'I suppose you will now offer me some needless objections about how things must be between us,' he told her, making a half-hearted offer to let her leave.

And leave she should—rushing from the little alcove after giving him a sharp word and a slap for his insolence. He deserved nothing less for behaving in a way that was everything despicable, everything he despised about himself and other men who would abuse their power over those in their debt.

But as he said it he reached around her and his fingers tightened on her bottom, flexed and then tightened again. She was round and lush, and he could imagine the feel of her naked flesh, cradling her in his lap as he pushed into her. His body gave a jump of desire in response.

With that little encouragement, she pulled him close again, and he felt another tremble as her body gave an answering surge.

He buried his face in her hair. 'No objections, then. Very good.' He forced her back with him, further into the darkness of the alcove and of his own soul.

He could hear the faint murmuring of couples in the refreshment room and a low moan from his partner, her quickening of breath and the shift of her gown against his coat. 'Someone might hear us,' she whispered.

He touched a finger to her lips. 'Then we will be careful.' He bent to kiss the slope of her breast, then tugged gently at the neckline of her gown, pushing the lace out of the way and probing beneath it to where her chemise had been tucked low and her breasts forced high to the top of her stays. At last his fingers found a nipple and coaxed it upwards to rest just outside her dress, so that he could latch upon it with a sigh.

She should be fighting for her virtue, or at least pretending to resist. He should be racked with guilt at his easy betrayal of Anne. But it felt so good to touch, and to feel a response. This was no mannequin but a living, breathing woman. The sort that a man could make a future with, have a house full of life and love and children.

She gave another gasp at the sudden shock of delight when his teeth closed upon the tip of her breast, and he swirled his tongue as he nipped and sucked. It was tender and sweet, and along with lust he felt the power of bringing her to life. And the bitterness of knowing that he had no right to this—that he was stealing it for his own pleasure, just as the villagers accused him of stealing their livelihoods.

'Tell me to stop,' he said, into her skin. For a moment he did, and looked up at her, admiring the fine line of her chin and cheekbones, for her head was thrown back as she panted in excitement.

'No.' She gasped, her face twisted as though it was agony to feel what he was making her feel. 'I want more.'

'I thought you did. When I saw you at the factory that first day I knew.' Even then her energy, her passion and her anger had shown, in that dull crowd, like a jewel in dross. She deserved more than this little village could offer her. She needed someone who could match her heat for heat. 'I want more as well. I want everything. I want to give you that as well. Everything you ever dreamt of. Let me set you free.' He dropped his head to her breast again.

He could feel that the intensity of his words frightened her. For a moment she seemed almost frozen by them, her frame stiff and rigid, neither welcoming nor resisting. But as he sucked rhythmically upon her he drew a greater response with each pull. Her hands rose to his shoulders, clutching, and then digging in with the sort of hard, painful, rhythmic massage that he might have expected from a cat that didn't know the power of its own claws. He cupped his hands beneath her breasts, holding them to his face before smoothing his fingers down over her skirts, outlining hips and thighs, and reaching behind one of her knees to urge her foot up on the bench beside him.

And she allowed him to do it. Her legs fell open to his touch. Her raised knee pressed encouragingly into his side as he stepped between them. His hand hovered at the fastenings of his trousers for only a moment before rejecting his own pleasure. There was not time, and this was not the place. She deserved more than a selfish coupling against a wall in a common passageway.

He pressed his lips to her ear and whispered, 'Relax for me. Trust me. Let me touch you.'

His hand went to her ankle, then slid up the silk of her stocking and higher, to the silk of her skin. He was teasing her gently, with playful strokes, between her legs, and he felt her surprised intake of breath cut short in an effort to keep quiet. Then he kissed her, and delved his fingers into the wonderfully warm, wet softness at their apex, circling and then pressing, pushing against the opening and then into it, gently, and then with more force. He deepened into a slow slide and thrust that matched the rhythm of his mouth.

She stifled her cry of surprise inside their kiss. There were people passing in the hall, barely feet from where they were. Discovery was inevitable if she could not keep silent, and she knew it.

He did not care. It would mean ruin for both of them. Anne and her family would leave in shame. The schemes he had built, largely from air, would collapse around him, leaving him with nothing but the woman in his arms.

But that would be more than enough. More than he deserved. He withdrew his hand and dropped to his knees before her, pleasuring her body with his mouth, first coaxing and then demanding a response from her. The harder she fought to keep silent, the more he teased, sucking the petals of her into his mouth and nursing upon them as he had at her breast. She bucked her hips against his tongue until he trapped them with his hands, held them still and had his way with her as her fingers twined in his hair, holding him close. Her trembling increased and he reached up again and gave a single hard thrust of his fingers. Her world unravelled, leaving her body throbbing and shaking, totally in his control.

He relaxed, letting his head loll against her thigh, planting gentle kisses on the skin above her garter as he fought for mastery of his own body.

Above him, his lover turned her head and laid her

cheek against the stone wall, as though trying to cool the heat in her blood. But her hands still played in his hair and stroked his temples, and her legs were still spread wide in welcome. She breathed slowly, deeply, in and out, waiting for him to accept the final gift she could offer.

In the silence he felt reality pressing against him, as it had when he'd come here to hide. He had thought only yesterday that he knew what he wanted. Wealth, power, respect, success. A moment ago he had been willing to risk it all—playing games with a woman who had been a stranger to him a week ago.

He reached with one hand to disentangle himself from her arms, and rose to his feet. But for a moment his other hand remained just where it was, fingers buried deep within her clenching body, to remind her who was controlling and who controlled, who was possessed and who possessed.

As though to confirm the truth, her body tightened on his fingers.

His gave an answering lurch of pleasure, even while he tried to regret what had happened. Then he withdrew his hand and stared silently into her eyes, which glittered in the darkness. He could not trust himself to speak. He dared not offer words of comfort or love. But neither could he dismiss her.

She read what she wished to into that silence and pulled away from him, as far into the corner of the little space as she could. She gave a snap of her skirt, to let it drop back into place, and straightened her bodice—which was in sore disarray and barely covering her luscious body.

'You are despicable. You know that, don't you?' she whispered, making sure that her voice was cold and controlled, even if it was the only part of her that was. 'You were trying to make me cry out just when the risk would have been greatest. You wanted discovery.'

'And you love me for it,' he said. 'The risk excited you. You climaxed. No harm was done. If I was as bad as you claim, I'd have taken the same pleasure. I could, even now, take the step that you could not retreat from, and you would go to whatever cold marriage bed fate has planned for you thinking not of your husband but of me.' It was an idle threat. For he would be damned before he'd let another man touch her from this night on.

'You flatter yourself, Mr Stratford.' She raised her chin, arrogant even in confusion.

'Frequently,' he admitted. 'But I am honest about it. I was born low, and not graced with connections or education. I would never call myself a handsome man. But I am the cleverest man in the room, and rich as Croesus. And I know that you want me.'

'That is quite different from loving you,' she said.

'Perhaps. But not for you. It is all of a thing to you. For you could not love a man without wanting him, and you would never want a man that you did not love. At least a little,' he qualified, allowing her some pride.

'We have barely met, and yet you think you know me well.'

'I think I do,' he said. 'And I like what I know. I wish to know more of you. Come to my room tonight.' There would be no more ghosts with her at his side, and no fears of a cold and passionless future.

She shook her head and turned her face from his. 'After this shameful incident there is little left for you to learn of me. You must allow me to keep some secrets for myself, Mr Stratford. Now, if you will ascertain that we are alone so that I may exit, I will go to the retiring room. And you, sir, should return to your fiancée. While she will be too polite to notice your absence, I suspect that you will find others in the community less forgiving of it.' She pushed past him, not bothering to check the emptiness of the hall, and ran.

He sank to the bench behind him, frustrated and confused. What the devil was he doing? Her set-down stung, but he had no right to complain of it. Even if there was a secret in her past that tainted her virtue, it gave him no right to treat her like an experienced London widow. He had been planning, just now, to set her up and keep her for his pleasure, forgetting who she was and who her father was. To take a mistress while taking a wife was not unheard of. But he could not have picked a worse one than Barbara Lampett.

He was lucky that she had not raised a cry that would end his hopes with Anne. Or burst into tears and aroused some guilt in him for the way he had treated her, forcing him to cry off and offer properly. Even if he had sought, in a careless moment, to ruin himself, he had no right to do it at her expense. To finish by demanding entrance to her bed proved he was as uncouth and deserving of scorn as she seemed to think him. He was a base, simple creature, who answered with an enthusiastic affirmative to any temptation that called to him, and he had demanded that she be the same.

But even then she had not rejected him. She had merely refused to confirm the truth. While he suspected that Anne would be just as content to be a widow as a bride, Barbara could not keep her body from responding to his—though she clearly wished to.

She deserved better. And he deserved exactly what he was getting: a big house, a successful business and a wife who neither loved nor wanted him. It should have been enough. More than enough. It was certainly more than he had expected out of life. He had no right to complain.

He felt the desire in him dying, and realised that Barbara had been wrong on that first day. It could not be coal in his veins, for coal was never this cold. He stood, straightened his coat and brushed the dust from the knees of his breeches. Then he drew back the curtain enough to let in a ray of light by which he could check his watch. There was still a quarter of an hour left before midnight. If he applied himself in that time, he suspected he could get quite drunk and still be in the ballroom before the clock chimed twelve.

Chapter Eleven

For the third time tonight Barbara was hiding. At least this time she had chosen the ladies' retiring room, which seemed a bit more dignified than returning to her childhood haunts in a stranger's home.

The alcove had seemed like a clever idea when she'd wanted to think undisturbed about what she was sure she'd discovered. That had been Anne in the doorway, gasping and crying over an innocent Christmas kiss. The reaction might have been appropriate had she come upon Barbara a few days earlier, in the arms of Joseph Stratford. But she had seemed unusually distraught that Robert Breton might kiss another.

It was interesting. And it had given her a flutter of hope. Despite what everyone might say was the future, there were other forces at work tonight. If Joseph asked, and Anne refused... Or if Breton asked first, as his reaction to Anne's tears said he might...

She had sat alone behind the curtain, thinking the most delicious thoughts, smiling to herself and imagining Joseph, either stunned or relieved, turning to her for comfort. Despite her father's feelings on the subject, she would give that comfort gladly. Not tonight, of course. They were still almost strangers. But in the coming months they might grow closer, while her father grew used to the idea.

Then the man she'd been imagining had burst in upon her and everything had changed.

She looked at herself in the mirror, watching the blood rushing to her cheeks and wondering what to think of what had occurred. Maybe it was not as significant as she made it out to be. She'd kept her maidenhead, after all. But it would be a lie to think of herself as innocent. Another shudder went through her body at the memory, and she gripped the edge of the little table before her until her knuckles went white, trying to regain control.

His words after had been harsh and hurtful—but exciting as well. She had tried to respond in kind, aloof and yet passionate, not wanting to reveal her heart lest this all be a game to him. But she hoped it was not. She could not help but love Joseph. His passion and enthusiasm for his work drew her, and they were tempered with a kindness and generosity that few had seen but her. Given time, he could be made to see the errors he was making. Or perhaps it was he who was right, and her father in the wrong. There had to be a compromise of some kind to avert disaster. And she might be the only one who could bring it about.

The door opened behind her. When she glanced into the mirror she saw Anne Clairemont enter. Just for a moment the other girl shot a look of unvarnished loathing at the back of her head. Then she seemed to realise that it had been observed. Her features softened and her expression reformed into the placid mask that she so often wore. She went to a little bench on the opposite side of the room and began straightening hairpins, dabbing lightly at her eyes in an effort to disguise the tears she'd shed earlier, powdering her cheeks until the face in her own mirror was a deathly white.

'Here, let me help you.' Barbara turned and went to her, smoothing the loose curls at the back of her head and rubbing gently at the other girl's cheeks to get some colour back into them.

'Thank you,' Anne said, a little coldly. 'I fear this evening you are not seeing me at my best.'

'What you saw in the refreshment room was nothing,' Barbara said, wondering even now if she was apologising for the correct offence. 'Mr Breton was attempting to be kind to me, I think. I am grateful, of course. But that is all.'

'It does not matter,' Anne said quickly, but there was a flash of spirit in her eyes that quickly died again.

'I think it might,' Barbara said. 'Perhaps we could call the carriage and return home rather than going back to the party. If it would help, I could pretend an indisposition and you could pretend to help me.'

'No,' Anne said hurriedly. 'The snow has come, and I will be staying the night. You as well. Do not worry. Arrangements are being made. I will be quite all right—really. I must return to the ballroom. Father will be expecting me. And Joseph.'

'But what do *you* wish, Anne?' It was maddening to watch the girl, so obviously miserable, headed in lockstep towards the altar, unwilling to consider another option.

'I wish for everyone to be happy this Christmas,' the other girl said firmly. 'It does not matter what I want. That will not be possible. I think we can only hope to do as little harm as possible.' She lifted her chin, inspecting herself in the mirror. 'That is much better. Thank you, Barbara. Now, if you would be so kind, I would like to return to the ballroom, and I do not wish to walk alone.'

They linked arms and proceeded down the corridor towards the ballroom, chatting amiably of nothing in particular. And if Barbara felt Anne's arm tensing as they passed the kissing bough in the doorway of the refreshment room, then she ignored it—just as Anne needed to ignore Barbara's flinch as they passed the alcove.

Then they were back in the ballroom, and little knots of people glanced in their direction, Anne's father giving an approving look. There was Joseph, standing near the musicians, holding out a welcoming hand.

For a single, foolish instant Barbara thought that he was looking to *her*, offering that friendly gesture to coax her near. Then the moment passed and she realised that it was intended for the woman at her side.

Anne stiffened in a way that was imperceptible to any but Barbara. Then she fixed the serene smile more firmly in her lips and stepped forwards to take the offered hand and her proper place at Joseph Stratford's side.

He gave a nod of approval and cleared his throat. Although the noise was not particularly loud, it caught the attention of everyone in the room. They turned to look at him expectantly, and Barbara watched in admiration at his easy mastery of the crowd.

But in horror as well. For, despite all his vague words, and his actions towards her, and Anne's obvious penchant for another, Barbara could see what was about to happen—just as everyone else could.

'My pleasure to announce…done me…honour…hand in marriage.'

The words seemed to fade in and out of her hearing. It was clear that the others had no problem, for they smiled and clapped politely. Champagne was pressed into her hand by a ready servant. Barbara accepted it with a numb nod. All around her glasses were raised and toasts made to the happy couple—for that was what they appeared to be.

Just before her knees gave way she took a half-step back to the little chair against the wall, so that it would seem she sat rather than collapsed. As the music began again she shrank back, pulling it behind a pot of ivy, and sipped wine that seemed like vinegar on her tongue.

Chapter Twelve

Too late, too late, too late.

It should have been a triumph. Joseph had acquitted himself as well as could be expected amongst the gentry who had accepted his invitation. He'd secured financing for his business plans, he had found himself a wife to secure his position in the area, and his truce with Lampett had lasted long enough to avoid embarrassment.

That he was well on the way to making the man's daughter into his mistress was a point that did not bear close observation. Nothing must come of that—no more than the extremely pleasant dalliance they had experienced in the hall. Surely she knew it was no more than that.

But he had seen the stricken look in her eyes even through the brandy-soaked haze he'd created to steel his nerves for the announcement. Even if she had done similar things before, she had allowed him to do what he had done because she loved him—or thought she did. He had taunted her with his knowledge of her feelings, cheapening them to hurt her. Then he had publicly pledged himself to someone else minutes after leaving her.

So he was marrying the wrong woman for the right reasons. What of it? The move was very like unto himself. He always seemed to be turning a good idea into a bad one. Though they suited perfectly, Bob and Anne would be parted so that he might advance in society and in business. After her brief visit to the manor he would pack Barbara Lampett back off to the village. She would stay as a virtuous spinster, so long as he kept his hands off her.

He remembered the vague promises he had made to the ghostly coachman of how things would change now that he knew of the problems. But for the life of him, he could not think what he might have done to make any difference. If the visions he had seen the previous evening were true, they would all be the sadder for what had occurred tonight, and he was to blame for that misery.

Too late. Too late.

His valet laid out his things and prepared him for bed. All the while Joseph listened to the ticking of the clock, which seemed to chant the words to him as each second passed. It was a wonder that man had invented such a clear measure of the passage of time—one that could be felt almost to the bone on silent nights like this.

It was not as if he needed a further reminder of his mortality. Lord knew, his father had seen to that in recent nights. And tonight's visitor would be the worst of all. For why would this charade have been needed if the future was a happy one? And it was almost three o'clock.

Too late.

The edges of the room seemed to darken and chill. Though it was well stocked with coal, the fire burned low in the grate. It was the spirit coming for him, he was sure. And he did not wish to see what it foretold.

He had made a mistake. Nothing unusual. He'd made many over the course of twenty-five years. But the mistakes of late were irrevocable. He was marrying a woman he did not love. Toying with one he did. Upending an already fragile community with the arrogant assurance that his plans would set everything right, given time.

But now it seemed that only his own death could call a halt to what had begun. He was unsure whether he was likely to be taken by the night's spirit, or simply driven to make his own end by the grim future that lay ahead.

Too. Late.

His valet withdrew in silence, leaving him alone.

Joseph sat on the edge of the bed, waiting for the end, disgusted with his cowardice. Perhaps his father's real plan had been that he meekly accept judgement on this last night. But there had to be something he could do. There must be some fact he was missing that might explain the village and the women in it, for they were a mystery to him. When Lady Clairemont had announced that they would be staying tonight, rather than fighting the weather, he had asked if it was her intention that Miss Lampett stay as well. He had been greeted with a look of such cold hostility that he could not believe it had risen from a simple indiscretion.

If tonight was to be his end, he would never know the truth. Nor would he know the woman who was sleeping just down the hall from him, in the smallest of the guest bedrooms. He could wait in his own room for the angel of death or the very devil himself to take him. Or he could go to her, demand the truth and love her—just once.

There would never be a better time for it, he was sure. If he was already damned, one more sin was not likely to make things any worse. He dared not miss the chance and leave her thinking he felt nothing.

He stood and threw off the nightshirt, grabbing a dressing gown and wrapping it about his naked body. Then he threw open the door and walked down the hall to seal his fate.

Chapter Thirteen

It had been a miserable evening, and one that Barbara would repeat in memory for the rest of her life. Each time she saw the happy couple who were lord and lady of Clairemont Manor her stomach would twist as she wondered how much Joseph remembered, and how much Anne knew of it. And if that brief interlude in the alcove had meant anything at all.

Then there was Robert Breton, who had been too cowardly to seize the opportunity when he'd had his chance. She hoped he would fade into obscurity rather than continue to haunt the area. If he stayed, she rather feared that they would become friends and spend long days brooding jealously over the lives they might have had. Perhaps they might marry, and have the same kind of dreary and passionless union that Joseph and Anne shared.

Why could she not just go back to her loneliness of a day ago? It had been so much simpler.

There was a knock at the door.

She sat up in bed and pulled the covers up to her chin. This was not the scratch of a servant, nor the polite tap of Anne, come to share a quiet conversation before bed. This was the firm rapping of the master of the house. He was standing in front of her door, probably one more knock away from calling out to her, which might wake a neighbour or alert a servant. The resultant scene would be almost as bad for him as for her.

She pushed aside the covers, hurried across the room and threw open the door before the night could become any worse. 'What are you doing here?' she whispered, not wanting to draw further attention.

'I have come for answers,' Joseph said, in a voice that was loud and unembarrassed.

'As if you are the one who needs them. Talk to me tomorrow over breakfast, if you must.' Preferably in the presence of chaperones, to ensure that she did not do anything more foolish than she already had.

'I don't have tomorrow.' As usual, he could think of no further than himself.

'Be quiet,' she whispered. 'Someone will hear.'

'If you do not wish to draw attention, you had best let me in,' he said, with a strange tight smile.

She grabbed him by the lapel and pulled him into the room, closing the door quickly, silently, regretting that she had touched him at all, for her hand seemed to burn with the contact. And now he was in front of her, blocking her way into her own room, and she was planted, shoulders to the door panel, in a way that half reminded her of those scandalous moments in the alcove. Except now she was wearing nothing but her chemise—not that there was much of her body he had not seen.

'What do you want?'

She tried not to squirm at the memory, and the traitorous desire to step forwards, to relax and to go to him. But perhaps that was not what he wanted. He did not reach for her. He was frowning, as though deep in thought.

'Tell me what has happened here.'

'I beg your pardon?'

'Here. In this community. Before I arrived. I need to know about the people right now, before I can go another step.'

She laughed, for it was so far outside what she had expected to hear that she could hardly credit it. 'You wish to know now—after moving here, building here and spending untold sums of money to achieve your ends—what the people might think of it?'

'I know what they think of it,' he said dismissively. 'They hate it—as they would hate any change. That is not what I mean and you know it. Tell me about Mary. Tell me about the mill fire. And your father's accident. Help me make sense of it all.'

'Help you to make sense of it?' She pushed past him to return to her bed. 'There is nothing to make sense of.

No blame to assess. Accidents happen. People are hurt. They die. Time passes. The survivors are changed, but they live on. For what else is there to do?' She turned back to face him. 'If that is all you have come here to say, then you are wrong. It *can* wait until morning, and a setting not so completely inappropriate. Goodnight, Mr Stratford.' She climbed into bed, turning away from him and pulling up the covers. He could make his retreat in anger or embarrassment. She did not care. But she should not be forced to watch it.

But he did not leave. She felt the weight of him, sitting on the edge of her bed, not touching, just out of reach of her. 'Tell me.'

'You are selfish and horrible to come and remind me of these things, tonight of all nights.' Even knowing the stupidity of it, after their time in the alcove she had cherished some small fantasy that he would come to her, attempting to continue what they had begun. Perhaps he would speak of love, and even though she would recognise the words for lies, it would be better than nothing.

'Barbara.' He laid his hand on her shoulder, and through the covers the weight of it was warm, heavy and soothing—as was the sound of her name on his lips. 'Tell me the truth. You have held things back from me. I would have no more secrets with you.'

'Like the fact that your engagement to Anne was in place even as you fondled me?' she shot back, the humiliation still fresh. 'Go to her, if you want a bed partner. Let me have some peace.'

'That is not what I mean. Not at all. Or at least that is not all.' He fumbled with his words, as though he could make no sense to her or himself. 'I need to know everything. I need to know about *you*.' He said it with such curious emphasis that for a moment she believed that he really cared. 'Why are the Clairemonts so cold to you? Tell me.'

He stretched out behind her on the mattress, the covers separating them, and the hand that had shaken her shoulder was wrapped about her waist, drawing her close as he buried his face in her hair. He would not leave until she spoke. She was sure of it. If she must give him the truth, it would be easier while lying in his arms, pretending that his strength was her own.

'Because I killed their daughter, six years ago at Christmas time. It is my fault that Mary is dead. They hate me for it, and I do not blame them.'

He did not move away from her, not even to breathe. If anything, his arms held her tighter, and his lips pressed to the back of her throat, close to her ear. 'You said she was ill.'

She sighed. 'And so she was—because of me. My friend Mary Clairemont died of influenza. There is no story. Many of us were sick that season. But none so bad as her,' Barbara admitted. 'We were the best of friends and spent all our time together. When I sickened she brought me broth and calf's-foot jelly. She read to me to pass the time. Her mother came as well. They took the illness back to their own home. Mary died of it.'

'You blamed yourself?'

'Not at first. But Mr Clairemont came and argued with Father. I heard them. He said that I should have been the one to die. It was horrible. After that, we were no longer welcome at the manor.'

'That was unfair,' Joseph said from behind her. 'But from what I have seen of Mr Clairemont it is not so very surprising.'

'Mrs Clairemont was distraught, and still weak from her own illness. It was a cold winter, and she did not recover until nearly spring. Christmas, which had been such a merry time at the manor, was silent.'

'I understand there were parties here?'

'Like this one. But bigger.' She could not help but smile at the memory. 'Not for years, now. Their sadness cut the heart out of them. They could not celebrate without thinking of Mary.'

'Time to move on, then,' Joseph said. His voice was gruff, as though it were possible to reject the softer emotions.

'One cannot just push away grief when everything about the Christmas holiday is a reminder,' she informed him, rolling to face him and leaning on her elbow. 'You must show more compassion for Mrs Clairemont. The family was forced to strip the greenery from the house and use the feasting foods for a funeral. It was a great shock to them.'

'But wrong to blame you for it,' he said, touching her hair with his hand.

'And Mr Clairemont lost his grip on his business. The war took its toll as well. Mr Mackay leased the land from him, but was not able to sell his goods. He bought the new looms to save money at the expense of the workers.'

'If Clairemont had been smart, he would have noticed before things got bad,' Joseph said, reasoning like a machine even while looking at her like a lover and lying near naked at her side. 'He lost a building because of it. A valuable tenant as well. That allowed me to capitalise…'

'Always business,' she said with a sigh. 'Father tried to help him at the last. Despite their differences, he ran to help save the mill with the rest of Mr Clairemont's friends. But he was the one who was struck down by a falling beam. He was unconscious for three days. We were sure he would die. And now…'

'His thoughts are addled,' Joseph finished. 'He blames the mill for it. He blames me as well.'

'But really it is my fault,' Barbara said. 'From the very first. If I had been the one to die, and not Mary…'

Before she could finish the sentence his arms had tightened upon her, drawing her into a breath-taking hug. 'Then things would have been different. But they would have been no better for the majority of people here.' His lips touched her cheek, kissing away a tear that she did not remember shedding. 'I have travelled the country, north and south, and seen what the war has done to trade, and what the new looms have done to tradesmen. It would have been uneasy here no matter what had happened. If your father had not been the one to speak against me then someone else would.'

She wanted to believe that almost as much as she wished that things could have been simpler—young and clean and pleasant, just as they had been a few years ago. 'There are a great many ifs,' she said. 'I think of them often. Sometimes it is only necessary to change the life of one person to set the world upon a different course.'

He stiffened. 'So I have been told. But I do not think that you are that person who must change.'

She laughed softly. 'And so I am put in my place, sir. It is good to know that you think me of so little importance in God's great scheme.'

'On the contrary. You are surprisingly important to...' He paused. 'To many people. But you are also blameless of anything that has happened here. Do not change. You are just right as you are. I would not alter an atom of you. But I owe you an apology. I assumed that the trouble was something quite different. A dispute over a suitor, perhaps.'

'There has never been anyone,' she admitted, then took a breath to gather courage. 'Other than you.'

He lay very still beside her. 'I never would have done what I did had I understood.'

'Did you think I was the village whore, then?' she

asked, struggling to escape his arms. 'It is a wonder you allowed me to associate with your guests.'

'No.' He said the word in a groan, and his arms were no longer gentle but holding her like iron as she fought against him. The lips that had been pressed softly to her cheek were taking her mouth, until she stilled and allowed his kiss, which was as rough and improper as he was. He filled her mouth with his tongue, making the rest of her body feel empty in comparison. The thin blanket that separated them was like a million miles of desert. And suddenly she was fighting not to get away but to be closer to him, praying that in total surrender he might finally admit what he felt for her.

'No,' he whispered, staying her hand and keeping the barrier between them. 'My guests are not worthy of you. Neither am I. I am a villain, a rogue, a debaucher. But I cannot seem to let you go. I only wanted to make things better, I swear. But with each turn I dig deeper. After tonight I will never get free.'

'If it is me you seek to be free from, then I hope you never succeed,' she whispered.

Perhaps it would have been better had he been right. If she had already fallen she would know how to proceed now, to find the thing that would make him happy, would make him stay. She pressed her lips to his earlobe and then his cheek, licking the dark stubble and following it to his jaw. He looked even more tired than he had before. She remembered that he complained he could not sleep. It must be true, for it was well past three and he was still awake and worrying about her.

Whatever he felt for her, he needed a comfort that only she could give him. She nestled her head against his throat and kissed the places that had been covered with his cravat. Then she found his fingers with hers and untangled them from the sheet he held, pushing the covers down so that they could be together.

He sighed and stopped resisting. Then he kicked away the last of the blankets and yanked at the tie of his robe, to be free of that as well. Suddenly she was sharing a bed with a naked man.

Though it was of her own choosing, she found that she was afraid to look on him. So she stared into his eyes, and found them to be infinitely sad, and perhaps a little frightened.

'No matter what happens, no matter how it appears,' he whispered, 'I am yours until I die. Do you understand that? And I am afraid of that. Because I know I will hurt you.'

'You never shall,' she said. It was another lie, of course. But she decided she would believe it, just for tonight. 'Would you help me to remove my chemise, please? For I think I would like to feel...'

His shoulders shook from laughing as he reached for the hem. 'Is that what it is like to make love to a lady? All "please" and "thank you"? I will give you a reason for those words.' He stripped her last garment from her and held her away from him for a moment, so that he could admire her body and kiss each of her peaking nipples.

'Cold?' he asked, smiling against her breast.

'A little,' she admitted, with a delicious shiver as he blew a cooling breath on her damp skin.

'I will take care of you.' He spread his robe over her shoulders and it was still warm with the heat of his body, the quilted silk arousing her body where it touched her. If she had been hoping for some deeper declaration she ought to be disappointed. But it felt good to be cared for, decadent and exciting.

Then he kissed her again. At first his lips pressed innocently to her forehead. Then they slipped down her face in a trail of small kisses on her eyelids and cheeks, coming to rest upon her mouth. It was not precisely chaste. But neither was it as unbridled as it had been a moment ago. His lips had lowered to hers in an almost leisurely fashion, brushing her face before settling, opening, deepening and taking her tongue into his mouth.

She kissed him back, as he had been kissing her, touching each feature of his face with her lips and tongue before settling on his mouth and losing herself in it. Being with Joseph was more than just passion. It was a solution, an answer, the opening of a locked door. It was right, no matter what her head should be telling her.

They parted for breath and he touched her cheek with his finger. 'May I stay with you until dawn?' he whispered. 'We do not have to lie together, if you do not wish…'

It was an odd thing to say. But she did not take the time to wonder at it, for there were far more interesting things to notice. 'It is what I wish,' she admitted. It was yet another point of no return—to say aloud that she wanted him. Before she could lose her nerve, she ran her hand once down the length of him, over his chest to rest near his sex, afraid to do more than that. She took a deep breath, and then spoke what was in her heart. 'Because I want to show you what I feel. Whatever happens tonight, tomorrow or in the distant future, you must know that I love you.'

'You have known me for such a short time that you cannot know the truth of your feelings.'

'I know that as well,' she said. 'And I know that you do not want my love. But I think it is important that you hear the truth. You do not love me. But I love you.'

'You should not,' he said, a little uneasily.

'I cannot help it.' She leaned back into the pillows and closed her eyes. With his body, he followed her, throwing a leg over her hip so that they could lie together, skin to skin.

She felt her body wakening as though it were newly born, every sensation a first. Despite the danger to her reputation, and to her heart, she felt warm and safe, and more sure of her love than ever. She must have been meant for him, and he for her. Why else would their bodies fit so well together? Why else would they respond so quickly? She could feel him, hard between her legs. And her hips gave an answering push against him, wet with invitation. The act of love, which had seemed most unusual when her mother explained it to her, now seemed like the most right and natural thing in the world.

Joseph understood, and gave a little shake of his head. 'Wait. There is more.'

'More?' After what had happened in the alcove this evening, what was left for them but to finish what they had started?

'I wish to know every inch of you.' His hands began to explore, smoothing down her shoulders and spine, and up the backs of her arms. His leg moved against hers, the hairs of it tingling as they brushed her. Then his mouth left hers to kiss her fingertips, her elbows and her ribs. He took one of her nipples into his mouth and gave it the softest of kisses. Then he rubbed his face gently between her breasts, so she could feel the roughness of his cheeks, grating ever so slightly against her skin. Then he turned his head to take the second breast less gently than the first, turning the soft kiss into a series of nips that made her cup his face in her hands, arch her back and press her body into his open mouth.

His fingers stroked her as his eagerness grew, gripping her thighs and parting them, and then giving one single touch of a fingertip in the place where they met. It hovered for a moment, and then slid down, and in.

She gasped. She had thought, after the sample he had given her by the ballroom, that she understood what it must be like to make love. But though he touched her in the same way she felt different now, as though every part of her body burned.

He slid up her body again, so that he could kiss her on the lips, and the passage of his rougher skin against her body was maddening. She wanted to writhe against him, purring and winding herself about him like a kitten, demanding to be stroked.

'If I can do nothing else, I want to make you feel as you do me, when I look at you.' He smiled. 'I will make you want me to the point of madness. And together we will take the want away with having.'

'You have.' It seemed that now he was nude he was larger. Not just... She looked down and then hurriedly up at his face again. Not just the increase she had expected. It was the whole of him, as though the power and energy which had been hidden beneath his clothing was suddenly released. She was awash in it, tingling from the tips of her toes to the top of her head.

She looked down again, at the pair of them naked and side by side on the bed. For a moment she was more amazed than aroused. It was natural and right to be this way with him, just as it had from the first moment they'd been alone together, when he'd grabbed her by the arm and pulled her to safety. He reached for her now and caught her suddenly under the arms, rolling and pulling her close. Then he was on his back, and she was being pulled down, over and against him, sprawling over his body, covering him like a blanket.

It was his turn to lie back into the pillows, sighing contentedly. Then he pulled her head down to meet his and kissed her, with the tickle of his chest hair against her nipples and the stirrings of his erection between her legs. His hands were busy, adjusting, moulding, positioning, until his body was fitted to hers, his manhood nudging at her maidenhead.

Now she was waiting, fairly sure of what the next step would be, but unsure of how it would come about. 'Relax,' he murmured against her temple. 'We are still strangers, the pair of us. Touch me. Learn my body so that I may better know yours. I want to feel your hands.'

'Where?'

'Anywhere. You will know when it is time for more than that.'

How would she know anything of the sort? Perhaps he still thought she had some experience in the matter. If so, she was likely to embarrass herself soon enough. But all the same she ran her hands over his chest and felt the muscles move in response. She touched his arms and they moved to circle her, to stroke her, to hold her in place against him. She bit his shoulder and he clutched her bottom, grinding his hips into hers as she sucked upon his skin.

And so she dared to sit up, balancing on his thighs, and reached lower to touch the part of him that touched her. His hands slipped between her legs, spreading them wide, probing the opening of her body and taking it while she stroked him. He teased and thrust with his fingertips, leaving little spearings of pleasure that coalesced inside her, urging her to pull his sex, which had grown hard, towards her own. She hung there, on the edge of something, afraid to take the leap that would end in a flight or a fall.

And then she was sure. She wanted it. She wanted him. She wanted to be his, even if it was just for a night. She cried out to him, 'Help me. Please.'

'Barbara. Darling.' The hands that had been slow and gentle before moved lightning-quick, pulling her forwards and onto him. There was a lance of pain. Then he rolled so that she was beneath him.

When she looked up, into his face, the expression she saw was as surprising as anything else had been. It was as though he had changed, in a moment, to a different man. There was no trace of hardness in him, nothing frightening or aloof. The flaws had burned away in a burst of triumphant energy, leaving bliss, peace and desire.

Then he began to move in her. She felt a sense of connection to him that was beyond physical. They were working together towards some common goal, and she smoothed her hands over the muscles of his back, trying to go where he led her, sure that there would be pleasure enough for both of them when they arrived. Everything was alive in her—every inch of skin. The places that touched and rubbed were different from the bare places touched by night air and firelight. The place where their bodies met was the best of all. There was no feeling like this. No words to describe it. It was like springtime, full of promise, melting ice and birdsong, the stirrings of things that had been sleeping inside her.

Inside her body some part of him touched some part of her, and it was as though the whole world had lurched violently to one side and then righted itself. Then it happened again. She seemed to lose all control as her body turned upside down and inside out. And in all that confusion he was with her, holding her, feeling the same thing. He tensed, gasped and stilled.

He was lying on top of her. But it was not as she'd expected. Even though he was a large man, he seemed to weigh nothing, covering her like a shield, keeping her warm and safe. He was a part of her now, and would be even after they parted, as she was sure they must. He drew away from her, but only a little way, reaching towards the foot of the bed to pull the coverlet over the pair of them and then settling back at her side, wrapping his arms about her body and keeping her close.

'I should go,' he whispered.

She did not really wish him to. But it might be better for him to leave now, while they were both happy, than to stay too long, until that feeling changed.

'You should,' she agreed. 'But I do not mean to let you. Not just yet.' She held him close, and he turned her so her back was against his chest, wrapping himself around her in a different way, as though he wanted to know every inch of her body before he released it.

'I will see to it that I am back in my room before the house wakes in the morning. I will listen for the chiming of the clock. It is already well past four. I did not hear it strike at all. Perhaps that is late enough. Nothing has changed.' Then he relaxed, stroking her hair, his hand moving slower and slower as he lost consciousness.

And she dozed as well. But before she was lost to all she wondered what he had been expecting.

Chapter Fourteen

The next morning was much as any other visit to the manor had been, even though another man was master. A round of sleepy guests gathered in the breakfast room for steaming plates of eggs, thick slices of ham, toast, marmalade and subdued chatter.

It was all familiar except for their host, who sat at the head of the table looking like death and subsisting on nothing more than black coffee. If he had slept at all, it did not show. His skin was grey and there were hollows in his cheeks that the razor had not touched. Barbara wanted to go to his side and cut the food on his plate, feeding him like an invalid before sending him to bed.

But that was not her job. It was Anne's.

There could be no acknowledgement of what had happened between them—not even to share the fatigue they had felt while lying in each other's arms waiting out the hour between the clock chiming four and five, wondering if each minute would be the last they'd share. She was as tired as he, though she had made an effort to look lively so that no one might ask her about it. But it was a happy exhaustion. She had come to the table and smiled down into her plate, trying not to show the world how wonderful she felt.

Then Joseph had arrived. And the longer she'd sat with him the worse she'd felt. She found herself listening to the ticking clock once more. Eating mechanically and longing for the moment she could escape.

Morning had come and everything had changed—in that it was much the same as it might have been had nothing happened at all. Joseph was there at breakfast, greeting his guests, helping himself to more coffee and making sure that all needs were met. But he showed her no special favour, enquiring politely if she had slept well without a wink or a nod.

She responded in kind. If she seemed awkward, or somewhat chilly, it would be taken for a sign of the estrangement between her family and him. Nothing more, nothing less.

Then he turned his attention to Anne. He could at least manage a smile for her, though it was little better than a death mask. His concern was more pointed. Her plate was heaped full and taken away just as quickly when she did not seem pleased with it.

Barbara felt her own food curdling in her stomach, and reached very deliberately for the teacup in front of her. As she lifted her gaze to stare fixedly across the table she caught the eyes of Robert Breton. His expression was similar. Just as bland and unflappable. He was just as stubbornly uninterested in the proceedings at the end of the table as she was.

But as he looked at her there was the slightest rise at one corner of his lip, and an equally slight salute as he raised his teacup, as though he were toasting their shared misery.

To kindred spirits, she thought, and responded in kind.

'Will you be participating in today's activities, Miss Lampett?' he asked politely. 'I understand that the skating on the pond is quite pleasant. There will be games in the parlour, and the lighting of the Yule Log.'

'I had not given it thought,' she answered. 'When I arrived I was hardly prepared for more than an evening. If there is a way to return to the village...with a servant, perhaps.' Even now she sat at the table wearing her ridiculously unfashionable ballgown, because it was all she had. Today it was just one more thing to single her out from the group as not quite belonging to it.

'Oh, please do stay,' Anne insisted. 'And do not give me any excuses about lack of preparation. Your skates are still here, you know, from when we were young together. Anything else needed you might borrow from me. Or there are Mary's old things...'

There was a sharp intake of breath from Lady Clairemont, who was seated beside Joseph. Anne fell silent again.

'Yes. Please. Stay. I will accept no excuses.' Joseph made the offer mechanically, without even looking up, and Barbara took another hurried sip of tea to stop the words on the tip of her tongue.

What do you mean by that? Are you in any way sincere? Or is that sarcasm I hear? Even if it is a bald-faced lie, could it not be delivered with a smile?

'No,' she said softly. 'I thank you for your gracious offer of hospitality, but I must be getting back to Mother and Father. Perhaps, after Christmas, I might return. It has all been quite lovely and I am very glad that you invited me.'

'Very well, then,' Joseph said, not even bothering with a token resistance. 'I will see that the carriage is brought round—or perhaps there is a sledge.'

A spirited discussion erupted as to the delightful nature of sleigh rides, and what fun it might be to make an outing into the village, which was declared 'quaint' by the visitors from the South. It was a relief when the attention turned to more cheerful topics than the fate of the dowdy young woman at the foot of the table, leaving Barbara to excuse herself unnoticed.

She fled to her bedroom, counting on the privacy of a locked door. There were no belongings to gather before departure. Hiding above stairs would spare her any more awkward conversations. She could sit in the window seat and watch for the carriage that would take her away from the disaster that this visit had become.

But even there she was not alone. When she entered,

she startled the maid who had come to make up the room. The girl was the youngest daughter of the Stock family, who lived a scant quarter-mile from Barbara's home, and she was staring at the tangle of sheets on the bed, and the bloody smudge in the midst of them. She offered a quick curtsey, and muttered an apology for the interruption. Then she smiled, as though she had been presented with a tidbit juicier than any she might see with Christmas dinner, and hurried from the room.

Barbara almost turned to go after her, with a lame story of her restless night and the sudden monthly imposition that would explain the spots of blood. But there was no way gossip could be avoided. To deny it would be as good as admitting the truth: a couple had been sporting here, and the lady involved was the formerly virginal Miss Barbara Lampett.

They had been careful, or so she'd thought. Between kisses Joseph had assured her that the walls were thick, and that no one would see him come or go. She had consoled herself that if she was lucky enough to avoid pregnancy—and she dared not think about any other possibility—the secret would go to her grave.

She had not counted on the maids. While a bit of gossip about Mr Stratford's London guests would be harmless, and gossip about Anne would be avoided for the sake of her family, there was no magical protection that extended to Miss Lampett. She was a lady and should know better.

She gave one last look around the room to remember

that, however briefly, she had been supremely happy here. She had belonged to someone, if only for a few hours. Now she must return to her home and put the happy memory away, as she had so many others. She would not return after Christmas, for she doubted she could bear another visit.

And so she wandered, avoiding the breakfast room, where so many people were still gathered, and the salons and reception rooms, where plans for the day were being made. Instead she went to say goodbye to the portrait gallery, and to the ballroom, stopping to touch the curtain that covered the little alcove and wondering, if she pulled it back suddenly, if she would find the ghost of her younger self hiding there. Or had all those old times been supplanted by memories of Joseph?

With a little smile, she drew aside the curtain—only to hear a gasp, and the rustle of clothing falling back into place as the couple inside sprang apart.

'I'm sorry,' she said, 'I had no idea…' She turned quickly, shielding her eyes.

Anne stumbled forwards into the hall. Mr Breton acted almost as quickly to thrust her back into the recess and step in front of her, as though it were possible to shield her from view. He cursed very softly, and ran his fingers through his hair in an effort to compose himself. Then he bowed. 'I am sorry you were a witness to my disgraceful behaviour, Miss Lampett.' He bowed again to Anne. 'And that you had to experience it, Miss Clairemont. My actions were totally inappropriate, and no apology can be offered for them other than an excess of alcohol.'

He looked back at Barbara, knowing that she had seen him, sober as a judge, at the breakfast table, less than an hour ago.

He gave a helpless shrug. 'My fate is in your hands, miss, as is the honour of a lady. Though I would not wish what has occurred here to be known, I cannot demand that you keep my secret. Know that I will be leaving Mr Stratford's home early in the New Year and returning to London. There will be no further risk of another incident.' Then he walked hurriedly away from them, down the hall.

The moment he was gone Anne rushed forwards, seizing her hands. The polite pretence of soft, smiling apathy had disappeared. 'Please, Barbara. Please. I beg you. Say nothing to Joseph of this. I know that I have no reason to ask your help. My family has treated you horribly for a thing which was no fault of yours. But, please, say nothing.'

For a moment the frozen woman before her melted into the image of her lost sister, into something much more human than she had been: a woman with desires who was at least capable of making mistakes, if not yet able to admit to them.

There was so much that Barbara was not speaking of already. Why should there not be one more thing? 'I saw nothing, Anne. Nothing at all that I wish to remark upon to anyone. But just for a moment can you not be honest with me? Was this all his doing? Or is there feeling on both sides?'

And Anne, normally so reserved and in control, burst into tears in her arms.

Barbara glanced around, relieved to see that there was no one there to witness the outburst. Then she took a firmer grip on Anne's hands and dragged her back into the alcove, to sit on the bench, pinning back the curtain to allow some light into their sanctuary. 'Come, now. If you cannot get hold of yourself, then at least come where fewer people might see you. Now, tell me. Do you love him or not?'

Anne gave a hesitant nod. 'He is leaving. Even before you discovered us he was threatening. Now he will go for sure.'

Barbara stifled surprise. She had meant to ask about Joseph—the only man whose future mattered. She corrected herself. 'You will lose Mr Breton, if you do not cry off your engagement.'

'How can I?' Anne looked up at her from watery blue eyes. 'I am the only daughter left. Everyone is depending on me to do exactly what is needed. Joseph wishes a lady for the manor. My father wishes to get his foot back in the door. He would rather stay here as a doting father-in-law than learn to be comfortable in new surroundings.' For a moment there was uncharacteristic bitterness in the sweet voice. 'No one is particularly interested in what *I* want. I had thought, since I had no real objections to the character of the man, that it would be enough to be comfortable and back in my own home. But, Barbara. Oh, Barbara.' She smiled. 'That was before I met Robert. I did not know that I could feel like this. And now it will end.'

Then she was crying again, and Barbara could find nothing to do other than offer her shoulder and pat the girl ineffectually on the back. Would it do her any good to be assured that her future husband did not care about her either?

That could not possibly be a comfort. Though she did not seem to expect it of him, Barbara doubted that the girl in her arms wished to know the extent of his uninterest, or that an old friend was a co-conspirator in her betrayal. Love was not her reason for marrying. And there was nothing Barbara could say that would make the Clairemonts' desire to regain the manor any different than it was.

'There, there,' she said, and could not manage to sound the least bit enthusiastic about it. Success for Anne meant failure for her.

There was no way, in good conscience, that she could talk the girl into crying off. 'Would it help,' she asked cautiously, 'if I spoke to Mr Stratford for you? Perhaps if he understood how unhappy you are…'

'No.' Anne gripped her arm. 'You mustn't. He would be furious. So would my father.'

Barbara doubted that would be totally true. Though Lord Clairemont would be angry at having his plans thwarted, she'd seen no evidence that Joseph would be similarly affected at the loss of his impending marriage.

But then, she had seen no evidence to the contrary. In all that little time they'd spent together he'd said nothing about Anne, either positive or negative. She was sure that he'd said not a word about terminating the engagement.

'Very well, then. I will not expose you.'

Anne gave her a watery smile. 'I am sorry again for how my family has treated you. How I have treated you as well. You are good and kind. I will do anything I can to help you in the future if you will keep my secret.'

With secrets of her own, Barbara could feel nothing but sympathy for the sister of her dearest friend. 'I will do nothing to hurt you, I promise. And if I can find a way to help you, I will do so.'

'I can ask for nothing more than that,' Anne said, carefully drying her eyes with a handkerchief.

'Miss Lampett?' Mrs Davy the housekeeper called from the end of the hall. 'The carriage is ready to take you to the village. Dick says you had best leave soon, or the roads will turn to mud.'

Without another word Barbara dropped the curtain into place, pretending that she had been alone. 'Of course. I am ready.' She walked quickly to the front of the house, wondering if she was obligated to say a farewell to her host. She decided against it. He knew very well how she felt, and the reasons for her leave-taking.

'You will give my regards and my regrets to Mr Stratford, of course,' she said politely to the housekeeper.

'That will not be necessary, miss. He is waiting to see you off.'

'Oh,' she said weakly, forcing her steps not to falter on the way to the door.

He was waiting there, just as the housekeeper had said, looking more like a professional mourner than a party host, a few flakes of snow lying unmelted in his dark hair.

She nodded at him, trying not to show the fear she felt that he would try to stop her. If he revealed even one moment of true feeling she was likely to turn back on her plan and go meekly to the room he had given her.

'I've come to see you off,' he said, without expression. 'I am your host. It is appropriate, I think, to wish you well and see you safely from the premises. People will wonder, otherwise.'

'And it is appropriate for me to thank you for your hospitality,' she answered back. But she said nothing further.

'Well, then. Go.' He said it gruffly, as though he could turn her decision into his own wish.

'There is no reason to stay,' she said firmly.

He sighed, his composure breaking. 'And yet I do not want you to leave.' That was at least said with some tenderness, as though he actually meant it.

'You know I must. There is nothing for me here.'

He reached out and touched her arm. 'There is always tonight.'

'You think that because of last night I will allow you to make a habit of coming to me in secret?'

'There could be no other way. I cannot cry off from Anne without disgracing her.'

There. He had finally said it. He could not hurt Anne, but he thought nothing of what he might do to Barbara Lampett, who had far less protection than the daughter of the most honourable family in the area.

'You are horrible,' she said. Despite how wonderful she had felt, his touch now was torture. It made her want to cry. She pulled her arm from his grasp.

'You said you loved me.' He said it softly, urgently.

'And you have never said the same to me. Not even as a lie. I was foolish to tell you. And foolish to feel it as well. For you are unworthy. Cruel and selfish, just as my father tried to tell me.'

'It is not as you think,' he said.

'But you offer no further explanation to tell me how it might *be*, if it is not exactly as it appears. You are using me, and you will marry another.'

'I did not intend to,' he admitted. 'But I could not sit alone in my room, waiting for the end.'

'The end? That is a tad melodramatic, Mr Stratford. I suppose next you will tell me that you are afraid of the dark.' She laughed scornfully, hoping that it might hurt him just a little, so that he might feel some part of what she felt whenever she looked at him.

His look in response was strange. A little blank, a little panicked. And clearly saying that she had discovered some part of the truth. 'That is it, isn't it? You are afraid to sleep alone in a darkened bedroom. You used me for a night to solve the problem.' She shuddered. 'That is all I was to you. A warmer for your bed and a candle on a dark night.'

'It was more than that,' he said. But still he would not say what.

'I ruined myself in the hope that there was some affection on your part. But I could have been anyone at all.' Without his help, she heaved herself into the body of the carriage and tried to close the door.

'Barbara. Wait.' He was just behind her, his shoulders blocking the entrance.

'I have waited too long already.'

'Do not leave me.' He sounded almost plaintive now, as though he were actually afraid of facing another night alone.

'Tonight you must go to Anne for your comfort. It would make more sense. I am sure you have much to talk about.' She bit her tongue then, to keep back the spiteful revelation that she had been almost ready to share. 'But of course you will not, will you? She is a lady, and deserves better than to be treated as a receptacle for your carnality. And I? I was a lady once. But no longer, now that you are through with me. Now I am through with you. Good day, sir.'

She sat facing carefully forwards, ignoring his presence, until with an oath he slammed the door and signalled for the coachman to drive.

Chapter Fifteen

How much had the coachman heard? she wondered, huddling beneath the coach robe and pulling her shawl around her shoulders. How much had the grooms guessed? Between the bunch of them they would piece together the bits of her argument with Joseph and their secret would be no secret at all. The tragedy involving Mary had been the talk of the village for a while. Then most had decided that it could not have been helped, and that even if the Lampetts should have known better than to allow company in a sickroom, they'd meant no harm by it.

But now she would be infamous. The people would expect no less of Joseph, for he was a man. He was an outsider, as well, and already reviled. But *she* should have known better, and society would punish her for her lapse in judgement. Women would cut her, and avoid her mother as well. Her father, if he could be made to understand, would be devastated.

She would have to leave. As soon as she was sure that there would be no child she would advertise for a position as a governess, or a lady's companion. Perhaps, if she threw herself on the mercy of the vicar, he would write a letter of reference for her, assuring the world that she was gently brought up and properly educated. Even Lord Clairemont might help, if it was understood that her goal was to get as far away from Fiddleton as she could, so that she could create no further trouble. Her parents would be heartbroken at her leaving, but once she had managed to explain Mother would likely agree.

The carriage had pulled up to her house now, and a groom helped her down, seeming at a loss that there was no package or bag that she might be helped with. She thanked him, and went up the walk alone, without turning back.

Her mother greeted her in the front room, eyes sharp, discerning, not willing to let her pass without a challenge. 'I have sent your father to the bakery to get us bread for supper,' she said. It was an obvious ruse so that they could be alone, for Barbara had seen to the baking only yesterday. 'Did you enjoy your visit to the great house, then?'

'Of course,' she said. 'We stayed the night because of the weather, but I was not feeling quite myself this morning, and thought it best…' She had dropped her head as she spoke, unable to meet her mother's gaze. That was her undoing. She showed her guilt plainly by hiding the expression that she could not let her mother read.

'One of the maids from Clairemont has been to the market and gone already. But on the way she visited her mother, Mrs Stock. The entire family is in service up at the house. And they do like to gossip.'

'I gave them no reason to talk.'

'Do not try to lie to me, Barbara. You cannot trick me with words, like your father and his speeches. The maid says that there was a man in your room last night, sharing your bed. Who was it?'

The plans she had made as she'd ridden towards the village had not included this first, most difficult conversation. If she was to manage any of the scandal it would not do to fight now, against another who would bear the shame of it. She sighed and collapsed onto the bench by the fire, hanging her head in embarrassment. 'It is as bad as you think. Probably worse. I love him.'

'You cannot,' her mother said firmly. 'In my opinion, if you meant to lie with the man before marriage, love is the worst reason for it.'

She stared up at her mother in surprise and wondered just what she might know of such things, and why she was not more shocked than she was.

Her mother gave her a candid look. 'You are not some fainting schoolgirl, Barbara. You are a young lady, well on your way to spinsterhood. Sometimes these things happen. If you were seventeen and in your first season it might ruin your chances. Now there are no opportunities left to spoil.' She sat down beside Barbara and said, more quietly, 'Who was he? I hope it was not some London dandy. If so, his words were likely false ones, and there is little hope that he will stay past the New Year. Was it that nice Mr Breton I have seen occasionally in the village? He might be persuaded to do the right thing for the sake of your reputation. Or we could write his father and demand a settlement.' She sounded almost hopeful at the thought, as though there were a way to make something good come from her daughter's mistake.

'Joseph Stratford,' Barbara said, with a sinking heart.

The older woman slumped beside her, as though her last hope had been dashed. 'I suppose now you will tell me that, while he claims to have feelings for you, he has no intention of crying off from Anne Clairemont.'

'He does not love her.' But that was no defence at all.

'Neither does he love you, or we would not be having this conversation.' Her mother stared down at her hands, which were trembling in her lap. 'Do you understand, even for a moment, the predicament we are in? Your father is failing.' The last words came in a harsh whisper that made them all the more terrible. 'When he is gone, there will be nothing to save us from our fate. My own inheritance is running out. I bore no sons. What little we have from your father will go to his brother. Even a bad marriage is quite out of the question for you once it gets round that you've been bedded by the most hated man in Fiddleton.'

'I thought to leave,' Barbara said hopefully. 'If I take a position, I might send what money I earn back home.'

Her mother said nothing to this for a time. When she finally spoke her voice was even quieter, as though she was afraid that the house itself might hear. 'There is another solution—if you are not too proud to take it.'

'I do not understand.' Until a moment ago Barbara had not thought of herself as hopeless. Now she was not sure what her mother saw as a last salvation.

'Joseph Stratford has no intention of marrying you— not while he can have the lady that belongs in the great house he's bought,' her mother said bitterly. 'He is little better than a child playing with a dolls' house. It does not matter if he cares for her. He will have Anne Clairemont because she belongs there.'

She had not thought of it. But her mother was right. It was a chilling idea that Anne would sit, just as she wanted, in the chair at the end of the great dining table, writing her letters in the morning room, lounging in the salon with the careless grace she had affected with so many years' practice. But she would be little better than an ornament.

'But Stratford has proven himself to be a greedy and licentious man. He cares nothing for the people here.'

'He's not like that,' Barbara said. But, though she believed him to be different, there was ample evidence that her mother was right.

'Of course he is,' her mother said, more firmly. 'And isn't that the argument of every foolish young girl whose head is turned by broad shoulders and a kind word? *"To me, he is different."*'

But to her, he was. It would do no good to repeat what she knew to be true. But she remembered what it had been like, the previous night, as he'd comforted her when she spoke of Mary. He had needed her as much as she had needed him.

'He's had you, and there's little more to it than that, I am sure. He'll do the same again, if you let him.'

And now what had felt so wonderful felt wrong and shameful. Her mother was right. Even as she'd tried to escape him he'd been trying to lure her back. She wanted to bathe herself, scrub at her skin until there was no memory of it left. 'It will not happen again.'

'Oh, yes, it will,' her mother said, with a sad frown. 'If you love him, you will go when he sends for you. You will not be able to help yourself. That is the nature of love, after all. In the face of it, my warnings will mean nothing to you.'

She put an arm around her daughter, drawing her close and untying her bonnet so that that Barbara could lay her head on a comforting shoulder.

Her mother smoothed her hair and whispered, 'We cannot take back the past. I will not stop you if you go to him. But if you do, make sure there is an arrangement. One time and people will call you a fool. Twice and they will call you a whore. If Mr Stratford cares for you at all, make him give you your due. There will be little use for fancy dresses and frippery. But we will have need of a steady income before too much longer.' Her mother choked back a tiny sob, and then said in a firm voice, 'We need to be practical about the future.'

Barbara sank down into a chair, waiting for the room to stop spinning around her. It had all come to that, had it? And so soon. She had wanted to believe there was a respectable future ahead of her, with forged references and a quick trip to a place where no one would know that she'd disgraced herself. But her mother, always the most practical woman, had dismissed that fantasy without another thought. There would be no concealing the truth. She was ruined, and now she must make the best of it.

And she could do that by being honest and admitting that she wished to go back to Joseph. She would be a mistress: a rich man's whore. But she could still love him, and be with him, even if she could not have him for her own.

Joseph would marry Anne, just as he'd planned to do. He would have his great house, and his pretty wife, and his woman, too. Perhaps that was what he'd planned all along. He had silenced the opposition to his mill as well. For she would now be forced to make Father understand how unwise it was to anger the man who put bread upon their table. If Joseph tired of her, for whatever reason…

Barbara's future would be secure and her family would be safe as long as she pleased him. But when she did not? He would send her away. There were few men like him in this small backwater, but plenty would know her as a great man's cast-off. If she did not arrange for a settlement at the beginning she would have to find another protector.

One that she did not love.

Barbara searched her feelings, trying to remember the conversations they'd shared, the constant rescues, the way she had felt as they had danced, and as he'd held her last night. Perhaps it was not love on his part. But there was nothing to indicate a lack of generosity. If she was to be a fallen woman, she could do much worse than to fall for Joseph Stratford.

As long as she put her heart to one side and thought sensibly there was a way out of this. Her mother was right. But if she meant to survive she must remember that love had no part in it. And as she sat there, ridiculous in an out-of-fashion ballgown, though it was near to noon, she let that part of herself die. There would be no foolish tears over things that could not be changed. She would seize the opportunity that had presented itself, and work it to her best advantage.

Joseph would approve of that, she was sure. Was that not the way he did business as well? If nothing else, she would prove that they were more alike than he knew.

Chapter Sixteen

Christmas Eve dinner was excellent, with roast beef fair to melting from the bone, and a Yorkshire pudding to sop up the rich gravy. The Christmas pudding was so soaked in spirits that a man could feel drunk on the richness of it, his own soul licked with the blue flames that danced over the surface of it without consuming it.

To Joseph Stratford every bite tasted like sand.

The Yule Log was crackling in the grate, and beside it were pans of chestnuts. Tables were set with bowls of wine and currants ready for snapdragon. His guests lit the spirits and snatched at the little fruits, shrieking with laughter and shaking their singed fingers.

And yet Joseph was cold.

The music, though not as raucous as it had been the previous evening, was lively enough to satisfy. But all the songs in the world could not have chased the dullness from his own spirit. He had done nothing as the only person who could make a change in him had turned and left. He had not stopped her. And soon he would pay the price for that.

To avoid conversing with others, Joseph danced the better part of the evening with Anne. True to form, she had little to say to him, letting him stride through the patterns in silence. She wore the same serene smile she always did. But there was a slightly panicked look in her eyes, as though she was bearing up no better than he. In encouragement, he squeezed her hand.

She started. Then, her worried eyes darting to his, gave an answering squeeze as if to admit that, while they both might be trapped, there was some comfort in knowing she had his sympathy.

Not trapped for long, my dear, he wanted to say. He had his own suspicions on how this night was likely to end. Try as he might, he could not see a marriage—happy or otherwise—looming on his life's horizon. Though it had been his whole world just a few days ago, the opening of the mill now seemed a distant and unlikely thing that he would have no part in. He wondered if Breton had the nerve to take it on. But that would mean turning his back on his birth and taking on a real position. Perhaps he could find some man of business to run the place. More likely the whole of it would fall to ruin if Joseph was not alive to fight for it.

It made him wonder… Would it have seemed too fatalistic to draw a will? He had no heir. Perhaps the house could revert to the Clairemonts once he was out of the way. It would have been wise to leave some document stating that it was his wish, should the worst occur tonight.

Although he had thought to fear death, now that it was likely upon him he could not seem to care. Barbara was gone, and he felt the emptiness of it as he walked the corridors of the great house before bed. He should have said something to her when he'd had the chance.

But what? How did one find the words for something that came so suddenly, so illogically, so inappropriately into one's life, upsetting plans, breaking vows, subverting all sense and reason? If he had fallen in love with her a few short months ago it might have been difficult. Now that he had formalised the agreement with Anne and her family it was quite impossible.

But then, everything seemed impossible to him. Where once his head had been full of bright and ambitious plans, it was now totally empty. He could not have a future with Barbara Lampett. But neither was he able to imagine one without her.

After his valet left him, he lay in silent dread, waiting for the strike of the clock. His father had been unnecessarily vague about the purpose of these visits. But he had said there would be three of them.

If he had seen the past and the present, then there could be little doubt that next would be the future. What if he had no future? It was quite possible that there was no future to see. If death was coming to take him, then he would be an angry spirit for having been kept waiting a night longer than expected.

If vengeance was due, then it was little more than Joseph deserved. He thought of his recent treatment of those around him, and the way Barbara had turned from him in disgust after only one night. She was right. He had used her, clinging to her like a lifeline in a stormy sea, trying to postpone what he'd known was coming.

If the coming shadow was no more than his death, he had waited too long to tell her what she meant to him. He would go to his grave in silence, and she would never know. He had given her reason enough to hate him. Perhaps that would be easier. Then she would not grieve.

He opened his eyes, aware of a change in the room. There was movement, but none of the light that the other spirits had brought with them. This future, whatever it was, was darkness. And the greatest cold yet. The very air around him was as the touch of the previous spirits, and it froze the breath in his lungs and the soul at his core.

He reached out to the darkness in the corner. Tonight it suited his mood to embrace it. 'Whatever you are, come and be done with it. I deserve all the punishment you wish to deliver. But if this is the end, then I request a boon. Give me one more day to make right what needs mending. Do not take me to judgement, knowing what I have left undone.'

There was no answer.

'Very well, then.' He sighed. 'I suppose that all men facing this have regrets. And if you granted wishes then it would be one more day, and one more, in a never-ending string.'

A deeper silence was his only answer. He could sense nothing: no amusement, condescension or annoyance from the thing in the corner. Only a feeling of waiting.

He studied it. The dark thing was man-shaped, and yet not quite a man. As tall as he. Cloaked, perhaps, for the outline of the head had a hooded quality. But only that. It seemed the harder he tried to look at it the less he could see. This lack of definition made him uneasy, building a fear in him that was worse than anything he might have imagined. If it had simply been some horror, he would have catalogued the deformity and recovered from the shock of it.

But this nameless, faceless thing taunted him with the idea that, if he struggled for a while, he would know it for what it was. It drew the tension in him out like a fine wire, making him wait for the snap of recognition that would cause him to go mad.

He deliberately looked away and stood, walking towards it. 'Come on, then. Take me to wherever it is that you mean to, and let us end this.'

He touched its hand. Or thought he did. For when he looked down there was nothing there. Yet the feeling of cold dry bones in his hands remained. This time they did not fly. They walked slowly—out of the bedroom, down the stairs and into the front hall, marching towards the front door, which swung open before them, engulfing them in a chill mist. He could feel the December wind rattling the leafless trees until they scraped against the windows and rustled curtains. And high on the icy gusts he heard a cry that was not so much a wail as a low moan. It came not from outside, but within.

As they passed the door of the salon he heard voices, and turned to view the tableau. A couple wrestled on the couch in a passionate embrace, near to devouring each other with the intensity of their kisses.

Anne looked as he had never seen her, beautiful but dishevelled. Her hair was free, her bodice loosened and her expression hungry. 'We cannot. We must stop.' Even as she said it she tore at the neckcloth of the man who held her.

'So you have said, for ten long years. Yet we never do.' Robert Breton kissed her again, pushing her hands away to pull at his shirt collar. 'Some day he will discover us. He is not a man who takes lightly the violation of what he considers his.'

Joseph's wife laughed bitterly. 'I doubt he cares. He must know by now. There have been no children. Nor are there likely to be. But he barely even tries any more.'

'Do not speak of your time together. I cannot bear to think of it.' His oldest friend reached up to smooth the hair away from his wife's face. 'You never should have married him.'

'But I did. And now it is too late.'

'You are still young,' he assured her. 'And just as

beautiful as the day I fell in love with you, so many Christmases ago. Leave him. Run away with me.'

Do it, you faithless harlot. I do not want you. The words sounded clear in his mind, and in his heart. He wanted to scream at the harshness of them, even if they were true.

'I cannot.' Anne sighed. 'I do not love him, nor does he love me. But without me he would be alone.'

'You know that is not true.'

'I do not wish to think of that,' Anne whispered, with a sad little laugh.

'Then think of his work. He has the mill to occupy him. It is his one true love.'

'He takes no more pleasure in that than he does in me. When he is at home he wanders the halls at night, counting the rooms.'

Had the habit never changed, then? Even ten years later, was he still so unsure of himself that he needed evidence of his wealth?

'He drinks far too much.'

'All the more reason to leave him,' Breton encouraged her.

She shook her head. 'It is likely to be the death of him soon enough. I have looked into his eyes. He is not well. What harm would it do to wait a month? Maybe two? I will be a widow then. None will think it odd that we find each other.'

His old friend's jaw tightened imperceptibly at the thought of further inaction. 'I will wait, if I must, for the love of you. I know how difficult it would be for you to leave here, and to admit to the world what has been going on between us. But if he does not finish himself soon, then it is not the drink that will end him.'

Anne clung to his arm. 'You mustn't say such things.'

Bob Breton, who was the mildest and most pleasant man that Joseph could name, looked colder than December. 'I think them often enough. I find it difficult to stay silent, with the cancer of it eating me from the inside. I said I understand why you stay, and I cannot fault you for it. He is your husband, and can offer much beyond the legality of your union. But that does not mean that I like it.'

He kissed her again, until she was near to swooning with desire for him. Then he spoke. 'I love you, Anne. But I cannot wait much longer. If he does not let you go with his own timely death I will do what is necessary to achieve the end necessary so that you might be free.'

Joseph waited for the denial, the pleading from his wife that would spare his life. Instead she was silent, but worried. She leaned forwards into Breton's shoulder, as though her only fears were for him. Breton's arm went about her, offering her the support that a husband should have given her.

Strangely, he felt no real jealousy at the sight—only sadness that it had come to this, and that two people so obviously in love had been poisoned to desperation with it.

'Enough of this,' he said to the shadow at his side.

'They hate me. There is nothing more to see. I am a cuckold, but at least I am alive. Take me to the mill, for I wish to see how it fares.'

They continued down the hall and out through the front door, across the lawn and into a mist so thick that the walk might have been one mile or ten for all he knew of it. There was no landmark to show him the way. Nor did he feel the passage of time as he walked.

They were standing at the mill gates now. The silent spectre reached up, resting a wisp of a hand against the gatepost, tracing a divot where a bullet had struck brick.

'There was trouble here, then?' There was no other evidence of it. The mill still stood, even larger than it had been when he'd last seen it, a decade before. He released an awed breath. 'Let me go inside.'

They entered through the dock, to see goods rolled and stacked in neat rows along the wall, ready for delivery. The boilers chugged and rattled, letting off heat and clouds of steam and the stink of sizing and dye. On the factory floor the looms rattled and the shuttles clattered in and out of the warp in a sprightly rhythm—the deafening sound of industry.

Everywhere he looked he saw workers: silent, sullen women and children, operating as surely and mechanically as the machines he'd made for them. From time to time they looked up with quick, rat-like glances at the clock. Then they hurried back to their work with a nervous shudder, as though they did not want to be caught looking anywhere but at their assigned tasks. It was functioning exactly as he'd hoped. And the sight of it filled him with a misery he could not describe.

'Very well, then. All I have worked for, all my dreams, will be like a mouth full of ashes to me in ten years' time. Is there more? Or will you take me home to bed?'

The shadow moved on, out into the fog again. There was nothing he could do but follow.

They walked down the high street of the village, a little way behind a hunched figure that seemed strangely familiar. Joseph quickened his pace to catch the man and end the mystery. But then he watched the villagers look up from their daily doings, stiffen and turn away. 'They see me?' he asked the spirit. If they did, it was not a connection he welcomed. While he had not been well liked in his own time, their glares now held a level of animosity he was not prepared for. What had once been reserve and suspicion had hardened into cold hatred. And it was all the worse because it was mostly the women who stared at him—not just the men who had always been angry.

In fact there seemed to be an unusual number of females.

Then a woman stepped directly into the path of the man in front of him, blocking his way.

The man he was following stopped dead in his tracks. He did not push past the stranger, but neither did he say anything, either in apology or enquiry. It was as though this was a ritual that had occurred before.

'Merry Christmas, Mr Stratford,' she said to the man he followed. 'I hope you are glad of it.' Then she spat on the ground at his feet.

Without a word, this other, older him stepped around her and continued on his way to the edge of the village, past the church and into the little graveyard beside it.

Not so little any more, Joseph noticed. Not huge, by any means, but larger than he would have expected. Had there been an epidemic? Or some other disaster to account for the additional graves? With little warning, the spirit at his side turned in at the gate and walked through the headstones to the last row of stones.

They were all names he recognised, for he had seen the men gathered around him just a few days ago, with hammers and torches, eager to push through the gates and smash the frames on the mill floor. Wilkins, Mutter, Andrews—and the eponymous Weaver, whose family had been at the craft for so long that they shared its name. All dead. All on the same day.

Had he called the militia? Or some other branch of the law? It could have been hanging, or just as easily a pitched battle that the local men were overmatched to fight. But the arrival of troops would explain the crease a bullet had made in the stonework at the mill. No matter what it had been, the rebellion had been stopped. And he had been at the heart of it. Calling in the law to protect his rights, and wiping out families in the process.

'It seems I won the argument in the end,' he said to the spirit. 'But there is no joy in knowing it.'

He looked down at another grave, some way distant from the cluster, and found Jordan—the man whose family he had seen starving just two nights ago. This man's stone was flanked with two smaller ones, topped with stone lambs. Joseph felt a chill, and found he did not have the nerve to look closer, for he was already imagining that table of hungry children, and the likelihood that whatever food was offered there now did not have as far to stretch.

The spectre gestured that it was time to withdraw, but he shook his head. Joseph searched the gravestones for one name in particular, knowing that if these men were here Barbara's father had likely died at their side, a victim of violence. She might have been hurt or killed, and the fault would lie with him.

'Where is Bernard Lampett? He must be dead as well. Why does he not lie with his friends?'

The ghost led him back to a monument worthy of a lord: a marble tomb, with brass fittings and a weeping angel at the top that shone with gilt. It was just the sort of grand thing he'd have ordered, had he the choice. It was garish and horrible next to the sad simplicity he had visited, but at one time he would not have been able to resist this final display of wealth. He fingered the letters carved in the side.

'Lampett. Dead the same day as the rest. And his

wife three months later.' Whether she had passed from poverty or grief, he did not know.

There was no sign here of what had happened to Barbara. But he could read the truth in the marble. Whatever had occurred, she had been there to see her father fall and to know that Joseph was to blame for it. The crypt he stood before was the product of his own guilty conscience. He had buried her parents properly, hoping to assuage whatever obligation he had incurred from the deaths.

He would only have done that if Barbara were still alive.

'Take me to her. I need to know what has happened,' he said, not bothering with a name. If the spirit knew to show him this, then it knew everything. He glanced helplessly as it raised a hand in the direction of the village, and they set off down the road together.

They would not be walking if there was nothing to see. He tensed, knowing that if the lessons held to form the spirit had likely saved the worst for last. But he had to know the truth, and so he set an eager pace.

'If you have something to show me, then be quick about it. I think you have managed to teach the lesson you wished. I must change. Although how I will do it I am not sure. There are expectations on me, you know. I cannot throw aside my engagement with the promise that she will be better off. Nor can I let the profits go hang and the equipment be destroyed. I cannot just walk away from it all.'

In response, the spirit said nothing.

'And now you will show me Barbara. What has become of her, then? Has she forgiven me? I seriously doubt it. Does she hate me? What misery am I likely to see? How will you lay it all at my door? Surely these people deserve some credit in their futures?' he said. 'She could just as easily have made a hash of things on her own, without my help. She was well on the way to that when I met her.'

He might as well have been arguing with the fog, for all he heard was the echo of his own empty words. But even he did not believe them. Even if he could convince himself that her misfortunes were her own doing, or her father's, it would pain him to see them.

At least they were going back to the village and not searching the graveyard for another stone. Surely that meant there was hope.

If he could just see her, it would be all right. What he saw—whatever its cause—could be changed for the better, even if he had to move heaven and earth—he glanced at the spectre beside him—or perhaps heaven and hell.

They were stopping at the same cottage she lived in now, as quietly cheerful as it had ever been, despite what he had just seen of her family. It held the same air of peace that he had seen just the other day, with the path swept of snow and the holly bushes by the door carefully trimmed. But it was as if, with the passage of time, the presence of the two others who had lived there had evaporated. If he searched, he would find no pipe ash in the garden, nor papers scattered on the writing desk. And there would be no Christmas dinner big enough for three and whatever guests might stop.

They drifted through the door as though it was nothing more than mist, and he was glad. He was sure that the cold tended to get in with each opening of the door, and it had a way of lingering like an unwanted guest. At least she should be warm and comfortable in her own home.

She was not in the front room, or the little kitchen, and he drifted with the spirit towards the bedrooms, feeling like a voyeur but unable to contain his curiosity.

He was right to be ashamed, for she was not alone. Though it was the middle of the day she was in bed, the sheet pooling around her waist as she stroked the back of the man lying beside her. She was older, as Anne had been, but still as beautiful as he remembered her from the previous night. Her breasts larger, heavier, her waist thickening. He wondered, if he passed through the cloth that hung over the doorframe of the other room, whether he would find a cradle in use, or a row of tiny cots. Were there children playing in the garden behind the cottage?

But there was no sound of laughter in the house or the garden.

He did not like to think that she had made no family for herself. But she was looking up at the man beside her with such warmth that perhaps the future was not so very grim. If he had nothing else, he would know that she was safe.

Then her lover turned, and Joseph saw his older self, rising from the bed.

Without thinking, Joseph ran his hands over his own body, seeking reassurance of sound mind and limbs. Was this really what he would look like? Or did he have some bit of that in him now? Vanity had made him sure that he was handsome, and ladies had done nothing to dissuade him from the belief. But this new him was a strange thing—pale, hair shot with grey, face hardened into a frown, body spider-thin and beginning to stoop.

The other him rose from the bed, not even looking down at the lovely woman who reached for him, pulling on trousers, tugging a shirt back into place and hurriedly tying his neckcloth.

'You cannot stay?' Barbara held out a hand to him, inviting.

'Why would I wish to? You could not even manage to heat the room, though you knew I would be coming.'

If the words hurt her, she gave no sign of it. 'It is warm enough in my bed, is it not?'

'It would be even warmer in a larger bed, with softer sheets. I have given you ample opportunity to move to more hospitable lodgings, and yet you insist on remaining in this hovel.'

'It is my home,' she said simply.

'It forces me to come into the village in the middle

of the day. You know how the people treat me. And we both know what they think of you because of my visits.'

She smiled sadly. 'I cannot help how they treat you. What they think of me is no less than the truth. I fail to see, after all this time, how I can change that.'

Joseph felt a hint of dread. How had it come to this? Just this morning she had left him with her pride intact. Lying with her had been a mistake. But he had intended something different by it. Surely it meant more than this?

The older Stratford scowled. 'I do not like it.'

At last he was showing some compassion, and Joseph looked on anxiously.

'It reflects poorly on me. I will build you a house—a fine one—with servants and proper receiving rooms. I will place it closer to the mill so that it will be more convenient.'

Joseph winced, for he could guess the sharp rejoinder he would receive. Barbara would put him in his place, right enough. Then he would apologise for his foolishness.

'But it would not be as convenient for me,' Barbara said softly, with a lying smile that was close to the one he'd seen most often on Anne Clairemont. 'It would cost you nothing if I remained here and you came more often, rather than staying so long at the mill.'

'You know I cannot put aside my work for you.' His own voice was deeper, rougher and annoyed. 'If I leave the floor even for a minute there is mischief. Thieves and ruffians, the lot of them.'

'You work too hard,' she chided gently. 'And you are hard on those who work for you. Perhaps if you showed compassion…'

'There is no place for compassion in business,' he barked. 'Since you know nothing about it, it would be better if you learned to keep silent, instead of parading your ignorance.'

Her smile faltered. 'Of course. But if I speak it is only because I care too much for you.'

Why do you bother? This man was hardly worthy of her affection. Suddenly, Joseph realised that he was thinking of himself as a stranger, and feeling jealous of and angered by the way that individual had squandered the trust that he was working so hard to earn. Apparently he had not even the courtesy to come to her in the night, to conceal what they did from the eyes of her neighbours.

And Barbara accepted it from him. She allowed him to treat her so after all the things he had done to hurt her, soaking up his cruelty like a sponge.

The other him looked down at her, eyes narrowed in suspicion, as though he had no reason to take her kindness for what it was. 'I give you no reason to care. But thank you.' He reached into his pocket and withdrew a jewel case. 'For you. A tiara to complete your parure.'

'Thank you,' she said, with a misery that the older Joseph Stratford did not seem to notice. She did not bother to open the box, merely set it on a table at the side of the bed.

'You idiot,' he said to his other self. 'I have no taste to speak of. But even I know that she would have no use for a crown. How could you? You are treating her...'

Like a whore.

'You're welcome,' said the other Stratford, and his response was as false as her thanks. 'And good day.' He turned to go.

Barbara's shoulders slumped in defeat, but she did not rise to see him out.

Joseph stepped forwards, unable to stand it any longer. He tried to catch the arm of the man at the door and his fingers passed through it. He swung again, in frustration, with enough force to bruise, and yet felt nothing but the passing of the air.

'Stay with her,' he demanded. 'Hear me, you bastard. I know you can. I am the sound of your own voice in your head. Listen to me.'

There was the slightest flinch in the shoulders of the man, as though he had felt a slap.

'Stay with her, damn you. Or at least take back that jewellery. You cheapen her with such a gift.'

The man he would become twitched again, as though he were throwing off a lead, and strode through the door and out of the cottage, letting the door slam behind him.

Slowly Barbara leaned back into the bed, as though it were an effort to stay upright and maintain the pretence of happiness when he was not there to see it. Without a word, or so much as a whimper, her tears began to fall. He knew the meaning of tears like that, shed in such utter silence. He had cried like that as a boy, when he had been convinced that there was no future for him.

He could bear it no longer, and reached out to touch her. But when his hand touched her face it seemed to glide through, leaving only a momentary warmth on his fingertips. There would be no comfort in this for either of them. He moved to sit on the edge of the bed, so close that he should have been able to feel the warmth of her body against his leg.

Apparently she felt the cold in him, for she shivered. 'It will be all right,' he said softly, hearing the trembling in his own voice. 'I will make it better. It will never come to this. I swear to you. You will not cry, damn me for each tear. You will not cry.'

He leaned closer, letting the shadow of himself fall onto the shadow of her until they were as one body. He felt the fear and pain and confusion that was in her as though it were his own. Worst of all, he felt her despair. She knew with certainty that it would never be better than it was at this moment, and would most likely be worse. He was slipping away a little more with each visit. She could sell the jewellery. She did not need it. She would never know want. But she would never know love. How had it come to this? He had sworn to take care of her.

He felt her own guilt at her weakness, and her shame at betraying her parents' memories each time she touched him. But she had loved him from the first. She still loved him. It had never meant more than money to him, but she had wanted to believe otherwise.

And Joseph realised with a shock that there was no blame here for anyone but him. He had done this to her—had changed every element of her life, had taken her family from her. And what he had put in the empty place was nothing more than cold comfort.

He could feel the increasing impatience of the silent spirit at his back, tugging him free. He fought, trying to stay with her, wishing she could feel some bit of him and take comfort in it, or that he could take away with him some small part of the burden she carried.

But he was gone with a wrench, being dragged back down the street towards the manor. He looked back at the haze of the spirit, feeling tears wet his own cheeks, and he said, 'I can change. Let me change.' He reached out to grab at the hood of the spirit, forcing it to face him as he had been afraid to before.

It turned to him then, reaching a thin, pale hand to uncover its face and stare at him.

It was his own face staring back. Not the one he saw in the mirror each morning, nor even the hardened man that was stalking through this unhappy future. This was him as he would be fifty years hence—still breathing, but near the end. He would be strong and healthy, but nearer to a century than to fifty.

And his eyes. At first he thought them soulless. But there was a flickering of pain, like a tormented thing racing about in his head, and a twitch at the corner of his mouth that he could not seem to control.

Joseph stared at him, into those familiar gray eyes, into the darkest part of his own soul. 'I have seen enough. Take me back. It will be different. As it should be. I promise.'

The ghost's shoulders slumped, as though relieved of a weight. The tension in his mouth relaxed. His eyes closed. And an empty cloak dropped to the floor.

It was a blanket. Nothing more than that. It had slipped from his own bed, in his own room. He had chased it to the rug and was sitting upon the floor and staring at it in the light of Christmas dawn as though he had never seen the thing before.

Joseph gave a nervous laugh and shook it, as though he expected to see some remnant of his vision. 'All over. Merry Christmas.' He said it almost as an oath more than a greeting. 'It is over, and I live to tell the tale.' Not that he could, lest he be thought mad. But he was indeed alive.

To the open and empty air, he said, 'And I will remember it all, whether it be dream or no.'

He reached for the bell-pull and rang for butler as well as valet, thinking it would be easier to rouse the housekeeper through an intermediary rather than directly. It would take more than one hand to set his plan in motion. The whole house might be needed, even though it was just past dawn on Christmas Day.

Chapter Seventeen

Joseph stumbled down the stairs one step ahead of his valet, who was still holding his coat. The shave Hobson had given him had been haphazard at best. But there was much to do, and he could not wait any longer for the butler to deliver his message.

'Mrs Davy!' He stood in the centre of the main hall and shouted for the housekeeper. It felt as though he were taking his first deep breath in an age, after being deep underwater.

The poor woman hustled into the room, hurriedly tying her apron, a look of alarm on her rosy face.

He gasped again and grinned at her, amazed at the elation that seemed to rush in along with the plan. It made him feel as he had on the day he had first thought of the new loom—full of bright promise. Only this was better.

'Mrs Davy,' he said again. 'My dear Mrs Davy!' And then he laughed at the look on her face.

She took a step back. 'Sir?'

He had worried her now. Though he was not a cruel master, when had he ever taken the time to call anyone dear?

'I have more work for you. I take it the larders are still full, and ready to feed my non-existent guests?'

She gave a hesitant nod. 'There was much more than was needed, sir.'

'Then we need to do something with the bounty. Baskets. Baskets and boxes—and bags. Bowls, if you must. I want you to search the house and fill every container available with the excess. Enough to feed every family in the village. While you are about it make enough for a box for every servant here. Make sure that you and your helpers take enough for yourselves as well. Empty the pantry. I wish to give it away.'

'Sir?'

Had he really become so ungenerous as to cause this look of surprise? If so, it was all the more reason to change his ways—with or without the intervention of ghosts.

'I want,' he said, more slowly and with emphasis, 'everyone in the village to have as happy a New Year as I am likely to. It will not happen for any of us if I sit alone in a house that is barely half full, and they sit in the village with empty cupboards and fears for the future. I have broken a tradition. I mean to mend it now. As quickly as possible.'

'Oh, sir.' She was grinning at him now, as though he had fulfilled her fondest wish by forcing her to labour on Christmas Day.

'If you can fill the baskets, I will take the carriage into the village. And a wagon as well. I will see to it that they are delivered. And with them I will send an invitation for this evening. All who wish to come must dance and drink and be merry.'

'Yes, sir!' She was already bustling back towards the kitchen, disappearing as quickly as she had appeared, as though borne on a cloud of enthusiasm.

'What the devil is going on?' Breton was approaching from the stairs, still wiping the sleep from his eyes. 'Stop making such a racket, Stratford, or you will wake the whole house.'

Joseph grinned at him. Good old Robert. Loyal Bob, who must be sorely conflicted by his feelings of late. 'A Merry Christmas to you, Breton.' He seized the man's hand and shook it vigorously. 'And may I take this moment to say I never had a truer friend, nor a better partner?'

'I might say the same of you,' Breton said, looking quite miserable. Then he took a deep breath. 'That is why I must speak. I know it is not the time or place, but there is something I wish to discuss. I did not get a wink of sleep last night, and I do not think I can stand...'

'Not another word.' Joseph held up his hand to stop

the confession that he suspected was coming. 'I wish nothing more for this Christmas than that you save any difficult revelations for after New Year's Eve. If you feel the same way—'

'I doubt a few days will change my mind on what I wish to tell you,' the man interrupted. 'For I wish—'

'...after I break my engagement with Anne.'

'...to go back to London. I...' They'd spoken on top of each other. And now Breton looked as if he wished to suck his last words back into his mouth. 'I beg your pardon?'

'I am going to speak to Anne. We both know that she does not love me. I am quite sure I will not make her happy. No matter how much business sense it might make, it is wrong to catch her up in it and force a union which might be disagreeable to her.'

'There are certain expectations...' Breton said cautiously.

'And they are all about this house. Well, damn the house. I do not want it,' Joseph said firmly. 'I would be quite content with something smaller. With fewer rooms, and not so many ghosts.' He laughed again. 'Her father can have it off me for a breach of promise settlement. That is what he wants, after all. Unless...' He grinned at Breton. 'Unless you would be willing to take the thing off my hands? I expect you would be troubled endlessly by Clairemont, of course. He seems to have the daft idea that his daughter shall be mistress, no matter what she wants. You'll be in his sights for a husband then, I am sure. You'll likely have to take her with the deal.'

'How dare you speak of her in that way? As though she were property to be traded!' Breton was simmering with rage and quite missing the point.

'I cannot trade a thing I never possessed, Bob.' He gave his friend a significant look. 'I doubt that my leaving will create much heartache for Miss Anne Clairemont. But can there be any doubt that such a lovely girl will be married by spring? I should think there is some gentleman who would wish to fill the void I leave. If I knew of him, I would urge him to act quickly—use the disarray I'm likely to leave in the Clairemont household to good advantage and whatever bait might come to hand to clinch the deal.'

'I see.' But he did not seem to. Breton's face was still wary.

'If there is a man who loves her as she deserves, I would wish him well.' To finish, he gave Bob a hearty clap upon the back, as though to jolt the man out of his lethargy.

'I see. Yes, I think I do.' The grin spread slowly across his friend's face as his plans for the future came clear.

'I think you do.' Joseph grinned back at him. 'And a Merry Christmas to you, sir.'

'I think it shall be.'

'Now, what was it that you wished to say to me earlier? For I do not think I quite heard it.'

'Nothing,' Bob said, waving a hand to scrub the air of his words. 'Nothing at all other than to wish you well.'

'That is good. For this might be a trying day for you. What do you think our London friends are likely to say if I bring the whole of the village back with me for Christmas dinner?'

Breton thought for a moment. 'I expect they will be horrified.'

'Well, apparently, it is the custom in these parts. I cannot keep alienating the workers, or there shall be hell to pay.'

'You might lose some investors,' Breton warned. 'Feathers are likely to be ruffled on your fat pigeons.'

'Then I shall have to win them back another way. Or I shall find others. But let us see, shall we? I mean to visit Anne next. Perhaps I can enlist the aid of her father in smoothing the way with the Londoners. If he does not throw me bodily from his house first.'

Joseph's carriage pulled up to the door of the Clairemonts' new home and he wondered why he had not taken the place for himself. He had deemed it too far from the mill and rejected it out of hand. But, even with the addition of a wife and children, twelve rooms and a modest staff would be much closer to his needs than the monstrosity he now owned. How had he been so foolish?

He was admitted, and waited patiently in the parlour for Miss Anne, who was preparing for church, relieved that their current bond would make his appearance seem somewhat less alarming to the household. How they would feel about him in a quarter-hour was likely to be a different story. He wondered with a smile if he should have instructed his coachman to keep in his seat, whip in hand, for the hasty escape they would need to make.

There was a wild scrambling in the hall, followed by a sudden pause and the sedate entrance of Miss Anne Clairemont. The single curl out of place on her beautiful head and the lopsided bow of her sash were the only evidence that he had caught her unawares. She gave a graceful curtsey, as though allowing him the moment to admire her, and then asked sweetly, 'Did you want me, Mr Stratford?'

'I have come to ask you the same thing, Miss Clairemont.' It was a bold question, but his morning was a busy one, and there was no point in beating around the bush. He watched as her pretty face registered confusion. 'Come, let us sit down and talk awhile.' He sat. Bob would have been horrified, and reminded him that he could not go ordering young ladies about in their own homes, nor sitting when they stood.

But this one did not seem to notice his lapse, and perched nervously on the couch at his side, waiting for him to speak.

He took her hand. 'Before we go another step on life's road, Anne, I must know the truth. Do you want me?'

'I…I don't understand,' Anne said firmly. But the truth of it was plain on her face—if only he could get her to admit it. 'In what way? Your visit is unexpected, of course, but not unwelcome.'

'I do not mean to ask if you want me now—this instant. I mean as a husband, and for life. Do you desire my company? I wish to know the reason for our upcoming union.'

'You wish to cry off?' Now her face was a mix of hope and dread, and a trembling that was the probable beginning of tears.

'I have asked and you have answered,' he said, as gently as possible. 'And that is how it will remain, if you truly wish it. Do not think I will cry off and leave you.' He paused and looked her clearly in the eye. 'If to have me is the thing that will truly make you happy.'

'Of course I am happy.' Her face fell.

If she persisted in this way he would have no choice but to marry her. Or perhaps he should arrange a match between her and the Aubusson. As she was making her heartfelt declaration she could not seem to take her eyes from the rug at their feet.

'You have honoured me with your proposal. My family stands to gain much by it. It will secure my future. Why would I not be happy?'

That sounded almost as if she asked herself the same question. It gave him reason to hope.

'Then now you must do something for me,' he said. 'Consider it a gift for our first Christmas.'

She looked up, quite terrified. 'I do not think… After

we are married…of course…but now? It is Christmas morning, Mr Stratford. And this is my parents' parlour.'

He laughed at her total misunderstanding of him, and at her obvious horror at the prospect of the conjugal act, wondering about how much she might have already learned from his friend about inappropriate acts of passion. If this was her view of him it was quite beyond a display of maidenly resistance, and much closer to active distaste. 'What I am requesting is nothing like what you expect. If we are to marry, we will be together for a long time. The rest of our lives, perhaps.'

He should not have said *perhaps*. He should have been more definite. That alone should have told him of his own heart. For once they were joined there would be no reprieve.

'And I should think, if we can give each other nothing else, we deserve mutual honesty—to be given without fear of recrimination. I have reason to suspect that you might be happier if you had been able to accept another. And that the primary goal in taking me is to help your family return to the place of social prominence it once held. If that is the truth, there is no shame in it. But would it not be better to state it outright, so that there can be no confusion?'

She blinked at him, unable to speak. But neither did she offer the quick denial that would have corrected a mistake.

'Now, tell me the truth. In one word. Do you love me?'

'It is not really expected, when one is of a certain

class, that one will marry for love,' she said, as though by rote.

'Nor is it expected that they will give a simple answer to a direct question,' he countered, but without any real irritation. 'But am I to assume, from your misdirection, that your answer is no?'

'I respect you, of course. You have many worthy and admirable qualities that would make a woman proud to be your wife.'

He sighed, for she was not making this easy. 'Then I am sure, since you have such respect for me, that you will be happy to hear that this morning I have taken the first step towards selling your old house to Mr Robert Breton.'

There was a moment of blankness on her face, a deliciously unattractive drop of her jaw and a sudden and complete lack of composure. It was the first sign of humanity he had seen in her. Then she spoke—not in the decorous half-whisper that he had grown accustomed to, but a full-throated, unladylike shout.

'Father!' She stood and shouted again. 'Father! Come downstairs immediately. I am about to break my engagement with Mr Stratford.'

Next, the carriage stopped at the first door in the village. His groom made to get down and take a package, but Joseph held up a hand. 'It must be me, I think. At least for the first few houses. Simply hand things to me, and I will be the one to knock.'

The first door was opened by a child. Before she

could run for Mama, Joseph thrust the basket into her arms and shouted, 'Merry Christmas!' and then turned away to receive the next hamper and walked the few steps to the next door.

There. Not so bad, he told himself. He had half feared that there would be a punch upon the nose and a slammed door before he could get his gift across the threshold. At the next house he saw a wife. After that he found one of the weavers most vocal in opposition to him still in nightshirt and cap.

Joseph pushed the basket into his arms, with a hurried 'Season's Greetings!'

'I suppose this is to make up for the trouble you've caused?' the man said sceptically.

'It is mince pies,' Joseph answered, lifting the corner of the cloth. 'And a ham. While it lacks the supernatural power to mend our differences, it will at least be good with warm bread. I believe there is some wine as well. More concrete and useful than an apology, I should think. But you can have one of those as well. The rest can wait until Twelfth Night.' He turned away to get another basket.

With the man still standing dumbstruck in the open doorway, Joseph began to walk down the street. From the corner of his eye he saw the man turn as well, shouting back into his house. As Joseph walked he could see the man darting down a side street, and heard a pounding on a back door somewhere ahead of him.

He delivered his next basket, and the good wife who

took it accepted it with a hesitant smile and a nod of confirmation—but none of the surprise that he had seen in the first houses. From then on he could almost hear the buzz as the news preceded him down the street with shouts, pounding footsteps and lads panting in kitchens to relay that the old dragon Stratford had gone mad and was giving away his hoard. A crowd was growing behind him as well, for just as the news ran ahead, out through back doors and down alleys, the consequences were trailing him like a parade.

At last he came to the Jordan house, and pushed a particularly large package into the man's hands as the door opened. 'Mr Jordan,' he said happily. 'A Merry Christmas to you. And—' he lifted the corner of the napkin that covered the gift '—a brace of partridge, cheese, oranges, sweets for the children, mince and a bottle of milk with the cream still floating on the top. Children need milk, Mr Jordan. And yours will not want for it once you have accepted the position of foreman at my mill.'

'Mr Stratford?' The man could not manage anything else, not even a thank-you.

'You needn't say more right now,' Joseph assured him. 'But you might help with the distribution of the rest of the packages in the wagon that is following my carriage. I have another important errand to run that will take me away from it. While you are about it, could you be so kind as to invite your neighbours to the manor this evening? The doors will be open, just as they always used to be.'

Jordan managed a weak nod.

'There's a good man. I will see you this evening, shall I?' Joseph looked at his watch.

Then he turned and ran.

The Lampett cottage was on the edge of the village, almost into the country, and set back at the end of a short drive. Joseph could feel the collective eyes of the people on him as he went. It was very near the same crowd as he had seen rioting at the mill. But where he had felt rage and distrust on that occasion he now felt a kind of wary encouragement pressing him forwards. The gifts he had offered had done much to disperse their ill will. But how they felt about him in the future would depend on his reception at this last and most vital of houses.

And none of it mattered, really. Not for the reasons they thought. While he might argue trade and tariffs until the last trump, he would have to agree to disagree with her father, and manage his troubled mind as well. But as long as they could be in agreement on one thing none of it would matter to him.

The winter air was sharp, and he ran until he could feel the pain of it in his lungs, in his side. Then he ran further, as he had when he was a boy and had no money for horses and no use for them either. It was good to be alive—to see the robins flitting in the bare branches of the few small trees in the garden, to kick the hoarfrost from the twigs and see it shower to the ground in a sparkle, and to hear the sound of the Christmas church bells growing louder as he neared the front gate and ran through it and up the drive towards the house. He did not stop even as he reached the door, but banged his body against it, striking knees and palms flat against the wood as he might have when playing tag as a child.

He peeled himself away to knock properly. Then he laughed and hammered on the door with his fists, heedless of the way it must look.

And then the door opened.

Chapter Eighteen

From her bedroom, Barbara could hear the pounding on the door, and then her father arguing with someone in the parlour.

Why must he act up on Christmas morning? It did not help that she was already feeling quite fragile, nerving herself for the curious glances she was likely to receive in church today. She did not think she could stand a scene from him as well. Mixed in with his rising voice she could hear the chill tones of her mother, who was never able to soothe him.

She looked in the mirror, straightening her brown merino church dress with trembling hands. She could think of only one thing that would cause such strife and anger to both of her parents. But would anyone be cruel enough to tell tales about her on this of all days? If that was the problem, she had best go and face it herself, for neither parent was likely to be up to the task.

When she went into the parlour she saw her father standing in the doorway, his shirt collar open, neckcloth in hand. Mr Joseph Stratford was crumpling the linen of Father's cravat with a vigorous handshake. Her mother stood to the side, looking like nothing so much as an outraged hen when a cat was stalking in the chicken house.

Joseph glanced past her father to her, smiling as though he had not a care in the world. 'Good morning to you, Miss Lampett. And a Merry Christmas.'

'What are you doing here?' she asked, rooted to her spot in the doorway to the hall. Why could she not stop looking at him, cross the room, push him out of the house and shut the door? Why did he have to look so well, so handsome and so much more vital and alive than he had after their night together? Did he mean to show her how well he did without her? Surely he must know that she drank in every detail whenever she looked at him.

Joseph realised that he had not released her father, and let the hand drop suddenly, turning to her mother with a deep bow. 'And to you, Mrs Lampett. A Merry Christmas. I do not think we have been formally introduced.'

'I know just who you are.' Her mother said it in a way that would tell him where he stood with the whole of the family.

He grinned in her direction, as though to say, *Just you wait. Things are about to get interesting.*

Remembering how purposely obtuse he could be when he had a goal in sight, how utterly heedless of others, she gave a warning shake of her head.

'I suppose you are wondering why I have come here in this way, at this hour, on this day.'

'I am wondering if I shall have to put you out,' said her father. 'I assure you that I am quite capable of it, should you make any more trouble.'

Father was no more capable of success in that than in flying to the moon. But this was hardly the time to call attention to it, so Barbara put in, as meekly as possible, 'I certainly hope that will not be necessary.' She shot Joseph an evil glare. 'If I could just talk to you outside for a moment, Mr Stratford? We might settle whatever it is that brings you here, and continue our preparations for church.'

'But I did not come to speak to you, Miss Lampett. At least not just yet. I promise I will be brief.' He gave her the quickest of apologetic smiles, and then returned to her father. And, if she was not mistaken, she saw a twinkle in his eye.

He was making fun of her. After all that had happened he was amusing himself at her expense. She would be sure he was brief, indeed. The first time he stopped speaking to take a breath, she would haul him by the neck from the room.

'Then proceed, sir. Have you have come to threaten me with arrest again?'

Oh, dear. This would be one of the days when Father

was clear of memory and in a foul temper. Barbara's mind worked furiously to come up with a distraction that would separate the pair of them.

'On the contrary, Mr Lampett. I have come to ask for your help.'

This was so shocking a request that it reduced the whole Lampett family to silence.

Mr Stratford used the pause to his advantage. 'You know that I mean to reopen the mill in a few weeks, and that there are likely to be more workers than positions available? This concerns me greatly.'

'It does?' her father said, stupefied at this reversal of positions.

'You know the people better than I, for I am near to a stranger. I can think of no one better qualified to help me find other employment for them. I would compensate you, of course, for it would take a fair amount of your time. Then, if I can persuade Robert Breton to be its patron, we will likely be reopening the school. You would be needed there as well—either as a teacher, or in an advisory capacity.'

'I don't know what to say.' And clearly her father did not. The onslaught of new ideas had stopped his anger in its tracks.

'You need not make a decision now. Think on it for a time. I am opening Clairemont Manor this evening for the annual Tenants' Ball. Perhaps there will be time for us to discuss it then. But feel free to share my ideas with any in the village you might meet. They are in no way secret. I mean to find employment of some kind for all those who are willing to work.'

'I will. I will at that. Margaret!' He gestured to his wife. 'We must go to church immediately. We will see many of the men affected. I will broach the subject to the vicar as well.'

'You will broach it after the last hymn,' her mother said severely.

'Of course.'

But Barbara could see by the look in her father's eye that he was unlikely to hear much of what was preached, and would spend the next hour scribbling pencil notes in the back of his prayer book that would become a stirring and inspiring speech on the subject.

Father grabbed for his hat and opened the door, as though he'd quite forgotten that there was a guest present.

'One more thing before you go, sir.' Stratford touched his arm. 'Might I request your daughter's hand in marriage?'

'Certainly,' her father muttered. 'Margaret, what have I done with my muffler?'

But her mother could manage nothing more than a squeak of surprise.

'It is on your neck, Father,' Barbara said weakly.

'Very good, then. Let us go to church.'

Her mother recovered her composure and shot an exasperated look around the room. 'After we have tied your neckcloth, Bernard.' She struggled with his collar button and the rumpled linen. 'We shall go on ahead—and you, Barbara, shall meet us there. Mr Stratford, if we do not see the pair of you in the family pew before the end of the first hymn... Well, I do not know what we shall do. But I trust you to behave as a gentleman.'

'I do not know why you would, ma'am,' Joseph said with a smile. 'Perhaps you do not know me as well as the rest of your family does. But you can trust me in this, at least. I will take good care of your daughter.' He gave another respectful bow as Barbara's parents withdrew, leaving them alone.

Barbara shot a helpless look after them as the door shut. Then she turned to face Joseph. 'And just *what* is the meaning of this, Mr Stratford?'

'I should think that would be obvious,' he said, with another smile. But there was no mischief in it. He was looking at her as if he had never seen anything so wonderful.

'There is nothing obvious about it. Was it not just two days ago that you made public your betrothal to Anne Clairemont?'

'And this morning I broke it.' He reached out to take her hand, running a weather-roughened finger across the back of her knuckles.

'You did not,' she said, pulling her hand away from him. 'Anne will be heartbroken.'

'She most certainly will not,' he answered back. 'She is utterly besotted with my friend Robert, and thoroughly glad to be rid of me.'

'You knew?' She breathed a little deeper knowing that the dark secret she had uncovered was no secret at all.

'I concur with her. They are very well suited. But to make sure that there is no trouble with her father I am selling Bob the house. Lord Clairemont will have what he wants, and Anne will marry the son of an earl and the man she loves. And no one will be forced to marry into trade.' Then he looked at her more seriously. 'Not even you, if you do not wish to. Marry me, that is.'

'It might be the wisest thing,' she admitted quietly. 'After what happened the other night.'

'You could marry me because it is the wisest thing to do,' he agreed. 'But I would rather you didn't. If it is only out of concern for your reputation I would understand. But I was rather under the impression that you had strong feelings for me.'

Must I confess everything again? Though it is true that I love you, I am tired of being your plaything. She bit back the foolish words that she wanted to say, and fought the desire to throw herself into his arms quickly, before he found a way to ruin it all again. 'I would much rather hear your reason for wanting to marry me. What could I possibly have that you need, Mr Stratford?'

'My heart,' he said simply. 'I think you must have taken it with you when you left yesterday. It is not clockwork, as you said. If it was, I should be able to replace it.'

'You are clever with machines,' she admitted, doing her best to still the fluttering in her own breast.

'It turns out I am flesh and blood, after all. And likely to make quite a mess of things if I am allowed to go on like this. I have given up my fiancée and my manor. I have walked through the village handing over so much food that I am not sure there will be anything left for supper—nor money to buy more, now that I have promised to employ the whole village. And to top it off I will likely frighten my London investors by letting the rabble into the house this evening.' He held out his open arms. 'I am a disaster in the making, Miss Lampett. Someone should take me in hand while I still have a penny left in my pocket.'

'Not me, surely,' she said with a little smile. 'For I would not change a bit of you. It was a wonderful thing you just did for Father.'

'I doubt it will solve all his problems,' Joseph said, taking her hand again. 'But perhaps, if he has a purpose and a different direction for his energies, we might harness a portion of his madness and do some good with it.'

'That is a far cry from threatening him with a one-way trip to Australia,' Barbara noted. 'That was the tune you were singing to me just a few days ago.'

'I find I cannot stomach the idea of a father-in-law who is a convict,' he said, with a wry twist of his mouth. 'I might be in trade, Miss Lampett, but even I have some standards.'

'You seem quite sure I will accept you.'

'Because I will not take no for an answer.' He dropped to one knee then, and gave her hand a squeeze. 'I have seen the future, Barbara. While I cannot claim that I will die if you do not have me, I am quite certain that it would not be worth my living without you.' He dropped his head to plant a kiss on the back of her hand, humbled and at her feet.

'Oh, do get up.' She nudged at him with the toe of her shoe. For she'd had a sudden memory of what had occurred in the little alcove the last time he'd knelt before her. And she was sure her face was burning bright red.

'Not until you say yes.' He looked up hopefully. 'I have no ring to offer you, but you may have whatever you like. And I promise that I will not waste money on a gaudy parure with a tiara that you do not need.'

'That is the most outlandish thing I have ever heard,' she said. 'What sort of man gets down on his knees and swears that he will *not* buy his wife jewellery?'

'One who is so totally undone by love that he is no longer sure what he is saying.'

'You are undone by love?' She was not sure she believed him. But she quite liked the sound of it.

He nodded. 'And running out of time to plead my case. The church bells have stopped. Soon your mother will be coming back to box my ears.'

'Then I had best take you, hadn't I?' She stepped

back and tried to tug him to his feet. 'For I rather like your ears just as they are.'

'Do you, now?' He stood and caught her around the waist, pulling her close for a kiss. 'I like yours as well. And your nose. And your eyes. And your fingertips.' He followed each revelation with a brief kiss to the honoured feature, and then put his mouth to her ear and whispered several other things that he appreciated, but that she was quite sure she should not let him see again until the banns had been read.

'It is Christmas,' she reminded him. 'And broad daylight. We are expected elsewhere, and already late.'

He sighed. 'Then put on your bonnet and we will be off.'

'I suppose you've brought your carriage again?' she said, tying up the ribbon on her new hat.

Then he proved to her that he had truly changed. For he reached into his pocket and tugged on his gloves, before setting his hat upon his head. 'Actually, no. It is not far, and such a nice day I did not bring it. We shall have to walk.'

'Together?' she said with a smile.

'I would have it no other way.'

* * * * *

LET'S TALK
Romance

For exclusive extracts, competitions
and special offers, find us online:

MILLS & BOON

HISTORICAL

Awaken the romance of the past

Escape with historical heroes from time gone by.
Whether your passion is for wicked
Regency Rakes, muscled Viking warriors or
rugged Highlanders, indulge your fantasies and
awaken the romance of the past.